PENGUIN BOOKS

CASHEL BYRON'S PROFESSION

George Bernard Shaw was born in Dublin in 1856. Essentially shy, he yet created the persona of G.B.S., the showman, satirist, controversialist, critic, pundit, wit, intellectual buffoon and dramatist. Commentators brought a new adjective into English: Shavian, a term used to embody all his brilliant qualities.

After his arrival in London in 1876 he became an active Socialist and a brilliant platform speaker. He wrote on many social aspects of the day: on *Commonsense about the War* (1914), *How to Settle the Irish Question* (1917) and *The Intelligent Woman's Guide to Socialism and Capitalism* (1928). He undertook his own education at the British Museum and consequently became keenly interested in cultural subjects. Thus his prolific output included music, art and theatre reviews, which were collected into several volumes: *Music in London 1890–1894* (3 vols., 1931); *Pen Portraits and Reviews* (1931); and *Our Theatre in the Nineties* (3 vols., 1931).

He conducted a strong attack on the London theatre and was closely associated with the intellectual revival of British theatre. His many plays fall into several categories: his 'Plays Unpleasant'; 'Plays Pleasant'; his comedies; chronicle-plays; 'metabiological Pentateuch' (*Back to Methuselah*, a series of plays) and 'political extravaganzas'. G.B.S. died in 1950.

BERNARD SHAW

CASHEL BYRON'S
PROFESSION

DEFINITIVE TEXT
under the editorial
supervision of
DAN H. LAURENCE

PENGUIN BOOKS

Penguin Books Ltd, Harmondsworth, Middlesex, England
Penguin Books, 625 Madison Avenue, New York, New York 10022, U.S.A.
Penguin Books Australia Ltd, Ringwood, Victoria, Australia
Penguin Books Canada Ltd, 2801 John Street, Markham, Ontario, Canada L3R 1B4
Penguin Books (N.Z.) Ltd, 182–190 Wairau Road, Auckland 10, New Zealand

—

First published in book form 1886
Revised 1889; further revised 1901
The 1901 definitive text published in the Collected Edition 1930 and in the
Standard Edition 1932 in Great Britain by Constable and Co.
Published in Penguin Books 1979

—

—

Made and printed in Great Britain
by C. Nicholls & Company Ltd
Set in Monotype Baskerville

PREFACE

NOVELS OF MY NONAGE

I NEVER think of Cashel Byron's Profession without a shudder at the narrowness of my escape from becoming a successful novelist at the age of twenty-six. At that moment an adventurous publisher might have ruined me. Fortunately for me, there were no adventurous publishers at that time; and I was forced to fight my way, instead of being ingloriously bought off at the first brush. Not that Cashel Byron's Profession was my very first novel. It was my fourth, and was followed by yet another. I recall these five remote products of my nonage as five heavy brown paper parcels which were always coming back to me from some publisher, and raising the very serious financial question of the sixpence to be paid to Messrs Carter, Paterson, and Co., the carriers, for passing them on to the next publisher. Eventually, Carter, Paterson, and Co. were the only gainers; for the publishers had to pay their readers' fees for nothing but a warning not to publish me; and I had to pay the sixpences for sending my parcels on a bootless errand. At last I grew out of novel-writing, and set to work to find out what the world was really like. The result of my investigations, so far, entirely confirms the observation of Goethe as to the amazement, the incredulity, the moral shock with which the poet discovers that what he supposed to be the real world does not exist, and that men and women are made by their own fancies in the image of the imaginary creatures in his youthful fictions, only much stupider.

Unfortunately for the immature poet, he has not in his nonage the satisfaction of knowing that his guesses at life are true. Bring a peasant into a drawing-room, and though his good sense may lead him to behave very properly, yet he will suffer torments of misgiving that everything he does must be a solecism. In my earlier excursions into literature I confess I felt like the peasant in the drawing-room. I was, on the whole, glad to get out of it. Looking back now with the eyes of experience, I find that I certainly did make blunders in matters outside the scope of poetic divination. To take a very mild example, I endowed the opulent heroine of this very book with a park of thirty acres in extent, being then fully persuaded that this was a reasonable estimate of the size of the Isle of Wight or thereabouts. But it is not by the solecisms of ignorance that the young man makes himself most ridiculous. Far more unnatural than these were my proprieties and accuracies and intelligences. I did not know my England then. I was young, raw from eighteenth century Ireland, modest, and anxious lest my poverty and provinciality should prevent me from correctly representing the intelligence, refinement, conscience, and good breeding which I supposed to be as natural and common in English society as in Scott's novels. I actually thought that educated people conscientiously learnt their manners and studied their opinions – were really educated, in short – instead of merely picking up the habits and prejudices of their set, and confidently presenting the resultant absurd equipment of class solecisms to the world as a perfect gentility. Consequently the only characters which were natural in my novels were the comic characters, because the island was (and is) populated exclusively by comic characters. Take them seriously in fiction, and the result is the Dickens heroine or the Sarah Grand hero: pathetically unattractive figments both of them. Thus my imaginary persons of quality became quite unlike any actual persons at large in England, being superior to them in a priggish manner which would nowadays rouse the humor of our younger publishers' readers very inopportunely. In 1882, however, the literary fashion which distinguished the virtuous and serious characters in a novel by a decorous stylishness and scrupulousness of composition, as if all their speeches had been corrected by their governesses and schoolmasters, had not yet been exploded by the 'New Journalism' of 1888 and the advent of a host of authors who had apparently never read anything, catering for a proletariat newly made literate by the Education Act. The distinction between the naturalness of Caleb Balderstone and the artificiality of Edgar and Lucy was still regarded as one of the social decencies by the seniors of literature; and this probably explains the fact that the only intimations I received that my work had made some impression, and had even been hesitatingly condemned, were from the older and more august houses whose readers were all grave elderly lovers of literature. And the more I progressed towards my own individual style and ventured upon the freer expression of my own ideas, the more I disappointed them. As to the regular novel-publishing houses, whose readers were merely on the scent of popularity, they gave me no quarter at all. And so between the old stool of my literary conscientiousness and the new stool of a view of life that did not reach publishing-point in England until about ten years later, when Ibsen drove it in, my novels fell to the ground.

I was to find later on that a book is like a child: it is easier to bring it into the world than to control it when it is launched there. As long as I kept sending my novels to the publishers, they were as safe from publicity as they would have been in the fire, where I had better, perhaps, have put them. But when I flung them aside as failures they almost instantly began to shew signs of life.

The Socialist revival of the eighties, into which I had plunged, produced the usual crop of propagandist magazines, in the conduct of which payment of the printer was the main problem, payment of contributors being quite out of the question. The editor of such a magazine can never count on a full supply of live matter to make up his tale of pages. But if he can collect a stock of unreadable novels, the refuse of the publishing trade, and a stock of minor poems (the world is full of such trash), an instalment of serial novel and a few verses will always make up the magazine to any required size. And this was how I found a use at last for my brown paper parcels. It seemed a matter of no more

7

consequence than stuffing so many broken window-panes with them; but it had momentous consequences; for in this way four of the five got printed and published in London, and thus incidentally became the common property of the citizens of the United States of America. These pioneers did not at first appreciate their new acquisition; and nothing particular happened except that the first novel (No. 5; for I ladled them out to the Socialist magazine editors in inverse order of composition) made me acquainted with William Morris, who, to my surprise, had been reading the monthly instalments with a certain relish. But that only proved how much easier it is to please a great man than a little one, especially when you share his politics. No. 5, called An Unsocial Socialist, was followed by No. 4, Cashel Byron's Profession; and Cashel Byron would not lie quiet in his serial grave, but presently rose and walked as a book.

It happened in this way. The name of the magazine was To-Day, not the present paper of that name, but one of the many To-days which are now Yesterdays. It had several editors, among them Mr Belfort Bax and the late James Leigh Joynes; but all the editors were in partnership with Mr Henry Hyde Champion who printed the magazine; and consequently went on for ever, whilst the others came and went. It was a fantastic business, Joynes having thrown up an Eton mastership, and Champion a commission in the army, at the call of Socialism. But Champion's pugnacity survived his abdicated adjutancy: he had an unregenerate taste for pugilism, and liked Cashel Byron so much that he stereotyped the pages of To-Day which it occupied, and in spite of my friendly remonstrances, hurled on the market a misshapen shilling edition. My friend Mr William Archer reviewed it prominently; the Saturday Review, always susceptible in those days to the arts of self-defence, unexpectedly declared it the novel of the age; Mr W. E. Henley wanted to have it dramatized; Stevenson wrote a letter about it, of which more presently; the other papers hastily searched their waste-paper baskets for it and reviewed it,

8

mostly rather disappointedly; and the public preserved its composure and did not seem to care.

That shilling edition began with a thousand copies; but it proved immortal. I never got anything out of it; and Mr Champion never got anything out of it; for he presently settled in Australia, and his printing presses and stereo plates were dispersed. But from that time forth the book was never really out of print; and though Messrs Walter Scott soon placed a revised shilling edition on the market, I suspect that still, in some obscure printing office, those old plates of Mr Champion's from time to time produce a 'remainder' of the original Modern Press edition, which is to the present what the Quarto Hamlet is to the Folio.

On the passing of To-Day, I became novelist in ordinary to a magazine called Our Corner, edited by Mrs Annie Besant. It had the singular habit of paying for its contributions, and was, I am afraid, to some extent a device of Mrs Besant's for relieving necessitous young propagandists without wounding their pride by open almsgiving. She was an incorrigible benefactress, and probably revenged herself for my freely expressed scorn for this weakness by drawing on her private account to pay me for my jejune novels. At last Our Corner went the way of all propagandist magazines, completing a second nonage novel and its own career at the same moment. This left me with only one unprinted masterpiece, my Opus 1, which had cost me an unconscionable quantity of paper, and was called, with merciless fitness, Immaturity. Part of it had by this time been devoured by mice, though even they had not been able to finish it. To this day it has never escaped from its old brown paper travelling suit; and I only mention it because some of its characters appear, Trollope fashion, in the later novels. I do not think any of them got so far as Cashel Byron's Profession; but the Mrs Hoskyn and her guests who appear in that absurd Chapter VI are all borrowed from previous works.

The unimportance of these particulars must be my

apology for detailing them to a world that finds something romantic in what are called literary struggles. However, I must most indignantly deny that I ever struggled. I wrote the books: it was the publishers who struggled with them, and struggled in vain. The public now takes up the struggle, impelled, not by any fresh operations of mine, but by Literary Destiny. For there is a third act to my tragedy.

Not long ago, when the memory of the brown paper parcels of 1879–1883 had been buried under twenty years of work, I learnt from the American papers that the list of book sales in one of the United States was headed by a certain novel called An Unsocial Socialist, by Bernard Shaw. This was unmistakably Opus 5 of the Novels of My Nonage. Columbia was beginning to look after her hitherto neglected acquisition. Apparently the result was encouraging; for presently the same publisher produced a new edition of Cashel Byron's Profession (Opus 4), in criticizing which the more thoughtful reviewers, unaware that the publisher was working backwards through the list, pointed out the marked advance in my style, the surer grip, the clearer form, the finer art, the maturer view of the world, and so forth. As it was clearly unfair that my own American publishers should be debarred by delicacy towards me from exploiting the new field of derelict fiction, I begged them to make the most of their national inheritance; and with my full approval, Opus 3, called Love Among the Artists (a paraphrase of the forgotten line Love Among the Roses) followed. No doubt it will pay its way: people who will read An Unsocial Socialist will read anything. But the new enthusiasm for Cashel Byron did not stop here. American ladies were seized with a desire to go on the stage and be Lydia Carew for two thrilling hours. American actors 'saw themselves' as Cashel. Mr James Corbett has actually appeared on the New York stage in the part. There can be no doubt now that my novels, so long left for dead in the forlorn-hope magazines of the eighties, have arisen and begun to propagate themselves vigorously throughout the new world at the rate of a dollar and a half per copy, free of all royalty to the flattered author.

Blame not me, then, reader, if these exercises of a raw apprentice break loose again and insist on their right to live. The world never did know chalk from cheese in matters of art; and, after all, since it is only the young and the old who have time to read, the rest being too busy living, my exercises may be fitter for the market than my masterpieces.

Cashel Byron's Profession is not a very venturesome republication, because, as I have said, the story has never been really out of print. But for some years after the expiration of my agreement with Messrs Walter Scott I did my best to suppress it, though by that time it had become the subject of proposals from a new generation of publishers. The truth is, the preference for this particular novel annoyed me. In novel-writing there are two trustworthy dodges for capturing the public. One is to slaughter a child and pathosticate over its deathbed for a whole chapter. The other is to describe either a fight or a murder. There is a fight in Cashel Byron's Profession: that profession itself is fighting; and here lay the whole schoolboy secret of the book's little vogue. I had the old grievance of the author: people will admire him for the feats that any fool can achieve, and bear malice against him for boring them with better work. Besides, my conscience was not quite easy in the matter. In spite of all my pains to present the prizefighter and his pursuits without any romantic glamor (for indeed the true artistic material of the story is the comedy of the contrast between the realities of the ring and the common romantic glorification or sentimental abhorrence of it), yet our non-combatant citizens are so fond of setting other people to fight that the only effect of such descriptions as I have incidentally given of Cashel's professional performances is to make people want to see something of the sort and take steps accordingly. This tendency of the book was repugnant to me; and if prizefighting were a sleeping dog, I should certainly let it lie, in spite of the American editions.

Unfortunately the dog is awake, barking and biting vigorously. Twenty years ago prizefighting was supposed to be dead. Few living men remembered the palmy days when Tom and Jerry went to Jackson's rooms (where Byron – not Cashel, but the poet – studied 'the noble art') to complete their education as Corinthians; when Cribb fought Molyneux and was to Tom Spring what Skene was to Cashel Byron; when Kemble engaged Dutch Sam to carry on the war with the O.P. rioters; when Sharples' portraits of leading bruisers were engraved on steel; when Bell's Life was a fashionable paper, and Pierce Egan's Boxiana a more expensive publishing enterprise than any modern Badminton volume. The sport was supposed to have died of its own blackguardism by the second quarter of the century; but the connoisseur who approaches the subject without moral bias will, I think, agree with me that it must have lived by its blackguardism and died of its intolerable tediousness; for all prizefighters are not Cashel Byrons, and in barren dreariness and futility no spectacle on earth can contend with that of two exhausted men trying for hours to tire one another out at fisticuffs for the sake of their backers. The Sayers revival in the sixties only left the ring more discredited than ever, since the injuries formerly reserved for the combatants began, after their culmination in the poisoning of Heenan, to be showered on the referee; and as the referee was usually the representative of the Bell's Life type of paper, which naturally organized the prizefights it lived by reporting, the ring went under again, this time undoubtedly through its blackguardism and violence driving away its only capable organizers.

In the eighties many apparently lost causes and dead enthusiasms unexpectedly revived: Imperialism, Patriotism, Religion, Socialism, and many other things, including prizefighting in an aggravated form, and on a scale of commercial profit and publicity which soon made its palmy days insignificant and ridiculous by contrast. A modern American pugilist makes more by a single defeat than Cribb made by all his victories. It is this fact that has decided me to give up my attempt to suppress Cashel Byron's Profession. Silence may be the right policy on a dropped subject; but on a burning one every word that can cool the fervor of idolatry with a dash of cold fact has its value.

I need not postpone a comment on the vast propaganda of pugnacity in modern fiction: a propaganda that must be met, not by shocked silence, but by counter-propaganda. And this counter-propaganda must not take the usual form of 'painting the horrors.' Horror is fascinating: the great criminal is always a popular hero. People are seduced by romance because they are ignorant of reality; and this is as true of the prize ring as of the battlefield. The intelligent prizefighter is not a knight-errant: he is a disillusioned man of business trying to make money at a certain weight and at certain risks, not of bodily injury (for a bruise is soon cured), but of pecuniary loss. When he is a Jew, a negro, a gypsy, or a recruit from that gypsified, nomadic, poaching, tinkering, tramping class which exists in all countries, he differs from the phlegmatic John Bull pugilist (an almost extinct species) exactly as he would differ from him in any other occupation: that is, he is a more imaginative liar, a more obvious poser, a more plausible talker, a vainer actor, a more reckless gambler, and more easily persuaded that he is beaten or even killed when he has only received an unusually hard punch. The unintelligent prizefighter is often the helpless tool of a gang of gamblers, backers, and showmen, who set him on to fight as they might set on a dog. And the spectacle of a poor human animal fighting faithfully for his backers, like a terrier killing rats, or a racehorse doing its best to win a race for its owner, is one which ought to persuade any sensible person of the folly of treating the actual combatants as 'the principals' in a prizefight. Cockfighting was not suppressed by imprisoning the cocks; and prizefighting will not be suppressed by imprisoning the pugilists. But, intelligent or unintelligent, first rate like Cashel Byron, second rate like Skene, or third rate like William Paradise in this story, the prizefighter is no more what the spectators imagine him to be than the lady with the wand and star in the pantomine is really a fairy queen. And since Cashel Byron's Profession, on its prizefighting side, is an attempt to take the reader behind the scenes without unfairly confusing professional pugilism with the blackguardly environment which is no more essential to it than to professional cricket, and which is now losing its hold on the pugilist through the substitution of gate-money at boxing exhibitions for stakes at prizefights as his means of living, I think I may let it go its way with a reasonable prospect of seeing it do more good than harm.

It may even help in the Herculean task of eliminating romantic fisticuffs from English novels, and so clear them from the reproach of childishness and crudity which they certainly deserve in this respect. Even in the best nineteenth century novels the heroes knock the villains down. Bulwer Lytton's Kenelm Chillingly was a 'scientific' pugilist, though his technique will hardly be recognized by experts. Thackeray, who, when defeated in a parliamentary election, publicly compared himself to Gregson beaten by Gully, loved a fight almost as much as he loved a fool. Even the great Dickens himself never quite got away from this sort of schoolboyishness; for though Joe Gargery knocking down Orlick is much more plausible than Oliver Twist punching the head of Noah Claypole, still the principle is the same: virtue still insists on victory, domination, and triumphant assault and battery. It is true that Dombey and Son contains a pious attempt to caricature a prizefighter; but no qualified authority will pretend that Dickens caught The Chicken's point of view, or did justice to the social accomplishments of the ring. Mr Toots's silly admiration of the poor boxer, and the manner in which the Chicken and other professors of the art of self-defence used to sponge on him, is perfectly true to life; but in the real pugilistic world so profitable a gull would soon have been taken out of the hands of the Chicken and preyed upon by much better company. It is true that if the Chicken had been an unconquerable fighter, he might have maintained a gloomy eminence in spite of his dulness and disagreeable manners; but Dickens gave away this one possible excuse by allowing The Larky Boy to defeat the Chicken with ignominy. That is what is called poetic justice. It is really poetic criminal law; and it is almost as dishonest and vindictive as real criminal law. In plain fact the pugilistic profession is like any other profession: common sense, good manners, and a social turn count for as much in it as they do elsewhere; and as the pugilist makes a good deal of money by teaching gentlemen to box, he has to learn to behave himself, and often succeeds very much better than the average middle-class professional man. Shakespear was much nearer the mark when he made Autolycus better company, and Charles the Wrestler a better-mannered man, than Ajax or Cloten. If Dickens had really known the ring, he would have made the Chicken either a Sayers in professional ability or a Sam Weller in sociability. A successful combination of personal repulsiveness with professional incompetence is as impossible there as at the bar or in the faculty. The episode of the Chicken, then, must be dismissed, in spite of its hero's tempting suggested remedy for Mr Dombey's stiffness, as a futile atonement for the heroic fisticuffs of Oliver Twist and Co.

There is an abominable vein of retaliatory violence all through the literature of the nineteenth century. Whether it is Macaulay describing the flogging of Titus Oates, or Dickens inventing the scene in which old Martin Chuzzlewit bludgeons Pecksniff, the curious childishness of the English character, its naughty relish for primitive brutalities and tolerance of physical indignities, its unreasoning destructiveness when incommoded, crop up in all directions. The childishness has its advantages: its want of foresight prevents the individual from carrying weapons, as it prevents the nation from being prepared for war; its forgetfulness prevents vendettas and prolonged malice-bearing; its simplicity and transparency save it from the more ingenious and complicated forms of political corruption. In short, it has those innocences of childhood which are a necessary result of its impotences. But it has no true sense of human dignity. The son of a Russian noble is not flogged at school, because he commits suicide sooner than survive the outrage to his self-respect. The son of an English noble has no more sense of dignity than the master who flogs him: flogging may be troublesome to the flogger and painful to the floggee; but the notion that the transaction is disgusting to the public and dishonorable and disgraceful to the parties is as unintelligible and fantastic in England as it is in a nursery anywhere. The moment the Englishman gets away from Eton, he begins to enjoy and boast of flogging as an institution. A school where boys are flogged and where they settle their quarrels by fighting with their fists he calls, not, as one might expect, a school of childishness, but a school of manliness. And he gradually persuades himself that all Englishmen can use their fists, which is about as true as the parallel theory that every Frenchman can handle a foil and that every Italian carries a stiletto. And so, though he himself has never fought a pitched battle at school, and does not, pugilistically speaking, know his right hand from his left; though his neighbors are as peaceful and as nervous as he; though if he knocked a man down or saw one of his friends do it, the event would stand out in his history like a fire or a murder; yet he not only tolerates unstinted knockings-down in fiction, but actually founds his conception of his nation and its destiny on these imaginary outrages, and at last comes to regard a plain statement of the plain fact that the average respectable Englishman knows rather less about fighting than he does about flying, as a paradoxical extravagance.

And so every popular English novel becomes a gospel of pugilism. Cashel Byron's Profession, then, is like any other novel in respect of its hero punching people's heads. Its novelty consists in the fact that an attempt is made to treat the art of punching seriously, and to detach it from the general elevation of moral character with which the ordinary novelist persists in associating it.

Here, therefore, the prizefighter is not idolized. I have given Cashel Byron every advantage a prizefighter can have: health and strength and pugilistic genius. But by pugilistic genius I mean nothing vague, imaginary, or glamorous. In all walks of life men are to be found who seem to have powers of divination. For example, you propound a complicated arithmetical problem: say the cubing of a number containing four digits. Give me a slate and half an hour's time, and I can produce a wrong answer. But there are men to whom the right answer is instantly obvious without any consciousness of calculation on their part. Ask such a man to write a description or put a somewhat complicated thought into words; and he will take my slate and blunder over it in search of words for half an hour, finally putting down the wrong ones; whilst for a Shakespear the words are there in due style and measure as soon as the consciousness of the thing to be described or the formation of the thought. Now there are pugilists to whom the process of aiming and estimating distance in hitting, of considering the evidence as to what their opponent is going to do, arriving at a conclusion, and devising and carrying out effective countermeasures, is as instantaneous and unconscious as the calculation of the born arithmetician or the verbal expression of the born writer. This is not more wonderful than the very complicated and deeply considered feats of breathing and circulating the blood, which everybody does continually without thinking; but it is much rarer, and so has a miraculous appearance. A man with this gift, and with no physical infirmities to disable him, is a born prizefighter. He need have no other exceptional qualities, courage least of all: indeed there are instances on record of prizefighters who have only consented to persevere with a winning fight when a mirror has been brought to convince them that their faces were undamaged and their injuries and terrors imaginary.

'Stage fright' is as common in the ring as elsewhere: I have myself seen a painful exhibition of it from a very rough customer who presently knocked out his opponent without effort, by instinct. The risks of the ring are limited by rules and conditions to such an extent that the experienced prize-fighter is much more afraid of the blackguardism of the spectators than of his opponent: he takes care to have a strong body of supporters in his corner, and to keep carefully away from the opposite corner. Courage is if anything rather scarcer, because less needed, in the ring than out of it; and there are civil occupations which many successful prize-fighters would fail in, or fear to enter, for want of nerve. For the ring, like all romantic institutions, has a natural attraction for hysterical people.

When a pugilistic genius of the Cashel Byron type appeared in the ring of his day, it soon became evident to the betting men on whom the institution depended, that it was useless to back clever boxers against him; for, as the second Lytton (Owen Meredith) wrote –

Talk not of genius baffled: genius is master of man.
Genius does what it must; and Talent does what it can.

But there is a well-known way of defeating the pugilistic genius. There are hard-fisted, hard-hitting men in the world, who will, with the callousness of a ship's figurehead, and almost with its helplessness in defence, take all the hammering that genius can give them, and, when genius can hammer no more from mere exhaustion, give it back its blows with interest and vanquish it. All pugilism lies between these two extremes typified by Cashel Byron and William Paradise; and it is because the Paradises are as likely to win as the Byrons, and are by no means so scarce, that the case for fist fighting, with gloves or without, as a discipline in the higher athletic qualities, moral and physical, imposes only on people who have no practical knowledge of the subject.

*

On a previous page I have alluded to a letter from Robert Louis Stevenson to Mr William Archer about Cashel Byron's Profession. Part of that letter has been given to the public in the second volume of Mr Sidney Colvin's edition of Stevenson's letters (Methuen, 1900). But no document concerning a living person of any consequence (by which I mean a person with money enough to take an action for libel) is ever published in England unless its contents are wholly complimentary. Stevenson's letters were probably all unfit for publication in this respect. Certainly the one about Cashel Byron's Profession was; and Mr Sidney Colvin, out of consideration for me and for his publishers and printers, politely abbreviated it. Fortunately the original letter is still in the hands of Mr Archer. I need not quote the handsome things which Mr Colvin selected, as they have been extensively reprinted in America to help the sale of the reprints there. But here is the suppressed portion, to which I leave the last word, having no more to say than that the book is now reprinted, not from the old Modern Press edition which Stevenson read, but from the revised text issued afterwards by Messrs Walter Scott, from which certain 'little bits of Socialism daubed in' for the edification of the readers of To-Day were either painted out or better harmonized with the rest. I had intended to make no further revision; and I have in fact made none of any importance; but in reading the proofs my pen positively jumped to humanize a few passages in which the literary professionalism with which my heroine expresses herself (this professionalism is usually called 'style' in England) went past all bearing. I have also indulged myself by varying a few sentences, and inserting one or two new ones, so as to enable the American publisher to secure copyright in this edition. But I have made no attempt to turn an 1882 novel into a twentieth century one; and the few alterations are, except for legal purposes, quite negligible.

And now for the suppressed part of Stevenson's verdict, which is in the form of an analysis of the book's composition.

'Charles Reade	1 part
Henry James or some kindred author, badly assimilated	1 part
Disraeli (perhaps unconscious) . . .	½ part
Struggling, overlaid original talent . .	1½ part
Blooming gaseous folly	1 part

'That is the equation as it stands. What it may become, I dont know, nor any other man. *Vixere fortes* – O, let him remember that – let him beware of his damned century: his gifts of insane chivalry and animated narration are just those that might be slain and thrown out like an untimely birth by the Dæmon of the Epoch.

'And if he only knew how I had enjoyed the chivalry! Bashville – O Bashville! *j'en chortle!* (which is finely polyglot).'

1901.

POSTSCRIPT TWENTYNINE YEARS LATER. Portions of this preface must be read with some reservations. Belfort Bax, Henry Hyde Champion, William Archer, and W. E. Henley are no longer Misters: they are all dead. And the novel that 'never escaped from its brown travelling suit' has at last escaped, to be published for the first time in the Collected Edition of my works fifty years after I wrote Finis on its last page.

1930.

CASHEL BYRON'S PROFESSION

PROLOGUE

I

MONCRIEF HOUSE, Panley Common. Scholastic establishment for the sons of gentlemen, etc.

Panley Common, viewed from the back windows of Moncrief House, is a tract of grass, furze, and rushes, stretching away to the western horizon.

One wet spring afternoon the sky was full of broken clouds; and the common was swept by their shadows, between which patches of green and yellow gorse were bright in the broken sunlight. The hills to the northward were obscured by a heavy shower, traces of which were drying off the slates of the school, a square white building, formerly a gentleman's country house. In front of it was a well-kept lawn with a few clipt holly trees: at the rear, quarter of an acre of land enclosed for the use of the boys. Strollers on the common could hear, at certain hours, a hubbub of voices and racing footsteps within the boundary wall. Sometimes, when the strollers were boys themselves, they climbed to the coping, and saw on the other side a piece of common trampled bare and brown, with a few square yards of concrete, so worn into hollows as to be unfit for its original use as a ball alley. Also a long shed, a pump, a door defaced by innumerable incised inscriptions, the back of the house in much worse repair than the front, and about fifty boys in tailless jackets and broad turned-down collars. Whenever the fifty boys perceived a young stranger on the wall, they rushed to the spot with a wild halloo; overwhelmed him with insult and defiance; and dislodged him by a volley of clods, stones, lumps of bread, and such other projectiles as were at hand.

On this rainy spring afternoon, a brougham stood at the door of Moncrief House. The coachman, enveloped in a white india-rubber coat, was bestirring himself a little after the recent shower. Withindoors, in the drawing room, Dr

Moncrief was conversing with a stately lady aged about thirty-five, elegantly dressed, of attractive manner, and beautiful at all points except her complexion, which was deficient in freshness.

'No progress whatever, I am sorry to say,' the doctor was remarking.

'That is very disappointing,' said the lady, contracting her brows.

'It is natural that you should feel disappointed,' replied the doctor. 'I should myself earnestly advise you to try the effect of placing him at some other – ' The doctor stopped. The lady's face had lit with a wonderful smile; and her hand was up with a bewitching gesture of protest.

'Oh no, Dr Moncrief,' she said: 'I am not disappointed with *you*; but I am all the more angry with Cashel because I know that if he makes no progress here, it must be his own fault. As to taking him away, that is out of the question. I should not have a moment's peace if he were out of your care. I will speak to him very seriously about his conduct before I leave today. You will give him another trial, will you not?'

'Certainly. With the greatest pleasure,' said the doctor, confusing himself by an inept attempt at gallantry. 'He shall stay as long as you please. But' – here the doctor became grave again – 'you cannot too strongly urge upon him the importance of hard work at the present time, which may be said to be the turning point of his career as a student. He is now nearly seventeen; and he has so little inclination for study that I doubt whether he could pass the examination necessary to enter one of the universities. You probably wish him to take a degree before he chooses a profession.'

'Yes, of course,' said the lady vaguely, evidently assenting to the doctor's remark rather than expressing a conviction of her own. 'What profession would you advise for him? You know so much better than I.'

'Hum!' said Dr Moncrief, puzzled. 'That would doubtless depend to some extent on his own taste – '

'Not at all,' said the lady, interrupting him vivaciously. 'What does he know about the world, poor boy? His own taste is sure to be something ridiculous. Very likely he would want to go on the stage, like me.'

'Oh! Then you would not encourage any tendency of that sort?'

'Most decidedly not. I hope he has no such idea.'

'Not that I am aware of. He shews so little ambition to excel in any particular branch, that I should say his choice of a profession may be best determined by his parents. I am, of course, ignorant whether his relatives possess influence likely to be of use to him. That is often the chief point to be considered, particularly in cases like your son's, where no special aptitude manifests itself.'

'I am the only relative he ever had, poor fellow,' said the lady, with a pensive smile. Then, seeing an expression of astonishment on the doctor's face, she added quickly, 'They are all dead.'

'Dear me!'

'However,' she continued, 'I have no doubt I can make plenty of interest for him. But I suppose it is difficult to get anything nowadays without passing competitive examinations. He really must work. If he is lazy he ought to be punished.'

The doctor looked perplexed. 'The fact is,' he said, 'your son can hardly be dealt with as a child any longer. He is still quite a boy in his habits and ideas; but physically he is rapidly springing up into a young man. That reminds me of another point on which I will ask you to speak earnestly to him. I must tell you that he has attained some distinction among his school-fellows here as an athlete. Within due bounds I do not discourage bodily exercises: they are a recognized part of our system. But I am sorry to say that Cashel has not escaped that tendency to violence which sometimes results from the possession of unusual strength and dexterity. He actually fought with one of the village youths in the main street of Panley some months ago, I am told, though the matter did not come to my ears immediately. He was guilty of a much more serious fault a little later. He and a companion of his obtained leave from me to walk to Panley Abbey together; but I afterwards found that their real object was to witness a prizefight that took place – illegally, of course – on the common. Apart from the deception practised, I think the taste they betrayed a dangerous one; and I felt bound to punish them by a severe imposition, and restriction to the grounds for six weeks. I do not hold, however, that everything has been done in these cases when a boy has been punished. I set a high value on a mother's influence by softening the natural roughness of boys.'

'I dont think he minds what I say to him in the least,' said the lady, with a sympathetic air, as if she pitied the doctor in a matter that chiefly concerned him. 'I will speak to him about it, certainly. Fighting is an unbearable habit. His father's people were always fighting; and they never did any good in the world.'

'If you will be so kind. There are just the three points: the necessity for greater – much greater – application to his studies; a word to him on the subject of rough habits; and to sound him as to his choice of a career. I agree with you in not attaching much importance to his ideas on that subject as yet. Still, even a boyish fancy may be turned to account in rousing the energies of a lad.'

'Quite so,' assented the lady. 'I shall take care to give him a lecture.'

The doctor looked at her mistrustfully, thinking perhaps that she herself would be the better for a lecture on her duties as a mother. But he did not dare to tell her so: indeed, having a prejudice that actresses were deficient in natural feeling, he doubted the use of daring. He also feared that the subject of her son was beginning to bore her; and, though a doctor of divinity, he was as reluctant as other men to be found wanting in address by a pretty woman. So he rang the bell, and bade the servant send Master Cashel Byron. Presently a door was heard to open below; and a buzz of distant voices became audible. The doctor fidgeted and tried to think of something to say; but his invention failed him: he sat in silence whilst the inarticulate buzz rose into a shouting of 'By-ron! Cash!' the latter cry imitated from the summons usually addressed to cashiers in haberdashers' shops. Finally there was a piercing yell of 'Mam-ma-a-a-a-ah!' apparently in explanation of the demand for Byron's attendance in the drawing room. The doctor reddened. Mrs Byron smiled. Then the door below closed, shutting out the tumult; and footsteps were heard on the stairs.

'Come in,' cried the doctor encouragingly.

Master Cashel Byron entered blushing; made his way awkwardly to his mother; and kissed the critical expression which was on her upturned face as she examined his appearance. Being only seventeen, he had not yet acquired a taste for kissing. He inexpertly gave Mrs Byron quite a shock by the collision of their teeth. Conscious of the failure, he drew himself upright, and tried to hide his hands, which were exceedingly dirty, in the scanty folds of his jacket. He was a well-grown youth, with strong neck and shoulders, and short auburn hair curling in little rings close to his scalp. He had blue eyes, and an expression of boyish good humor, which, however, did not convey any assurance of good temper.

'How do you do, Cashel?' said Mrs Byron, with queenly patronage, after a prolonged look at him.

'Very well, thanks,' said he, grinning and avoiding her eye.

'Sit down, Byron,' said the doctor. Byron suddenly forgot how to sit down, and looked irresolutely from one chair to another. The doctor made a brief excuse, and left the room, much to the relief of his pupil.

'You have grown greatly, Cashel. And I am afraid you are very awkward.' Cashel colored and looked gloomy.

'I do not know what to do with you,' continued Mrs Byron. 'Dr Moncrief tells me that you are very idle and rough.'

'I am not,' said Cashel sulkily. 'It is bec—'

'There is no use in contradicting me in that fashion,' said Mrs Byron, interrupting him sharply. 'I am sure that whatever Dr Moncrief says is perfectly true.'

'He is always talking like that,' said Cashel plaintively. 'I cant learn Latin and Greek; and I dont see what good they are. I work as hard as any of the rest – except the regular stews perhaps. As to my being rough, that is all because I was out one day with Gully Molesworth; and we saw a crowd on the common; and when we went to see what was up it was two men fighting. It wasnt our fault that they came there to fight.'

'Yes: I have no doubt that you have fifty good excuses, Cashel. But I will not allow any fighting; and you really must work harder. Do you ever think of how hard *I* have to work to pay Dr Moncrief one hundred and twenty pounds a year for you?'

'I work as hard as I can. Old Moncrief seems to think that a fellow ought to do nothing else from morning till night but write Latin verses. Tatham, that the doctor thinks such a genius, does all his constering from cribs. If I had a crib I could conster as well – very likely better.'

'You are very idle, Cashel: I am sure of that. It is too provoking to throw away so much money every year for nothing. Besides, you must soon be thinking of a profession.'

'I shall go into the army,' said Cashel. 'It is the only profession for a gentleman.'

Mrs Byron looked at him for a moment as if amazed at his presumption. But she checked herself and only said, 'I am afraid you will have to choose some less expensive profession than that. Besides, you would have to pass an examination to enable you to enter the army; and how can you do that unless you study?'

'Oh, I shall do that all right enough when the time comes.'

'Dear, dear! You are beginning to speak so coarsely, Cashel. After all the pains I took with you at home!'

'I speak the same as other people,' he replied sullenly. 'I

dont see the use of being so jolly particular over every syllable. I used to have to stand no end of chaff about my way of speaking. The fellows here know all about you, of course.'

'All about me?' repeated Mrs Byron, looking at him curiously.

'All about your being on the stage, I mean,' said Cashel. 'You complain of my being rough; but I should have a precious bad time of it if I didnt lick the chaff out of some of them.'

Mrs Byron smiled doubtfully to herself, and remained silent and thoughtful for a moment. Then she rose and said, glancing at the weather, 'I must go now, Cashel, before another shower begins. And do, pray, try to learn something and to polish your manners a little. You will have to go to Cambridge soon, you know.'

'Cambridge!' exclaimed Cashel, excited. 'When, mamma? When?'

'Oh, I dont know. Not yet. As soon as Dr Moncrief says you are fit to go.'

'That will be long enough,' said Cashel, much dejected by this reply. 'He will not turn £120 a year out of doors in a hurry. He kept big Inglis here until he was past twenty. Look here, mamma: might I go at the end of this half? I feel sure I should do better at Cambridge than here.'

'Nonsense,' said Mrs Byron decidedly. 'I do not expect to have to take you away from Dr Moncrief for the next eighteen months at least, and not then unless you work properly. Now dont grumble, Cashel: you annoy me exceedingly when you do. I am sorry I mentioned Cambridge to you.'

'I would rather go to some other school, then,' said Cashel ruefully. 'Old Moncrief is so awfully down on me.'

'You only want to leave because you are expected to work here; and that is the very reason I wish you to stay.'

Cashel made no reply; but his face darkened ominously.

'I have a word to say to the doctor before I go,' she added, reseating herself. 'You may return to your play now.

Goodbye, Cashel.' And she again raised her face to be kissed.

'Goodbye,' said Cashel huskily, as he turned towards the door, pretending that he had not noticed her action.

'Cashel!' she said, with emphatic surprise. 'Are you sulky?'

'No,' he retorted angrily. 'I havnt said anything. I suppose my manners are not good enough. I'm very sorry; but I cant help it.'

'Very well,' said Mrs Byron firmly. 'You can go. I am not pleased with you.'

Cashel walked out of the room and slammed the door. At the foot of the stairs he was stopped by a boy about a year younger than himself, who accosted him eagerly.

'How much did she give you?' he whispered.

'Not a halfpenny,' replied Cashel, grinding his teeth.

'Oh, I say!' exclaimed the other, deeply disappointed. 'That was beastly mean.'

'She's as mean as she can be,' said Cashel. 'It's all old Monkey's fault. He has been cramming her with lies about me. But she's just as bad as he is. I tell you, Gully, I hate my mother.'

'Oh, come!' said Gully, shocked. 'Thats a little too strong, old chap. But she certainly ought to have stood something.'

'I dont know what you intend to do, Gully; but I mean to bolt. If she thinks I am going to stick here for the next two years, she is jolly much mistaken.'

'It would be an awful lark to bolt,' said Gully, with a chuckle. 'But,' he added seriously, 'if you really mean it, by George, I'll go too! Wilson has just given me a thousand lines; and I'll be hanged if I do them.'

'Gully,' said Cashel, his frown deepening and fixing itself forbiddingly: 'I should like to see one of those chaps we saw on the common pitch into the doctor – get him on the ropes, you know.'

Gully's mouth watered. 'Yes,' he said breathlessly;

'particularly the fellow they called the Fibber. Just one round would be enough for the old beggar. Lets come out into the playground: I shall catch it if I am found here.'

II

That night there was just sufficient light struggling through the clouds to make Panley Common visible as a black expanse, against the lightest tone of which a piece of ebony would have appeared pale. Not a human being was stirring within a mile of Moncrief House, the chimneys of which, ghostly white on the side next the moon, threw long shadows on the silver-grey slates. The stillness had just been broken by the stroke of a quarter-past twelve from a distant church tower, when, from the obscurity of one of these chimney shadows, a head emerged. It belonged to a boy, whose body presently came wriggling through an open skylight. When his shoulders were through, he turned himself face upwards; seized the miniature gable in which the skylight was set; drew himself completely out; and made his way stealthily down to the parapet. He was immediately followed by another boy.

The door of Moncrief House was at the left hand corner of the front, and was surmounted by a tall porch, the top of which was flat and could be used as a balcony. A wall, of the same height as the porch, connected the house front with the boundary wall, and formed part of the inclosure of a fruit garden which lay at the side of the house between the lawn and the playground. When the two boys had crept along the parapet to a point directly above the porch, they stopped; and each lowered a pair of boots to the balcony by means of fishing lines. When the boots were safely landed, their owners let the lines drop, and re-entered the house by another skylight. A minute elapsed. Then they reappeared on the top of the porch, having come out through the window to which it served as a balcony. Here they put on their boots, and made for the wall of the fruit garden. As they crawled along it, the hindmost boy whispered,

'I say, Cashy.'

'Shut up, will you,' replied the other under his breath. 'Whats wrong?'

'I should like to have one more go at old mother Moncrief's pear tree: thats all.'

'There are no pears on it at this time of year, you fool.'

'I know. This is the last time we shall go this road, Cashy. Usent it to be a lark? Eh?'

'If you dont shut up, it wont be the last time; for youll be caught. Now for it.'

Cashel had reached the outer wall; and he finished his sentence by dropping from the coping to the common. Gully held his breath for some moments after the noise made by his companion's striking the ground. Then he demanded in a whisper whether all was right.

'Yes,' returned Cashel impatiently. 'Drop as soft as you can.'

Gully obeyed; and was so careful lest his descent should shake the earth and awake the doctor, that his feet shrank from the concussion. He alighted in a sitting posture, and remained there, looking up at Cashel with a stunned expression.

'Crickey!' he ejaculated presently. 'That was a buster.'

'Get up, I tell you,' said Cashel. 'I never saw such a jolly ass as you are. Here, up with you! Have you got your wind back?'

'I should think so. Bet you twopence I'll be first at the cross roads. I say: lets pull the bell at the front gate and give an awful yell before we start. Theyll never catch us.'

'Yes,' said Cashel ironically: 'I fancy I see myself doing it, or you either. Now then. One, two, three, and away.'

They ran off together, and reached the cross roads about eight minutes later: Gully completely out of breath, and Cashel nearly so. Here, according to their plan, Gully was to take the north road and run to Scotland, where he felt sure his uncle's gamekeeper would hide him. Cashel was to go to sea, so that if his affairs became desperate, he could at least turn pirate, and achieve eminence in that profession by adding a chivalrous humanity to the ruder virtues for which it is already famous.

Cashel waited until Gully had recovered from his race. Then he said,

'Now, old fellow. Weve got to separate.'

Gully, confronted with the lonely realities of his scheme, did not like the prospect. After a moment's reflection he exclaimed,

'Damme, old chap, I'll come with you. Scotland may go and be hanged.'

But Cashel, being the stronger of the two, was as anxious to get rid of Gully as Gully was to cling to him. 'No,' he said, 'I'm going to rough it; and you wouldnt be able for that. Youre not strong enough for a sea life. Why, man, those sailor fellows are as hard as nails; and even they can hardly stand it.'

'Well, then, do you come with me,' urged Gully. 'My uncle's gamekeeper wont mind. He's a jolly good sort; and we shall have no end of shooting.'

'Thats all very well for you, Gully; but I dont know your uncle; and I'm not going to put myself under a compliment to his gamekeeper. Besides, we should run too much risk of being caught if we went through the country together. Of course I should be only too glad if we could stick to one another; but it wouldnt do: I feel certain we should be nabbed. Goodbye.'

'But wait a minute,' pleaded Gully. 'Suppose they do try to catch us: we shall have a better chance against them if there are two of us.'

'Stuff!' said Cashel. 'Thats all boyish nonsense. There will be at least six policemen sent after us; and even if I did my very best, I could barely lick two if they came on together. And you would hardly be able for one. You just keep moving, and dont go near any railway station; and you will get to Scotland all safe enough. Look here: weve wasted five minutes already. Ive got my wind now; and I must be off. Goodbye.'

Gully disdained to press his company on Cashel any further. 'Goodbye,' he said, mournfully shaking his hand. 'Success, old chap.'

'Success!' echoed Cashel, grasping Gully's hand with a pang of remorse for leaving him. 'I'll write to you as soon as I have anything to tell you. I may be some months, you know, before I get regularly settled.'

He gave Gully a final squeeze; released him; and darted off along the road leading to Panley Village. Gully looked after him a moment, and then ran away Scotlandwards.

Panley Village is nothing but a High Street, with an old-fashioned inn at one end, a modern railway station and bridge at the other, and a pump and pound midway between. Cashel stood for a while in the shadow under the bridge before venturing along the broad moonlit street. Seeing no one, he stepped out at a brisk walking pace; for he had by this time reflected that it was not possible to run all the way to the Spanish main. There was, however, another person stirring in the village besides Cashel. This was Mr Wilson, Dr Moncrief's professor of mathematics, who was returning from a visit to the theatre. Mr Wilson believed that theatres were wicked places, to be visited by respectable men only on rare occasions and by stealth. The only plays he went openly to witness were those of Shakespear; and his favorite was As You Like It: Rosalind in tights having an attraction for him which he missed from Lady Macbeth in petticoats. This evening he had seen Rosalind impersonated by a famous actress, who had come to a neighboring town on a starring tour. After the performance he had returned to Panley to sup there with a friend, and was now making his way back to Moncrief House. He was in a frame of mind favorable for the capture of a runaway boy. An habitual delight in being too clever for his pupils, fostered by frequently overreaching them in mathematics, was just now stimulated by the effect of a liberal supper and the roguish consciousness of having been to the play. He saw and recognized Cashel as he approached the village pound. Understanding the situation at once, he hid behind the pump; waited until the unsuspecting truant was passing within arm's length; and then pounced out and seized him by the collar of his jacket.

'Well, sir,' he said. 'What are you doing here at this hour? Eh?'

Cashel, scared and white, looked at him, and could not answer a word.

'Come along with me,' said Wilson sternly.

Cashel suffered himself to be led some twenty yards. Then he stopped and burst into tears.

'There is no use in my going back,' he said. 'I have never done any good there. I cant go back.'

'Indeed,' said Wilson, with magisterial sarcasm. 'We shall try to make you do better in future.' And he forced the fugitive to resume his march.

Cashel, bitterly humiliated by his own tears, and exasperated by a certain cold triumph which Wilson evinced on witnessing them, did not go many steps further without protest.

'You neednt hold me,' he said angrily: 'I can walk without being held.' The master tightened his grasp and pushed his captive forward. 'I wont run away, sir,' said Cashel more humbly, shedding fresh tears. 'Please let me go,' he added in a suffocated voice, trying to turn his face towards his captor. But Wilson twisted him back again, and still urged him onwards. Cashel cried out passionately, 'Let me go,' and struggled to break loose.

'Come, come, Byron,' said the master, controlling him with a broad strong hand: 'none of your nonsense, sir.'

Then Cashel suddenly slipped out of his jacket; turned on Wilson; and struck up at him savagely with his right fist. The master received the blow just beside the point of his chin; and his eyes seemed to Cashel to roll up and fall back into his head with the shock. He drooped forward for a moment, and fell in a heap face downwards. Cashel recoiled, wringing his hand to relieve the tingling of his knuckles, and terrified by the possibility that he had committed murder. But Wilson presently moved and dispelled that misgiving. Some of Cashel's fury returned as he shook his fist at his prostrate adversary, and, exclaiming, ' *You* wont brag much of having seen me cry,' wrenched the jacket from him with unnecessary violence, and darted away at full speed.

Mr Wilson, though he was soon conscious and able to rise, did not at first feel disposed to stir. He began to moan, with a dazed faith that some one would eventually come to him with sympathy and assistance. But the lapse of time brought nothing but increased cold and pain. It occurred to him that if the police found him they might suppose him to be drunk; also that it was his duty to go to them and give the alarm. He rose, and, after a struggle with dizziness and nausea, concluded that his most pressing duty was to get to bed, and leave Dr Moncrief to recapture his ruffianly pupil as best he could.

At half-past one o'clock the doctor was roused by a knocking at his chamber-door, outside which he found his professor of mathematics, bruised, muddy, and apparently inebriated. Some minutes were lost before Wilson could get his principal's mind on the right track. Then the boys were awakened and the roll called. Byron and Molesworth were reported absent. No one had seen them go: no one had the least suspicion of how they had got out of the house. One little boy mentioned the skylight; but, observing a threatening e xpression on the faces of a few of the bigger boys, who were fond of fruit, he did not press his suggestion, and submitted to be snubbed by the doctor for having made it. It was nearly three o'clock before the alarm reached the village, where the authorities tacitly declined to trouble themselves about it until morning. The doctor, convinced that the lad had gone to his mother, did not believe that any search was necessary, and contented himself with writing a note to Mrs Byron describing the attack on Mr Wilson, and expressing regret that no proposal having for its object the readmission of Master Byron to the academy could be entertained.

The pursuit was now directed entirely after Molesworth, as it was plain, from Mr Wilson's narrative, that he had separated from Cashel outside Panley. Information was soon forthcoming. Peasants in all parts of the country had seen, they said, 'a lad that might be him.' The search lasted until five o'clock next afternoon, when it was terminated by the appearance of Gully in person, footsore and repentant. After parting from Cashel and walking two miles, he had lost heart and turned back. Half way to the cross roads he had reproached himself with cowardice, and resumed his flight. This time he placed eight miles betwixt himself and Moncrief House. Then he left the road to make a short cut through a plantation, and went astray. After wandering dejectedly until morning, he saw a woman working in a field, and asked her the shortest way to Scotland. She had never heard of Scotland; and when he asked the way to Panley, she grew suspicious and threatened to set her dog at him. This discouraged him so much that he was afraid to speak to the other strangers whom he met. Steering by the sun, he oscillated between Scotland and Panley according to the fluctuation of his courage. At last he yielded to hunger, fatigue, and loneliness; devoted his remaining energy to the task of getting back to school; struck the common at last; and hastened to surrender himself to the doctor, who menaced him with immediate expulsion. Gully was greatly concerned at the prospect of being compelled to leave the place he had just run away from; and earnestly begged the doctor to give him another chance. His prayer was granted. After a prolonged lecture, the doctor, in consideration of the facts that Gully, though corrupted by the example of a desperate associate, had proved the sincerity of his repentance by coming back of his own accord, and had not been accessory to the concussion of the brain from which Mr Wilson supposed himself to be suffering, accepted his promise of amendment and gave him a free pardon. Gully accordingly attempted for the first time in his life to play the part of the studious and sensible boy; and was so much struck by the safety, credit, and self-satisfaction which it gained for him, that he kept it up to the end of his schooldays. Yet he did not lose the esteem of his comrades; for he succeeded in convincing them, by the license of his private conversation, that his reformation was only a consummate imposture, of which that common enemy, the principal, was the unpitied dupe.

Meanwhile, Mrs Byron, not suspecting the importance of the doctor's note, and happening to be in a hurry when it arrived, laid it by unopened, intending to read it at her leisure. She would have forgotten it altogether but for a second note which came two days later, requesting some acknowledgment of the previous communication. On learning the truth she immediately drove to Moncrief House, and there abused the doctor as he had never been abused in his life before; after which she begged his pardon, and implored him to assist her to recover her darling boy. When he suggested that she should offer a reward for information and capture, she indignantly refused to spend a farthing on the little ingrate; wept and accused herself of having driven him away by her unkindness; stormed and accused the doctor of having treated him harshly; and finally said that she would give £100 to have him back, but that she would never speak to him again. The doctor promised to undertake the search, and would have promised anything to get rid of his visitor. A reward of £50 was offered. But whether the fear of falling into the clutches of the law for murderous assault stimulated Cashel to extraordinary precaution, or whether he had contrived to leave the country in the four days between his flight and the offer of the reward, the doctor's efforts were unsuccessful; and he had to confess their failure to Mrs Byron. She agreeably surprised him by writing a pleasant letter to the effect that it was very provoking, and that she could never thank him sufficiently for all the trouble he had taken. And so the matter dropped.

III

There was at this time in the city of Melbourne, in Australia, a wooden building, above the door of which was a board inscribed GYMNASIUM AND SCHOOL OF ARMS. In the long narrow entry hung a framed manuscript which set forth that Ned Skene, ex-champion of England and the Colonies, was to be heard of within by gentlemen desirous of becoming proficient in the art of self-defence. Also the terms on which Mrs Skene, assisted by a competent staff of professors, would give lessons in dancing, deportment, and calisthenics.

One evening a man sat smoking on a common kitchen-chair on the threshold of this establishment. Beside him were some tin tacks and a hammer. He had just nailed to the doorpost a card on which was written in a woman's handwriting: '*Wanted, a male attendant who can keep accounts. Inquire within.*' The smoker was a powerful man, with a thick neck that swelled out beneath his broad flat ear-lobes. He had small eyes, and large teeth over which his lips were slightly parted in a smile, good-humored but affectedly cunning. His hair was black and close cut, his skin indurated, and the bridge of his nose smashed level with his face. The tip, however, was uninjured. It was squab and glossy, and, by giving the whole feature an air of being on the point of expanding to its original shape, produced a snubbed expression which relieved the otherwise formidable aspect of the man, and recommended him as probably a modest and affable fellow when sober and unprovoked. He seemed about fifty years of age, and was clad in a straw hat and a suit of white linen.

Before he had finished his pipe, the card on the doorpost attracted the attention of a youth attired in a coarse sailor's jersey and a pair of grey tweed trousers which he had outgrown.

'Looking for a job?' inquired the ex-champion of England and the Colonies.

The youth blushed and replied, 'Yes. I should like to get something to do.'

Mr Skene stared at him with stern curiosity. His professional pursuits had familiarized him with the manners and speech of English gentlemen; and he immediately recognized the shabby sailor lad as one of that class.

'Perhaps youre a scholar,' said the prizefighter, after a moment's reflection.

'I have been at school; but I didnt learn much there. I think I could book-keep by double entry.'

'Double entry! Whats that?'

'It's the way merchants' books are kept. It is called so because everything is entered twice over.'

'Ah!' said Skene, unfavorably impressed by the system: 'once is enough for me. Whats your weight?'

'I dont know,' said the lad with a grin.

'Not know your own weight! That aint the way to get on in life.'

'I havnt been weighed since a long time ago in England,' said the other, beginning to get the better of his shyness. 'I was eight stone four then; so you see I am only a light weight.'

'And what do you know about light weights? Perhaps, being so well educated, you know how to fight. Eh?'

'I dont think I could fight you,' said the youth, with another grin.

Skene chuckled; and the stranger, with boyish communicativeness, gave him an account of a real fight (meaning apparently one between professional pugilists) which he had seen in England. He went on to describe how he had himself knocked down a master with one blow when running away from school. Skene received this sceptically, and cross-examined the narrator as to the manner and effect of the blow, with the result of convincing himself that the story was true. At the end of quarter of an hour, the lad had commended himself so acceptably by his conversation that the champion took him into the gymnasium, where he weighed him; measured him; and finally handed him a pair of boxing gloves and invited him to shew what he was made of. The youth, though impressed by the prizefighter's attitude with a hopeless sense of the impossibility of reaching him, rushed boldly at him several times, knocking his face on each occasion against Skene's left fist, which seemed to be ubiquitous, and to have the power of imparting the consistency of iron to padded leather. At last the novice directed a frantic assault at the champion's nose, rising on his toes in that aspiration. Skene stopped the blow with a jerk of his right elbow; and the impetuous youth spun and stumbled away until he fell supine in a corner, rapping his head smartly on the floor at the same time. He rose with unabated cheerfulness and offered to continue the combat; but Skene declined any further exercise just then, though he was so much pleased with his novice's game that he promised to give him a scientific education and make a man of him.

The champion now sent for his wife, whom he revered as a pre-eminently sensible and well-mannered woman. The newcomer could see in her only a ridiculous dancing mistress; but he treated her with great deference, and thereby improved the high opinion which Skene had already formed of him. He related to her how, after running away from school, he had made his way to Liverpool; gone to the docks; and contrived to hide himself on board a ship bound for Australia. Also how he had suffered severely from hunger and thirst before he discovered himself; and how, notwithstanding his unpopular position as stowaway, he had been fairly treated as soon as he had shewn that he was willing to work. And in proof that he was still willing, and had profited by his maritime experience, he offered to sweep the floor of the gymnasium then and there. This proposal convinced the Skenes, who had listened to his story like children listening to a fairy tale, that he was not too much of a gentleman to do rough work; and it was presently arranged that he should thenceforth board and lodge with them; have five shillings a week for pocket money; and be man of all work, servant, gymnasium attendant, clerk, and apprentice to the ex-champion of England and the Colonies.

He soon found his bargain no easy one. The gymnasium was open from nine in the morning until eleven at night; and the athletic gentlemen who came there not only ordered him about without ceremony, but varied the monotony of vainly opposing the invincible Skene, by practising what he taught them on the person of his apprentice, whom they pounded with great relish, and threw backwards, forwards, and over their shoulders as though he had been but a senseless effigy provided for that purpose. The champion looked on and laughed, being too lazy to redeem his promise of teaching the novice to defend himself. The latter, however, watched the lessons he saw daily given to the others; and before the end of the month he so completely turned the tables on the amateur pugilists of Melbourne that Skene one day took occasion to remark that he was growing uncommon clever, but that gentlemen liked to be played easy with, and that he should be careful not to knock them about too much. Besides these bodily exertions, he had to keep account of gloves and foils sold and bought, and of the fees due both to Mr and Mrs Skene. This was the most irksome part of his duty; for he wrote a large schoolboy hand, and was not quick at figures. When he at last began to assist his master in giving lessons, the accounts had fallen into arrear; and Mrs Skene had to resume her former care of them: a circumstance which gratified her husband, who regarded it as a fresh triumph of her superior intelligence. Then a Chinaman was engaged to do the more menial work of the establishment. 'Skene's Novice,' as he was now generally called, was elevated to the rank of assistant professor to the champion, and became a person of some consequence in the gymnasium.

He had been there more than nine months, and had

developed into an athletic young man of eighteen with a
keen eye for a tip, and a scale of 'Thank you, sirs' nicely
graduated from half-a-crown to a sovereign, when an important conversation took place between him and his
principal. It was evening; and the only persons in the gymnasium were Ned Skene, who sat smoking at his ease with
his coat off, and the novice, who had just come downstairs
from his bedroom, where he had been preparing for a visit
to the theatre.

'Well, my gentleman,' said Skene mockingly: 'youre a
fancy man, you are. Gloves, too! Theyre too small for you.
Dont you get hittin nobody with them on, or youll mebbe
sprain your wrist.'

'Not much fear of that,' said the novice, looking at his
watch. Finding that he had some minutes to spare, he sat
down opposite Skene.

'No,' assented the champion. 'When you rise to be a
regular professional, you wont care to spar with nobody
without youre well paid for it.'

'I may say I am in the profession already. You dont call
me an amateur, do you?'

'Oh no,' said Skene: 'not so bad as that. But mind you,
my boy, I dont call no man a fighting man what aint been
in the ring. Youre a sparrer, and a clever, pretty sparrer;
but sparring aint the real thing. Some day, please God,
we'll make up a little match for you, and shew what you
can do without the gloves.'

'I would just as soon have the gloves off as on,' said the
novice a little sulkily.

'Thats because you have a heart as big as a lion,' said
Skene soothingly. But the novice, accustomed to hear his
master pay the same compliment to his patrons whenever
they were seized with fits of boasting (which usually happened when they got worsted), looked obdurate and said
nothing.

'Sam Ducket of Milltown was here today while you was
out giving Captain Noble his lesson,' continued Skene,

watching his apprentice's face. 'Now Sam is a real fighting man, if you like.'

'I dont think much of him. He's a liar, for one thing.'

'Thats a failing of the profession. I dont mind telling *you* so,' said Skene mournfully. Now the novice had found out this for himself already. He never, for instance, believed the accounts which his master gave of the accidents and conspiracies which had led to his being defeated three times in the ring. However, as Skene had won fifteen battles, his next remark was undeniable. 'Men fight none the worse for being liars. Sam Ducket bet Ebony Muley in twenty minutes.'

'Yes,' said the novice scornfully; 'and what is Ebony Muley? A wretched old nigger nearly sixty years old, who is drunk seven days in the week, and would sell a fight for a glass of brandy! Ducket ought to have knocked him out of time in twenty seconds. Ducket has no science.'

'Not a bit,' said Ned. 'But he has lots of game.'

'Pshaw! Thats what they always try to make out. If a fellow knows how to box, they say he has science but no pluck. If he doesnt know his right hand from his left, they say that he isnt clever, but that he's full of game.'

Skene looked with secret wonder at his pupil, whose powers of observation and expression sometimes seemed to him almost to rival those of Mrs Skene. 'Sam was sayin something like that today,' he remarked. 'He says youre only a sparrer, and that youd fall down with fright if you was put into a twenty-four foot ring.'

The novice flushed. 'I wish I had been here when Sam Ducket said that.'

'Why, what could you ha' done to him?' said Skene, his small eyes twinkling.

'I'd have punched his head: thats what I could and would have done to him.'

'Why, man, he'd eat you.'

'He might. And he might eat you too, Ned, if he had salt enough with you. He talks big because he knows I have no money; and he pretends he wont strip for less than fifty pounds a side.'

'No money!' cried Skene. 'I know them as'll make up fifty pound before twelve tomorrow for any man as I will answer for. *There'd* be a start for a young man! Why, my fust fight was for five shillings in Tott'nam Fields; and proud I was when I won it. I dont want to set you on to fight a crack like Sam Ducket anyway against your inclinations; but dont go to say that money isnt to be had. Let Ned Skene pint to a young man and say, "Thats the young man that Ned backs"; and others'll come forard with the stakes – aye, crowds of em.'

The novice hesitated. 'Do you think I ought to, Ned?' he said.

'That aint for me to say,' said Skene doggedly. 'I know what I would ha' said at your age. But perhaps youre right to be cautious. I tell you the truth, I wouldnt care to see you whipped by the like of Sam Ducket.'

'Will you train me if I challenge him?'

'Will I train you!' echoed Skene, rising with enthusiasm. 'Aye will I train you, and put my money on you too; and you shall knock fireworks out of him, my boy, as sure as my name's Ned Skene.'

'Then,' cried the novice, reddening with excitement, 'I'll fight him. And if I lick him, you will have to hand over your belt as champion of the colonies to me.'

'So I will,' said Skene affectionately. 'Dont stay out late; and dont for your life touch a drop of liquor. You must go into training tomorrow.'

This was Cashel Byron's first professional engagement.

END OF THE PROLOGUE

WILTSTOKEN CASTLE was a square building with circular bastions at the corners: each bastion terminating skyward in a Turkish minaret. The south-west face was the front, pierced by a Moorish arch fitted with glass doors, which could be secured on occasion by gates of fantastically hammered iron. The arch was enshrined by a Palladian portico, which rose to the roof, and was surmounted by an open pediment, in the cleft of which stood a black marble figure of an Egyptian, erect, and gazing steadfastly at the midday sun. On the ground beneath was an Italian terrace with two great stone elephants at the ends of the balustrade. The windows of the upper storey were, like the entrance, Moorish; but the principal ones below were square bays, mullioned. The castle was considered grand by the illiterate; but architects, and readers of books on architecture, condemned it as a nondescript mixture of styles in the worst possible taste. It stood on an eminence surrounded by hilly woodland, thirty acres of which were enclosed as Wiltstoken Park. Half a mile south was the little town of Wiltstoken, accessible by rail from London in about two hours.

Most of the inhabitants of Wiltstoken were Conservatives. They stood in awe of the Castle; and some of them would at any time have cut half a dozen of their oldest friends to obtain an invitation to dinner, or even a bow in public, from Miss Lydia Carew, its orphan mistress. This Miss Carew was a remarkable person. She had inherited the Castle and park from her aunt, who had considered her niece's large fortune in railways and mines incomplete without land. So many other legacies had Lydia received from kinsfolk who hated poor relations, that she was now, in her twenty-fifth year, the independent possessor of an annual income equal to the year's earnings of five hundred workmen, and under no external compulsion to do anything in return for it. In addition to the advantage of being a single woman with unusually large means, she enjoyed a reputation for vast learning and exquisite culture. It was said in Wiltstoken that she knew forty-eight living languages and all the dead ones; could play on every known musical instrument; was an accomplished painter; and had written poetry. All this might as well have been true as far as the Wiltstokeners were concerned, since she knew more than they. She had spent her life travelling with her father, a man of active mind and bad digestion, with an independent income, and a taste for sociology, science in general, and the fine arts. On these subjects he had written books, mostly about the Renaissance, by which he had earned a reputation as a sort of culture merchant for tourists. They involved much reading, travelling, sight-seeing, and theorizing, of all which, except the theorizing, his daughter had done her share, and indeed, as she grew more competent, and he weaker and older, more than her share. Having had to combine health-hunting with culture-distillation, and being very irritable and fastidious, he had schooled her in self-control and endurance by harder lessons than those which had made her acquainted with the works of Greek and German philosophers long before she understood the English into which she translated them.

When Lydia was in her twenty-first year, her father's health failed seriously. He became more dependent on her; and she anticipated that he would also become more exacting in his demands on her time. But one day, at Naples, she had arranged to go riding with a newly arrived and rather pleasant English party. Shortly before the appointed hour, he asked her to make a translation of a long extract from Lessing. Lydia, in whom self-questionings as to the justness of her father's yoke had for some time been stirring, paused thoughtfully for perhaps two seconds before she consented. Carew said nothing; but he presently intercepted a servant who was bearing an apology to the English party; read the note; and went back to his daughter, who was already busy at Lessing.

'Lydia,' he said, with a certain hesitation which she would have ascribed to shyness had that been at all credible of her father when addressing her: 'I wish you never to postpone your business to literary trifling.'

She looked at him with the vague fear that accompanies a new and doubtful experience; and he, dissatisfied with his way of putting the case, added, 'It is of greater importance that you should enjoy yourself for an hour than that my book should be advanced. Far greater!'

Lydia, after some consideration, put down her pen and said, 'I shall not enjoy riding if there is anything else left undone.'

'I shall not enjoy your writing if your excursion is given up for it,' he said. 'I prefer your going.'

Lydia obeyed silently. An odd thought struck her that she might end the matter gracefully by kissing him. But they were unaccustomed to make demonstrations of this kind; so nothing came of the impulse. She spent the day on horseback; reconsidered her late rebellious thoughts; and made the translation in the evening.

Thenceforth, Lydia had a growing sense of the power she had unwittingly been acquiring during her long subordination. Timidly at first, and more boldly as she became used to dispense with the parental leading strings, she began to follow her own bent in selecting subjects for study, and even to defend certain recent developments in music and painting against her father's conservatism. He approved of this independent mental activity on her part, and repeatedly warned her not to pin her faith more on him than on any other critic. She once told him that one of her incentives to disagree with him was the pleasure it gave her to find out ultimately that he was right. He replied gravely,

'That pleases me, Lydia, because I believe you. But such things are better left unsaid. They seem to belong to the art of pleasing, which you will perhaps soon be tempted to practise, because it seems to all young people easy, well-paid, amiable, and a mark of good breeding. In truth it is vulgar, cowardly, egotistical, and insincere: a virtue in a shopman: a vice in a free woman. It is better to leave genuine praise unspoken than to expose yourself to the suspicion of flattery.'

Shortly after this, at his desire, she spent a season in London, and went into English polite society, which she found to be in the main a temple for the worship of riches and a market for the sale of virgins. Having become familiar with both the cult and the trade elsewhere, she found nothing to interest her except the English manner of conducting them; and the novelty of this soon wore off. She was also incommoded by her involuntary power of inspiring affection in her own sex. Impulsive girls she could keep in awe; but old women, notably two aunts who had never paid her any attention during her childhood, now persecuted her with slavish fondness, and tempted her by mingled entreaties and bribes to desert her father and live with them for the remainder of their lives. Her reserve fanned their longing to have her for a pet; and, to escape them, she returned to the continent with her father, and ceased to hold any correspondence with London. Her aunts declared themselves deeply hurt; and Lydia was held to have treated them very injudiciously; but when they died, and their wills became public, it was found that they had vied with one another in enriching her.

When she was twenty-five years old, the first startling event of her life took place. This was the death of her father at Avignon. No endearments passed between them even on that occasion. She was sitting opposite to him at the fireside one evening, reading aloud, when he suddenly said, 'My heart has stopped, Lydia. Goodbye!' and immediately died. She had some difficulty in quelling the tumult that arose when the bell was answered. The whole household felt bound to be overwhelmed, and took it rather ill that she seemed neither grateful to them nor disposed to imitate their behavior.

Carew's relatives agreed that he had made a most unbecoming will. It was a brief document, dated five years before his death, and was to the effect that he bequeathed to his dear daughter Lydia all he possessed. He had, however, left her certain private instructions. One of these, which excited great indignation in his family, was that his body should be conveyed to Milan, and there cremated. Having disposed of her father's remains as he had directed, she came to set her affairs in order in England, where she inspired much hopeless passion in the toilers in Lincoln's Inn Fields and Chancery Lane, and disconcerted her solicitors by evincing a capacity for business hardly compatible with the docility they expected from a rich and unprotected young lady. When all was arranged, and she was once more able to enjoy a settled tranquillity, she returned to Avignon, and there discharged her last duty to her father. This was to open a letter she had found in his desk, inscribed by his hand, 'For Lydia. To be read by her at leisure when I and my affairs shall be finally disposed of.' The letter ran thus:—

'My Dear Lydia – I belong to the great company of disappointed men. But for you, I should now write myself down a failure like the rest. It is only a few years since it first struck me that although I had failed in many vain ambitions with which (having failed) I need not trouble you now, I had been of some use as a father. Upon this it came into my mind that you could draw no other conclusion from the course of our life together than that I have, with entire selfishness, used you throughout as my mere amanuensis and clerk, and that you are under no more obligation to me for your attainments than a slave is to his master for the strength which enforced labor has given to his muscles. Lest I should leave you suffering from so mischievous and oppressive an influence as a sense of injustice, I now justify myself to you.

'I have never asked you whether you remember your

49

mother. Had you at any time broached the subject, I should have spoken quite freely to you on it; but as some wise instinct led you to avoid it, I was content to let it rest until circumstances such as the present should render further reserve unnecessary. If any regret at having known so little of the woman who gave you birth troubles you, shake it off without remorse. She was an egotist who could keep neither husband, child, servant, nor friend, under the same roof with her. I speak dispassionately. All my bitter personal feeling against her is as dead whilst I write as it will be when you read. I have even come to regard tenderly certain of her characteristics which you inherit; so that I can confidently say that I never, since the perishing of the infatuation in which I married, felt more kindly towards her than I do now. I made the best, and she the worst, of our union for six years; and then we parted. I permitted her to give what account of the separation she pleased, and made her a much more liberal allowance than she had any right to expect. By these means I induced her to leave me in undisturbed possession of you, whom I had already, as a measure of precaution, carried off to Belgium. The reason why we never visited England during her lifetime was that she could, and probably would, have made my previous conduct and my hostility to popular religion an excuse for wresting you from me. I need say no more of her, and am sorry it was necessary to mention her at all.

'I will now tell you what induced me to secure you for myself. It was not natural affection: I did not love you then; and I knew that you would be a serious encumbrance to me. But having brought you into the world, and then broken through my engagements with your mother, I felt bound to see that you should not suffer for my mistake. Gladly would I have persuaded myself tht she was (as the gossips said) the fittest person to have charge of you; but I knew better, and made up my mind to discharge my responsibility as well as I could. In course of time you became useful to me; and, as you know, I made use of you without scruple, but never without regard to your own advantage. I always kept a secretary to do whatever I considered mere copyist's work. Much as you did for me, I think I may say with truth that I never imposed a task of no educational value on you. I fear you found the hours you spent over my money affairs very irksome; but I need not apologize for that now: you must already know by experience how necessary a knowledge of business is to the possessor of a large fortune.

'I did not think, when I undertook your education, that I was laying the foundation of any comfort for myself. For a long time you were only a good girl, and what ignorant people called a prodigy of learning. In your circumstances a commonplace child might have been both. I subsequently came to contemplate your existence with a pleasure which I never derived from the contemplation of my own. I have not succeeded, and shall not succeed in expressing the affection I feel for you, or the triumph with which I find that what I undertook as a distasteful and thankless duty has rescued my life and labor from waste. My literary travail, much as it has occupied us both, I now value only for the share it has had in educating you; and you will be guilty of no disloyalty to me when you come to see that though I sifted as much sand as most men, I found no gold. I ask you to remember then that I did my duty to you long before it became pleasurable or even hopeful. And, when you are older and have learned from your mother's friends how I failed in my duty to her, you will perhaps give me some credit for having conciliated the world for your sake by abandoning habits and acquaintances which, whatever others may have thought of them, did much whilst they lasted to make life endurable to me.

'Although your future will not concern me, I often find myself thinking of it. I fear you will soon find that the world has not yet provided a place and a sphere of action for well-instructed women. In my younger days, when the companionship of my fellows was a necessity to me, I tried to set aside my culture; relax my principles; and acquire common tastes, in order to fit myself for the society of the only men within my reach; for, if I had to live among bears, I had rather be a bear than a man. The effort made me more miserable than any other mistake I have ever made. It was lonely to be myself; but not to be myself was death in life. Take warning, Lydia: do not be tempted to accommodate yourself to the world by moral suicide.

'Some day, I expect and hope, you will marry. You will then have an opportunity of making an irremediable mistake, against the possibility of which no advice of mine or subtlety of yours can guard you. I think you will not easily find a man able to satisfy in you that desire to be relieved of the responsibility of thinking out and ordering our course of life that makes us each long for a guide whom we can thoroughly trust. If you fail, remember that your father, after suffering a bitter and complete disappointment in his wife, yet came to regard his marriage as the only fruitful event in his career. Let me remind you also since you are so rich, that you need not, in jealousy of your own income, limit your choice of a husband to those already too rich to marry for money. No vulgar adventurer, I hope, will be able to recommend himself to you; and better men will be at least as much frightened as attracted by your wealth. The only class against which I need warn you is that to which I myself am supposed to belong. Never think that a man must prove a suitable and satisfying friend for you merely because he has read much criticism; that he must feel the influences of Art as you do, because he knows and adopts the classification of names and schools with which you are familiar; or that because he agrees with your favorite authors he must necessarily interpret their words to himself as you understand them. Beware of men who have read more than they have worked, or who love to read better than to work. Do not forget that where the man is always at home, the woman is never happy. Beware of painters, poets, musicians, and artists of all sorts, except very great artists; beware even of them as husbands and fathers. Self-satisfied workmen who have learnt their business well, whether they be chancellors of the exchequer or farmers, I recommend to you as, on the whole, the most tolerable class of men I have met.

'I shall make no further attempt to advise you. As fast as my counsels rise to my mind follow reflections that convince me of their futility.

'You may perhaps wonder why I never said to you what I have written down here. I have tried to do so and failed. If I understand myself aright, I have written these lines mainly to relieve a craving to express my affection for you. The awkwardness which an overcivilized man experiences in admitting that he is something more than an educated stone prevented me from confusing you by demonstrations of a kind I had never accustomed you to. Besides, I wish this assurance of my love – my last word – to reach you when no further commonplaces to blur the impressiveness of its simple truth are possible.

'I know I have said too much; and I feel that I have not said enough. But the writing of this letter has been a difficult task. Practised as I am with my pen, I have never, even in my earliest efforts, composed with such labor and sense of inadequacy –'

Here the manuscript broke off. The letter had never been finished.

CHAPTER II

IN the month of May, seven years after the flight of the two boys from Moncrief House, a lady sat in an island of shadow made by a cedar tree in the midst of a glittering green lawn. She did womanly to avoid the sun; for her complexion was as delicately tinted as mother-of-pearl. She was a small, graceful woman with sensitive lips and nostrils, green eyes with quiet unarched brows, and ruddy gold hair, now shaded by a large untrimmed straw hat. Her dress of Indian muslin, with half sleeves ending in wide ruffles at the elbows, hardly covered her shoulders, where it was supplemented by a fleecy white scarf which made a nest of soft woollen lace for her throat. She was reading a little ivory-bound volume – a miniature edition of the second part of Goethe's Faust.

As the afternoon wore on and the light mellowed, the lady dropped her book and began to think and dream, unconscious of a prosaic black object crossing the lawn towards her. This was a young gentleman in a frock coat. He was dark, and had a long, grave face, with a reserved expression, but not ill-looking.

'Going so soon, Lucian?' said the lady, looking up as he came into the shadow.

Lucian looked at her wistfully. His name, as she uttered it, always stirred him vaguely. He was fond of finding reasons for things, and had long ago decided that this inward stir was due to her fine pronunciation. His other intimates called him Looshn.

'Yes,' he said. 'I have arranged everything, and have come to give an account of my stewardship, and to say goodbye.'

He placed a garden chair near her and sat down. She laid her hands one on the other in her lap, and composed herself to listen.

'First,' he said, 'as to the Warren Lodge. It is let for a month only; so you can allow Mrs Goff to have it rent free in July if you wish to. I hope you will not act so unwisely.'

She smiled, and said, 'Who are the present tenants? I hear that they object to the dairymaids and men crossing the elm vista.'

'We must not complain of that. It was expressly stipulated when they took the lodge that the vista should be kept private for them. I had no idea at that time that you were coming to the Castle, or I should of course have declined such a condition.'

'But we do keep it private for them: strangers are not admitted. Our people pass and repass once a day on their way to and from the dairy: that is all.'

'It seems churlish, Lydia; but this is a special case – a young gentleman who has come to recruit his health. He needs daily exercise in the open air; but he cannot bear observation: indeed I have not seen him myself; and he has only a single attendant with him. Under these circumstances, I agreed that they should have the sole use of the elm vista. In fact they are paying more rent than would be reasonable without this privilege.'

'I hope the young gentleman is not mad.'

'I satisfied myself, before I let the lodge to him, that he would be a proper tenant,' said Lucian, with reproachful gravity. 'He was strongly recommended to me by Lord Worthington, who spoke quite warmly of him. As it happens, I expressed to him the suspicion you have just suggested. Worthington vouched for the tenant's sanity as well as for his solvency, and offered to take the lodge in his own name and be personally responsible for the good behavior of the invalid. You need have no fear: it is only some young fellow who has upset his nerves by hard reading. Probably some college friend of Worthington's.'

'Perhaps so. But I should expect a college friend of Lord Worthington's to be a hard rider or drinker rather than a hard reader.'

'You may be quite at ease, Lydia. I took Lord Worthington at his word so far as to make the letting to him.'

'I am quite satisfied, Lucian; and I am greatly obliged to you. I will give orders that no one is to go to the dairy by way of the warren.'

'The next point,' resumed Lucian, 'is more important, as it concerns you personally. Miss Goff is willing to accept your offer. And a most unsuitable companion she will be for you!'

'Why, Lucian?'

'On all accounts. She is younger than you, and therefore cannot chaperone you. She has received only an ordinary education; and her experience of society is derived from local subscription balls. And as she is not unattractive, and is considered a beauty in Wiltstoken, she is self-willed, and will probably take your patronage in bad part.'

'Is she more self-willed than I?'

'You are not self-willed, Lydia; except that you are deaf to advice.'

'You mean that I seldom follow it. And so you think I had better employ a professional companion – a decayed gentlewoman – than save this young girl from going out as a governess and beginning to decay at twenty-three?'

'The business of getting a suitable companion, and the duty of relieving poor people, are two different things, Lydia.'

'True, Lucian. When will Miss Goff call?'

'This evening. Mind: nothing is settled as yet. If you think better of it on seeing her, you have only to treat her as an ordinary visitor, and the subject will drop. For my own part, I prefer her sister; but she will not leave Mrs Goff, who has not yet recovered from the shock of her husband's death.'

Lydia looked reflectively at the little volume in her hand, and seemed to think out the question of Miss Goff. When she looked up again it was evidently settled; but she said nothing.

'Well?' said Lucian presently, embarrassed by her silence.

'Well?' said Lydia, not at all embarrassed.

'You have not said anything.'

'I have nothing to say.'

'Then,' said Lucian shortly, giving way to a sense of injury, 'I had better go.'

'Not at all,' said Lydia. 'I am enjoying your company in the Wiltstoken way. When two of our laborers here are friends, how do they shew it? They lean on the same gate for hours together every Sunday morning without exchanging a word. Surely thats better than the nervous horror o silence and self-consciousness called society in our unfortunate circle.'

'You have such extraordinary ideas, Lydia! An agricultural laborer is silent just as a dog is silent.'

'Dogs are very good company,' said Lydia.

To this he found nothing to say. The only relation to a woman in which he felt happy was one of intellectual condescension and explanation. Lydia never questioned his explanations; but as she did not draw the same moral from them, he seldom felt that they had been successful. As to maintaining a silence with her on the agricultural laborers' lines, that was beyond his utmost power of self-possession. He had to plead his train and say goodbye.

She gave him her hand; and a dull glow came into his grey jaws as he took it. Then he buttoned his coat and walked gravely away. As he went, she watched the sun flashing from his glossy hat, and drowning in his respectable coat. She sighed, and took up Goethe again.

But after a little while she tired of sitting still, and rose and wandered through the park for nearly an hour, trying to find the places where she had played in her childhood during a visit to her late aunt. She recognized a great toppling Druid's altar that had formerly reminded her of Mount Sinai threatening to fall on the head of Christian in The Pilgrim's Progress. Further on she saw and avoided a swamp in which she had once earned a scolding from her nurse by filling her stockings with mud. Then she found herself in a long avenue of green turf, running east and west, and apparently endless. This seemed the most delightful of all her possessions; and she had begun to plan a pavilion to build near it, when she suddenly recollected that this must be the elm vista of which the privacy was so stringently insisted upon by her invalid tenant at the Warren Lodge. She fled into the wood at once, and, when she was safe there, laughed at the oddity of being a trespasser in her own domain. A wide detour was needed to avoid intruding again: consequently, after walking a little time, she lost herself. The trees seemed never-ending: she began to think she must possess a forest as well as a park. At last she saw an opening. Hastening towards it, she came again into the sunlight, and stopped, dazzled by an apparition which she at first took to be a beautiful statue, but presently recognized, with a strange glow of delight, as a living man.

To so mistake a gentleman exercising himself in the open air on a nineteenth century afternoon would, under ordinary circumstances, imply incredible ignorance either of men or statues. But the circumstances in Miss Carew's case were not ordinary; for the man was clad in a jersey and knee breeches of white material; and his bare arms shone like those of a gladiator. His broad pectoral muscles, in their white covering, were like slabs of marble. Even his hair, short, crisp, and curly, seemed like burnished bronze in the evening light. It came into Lydia's mind that she had disturbed an antique god in his sylvan haunt. The fancy was only momentary; for her next glance fell on a third person, a groom-like man, impossible to associate with classic divinity, contemplating his companion much as a groom might contemplate an exceptionally fine horse. He was the first to see Lydia; and his expression as he did so plainly shewed that he regarded her as a most unwelcome intruder. The statue-man, following his sinister look, saw her too, but with different feelings; for his lips parted; his color rose; and he stared at her with undisguised admiration and wonder. Lydia's first impulse was to turn and fly; her next, to apologize for her presence. Finally she went away quietly through the trees.

The moment she was out of their sight, she increased her pace almost to a run. The day was warm for rapid movement; and she soon stopped and listened. There were the usual woodland sounds: leaves rustling, grasshoppers chirping, and birds singing; but not a human voice or footstep. She began to think that the god-like figure was only the Hermes of Praxiteles, suggested to her by Goethe's classical Sabbat, and changed by a daydream into the semblance of a living reality. The groom must have been one of those incongruities characteristic of dreams – probably a reminiscence of Lucian's statement that the tenant of the Warren Lodge had a single male attendant. It was impossible that this glorious vision of manly strength and beauty could be substantially a student broken down by excessive study. That irrational glow of delight too was one of the absurdities of dreamland: otherwise she would have been ashamed of it.

Lydia made her way back to the Castle in some alarm as to the state of her nerves, but dwelling on her vision with a pleasure that she would not have ventured to indulge had it concerned a creature of flesh and blood. Once or twice it recurred to her so vividly that she asked herself whether it could have been real. But a little reasoning convinced her that it must have been an hallucination.

'If you please, madam,' said one of her staff of domestics, a native of Wiltstoken, who stood in deep awe of the lady of the Castle, 'Miss Goff is waiting for you in the drawing room.'

The drawing room of the Castle was a circular apartment with a dome-shaped ceiling broken into gilt ornaments resembling thick bamboos, which projected vertically downward like stalagmites. The heavy chandeliers were loaded with flattened brass balls, magnified facsimiles of which crowned the uprights of the low, broad, massively-framed chairs, covered in leather stamped with Japanese dragon designs in copper-colored metal. Near the fireplace was a bronze bell of Chinese shape, mounted like a mortar on a black wooden carriage for use as a coal-scuttle. The wall was decorated with large gold crescents on a ground of light blue.

In this barbaric rotunda Miss Carew found awaiting her a young lady of twenty-three, with a well-developed resilient figure, and a clear complexion, porcelain surfaced, and with a fine red in the cheeks. The lofty pose of her head expressed the habitual sense of her own consequence given her by the admiration of the youth of the neighborhood, which was also, perhaps, the cause of the neatness of her inexpensive black dress and of her irreproachable gloves, boots, and hat. She had been waiting to introduce herself to the lady of the Castle for ten minutes in a state of nervousness that culminated as Lydia entered.

'How do you do, Miss Goff? Have I kept you waiting? I was out.'

'Not at all,' said Miss Goff, with a confused impression that red hair was aristocratic, and dark brown (the color of her own) vulgar. She had risen to shake hands, and now, after hesitating a moment to consider what etiquette required her to do next, resumed her seat. Miss Carew sat down too, and gazed thoughtfully at her visitor, who held herself rigidly erect, and, striving to mask her nervousness, unintentionally looked disdainful.

'Miss Goff,' said Lydia, after a silence that made her speech impressive: 'will you come to me on a long visit? In this lonely place, I am greatly in want of a friend and companion of my own age and position. I think you must be equally so.'

Alice Goff was very young, and very determined to accept no credit that she did not deserve. She proceeded to set Miss Carew right as to her social position, not considering that the lady of the Castle probably understood it better than she did herself, and indeed thinking it quite natural that she should be mistaken.

'You are very kind,' she replied stiffly; 'but our positions are quite different, Miss Carew. The fact is that I cannot afford to live an idle life. We are very poor; and my mother is partly dependent on my exertions.'

'I think you will be able to exert yourself to good purpose if you come to me,' said Lydia, unimpressed. 'It is true that I shall give you very expensive habits; but I will also enable you to support them.'

'I do not wish to contract expensive habits,' said Alice reproachfully. 'I shall have to content myself with frugal ones throughout my life.'

'Not necessarily. Tell me frankly: how had you proposed to exert yourself? As a teacher, was it not?'

Alice flushed, but assented.

'You are not at all fitted for it; and you will end by marrying. As a teacher you could not marry well. As an idle lady, with expensive habits, you will marry very well indeed. It is quite an art to know how to be rich – an indispensable art, if you mean to marry a rich man.'

'I have no intention of marrying,' said Alice loftily. She thought it time to check this cool aristocrat. 'If I come at all, I shall come without any ulterior object.'

'That is just what I had hoped. Come without conditions or second thought of any kind.'

'But –' began Alice, and stopped, bewildered by the pace at which the negotiation was proceeding. She murmured a few words, and waited for Lydia to proceed. But Lydia had said her say, and evidently expected a reply, though she seemed assured of having her own way, whatever Alice's views might be.

'I do not quite understand, Miss Carew. What duties? – what would you expect of me?'

'A great deal,' said Lydia gravely. 'Much more than I should from a mere professional companion.'

'But I shall be a professional companion,' protested Alice.

'Whose?'

Alice flushed again, angrily this time. 'I did not mean to say –'

'You do not mean to say that you will have nothing to do with me,' said Lydia, stopping her quietly. 'Why are you so scrupulous, Miss Goff? You will be close to your home, and can return to it at any moment if you become dissatisfied with your position here.'

Fearful that she had disgraced herself by bad manners; loth to be taken possession of as if her wishes were of no consequence when a rich lady's whim was to be gratified; suspicious – since she had often heard gossiping tales of the dishonesty of people in high positions – lest she should be cheated out of the substantial salary she had come resolved to demand; and withal unable to defend herself against Miss Carew, Alice caught at the first excuse that occurred to her.

'I should like a little time to consider,' she said.

'Time to accustom yourself to me, is it not? You can have as long as you plea—'

'Oh, I can let you know tomorrow,' interrupted Alice officiously.

'Thank you. I will send a note to Mrs Goff to say that she need not expect you back until tomorrow.'

'But I did not mean – I am not prepared to stay,' remonstrated Alice, feeling more and more entangled in Lydia's snare.

'We shall take a walk after dinner, then, and call at your house, where you can make your preparations. But I think I can lend you all you will require.'

Alice dared make no further objection. 'I am afraid,' she stammered, 'you will think me horribly rude; but I am so useless, and you are so sure to be disappointed, that – that –'

'You are not rude, Miss Goff; but I find you very shy.

You want to run away and hide from new faces and new surroundings.'

Alice, who was self-possessed and even overbearing in Wiltstoken society, felt that she was misunderstood, but did not know how to vindicate herself.

Lydia resumed. 'I have formed my habits in the course of my travels, and so live without ceremony. We dine early – at six.'

Alice had dined at two, but did not feel bound to confess it.

'Let me shew you your room,' said Lydia, rising. 'This is a curious drawing room,' she added, glancing around. 'I have never used it before.' She looked about her again with some interest, as if the apartment belonged to some one else; and then led the way to a room on the first floor, furnished as a lady's bed-chamber. 'If you dislike this,' she said, 'or cannot arrange it to suit you, there are others, of which you can have your choice. Come to my boudoir when you are ready.'

'Where is that?' said Alice anxiously.

'It is – You had better ring for some one to shew you. I will send you my maid.'

Alice, even more afraid of the maid than of the mistress, declined hastily. 'I am accustomed to attend to myself, Miss Carew,' she added, with proud humility.

'You will find it more convenient to call me Lydia,' said Miss Carew. 'Otherwise you will be supposed to refer to my grand-aunt, a very old lady.' She then left the room.

Alice was fond of thinking that she had a womanly taste and touch in making a room pretty. She was accustomed to survey with pride her mother's drawing room, which she had garnished with cheap cretonnes, Japanese paper fans, and nic-nacs in ornamental pottery. She felt now that if she slept once in the bed before her, she could never be content in her mother's house again. All that she had read and believed of the beauty of cheap and simple ornament, and the vulgarity of costliness, recurred to her as a paraphrase of the

'Sour grapes' of the fox in the fable. She pictured to herself with a shudder the effect of a sixpenny Chinese umbrella in that fireplace, a cretonne valance to that bed, or chintz curtains to those windows. There was in the room a series of mirrors consisting of a great glass in which she could see herself at full length, another framed in the carved oaken dressing table, and smaller ones of various shapes fixed to jointed arms that turned every way. To use them for the first time was like having eyes in the back of one's head. She had never seen herself from all points of view before. As she gazed, she strove not to be ashamed of her dress; but even her face and figure, which usually afforded her unqualified delight, seemed robust and middle-class in Miss Carew's mirrors.

'After all,' she said, seating herself on a chair that was even more luxurious to rest in than to look at; 'putting the lace out of the question – and my old lace that belongs to mamma is quite as valuable – her whole dress cannot have cost much more than mine. At any rate, it is not worth much more, whatever she may have chosen to pay for it.'

But Alice was clever enough to envy Miss Carew her manners more than her dress. She would not admit to herself that she was not thoroughly a lady; but she felt that Lydia, in the eye of a stranger, would answer that description better than she. Still, as far as she had observed, Miss Carew was exceedingly cool in her proceedings, and did not take any pains to please those with whom she conversed. Alice had often made compacts of friendship with young ladies, and had invited them to call her by her Christian name; but on such occasions she had always called them 'dear' or 'darling' and, whilst the friendship lasted, which was often longer than a month, had never met them without exchanging an embrace and a hearty kiss.

'And nothing,' she said, springing from the chair as she thought of this, and speaking very resolutely, 'shall tempt me to believe that there is anything vulgar in sincere affection. I shall be on my guard against this woman.'

Having settled that matter for the present, she went on with her examination of the room, and was more and more attracted by it as she proceeded. For, thanks to her eminence as a local beauty, she had not that fear of beautiful and rich things which renders abject people incapable of associating costliness with comfort. Had the counterpane of the bed been her own, she would unhesitatingly have converted it into a ball dress. There were toilet appliances of which she had never felt the need, and could only guess the use. She looked with despair into the two large closets, thinking how poor a show her three dresses, her ulster, and her few old jackets would make there. There was also a dressing room with a marble bath that made cleanliness a luxury instead of, as it seemed at home, one of the sternest of the virtues. Everything was appropriately elegant; but nothing had been placed in the rooms for the sake of ornament alone. Miss Carew, judged by her domestic arrangements, was a utilitarian before everything. There was a very handsome chimneypiece; but as there was nothing on the mantelshelf, Alice made a faint effort to believe that it was inferior in point of taste to that in her own bedroom, which was covered with blue cloth, bordered by a fringe and a row of brass-headed nails, and laden with photographs in plush frames.

The striking of the hour reminded her that she had forgotten to prepare for dinner. She hastily took off her hat; washed her hands; spent another minute among the mirrors; and was summoning courage to ring the bell, when a doubt occurred to her. Ought she to put on her gloves before going down or not? This kept her in perplexity for many seconds. At last she resolved to put her gloves in her pocket, and be guided as to their further disposal by the example of her hostess. Not daring to hesitate any longer, she rang the bell, and was presently joined by a French lady of polished manners – Miss Carew's maid – who conducted her to the boudoir, an hexagonal apartment that, Alice thought, a sultana might have envied. Lydia was there, reading. Alice noted with relief that she had not changed her dress, and was ungloved.

Miss Goff did not enjoy the dinner. There was a butler who seemed to have nothing to do but stand at a buffet and watch her. There was also a swift, noiseless footman who presented himself at her elbow at intervals, and compelled her to choose on the instant between unfamiliar things to eat and drink. She envied these men their knowledge of society, and shrank from their criticism. Once, after taking a piece of asparagus in her hand, she was deeply mortified to see her hostess consume the vegetable with the aid of a knife and fork; but the footman's back was turned to her just then; and the butler, oppressed by the heat of the weather, was in a state of abstraction bordering on slumber. On the whole, by dint of imitating Miss Carew, who did not plague her with any hostess-like vigilance, she came off without discredit to her breeding.

Lydia, on her part, acknowledged no obligation to entertain her guest by chatting, and enjoyed her thoughts and her dinner in silence. Alice began to be fascinated by her, and to wonder what she was thinking about. She fancied that the footman was not quite free from the same influence. Even the butler might have been meditating himself to sleep on the subject. Alice felt tempted to offer her a penny for her thoughts; but she dared not be so familiar as yet. Had the offer been made and accepted, butler, footman, and guest would have been plunged into equal confusion by the explanation, which would have run thus:

'I had a vision of the Hermes of Praxiteles in a sylvan haunt today; and I am thinking of that.'

NEXT day Alice accepted Miss Carew's invitation. Lydia, who seemed to regard all conclusions as foregone when she had once signified her approval of them, took the acceptance as a matter of course. Alice thereupon thought fit to remind her that there were other persons to be considered. She said,

'I should not have hesitated yesterday but for my mother. It seems so heartless to leave her.'

'You have a sister at home, have you not?'

'Yes. But she is not very strong; and my mother requires a great deal of attention.' Alice paused, and added in a lower voice, 'She has never recovered from the shock of my father's death.'

'Your father is then not long dead?' said Lydia in her usual tone.

'Only two years,' said Alice coldly. 'I hardly know how to tell my mother that I am going to desert her.'

'Go and tell her today, Alice. You need not be afraid of hurting her. Grief of two years' standing is only a bad habit.'

Alice started, outraged. Her mother's grief was sacred to her; and yet it was by her experience of her mother that she recognized the truth of Lydia's remark, and felt that it was unanswerable. She frowned; but the frown was lost: Miss Carew was not looking at her. Then she rose and went to the door, where she stopped to say,

'You do not know our family circumstances. I will go now and try to prevail on my mother to let me stay with you.'

'Please come back in good time for dinner,' said Lydia, unmoved. 'I will introduce you to my cousin Lucian Webber: I have just received a telegram from him. He is coming down with Lord Worthington. I do not know whether Lord

Worthington will come to dinner or not. He has an invalid friend at the Warren Lodge; and Lucian does not make it clear whether he is coming to visit him or me. However, it is of no consequence: Lord Worthington is only a young sportsman. Lucian is a clever man, and will be a well-known one some day. He is secretary to a Cabinet Minister, and is very busy; but we shall probably see him often whilst the Whitsuntide holidays last. Excuse my keeping you waiting at the door to hear that long history. Adieu!' She waved her hand; and Alice suddenly felt that it might be possible to become very fond of Miss Carew.

She spent an unhappy afternoon with her mother. It had been Mrs Goff's fortune to marry a man of whom she was afraid, and who made himself very disagreeable whenever his house or his children were neglected in the least particular. Making a virtue of necessity, she had come to be regarded in Wiltstoken as a model wife and mother. At last, when a drag ran over Mr Goff and killed him, she was left almost penniless, with two daughters on her hands. In this extremity, she took refuge in grief, and did nothing. Her daughters settled their father's affairs as best they could; moved into a cheap house; and procured a strange tenant for that in which they had lived during many years. Janet, the elder sister, a student by disposition, employed herself as a teacher of the latest fashions in female education, rumors of which had already reached Wiltstoken. Alice was unable to teach mathematics and moral science; but she formed a dancing class, and gave lessons in singing and in a language which she believed to be current in France, but which was not intelligible to natives of that country travelling through Wiltstoken. Both sisters were devoted to one another and to their mother. Alice, who had enjoyed the special affection of her self-indulgent father, preserved some regard for his memory, though she could not help wishing that his affection had been strong enough to induce him to save a provision for her. She was ashamed, too, of the very recollection of his habit of getting drunk at races, regattas, and other national festivals, by an accident at one of which he had met his death.

Alice went home from the Castle expecting to leave her family divided between joy at her good fortune and grief at losing her; for her views of human nature and parental feeling were as yet purely romantic. But Mrs Goff, at once becoming envious of the luxury her daughter was about to enjoy, overwhelmed her with accusations of want of feeling, eagerness to desert her mother, and vain love of pleasure. Alice, who, in spite of a stubborn sense of the duty of truth telling, had often told Mrs Goff half a dozen lies in one afternoon to spare her some unpleasant truth, and would have scouted as infamous any suggestion that her parent was more selfish than saintly, soon burst into tears, declaring that she would not return to the Castle, and that nothing would have induced her to stay there the night before had she thought that her doing so could give pain at home. This alarmed Mrs Goff, who knew by experience that it was easier to drive Alice upon rash resolves than to shake her in them afterwards. Fear of incurring blame in Wiltstoken for wantonly opposing her daughter's interests, and of losing her share of Miss Carew's money and countenance, got the better of her jealousy. She lectured Alice severely for her headstrong temper, and commanded her on her duty not only to her mother, but also and chiefly to her God, to accept Miss Carew's offer with thankfulness, and to insist upon a definite salary as soon as she had, by good behavior, made her society indispensable at the Castle. Alice, dutiful as she was, reduced Mrs Goff to entreaties, and even to symptoms of an outburst of violent grief for the late Mr Goff, before she consented to obey her. She would wait, she said, until Janet, who was absent teaching, came in, and promised to forgive her for staying away the previous night (Mrs Goff had falsely represented that Janet, deeply hurt, had lain awake weeping during the small hours of the morning). The mother, seeing nothing for it but either to get rid of Alice before Janet's return, or be detected in a spiteful untruth, had to pretend that Janet was spending the evening with some friends, and to urge the unkindness of leaving Miss Carew lonely. At last Alice washed away the traces of her tears, and returned to the Castle, feeling very miserable, and trying to comfort herself with the reflection that her sister had been spared the scene which had just passed.

Lucian Webber had not arrived when she reached the Castle. Miss Carew glanced at her melancholy face as she entered, but asked no questions. Presently, however, she put down her book; considered for a moment; and said,

'It is nearly three years since I have had a new dress.' Alice looked up with interest. 'Now that I have you to help me to choose, I think I will be extravagant enough to renew my entire wardrobe. I wish you would take this opportunity to get some things for yourself. You will find that my dressmaker, Madame Smith, is to be depended on for work, though she is expensive and dishonest. When we are tired of Wiltstoken we can go to Paris, and be millinered there; but in the meantime we can resort to Madame Smith.'

'I cannot afford expensive dresses,' said Alice.

'I should not ask you to get them if you could not afford them. I warned you that I should give you expensive habits.'

Alice hesitated. She had a healthy inclination to take whatever she could get on all occasions; and she had suffered too much from poverty not to be more thankful for her good fortune than humiliated by Miss Carew's bounty. But the thought of being driven, richly attired, in one of the Castle carriages, and meeting Janet trudging about her daily tasks in a cheap black serge and mended gloves, made Alice feel that she deserved all her mother's reproaches. However, it was obvious that a refusal would be of no material benefit to Janet; so she said,

'Really I could not think of imposing on your kindness in this wholesale fashion. You are too good to me.'

'I will write to Madame Smith this evening,' said Lydia.

Alice was about to renew her protest more faintly, when

Mr Webber was announced. She stiffened herself to receive the visitor. Lydia's manner did not alter in the least. Lucian, whose demeanor resembled Miss Goff's rather than his cousin's, went through the ceremony of introduction with solemnity, and was received with a dash of scorn; for Alice, though secretly awestricken, bore herself tyrannically towards men from habit.

In reply to Alice, Mr Webber thought the day cooler than yesterday. In reply to Lydia he admitted that the resolution of which the Leader of the Opposition had given notice was tantamount to a vote of censure on the Government. He was confident that Ministers would have a majority. He had no news of any importance. He had made the journey down with Lord Worthington, who had come to Wiltstoken to see the invalid at the Warren Lodge. He had promised to return with Lucian in the seven-thirty train.

When they went down to dinner, Alice, profiting by her experience of the day before, faced the servants with composure, and committed no solecisms. Unable to take part in the conversation, as she knew nothing of politics, which were the staple of Lucian's discourse, she sat silent, and re-considered an old opinion of hers that it was ridiculous and ill-bred in a lady to discuss anything that was in the news-papers. She was impressed by Lucian's cautious and some-what dogmatic style of conversation, and concluded that he knew everything. Lydia seemed interested in his informa-tion, but quite indifferent to his opinions.

Towards half-past seven, Lydia proposed that they should walk to the railway station, adding, as a reason for going, that she wished to learn bookmaking from Lord Worthington. Lucian looked grave at this; and Alice, to shew that she shared his notions of propriety, looked shocked. Neither demonstration had the slightest effect on Lydia. She led the way to the hall; took her untrimmed straw hat and her scarf from a stand there; and walked out, gloveless, into the fresh spring evening. Alice, aghast at these manlike proceedings, and deprived of the ten minutes upon which she had counted to pin on her hat and equip herself for public inspection, had to rush upstairs and down again with undignified haste. When she overtook them on the lawn, Lucian was saying,

'Worthington is afraid of you, Lydia – needlessly, as it seems.'

'Why?'

'Because you know so much more than he does,' said Lucian, rejoiced by an invitation to explain. 'But perhaps you have more sympathy with his tastes than he supposes.'

'I may explain to you, Alice, that Lord Worthington is a young gentleman whose calendar is the racing calendar, and who interests himself in favorites and outsiders much as Lucian does in prime ministers and independent radicals. He never reads anything, and never associates with people who read anything; so his conversation is bearable. Would you like to go to Ascot, Alice?'

Alice answered, as she felt Lucian expected her to answer, that she had never been to a race, and that she had no desire to go to one.

'You will change your mind in time for next year's meeting. A race interests every one, which is more than can be said for the opera or the Academy.'

'I have been at the Academy,' said Alice, who had been once with her father to London.

'Indeed!' said Lydia. 'Were you in the National Gallery?'

'The National Gallery! I think not. I forget.'

'Did you enjoy the pictures?'

'Oh, very much indeed.'

'You will find Ascot far more amusing.'

'Let me warn you,' said Lucian to Alice, 'that my cousin's pet caprice is to affect a distaste for art, to which she is passionately devoted; and for literature, in which she is profoundly read.'

'Cousin Lucian,' said Lydia: 'should you ever be cut off from your politics, and disappointed in your ambition, you will have an opportunity of living upon art and literature. Then I shall respect your opinion of their satisfactoriness as a staff of life. As yet you have only tried them as a sauce.'

'Discontented, as usual?' said Lucian.

'Your one idea respecting me, as usual,' replied Lydia with patient impatience, as they entered the station.

The train, three carriages and a van, was waiting at the platform. The engine was humming subduedly; and the driver and fireman were leaning out: the latter, a young man, eagerly watching two gentlemen standing before the first-class carriage; whilst the driver shared his curiosity in an elderly, preoccupied manner. One of the persons thus observed was a bullet-headed little man of about twenty-five, in the afternoon costume of metropolitan fashion. Lydia instantly recognized the other as the Hermes of the day before, in spite of his straw hat, canary-colored scarf, and a suit of minute black-and-white chessboard pattern, with a crimson silk handkerchief overflowing the breast pocket of the coat. His hands were unencumbered by stick or umbrella; he carried himself smartly, balancing himself so accurately that he seemed to have no weight; and his expression was self-satisfied and good-humored. But –! Lydia felt that there was a But somewhere about this handsome, powerful, and light-hearted young man.

'There is Lord Worthington,' she said, indicating the bullet-headed gentleman. 'Surely that cannot be his invalid friend with him?'

'He is the man who lives at the Warren Lodge,' said Alice. 'I know his appearance.'

'Which is certainly not suggestive of a valetudinarian,' remarked Lucian, looking hard at the stranger.

They had now come close to the two, and could hear Lord Worthington, as he opened the carriage door to get in, saying, 'Take care of yourself, like a good fellow, wont you? Remember! if it lasts a second over the fifteen minutes, I shall drop five hundred pounds.'

Hermes placed his arm round the shoulders of the young lord, and gave him an elder-brotherly roll. Then he said with correct accent and pronunciation, but with a certain rough quality of voice, and louder than English gentlemen usually speak: 'Your money is as safe as the Mint, my boy.'

Evidently, Alice thought, the stranger was an intimate friend of Lord Worthington. She resolved to be particular in her behavior before him, if introduced.

'Lord Worthington,' said Lydia.

Startled, he turned and climbed hastily down from the step of the carriage, saying in some confusion, 'How de do, Miss Carew? Lovely country and lovely weather – must agree awfully well with you. You look as if it did.'

'Thank you: I dare say I do. Your friend is a tenant of mine, I think.'

Lord Worthington looked at her with a countenance that expressed a sudden and vivid dread of detection, and answered not a word.

'You are going to introduce him to me, are you not?'

'You give me leave to?' he stipulated.

'Of course,' said Lydia. 'Is there any reason – '

'Oh, not the least in the world, since you wish it,' he replied quickly, his eyes twinkling mischievously as he turned to his companion, who was standing at the carriage door admiring Lydia, and being himself admired by the stoker. 'Mr Cashel Byron: Miss Carew.'

Mr Cashel Byron reddened a little as he raised his straw hat, but, on the whole, bore himself like an eminent man who was not proud. As, however, he seemed to have nothing to say for himself, Lydia set Lord Worthington talking about Ascot, and listened to him whilst she looked at her new acquaintance. Now that the constraint of society had banished his former expression of easy good humor, there was something formidable in him that gave her an unaccountable thrill of pleasure. The same impression of latent danger had occurred, less agreeably, to Lucian, who was affected much as he might have been by the proximity

74

of a large dog of doubtful temper. Lydia thought that Mr Byron did not, at first sight, like her cousin; for he was looking at him obliquely, as though stealthily measuring him.

The group was broken up by the guard calling to the passengers to take their seats. Farewells were exchanged; and Lord Worthington cried, 'Take care of yourself,' to Cashel Byron, who replied somewhat impatiently, and with an apprehensive glance at Miss Carew, 'All right, all right: never you fear, sir.' Then the train went off; and he was left on the platform with the two ladies.

'We are returning to the Park, Mr Cashel Byron,' said Lydia.

'So am I,' said he. 'Perhaps – ' Here he broke down, and looked at Alice to avoid Lydia's eye. Then they went out together.

When they had walked some distance in silence: Alice looking rigidly before her, recollecting with suspicion that he had just addressed Lord Worthington as 'sir'; whilst Lydia was observing his light step and perfect balance, and trying to read his troubled face: he said,

'I saw you in the park yesterday; and I thought you were a ghost. Old Mellish – my man, I mean – saw you too. I knew by that that you were genuine.'

'Strange!' said Lydia. 'I had the same fancy about you.'

'What! You had!' he exclaimed, looking at her. Whilst thus unmindful of his steps, he stumbled, and recovered himself with a stifled oath. Then he became very red, and remarked, to Miss Goff, that it was a warm evening.

Alice assented. 'I hope,' she added, 'that you are better.'

He looked puzzled. Concluding, after consideration, that she had referred to his stumble, he said,

'Thank you: I didnt hurt myself.'

'Lord Worthington has been telling us about you,' said Lydia. He halted suddenly, evidently deeply mortified. She hastened to add, 'He mentioned that you had come down here to recruit your health: that is all.'

Cashel's features relaxed into a curious smile; and he

walked on again. But presently he became suspicious, and said anxiously, 'He didnt tell you anything else about me, did he'?

Alice stared at him superciliously. Lydia replied, 'No. Nothing else.'

'I thought you might have heard my name somewhere,' he persisted.

'Perhaps I have; but I cannot recall in what connection. Why? Do you know any friends of mine?'

'Oh no. Only Lord Worthington.'

'I conclude then that you are celebrated, and that I have the misfortune not to know it, Mr Cashel Byron. Is it so?'

'Not a bit of it,' he replied hastily. 'Theres no reason why you should ever have heard of me. I am much obliged to you for your kind inquiries,' he continued, turning to Alice. 'I'm quite well now, thank you. The country has set me right again.'

Alice, who was beginning to have her doubts of Mr Byron, smiled falsely and drew herself up a little. He turned away from her, hurt by her manner, and so ill able to conceal his feelings that Miss Carew, always watching him, saw what he felt and knew with delight that he was turning to her for consolation. He looked at Lydia wistfully, as if trying to guess her thoughts, which seemed to be with the setting sun, or in some equally beautiful and mysterious region. But he could see that there was no reflection of Miss Goff's scorn in her face.

'And so you really took me for a ghost?' he said.

'Yes. At first I thought you were a statue.'

'A statue!'

'You do not seem flattered by that.'

'It is not flattering to be taken for a lump of stone,' he replied ruefully.

Here was a man whom she had mistaken for the finest image of manly strength and beauty known to her; and he was so void of artistic culture that he held a statue to be a distasteful lump of stone.

'I believe I was trespassing then,' she said; 'but I did so

unintentionally. I had gone astray; for I am comparatively a stranger here, and cannot find my way about my park yet.'

'It didnt matter a bit,' said Cashel impetuously. 'Come as often as you want. Mellish fancies that if any one gets a glimpse of me he wont get any odds. You see he would like people to think – ' Here Cashel, recollecting himself, broke off, and added in confusion, 'Mellish is mad: thats about where it is.'

Alice glanced significantly at Lydia. She had already suggested that madness was the real reason for the seclusion of the tenants at the Warren Lodge. Cashel saw the glance, and intercepted it by turning to her, and saying, with an attempt at conversational ease,

'How do you young ladies amuse yourselves in the country? Do you play billiards ever?'

'No,' said Alice indignantly. The question, she thought, implied that she was capable of spending her evenings on the first floor of a public-house. To her surprise, Lydia remarked,

'I play – a little. I do not care sufficiently for the game to make myself proficient. You were equipped for lawn-tennis, I think, when I saw you yesterday. Miss Goff is a celebrated lawn-tennis player. She vanquished the Australian champion last year.'

It seemed that Byron, after all, was something of a courtier; for he displayed great astonishment at this feat. 'The Australian champion!' he repeated. 'And who may *he* – Oh! you mean the lawn-tennis champion. To be sure. Well, Miss Goff, I congratulate you. It is not every ammichoor (amateur) that can brag of having shewn a professional champion to a back seat.'

Alice, outraged by the imputation of bragging, and certain that slang was vulgar, whatever billiards might be, bore herself still more loftily, and resolved to snub him explicitly if he addressed her again. But he did not; for they came just then to a narrow iron gate in the wall of the park, at which Lydia stopped.

'Let me open it for you,' said Cashel. She gave him the key; and he seized one of the bars of the gate with his left hand, and stooped as though he wanted to look into the keyhole. Yet he opened it smartly enough.

Alice was about to pass in with a cool bow when she saw Miss Carew offer Cashel her hand. Whatever Lydia did was done so that it seemed the right thing to do. He took the hand timidly, and gave it a little shake, not daring to meet her eyes. Alice put out her glove stiffly. Cashel immediately stepped forward with his right foot and enveloped her fingers with the hardest clump of knuckles she had ever felt. Glancing down at this remarkable fist, she saw that it was discolored almost to blackness. Then she went in through the gate, followed by Lydia, who turned to close it behind her. As she pushed, Cashel, standing outside, grasped a bar and pulled. She at once relinquished to him the shutting of the gate, and smiled her thanks as she turned away; but in that moment he plucked up the courage to look at her. The sensation of being so looked at was quite novel, and very curious. She was even a little out of countenance, but not so much so as Cashel, who nevertheless could not take his eyes away.

'Do you think,' said Alice, as they crossed the orchard, 'that that man is a gentleman?'

'How can I possibly tell? We hardly know him.'

'But what do you think? There is always a certain something about a gentleman that one recognizes by instinct.'

'Is there? I have never observed it.'

'Have you not?' said Alice, surprised, and beginning uneasily to fear that her superior perception of gentility was in some way the effect of her social inferiority to Miss Carew. 'I thought one could always tell.'

'Perhaps so,' said Lydia. 'For my own part I have found the same varieties of address in every class. Some people, no matter what the style of their particular set may be, have a native distinction and grace of manner –'

'That is what I mean,' said Alice.

' – but you find that as often among actors, gipsies, and peasants, as among ladies and gentlemen. One can make a fair guess with most people, but not with this Mr Cashel Byron. Are you curious about him?'

'I!' exclaimed Alice superbly. 'Not in the least.'

'I am. He interests me. I seldom see anything novel in humanity; and he is a very singular man.'

'I meant,' said Alice, crestfallen, 'that I take no special interest in him.'

Lydia, not being concerned as to the exact degree of Alice's interest, merely nodded, and continued, 'He may, as you suppose, be a man of humble origin, who has seen something of society; or he may be a gentleman unaccustomed to society. I feel no conviction either way.'

'But he speaks very roughly; and his slang is disgusting. His hands are hard and quite black. Did you not notice them?'

'I noticed it all; and I think that if he were a man of low condition he would be careful not to use slang. Self-made persons are usually precise in their language: they rarely break the formulated laws of society, whereas he breaks every one of them. His pronunciation of some words is so distinct that an idea crossed me once that he might be an actor. But then it is not uniformly distinct. I am sure that he has some object or occupation in life: he has not the air of an idler. Yet I have thought of all the ordinary professions; and he does not fit one of them. That is perhaps what makes him interesting. He is unaccountable.'

'He must have some position. He was very familiar with Lord Worthington.'

'Lord Worthington is a sportsman, and is familiar with all sorts of people.'

'Yes; but surely he would not let a jockey, or anybody of that class, put his arm round his neck, as we saw Mr Byron do.'

'Perhaps not,' said Lydia thoughtfully, 'Still,' she added,

clearing her brow and laughing, 'I dont believe he is an invalid student.'

'I will tell you what he is,' said Alice suddenly. 'He is companion and keeper to the man with whom he lives. Do you recollect his saying "Mellish is mad"?'

'That is possible,' said Lydia. 'At all events we have got somebody to talk about; and that is an important home-comfort in the country.'

Just then they reached the Castle. Lydia lingered for a moment on the terrace. The tall Tudor chimneys of the Warren Lodge stood up against the long crimson cloud into which the sun was sinking. She smiled as if some quaint idea had occurred to her; raised her eyes for a moment to the black marble Egyptian gazing with unwavering eyes into the sky; and followed Alice indoors.

Later on, when it was quite dark, Cashel sat in a spacious kitchen at the lodge, thinking. His companion, who had laid his coat aside, was at the fire, smoking, and watching a saucepan that simmered there. He broke the silence by remarking, after a glance at the clock, 'Time to go to roost.'

'Time to go to the devil,' said Cashel. 'I am going out.'

'Yes, and get a chill. Not if I know it, you dont.'

'Well, go to bed yourself; and then you wont know it. I want to take a walk round the place.'

'If you put your foot outside that door tonight, Lord Worthington will lose his five hundred pounds. You cant lick any one in fifteen minutes if you train on night air. Get licked yourself, more likely.'

'Will you lay two to one that I dont sleep on the grass and knock the Flying Dutchman out of time in the first round afterwards?'

'Come,' said Mellish coaxingly: 'have some common sense. I'm advising you for your good.'

'Suppose I dont want to be advised for my good. Eh? Hand me over that lemon. You neednt start a speech: I'm not going to eat it.'

'Blest if he aint rubbin is ands with it!' exclaimed Mellish, after watching him for some moments. 'Why, you bloomin fool, lemon wont arden your ands. Aint I took enough trouble with them?'

'I want to whiten them,' said Cashel, impatiently throwing the lemon under the grate; 'but it's no use. I cant go about with my fists like this. I'll go up to London tomorrow and buy a pair of gloves.'

'What! Real gloves? Wearin gloves?'

'You thundering old lunatic,' said Cashel, rising and putting on his hat: 'is it likely that I want a pair of mufflers? Perhaps you think *you* could teach me something with them. Ha! ha! By the bye – now mind this, Mellish – dont let it out down here that I'm a fighting man. Do you hear?'

'Me let it out!' cried Mellish indignantly. 'Is it likely? Now, I asts you, Cashel Byron, is it likely?'

'Likely or not, dont do it,' said Cashel. 'You might get talking with some of the chaps about the Castle stables. They are free with their liquor when they can get sporting news for it.'

Mellish looked at him reproachfully; and Cashel turned towards the door. The movement reminded the trainer of his professional duties. He renewed his remonstrances as to the folly of venturing into the night air, citing many examples of pugilists who had suffered defeat through neglecting the counsel of their trainers. Cashel expressed his disbelief in these anecdotes in brief and personal terms; and at last Mellish had to content himself with proposing to limit the duration of the walk to half an hour.

'Perhaps I shall come back in half an hour,' said Cashel. 'And perhaps I shant.'

'Well, look here,' said Mellish. 'Dont let us two pals quarrel about a minute or so. I feel the want of a walk myself; and I'll come with you.'

'I'm damned if you shall,' said Cashel. 'Here: let me out; and shut up. I'm not going further than the park. I have no intention of making a night of it in the village, which is what

81

you are afraid of. I know you, you old dodger. If you dont get out of my way, I'll seat you on the fire.'

'But dooty, Cashel, dooty,' pleaded Mellish persuasively. 'Every man oughter do his dooty. Consider your dooty to your backers.'

'Are you going to get out of my way; or must I put you out of it?' said Cashel, reddening ominously.

Mellish went back to his chair; bowed his head on his hands; and wept. 'I'd sooner be a dog nor a trainer,' he sobbed. 'Oh! the cussedness o' bein shut up for weeks with a fightin man! For the fust two days theyre as sweet as treacle; and then their contrairiness comes out. Their tempers is puffict 'ell.'

Cashel, additionally enraged by a sting of remorse, went out and slammed the door. He made straight towards the Castle, and watched its windows for nearly half an hour, keeping in constant motion so as to avert a chill. At last a bell struck the hour from one of the minarets. To Cashel, accustomed to the coarse jangling of ordinary English bells in too low belfries, the sound seemed to belong to fairyland. He went slowly back to the Warren Lodge, and found his trainer standing at the open door, smoking, and anxiously awaiting his return. Cashel rebuffed his conciliatory advances with a haughty reserve more dignified but much less acceptable to Mr Mellish than his former profane familiarity, and went thoughtfully to bed.

CHAPTER IV

MISS CAREW sat on the bank of a great pool in the park, throwing pebbles two by two into the water, and intently watching the intersection of the circles they made on its calm surface. Alice, who had rashly begun her companionship by a parade of all her accomplishments, was sketching the Castle. The woodland rose round them like the sides of an amphitheatre; but the trees did not extend to the water's edge: there was an ample margin of bright greensward and a narrow belt of gravel, from which Lydia was picking her pebbles.

Hearing a footstep, she looked back, and saw Cashel Byron standing behind Alice, apparently much interested in her drawing. He was dressed as she had last seen him, except that he wore gorgeous primrose gloves and an Egyptian red scarf. Alice turned, and surveyed him with haughty surprise; but he stood at ease with an inept swagger; and she, after glancing at Lydia to reassure herself that she was not alone, bade him good morning, and resumed her work.

'Queer place,' he remarked, after a pause, alluding to the Castle. 'Chinese looking, isnt it?'

'It is considered a very fine building,' said Alice.

'Oh, hang what it is considered!' said Cashel. 'What *is* it? That is the point to look at.'

'It is a matter of taste,' said Alice very coldly.

'Mr Cashel Byron.'

Cashel started and hastened to the bank. 'How d'ye do, Miss Carew,' he said. 'I didnt see you until you called me.' She looked at him quietly; and he quailed, convicted of a foolish falsehood. 'There is a splendid view of the Castle from here,' he continued, to change the subject. 'Miss Goff and I have just been talking about it.'

'Yes. Do you admire it?'

'Very much indeed. It is a beautiful place. Every one must acknowledge that.'

'It is considered kind to praise my house to me, and to ridicule it to other people. You do not say, "Hang what it is considered," now.'

Cashel, with an unaccustomed sense of getting the worst of an encounter, almost lost heart to reply. Then he brightened, and said, 'I can tell you how that is. As far as being a place to sketch, or for another person to look at, it is Chinese enough. But somehow your living in it makes a difference. That is what I meant: upon my soul it is.'

Lydia smiled; but he, looking down at her, did not see the smile because of her coronet of red hair, which seemed to flame in the sunlight. The obstruction was unsatisfactory to him: he wanted to see her face. He hesitated, and then sat down on the ground beside her cautiously, as if getting into a very hot bath.

'I hope you wont mind my sitting here,' he said timidly. 'It seems rude to talk down at you from a height.'

She shook her head and threw two more stones into the pool. He could think of nothing further to say; and as she did not speak, but gravely watched the circles in the water, he began to stare at them too; and they sat in silence for some minutes, steadfastly regarding the waves: she as if there were matter for infinite thought in them: he as though the spectacle wholly confounded him. At last she said,

'Have you ever realized what a vibration is?'

'No,' said Cashel, after a blank look at her.

'I am delighted to hear you confess that. We have reduced everything nowadays to vibration. Light – sound – sensation – all are either vibrations or interference of vibrations. There,' she said, throwing another pair of pebbles in, and pointing to the two sets of widening rings as they overlapped one another: 'the twinkling of a star, and the pulsation in a chord of music, are *that*. But I cannot picture the thing in my own mind. I wonder whether the hundreds of writers of text-books on physics, who talk so glibly of vibrations, realize them any better than I do.'

'Not a bit of it. Not one of them. Not half so well,' said Cashel cheerfully, replying to as much of her speech as he understood.

'Perhaps the subject does not interest you,' she said, turning to him.

'On the contrary: I like it of all things,' said he boldly.

'I can hardly say as much for my own interest in it. I am told that you are a student, Mr Cashel Byron. What are your favorite studies? – or rather, since that is generally a hard question to answer, what are your pursuits?'

Alice listened.

Cashel looked doggedly at Lydia, his color slowly deepening. 'I am a professor,' he said.

'A professor of what? I know I should ask of where; but that would only elicit the name of a college, which would convey no real information to me.'

'I am a professor of science,' said Cashel in a low voice, looking down at his left fist, which he was balancing in the air before him, and stealthily hitting his bent knee as if it were another person's face.

'Physical or moral science?' persisted Lydia.

'Physical science,' said Cashel. 'But theres more moral science in it than people think.'

'Yes,' said Lydia seriously. 'Though I have no real knowledge of physics, I can appreciate the truth of that. Perhaps all the science that is not at bottom physical science, is only formal nescience. I have read much of physics, and have often been tempted to make the experiments with my own hands – to furnish a laboratory – to wield the scalpel even. For to master science thoroughly, I suppose one must take one's gloves off. Is that your opinion?'

Cashel looked hard at her. 'You never spoke a truer word,' he said. 'But you can become a very respectable amateur by working with the gloves.'

'*I* never should. The many who believe they are the

85

wiser for reading accounts of experiments, deceive themselves. It is as impossible to learn science from hearsay as to gain wisdom from proverbs. Ah, it is so easy to follow a line of argument, and so difficult to grasp the facts that underlie it! Our popular lecturers on physics present us with chains of deductions so highly polished that it is a luxury to let them slip from end to end through our fingers. But they leave nothing behind but a vague memory of the sensation they afforded.'

'I wish I could talk like that,' said Cashel: '– like a book, I mean.'

'Heaven forbid!' said Lydia. 'I beg your pardon for it. Will you give me some lessons if I set to work in earnest at science?'

'Well,' said Cashel with a covert grin, 'I would rather you came to me than to another professor; but I dont think it would suit you. I should like to try my hand on your friend there. She's stronger and straighter than nine out of ten men.'

'You set a high value on physical qualifications, then. So do I.'

'Only from a practical point of view, mind you,' said Cashel earnestly. 'It isnt right to be always looking at men and women as you look at horses. If you want to back them in a race or in a fight, thats one thing; but if you want a friend or a sweetheart, thats another.'

'Quite so,' said Lydia, smiling. 'You do not wish to commit yourself to any warmer feeling towards Miss Goff than a critical appreciation of her form and condition.'

'Just that,' said Cashel, satisfied. '*You* understand me, Miss Carew. There are some people that you might talk to all day, and theyd be no wiser at the end of it than they were at the beginning. Youre not one of that sort.'

'I wonder do we ever succeed really in communicating our thoughts to one another. A thought must take a new shape to fit itself into a strange mind. You, Mr Professor, must have acquired special experience of the incommunicability of ideas in the course of your lectures and lessons.'

Cashel looked uneasily at the water, and said in a lower voice, 'Of course you may call me just whatever you like; but – if it's all the same to you – I wish you wouldnt call me Professor.'

'I have lived so much in countries where people expect to be addressed by even the most trivial titles on all occasions, that I may claim to be excused for having offended on that point. Thank you for telling me. But I am to blame for discussing science with you. Lord Worthington told us that you had come down here expressly to escape from it – to recruit yourself after an excess of work.'

'It doesnt matter,' said Cashel.

'I have not done harm enough to be greatly concerned; but I will not offend again. To change the subject, let us look at Miss Goff's sketch.'

Miss Carew had hardly uttered this suggestion, when Cashel, in a business-like manner, and without the slightest air of gallantry, expertly lifted her and placed her on her feet. This unexpected attention gave her a shock, followed by a thrill that was not disagreeable. She turned to him with a faint mantling in her cheeks.

'Thank you,' she said; 'but pray do not do that again. It is a little humiliating to be lifted like a child. You are very strong.'

'There is not much strength needed to lift such a feather-weight as you. Seven stone two, I should judge you to be about. But theres a great art in doing these things properly. I have often had to carry off a man of fourteen stone, resting him all the time as if he was in bed.'

'Ah,' said Lydia: 'I see you have had some hospital practice. I have often admired the skill with which trained nurses handle their patients.'

Cashel, without a word, followed her to where Alice sat.

'It is very foolish of me, I know,' said Alice presently; 'but I never can draw when any one is looking at me.'

'You fancy that everybody is thinking about how youre

doing it,' said Cashel encouragingly. 'Thats always the way with amateurs. But the truth is that not a soul except yourself is a bit concerned about it. *Ex*-cuse me,' he added, taking up the drawing, and proceeding to examine it leisurely.

'Please give me my sketch, Mr Byron,' she said, her cheeks red with anger. Puzzled, he turned to Lydia for an explanation, whilst Alice seized the sketch and packed it in her portfolio.

'It is getting rather warm,' said Lydia. 'Shall we return to the castle?'

'I think we had better,' said Alice, trembling with resentment as she walked away quickly, leaving Lydia alone with Cashel, who exclaimed,

'What in thunder have I done?'

'You have made an inconsiderate remark with unmistakeable sincerity.'

'I only tried to cheer her up. She must have mistaken what I said.'

'I think not. Do you believe that young ladies like to be told that there is no occasion for them to be ridiculously self-conscious?'

'I say that! I'll take my oath I never said anything of the sort.'

'You worded it differently. But you assured her that she need not object to have her drawing overlooked, as it is of no importance to any one.'

'Well, if she takes offence at that, she must be a born fool. Some people cant bear to be told anything. But they soon get all that thin-skinned nonsense knocked out of them.'

'Have you any sisters, Mr Cashel Byron?'

'No. Why?'

'Or a mother?'

'I have a mother; but I havnt seen her for years; and I dont much care if I never see her. It was through her that I came to be what I am.'

'Are you then dissatisfied with your profession?'

'No: I dont mean that. I am always saying stupid things.'

'Yes. That comes of your ignorance of a sex accustomed to have its silliness respected. You will find it hard to keep on good terms with my friend without learning a little more of womanly ways.'

'As to her, I wont give in that I'm wrong unless I *am* wrong. The truth's the truth.'

'Not even to please Miss Goff?'

'Not even to please you. Youd only think the worse of me afterwards.'

'Quite true, and quite right,' said Lydia cordially. 'Goodbye, Mr Cashel Byron. I must go back to Miss Goff.'

'I suppose you will take her part if she keeps a down on me for what I said to her.'

'What is a down? A grudge?'

'Yes. Something of that sort.'

'Colonial, is it not?' pursued Lydia, with the air of a philologist.

'Yes, I believe I picked it up in the colonies.' Then he added sullenly, 'I suppose I shouldnt use slang in speaking to you. I beg your pardon.'

'Not at all. I like finding out about things, especially about words. And I want to find out about you. You were not born in Australia, were you?'

'Good Lord! no. But are you out with me because I annoyed Miss Goff?'

'Not in the least. I sympathize with her annoyance at the manner, if not the matter, of your rebuke: that is all.'

'I cant, for the life of me, see what there was in what I said to raise such a fuss about. I wish you would give me a nudge whenever you see me making a fool of myself. I will shut up at once and ask no questions.'

'So that it will be understood that my nudge means "Shut up, Mr Cashel Byron: you are making a fool of yourself"?'

'Just so. *You* understand me. I told you that before, didnt I?'

'I am afraid,' said Lydia, her face bright with laughter,

'that I cannot take charge of your manners until we are a little better acquainted.'

He seemed disappointed. Then his face clouded; and he began, 'If you regard it as a liberty –'

'Of course I regard it as a liberty,' she said, neatly interrupting him. 'My own conduct gives me quite enough to take care of. Do you know that for so very strong a man and learned a professor, you seem to have very little sense?'

'By Jingo!' exclaimed Cashel, with sudden excitement, 'I dont care what you say to me. You have a way of giving things a turn that makes it a pleasure to be shut up by you; and if I were a gentleman as I ought to be, instead of a poor devil of a professional pug, I would –' He recollected himself, and turned quite pale. There was a pause.

'Let me remind you,' said Lydia composedly, though she too had changed color at the beginning of his outburst, 'that we are both wanted elsewhere at present: I by Miss Goff; and you by your servant, who has been hovering about us and looking at you anxiously for some minutes.'

Cashel turned fiercely, and saw Mellish standing a little way off, sulkily watching them. Lydia took the opportunity, and left the place. As she retreated, she could hear that they were at high words together; but she could not distinguish what they were saying. This was fortunate; for their language was abominable.

She found Alice in the library, seated bolt upright in a chair that would have tempted a good-humored person to recline. Lydia sat down in silence. Alice, looking at her, discovered that she was in a fit of noiseless laughter. The effect, in contrast to her habitual self-possession, was so strange that Alice almost forgot to be offended.

'I am glad to see that it is not hard to amuse you,' she said.

Lydia waited to recover herself thoroughly, and then replied, 'I have not laughed so three times in my life. Now, Alice, put aside your resentment of our neighbor's impudence for the moment; and tell me what you think of him.'

'I have not thought about him at all, I assure you,' said Alice disdainfully.

'Then think about him for a moment to oblige me; and let me know the result.'

'Really, you have had much more opportunity of judging than I. *I* have hardly spoken to him.'

Lydia rose patiently and went to the bookcase. 'You have a cousin at one of the universities, have you not?' she said, seeking along the shelf for a volume.

'Yes,' replied Alice, speaking very sweetly to atone for her want of amiability on the previous subject.

'Then perhaps you know something of university slang?'

'I never allow him to talk slang to me,' said Alice quickly.

'You may dictate modes of expression to a single man, perhaps, but not to a whole university,' said Lydia, with a quiet scorn that brought unexpected tears to Alice's eyes. 'Do you know what a pug is?'

'A pug!' said Alice vacantly. 'No: I have heard of a bull-dog – a proctor's bulldog, but never of a pug.'

'I must try my slang dictionary,' said Lydia, taking down a book. 'Here it is. "Pug – a fighting man's idea of the contracted word to be produced from pugilist." What an extraordinary definition! A fighting man's idea of a contraction! Why should a man have a special idea of a contraction when he is fighting; or why should he think of such a thing at all under such circumstances? Perhaps fighting man is slang too. No: it is not given here. Either I mistook the word, or it has some signification unknown to the compiler of my dictionary.'

'It seems quite plain to me,' said Alice. 'Pug means pugilist.'

'But pugilism is boxing: it is not a profession. I suppose all men are more or less pugilists. I want a sense of the word in which it denotes a calling or occupation of some kind. I fancy it means a demonstrator of anatomy. However, it does not matter.'

'Where did you meet with it?'

'Mr Byron used it just now.'

'Do you really like that man?' said Alice, returning to the subject more humbly than she had quitted it.

'So far, I do not dislike him. He puzzles me. If the roughness of his manner is an affectation, I have never seen one so successful before.'

'Perhaps he does not know any better. His coarseness did not strike me as being affected at all.'

'I should agree with you but for one or two remarks that fell from him. They shewed an insight into the real nature of scientific knowledge, and an instinctive sense of the truths underlying words, which I have never met with except in men of considerable culture and experience. I suspect that his manner is deliberately assumed in protest against the selfish vanity which is the common source of social polish. It is partly natural, no doubt. He seems too impatient to choose his words heedfully. Do you ever go to the theatre?'

'No,' said Alice, taken aback by this apparent irrelevance. 'My father disapproved of it. But I was there once. I saw The Lady of Lyons.'

'There is a famous actress, Adelaide Gisborne –'

'It was she whom I saw as the Lady of Lyons. She acted it beautifully.'

'Did Mr Byron remind you of her?'

Alice stared incredulously at Lydia. 'I dont believe there can be two people in the world less like one another,' she said.

'Nor do I,' said Lydia meditatively, dropping into the literary manner which Cashel admired. 'But I think their dissimilarity must owe its emphasis to some lurking likeness. Otherwise how could he have reminded me of her?' A long silence ensued, during which Alice, conscious of some unusual stir in her patroness, watched her furtively and wondered what would happen next.

'Alice.'

'Yes.'

'My mind is running on trifles – a sure symptom of failing mental health. My visit to Wiltstoken is only one of several attempts I have made to live idly since my father's death. They have all failed. Work is one of the necessaries of life to me. I will go up to London tomorrow.'

Alice's heart sank; for this seemed equivalent to a dismissal. But her face expressed nothing but polite indifference.

'We shall have time to run through all the follies of the season before June, when I hope to return here and set to work at a book I have planned. I must collect materials for it in London. If I leave town before the season is over, and you are unwilling to come away with me, I can easily find some one who will take care of you as long as you please to stay. I wish it were June already!'

Alice preferred Lydia's womanly impatience to her fatalistic calm. It relieved her sense of inferiority, which familiarity had increased rather than diminished. She did not yet dare to suspect her patroness of anything so vulgarly human as a sexual interest in Cashel; but she was beginning to persuade herself with some success that the propriety of Lydia's manners was at least questionable. That morning Miss Carew had not scrupled to ask a man what his profession was; and this, at least, Alice congratulated herself on being too well bred to do. She had quite lost her awe of the servants; and had begun to address them with an unconscious haughtiness and a conscious politeness that were making the word upstart frequent in the servants' hall. Bashville, the footman, had risked his popularity there by opining that Miss Goff was a fine young woman.

Bashville was in his twenty-fourth year, and stood five feet ten in his stockings. At The Green Man in the village all the rustic pretence of indifference to his metropolitan prestige had melted before his fluent oratory and his keenness in political debate. In the stables he was deferred to as an authority on sporting affairs, and an expert wrestler in the Cornish fashion. The women servants regarded him with undissembled admiration. They vied with one another in inventing expressions of delight when he recited before them, which, as he had a good memory and was fond of poetry, he often did. They were proud to go out walking with him. But his attentions never gave rise to jealousy; for it was an open secret in the servants' hall that he loved his mistress. He had never said anything to that effect; and no one dared allude to it in his presence, much less rally him on his weakness; but his passion was well known for all that; and it seemed by no means so hopeless to the younger members of the domestic staff as it did to the cook, the butler, and Bashville himself. Miss Carew, who knew the value of good servants, appreciated her footman's smartness, and paid him accordingly; but she had no suspicion that she was waited on by a versatile young student of poetry and public affairs, distinguished for his gallantry, his personal prowess, his eloquence, and his influence in local politics.

It was Bashville who now entered the library with a salver, which he proffered to Alice, saying, 'The gentleman is waiting in the round drawing room, Miss.'

Alice took the gentleman's card, and read, 'Mr Wallace Parker.'

'Oh!' she said, with vexation, glancing at Bashville as if to divine his impression of the visitor. 'My cousin – the one we were speaking of just now – has come to see me.'

'How fortunate!' said Lydia. 'He will tell me the meaning of pug. Ask him to lunch with us.'

'You would not care for him,' said Alice. 'He is not much used to society. I suppose I had better go and see him.'

Miss Carew did not reply, being plainly at a loss to understand how there could be any doubt about the matter. Alice went to the round drawing room, where she found Mr Parker examining a trophy of Indian armor, and presenting a back view of a short gentleman in a spruce blue frockcoat. A new hat and pair of gloves were also visible as he stood looking upward with his hands behind him. When he turned to greet Alice, he displayed a face expressive of resolute self-esteem, with eyes whose watery brightness, together with the bareness of his temples, from which the hair was worn away, suggested late hours and either very studious or very dissipated habits. He advanced confidently; pressed Alice's hand warmly for several seconds; and placed a chair for her, without noticing the marked coldness with which she received his attentions.

'I am not angry, Alice,' he said, when he had seated himself opposite to her; 'but I was surprised to learn from Aunt Emily that you had come to live here without consulting me. I –'

'Consult you!' she exclaimed, scornfully interrupting him. 'I never heard of such a thing! Why should I consult you as to my movements?'

'Well, I should not have used the word consult, particularly to such an independent little lady as sweet Alice Goff. Still, I think you might at least have gone through the form of acquainting me with the step you were taking. The relations that exist between us give me a right to your confidence.'

'What relations, pray?'

'What relations!' he repeated, with reproachful emphasis.

'Yes. What relations?'

He rose, and addressed her with tender solemnity. 'Alice,' he began: 'I have proposed to you six times –'

'And have I accepted you once?'

'Hear me to the end, Alice. I know that you have never explicitly accepted me; but it has always been understood that my needy circumstances were the only obstacle to our happiness. We – Dont interrupt me, Alice: you little know whats coming. That obstacle no longer exists. I have been made second master at Sunbury College, with £350 a year, a house, coals, and gas. In the course of time, I shall undoubtedly succeed to the head mastership – a splendid position, worth £1600 a year. You are now free from the troubles that have pressed so hard upon you since your father's death; and you can quit at once – now – instantly, your dependent position here.'

'Thank you: I am very comfortable here. I am staying on a visit with Miss Carew.'

Silence ensued; and he sat down slowly. Then she added, 'I am exceedingly glad that you have got something good at last. It must be a great relief to your poor mother.'

'I fancied, Alice – though it may have been only fancy – I fancied that *your* mother was colder than usual in her manner this morning. I hope the luxuries of this palatial mansion are powerless to corrupt your heart. I cannot lead you to a castle and place crowds of liveried servants at your beck and call; but I can make you mistress of an honorable English home, independent of the bounty of strangers. You can never be more than a lady, Alice.'

'It is very good of you to lecture me, I am sure.'

'You might be serious with me,' he said, rising in ill humor, and walking a little way down the room. 'I think the offer of a man's hand ought to be received with respect.'

'Oh! I did not quite understand. I thought we agreed that you are not to make me that offer every time we meet.'

'It was equally understood that the subject was only deferred until I should be in a position to resume it without binding you to a long engagement. That time has come now; and I expect a favorable answer at last. I am entitled to one, considering how patiently I have waited for it.'

'For my part, Wallace, I must say I do not think it wise for you to think of marrying with only £350 a year.'

'With a house: remember that; and coals, and gas! You are becoming very prudent now that you live with Miss Whatshername here. I fear you no longer love me, Alice.'

'I never said I loved you at any time.'

'Pshaw! You never said so, perhaps; but you always gave me to understand –'

'I did nothing of the sort, Wallace; and I wont have you say so.'

'In short,' he retorted bitterly, 'you think you will pick up some swell here who will be a better bargain than I am.'

'Wallace! How dare you?'

'You hurt my feelings, Alice; and I speak out. I know how to behave myself quite as well as those who have the *entrée* here; but when my entire happiness is at stake I do not stand on punctilio. Therefore I insist on a straightforward answer to my fair, honorable proposal.'

'Wallace,' said Alice, with dignity: 'I will not be forced into giving an answer against my will. I regard you as a cousin.'

'I do not wish to be regarded as a cousin. Have I ever regarded you as a cousin?'

'And do you suppose, Wallace, that I should permit you to call me by my Christian name, and be as familiar as we have always been together, if you were not my cousin? If so, you must have a very strange opinion of me.'

'I did not think that luxury could so corrupt –'

'You said that before,' said Alice pettishly. 'Do not keep repeating the same thing over and over: you know it is one of your bad habits. Will you stay to lunch? Miss Carew told me to ask you.'

'Indeed! Miss Carew is very kind. Please inform her that I am deeply honored, and that I feel quite disturbed at being unable to accept her patronage.'

Alice poised her head disdainfully. 'No doubt it amuses you to make yourself ridiculous,' she said; 'but I must say I do not see any occasion for it.'

'I am sorry that my behavior is not sufficiently good for you. You never found any cause to complain of it when our surroundings were less aristocratic. I am quite ashamed of taking so much of your valuable time. *Good* morning.'

'Good morning. But I do not see why you are in such a rage.'

'I am not in a rage. I am only grieved to find that you are corrupted by luxury. I thought your principles were higher. Good morning, Miss Goff. I shall not have the pleasure of seeing you again in this very choice mansion.'

'Are you really going, Wallace?' said Alice, rising.

'Yes. Why should I stay?'

She rang the bell, greatly disconcerting him; for he had expected her to detain him and make advances for a reconciliation. Before they could exchange more words, Bashville entered.

'Goodbye,' said Alice politely.

'Goodbye,' he replied, through his teeth. He walked loftily out, passing Bashville with marked scorn.

He had left the house, and was descending the terrace steps, when he was overtaken by the footman, who said civilly,

'Beg your pardon, sir. Youve forgotten this, I think.' And he handed him a walking stick.

Parker's first idea was that his stick had attracted the man's attention by the poor figure it made in the castle hall, and that Bashville was requesting him, with covert superciliousness, to remove his property. On second thoughts his self-esteem rejected this suspicion as too humiliating; but he resolved to shew Bashville that he had a gentleman to deal with. So he took the stick, and, instead of thanking Bashville, handed him five shillings.

Bashville smiled and shook his head. 'Oh no, sir,' he said: 'thank you all the same. Those are not my views.'

'The more fool you,' said Parker, pocketing the coins, and turning away.

Bashville's countenance changed. 'Come come, sir,' he said, following Parker to the foot of the steps: 'fair words deserve fair words. I am no more a fool than you are. A gentleman should know his place as well as a servant.'

'Oh, go to the devil,' muttered Parker, turning very red, and hurrying away.

'If you werent my mistress's guest,' said Bashville, looking menacingly after him, 'I'd send you to bed for a week for sending me to the devil.'

CHAPTER V

Miss Carew unhesitatingly carried out her intention of going to London, where she took a house in Regent's Park, to the disappointment of Alice, who had hoped to live in Mayfair, or at least in South Kensington. But Lydia set great store by the high northerly ground and open air of the Park; and Alice found almost perfect happiness in driving through London in a fine carriage and fine clothes. She liked that better than concerts of classical music, which she did not particularly relish, or even than the opera, to which they went often. The theatres pleased her more, though the amusements there were tamer than she had expected. 'Society' was delightful to her because it was real London society. She acquired a mania for dancing; went out every night; and seemed to herself far more distinguished and attractive than she had ever been in Wiltstoken, where she had nevertheless held a sufficiently favorable opinion of her own manners and person.

Lydia did not share all these dissipations. She easily procured invitations and chaperones for Alice, who wondered why so intelligent a woman would take the trouble to sit out a stupid concert, and then go home, just as the real pleasure of the evening was beginning.

One Saturday morning, at breakfast, Lydia said,

'Have you ever been to the Crystal Palace?'

'No,' said Alice, with some scorn, which she repented when Lydia rejoined sedately,

'I think I will go down there today and wander about the gardens for a while. There is to be a concert in the afternoon, at which Madame Szczympliça, whose playing you do not admire, will appear. Will you come with me?'

'Of course,' said Alice, resolutely dutiful.

'Of choice: not of course,' said Lydia. 'Are you engaged for tomorrow evening?'

'Sunday? Oh no. Besides, I consider all my engagements subject to your convenience.'

There was a pause, long enough for this assurance to fall perfectly flat. Alice bit her lip. Then Lydia said, 'Do you know Mrs Hoskyn?'

'Mrs Hoskyn who gives Sunday evenings? Shall we go there?' said Alice eagerly. 'People often ask me whether I have been at one of them. But I dont know her – though I have seen her. Is she nice?'

'She is a young woman who has read a great deal of art criticism, and been deeply impressed by it. She has made her house famous by bringing there all the clever people she meets, and making them so comfortable that they take care to go again. But she has not, fortunately for her, allowed her craze for art to get the better of her common sense. She has married a prosperous man of business, who probably never read anything but a newspaper since he left school; and I doubt if there is a happier pair in England.'

'I presume she had sense enough to know that she could not afford to choose,' said Alice complacently. 'She is very ugly.'

'Do you think so? She has many admirers, and was, I am told, engaged to Mr Herbert, the artist, before she met Mr Hoskyn. We shall meet Mr Herbert there tomorrow, and a number of celebrated persons besides: his wife Madame Szczympliça the pianiste, Owen Jack the composer, Conolly the inventor, and others. The occasion will be a special one, as Herr Abendgasse, a remarkable German socialist-of-the-chair and art critic, is to deliver a lecture on The True in Art. Be careful, in speaking of him in society, to refer to him as a sociologist, and not a socialist. Are you particularly anxious to hear him lecture?'

'No doubt it will be very interesting,' said Alice. 'I should not like to miss the opportunity of going to Mrs Hoskyn's. People so often ask me whether I have been there, and whether I know this, that, and the other celebrated person, that I feel rather out of it in my rustic ignorance.'

'Because,' pursued Lydia, 'I had intended not to go until after the lecture. Herr Abendgasse is enthusiastic and eloquent, but not original. I prefer to get his ideas direct from their inventors; so unless you are specially interested – '

'Not at all. If he is a socialist I had much rather not listen to him, particularly on Sunday evening.'

It was arranged accordingly that they should go to Mrs Hoskyn's after the lecture. Meanwhile they went to Sydenham, where Alice went through the Crystal Palace with provincial curiosity, and Lydia explained the place encyclopædically. In the afternoon there was a concert, at which a band played several long pieces of music, which Lydia seemed to enjoy, though she occasionally found fault with the performers. Alice, able to detect neither the faults in the execution nor the beauty of the music, did as she saw the others do – pretended to be pleased, and applauded decorously. Madame Szczympliça, whom she expected to meet at Mrs Hoskyn's, appeared, and played a fantasia for pianoforte and orchestra by the famous Jack, another of Mrs Hoskyn's circle. There was in the program an analysis of this composition, from which Alice learnt that by attentively listening to the *Adagio* she could hear the angels singing therein. She listened as attentively as she could, but heard no angels, and was astonished when, at the conclusion of the fantasia, the audience applauded Madame Szczympliça as if she had made them hear the music of the spheres. Even Lydia seemed moved, and said,

'Strange, that she is only a woman like the rest of us, with just the same narrow bounds to her existence, and just the same prosaic cares – that she will go by train to Victoria, and thence home in a common vehicle, instead of embarking in a great shell, and being drawn by swans to some enchanted island. Her playing reminds me of myself as I was when I believed in fairyland, and indeed knew little about any other land.'

'They say,' said Alice, 'that her husband is very jealous, and that she leads him a terrible life.'

'*They say* anything that brings gifted people to the level of their own experience. Doubtless they are right. I have not met Mr Herbert; but I have seen his pictures, which suggest that he reads everything and sees nothing; for they all represent scenes described in some poem. If one could only find an educated man who had never read a book, what a delightful companion he would be!'

When the concert was over, they did not return directly to town, as Lydia wished to walk awhile in the gardens. In consequence, when they left Sydenham they got into a Waterloo train, and so had to change at Clapham Junction. It was a fine summer evening; and Alice, though she thought that it became ladies to hide themselves from the public in waiting-rooms at railway stations, did not attempt to dissuade Lydia from walking to and fro at an unfrequented end of the platform, which ended in a bank covered with flowers.

'To my mind,' said Lydia, 'Clapham Junction is one of the prettiest places about London.'

'Indeed!' said Alice a little maliciously. 'I thought that all artistic people looked on junctions and railway lines as blots on the landscape.'

'Some of them do,' said Lydia; 'but they are not the artists of our generation; and those who take up their cry are no better than parrots. If every holiday recollection of my youth – every escape from town to country – be associated with the railway, I must feel towards it otherwise than my father did, upon whose middle age it came as a monstrous iron innovation. The locomotive is one of the wonders of modern childhood. Children crowd upon a bridge to see the train pass beneath. Little boys strut along the streets puffing and whistling in imitation of the engine. All that romance, silly as it looks, becomes sacred in after life. Besides, when it is not underground in a foul London tunnel, a train is a beautiful thing. Its pure white fleece of steam harmonizes with every variety of landscape. And its sound! Have you ever stood on a sea coast skirted by a railway, and listened as the train came into hearing in the far distance? At first it can hardly be distinguished from the noise of the sea; then you recognize it by its variation: one moment smothered in a deep cutting, and the next sent echoing from some hillside. Sometimes it runs smoothly for many minutes, and then breaks suddenly into a rhythmic clatter, always changing in distance and intensity. When it comes near, you should get into a tunnel, and stand there whilst it passes. I did that once; and it was like the last page of an overture by Beethoven, thunderingly impetuous. I cannot conceive how any person can hope to disparage a train by comparing it with a stage coach; and I know something of stage coaches, or, at least, of *diligences*. Their effect on the men employed about them ought to decide the superiority of steam without further argument. I never saw an engine driver who did not seem an exceptionally intelligent mechanic; whilst the very writers and artists who have preserved the memory of the coaching days for us do not appear to have taken coachmen seriously, or to have regarded them as responsible and civilized men. Abuse of the railway from a pastoral point of view is obsolete. There are millions of grown persons in England to whom the far sound of the train is as pleasantly suggestive as the piping of a blackbird. And then – is not that Lord Worthington getting out of the train? Yes, that one, at the third platform from this. He – ' She stopped. Alice looked, but could see neither Lord Worthington nor the cause of a subtle but perceptible change in Lydia, who said quickly,

'He is probably coming to our train. Come to the waiting-room.' She walked swiftly along the platform as she spoke. Alice hurried after her; and they had but just got into the room, the door of which was close to the staircase which gave access to the platform, when a coarse din of men's voices told them that a noisy party was ascending the steps. Presently a man emerged reeling, and at once began to execute a drunken dance, and to sing as well as his condition and musical faculty allowed. Lydia stood near the window of the room, and watched in silence. Alice, following her example, recognized the drunken dancer as Mellish. He was followed by three men, gaily attired and highly elated, but comparatively sober. After them came Cashel Byron, showily dressed in a velveteen coat and tightly fitting fawn-colored pantaloons that displayed the muscles of his legs. He also seemed quite sober; but he was dishevelled; and his left eye blinked frequently, the adjacent brow and cheek being much yellower than his natural complexion, which appeared to advantage on the right side of his face. Walking steadily to Mellish, who was now asking each of the bystanders in turn to come and drink at his expense, he seized him by the collar, and sternly bade him cease making a fool of himself. Mellish tried to embrace him.

'My own boy,' he exclaimed affectionately. 'He's my little nonpareil. Cashel Byron agin the world at catchweight. Bob Mellish's money – '

'You sot,' said Cashel, rolling him about until he was giddy as well as drunk, and then forcing him to sit down on a bench: 'one would think you never saw a mill or won a bet in your life before.'

'Steady, Byron,' said one of the others. 'Heres his lordship.' Lord Worthington was coming up the stairs, apparently the most excited of the party.

'Fine man!' he cried, patting Cashel on the shoulder. 'Splendid man! You have won a monkey for me today; and you shall have your share of it, old boy.'

'I trained him,' said Mellish, staggering forward again. 'I trained him. You know me, my lord. You know Bob Mellish. A word with your lordship in c – confidence. You jes ask who knows how to make the beef go and the muscle come. You ask – I ask your lorships par'n. What'll your lorship take?'

'Take care, for Heaven's sake!' exclaimed Lord Worthington, clutching at him as he reeled backwards towards the line. 'Dont you see the train?'

'*I* know,' said Mellish gravely. 'I am all right: no man more so. I am Bob Mellish. You ask –'

'Here. Come out of this,' said one of the party, a powerful man with a scarred face and crushed nose, grasping Mellish and thrusting him into the train. 'You want a beef-steak on that ogle of yours, where you napped the Dutchman's auctioneer, Byron. It's got more yellow paint on it than y'll like to shew in church tomorrow.'

At this they all gave a roar of laughter, and took an empty first-class compartment by storm. Lydia and Alice had hardly time to take their places in the train before it started.

'Really I must say,' said Alice, 'that if those were Mr Cashel Byron's and Lord Worthington's associates, their tastes are very peculiar.'

'Yes,' said Lydia almost grimly. 'I am a fair linguist; but I did not understand a single sentence of their conversation, though I heard it all distinctly.'

'They were not gentlemen,' said Alice. 'You say that no one can tell by a person's appearance whether he is a gentleman or not; but surely you cannot think that those men are Lord Worthington's equals.'

'I do not,' said Lydia. 'They are ruffians; and Cashel Byron is the most unmistakeable ruffian of them all.'

Alice, awestruck, did not venture to speak again until they left the train at Victoria. There was a crowd outside the carriage in which Cashel had travelled. Alice hastened past; but Lydia asked a guard whether anything was the matter. He replied that a drunken man, alighting from the train, had fallen down upon the rails, so that, had the carriage been in motion, he would have been killed. Lydia thanked the guard, and, as she turned from him, found Bashville standing before her, touching his hat. She had given him no instructions to attend. However, she accepted his presence as a matter of course, and inquired whether the carriage was there.

'No, madam,' replied Bashville. 'The coachman had no orders.'

'Quite right. A hansom, if you please.' When he was gone, she said to Alice, 'Did you tell Bashville to meet us?'

'Oh *dear* no! I should not think of doing such a thing.'

'Strange! However, he knows his duties better than I do; so I have no doubt that he has acted properly. He has been waiting all the afternoon, I suppose, poor fellow.'

'He has nothing else to do,' said Alice carelessly. 'Here he is. He has picked out a new hansom for us too.'

Meanwhile, Mellish had been dragged from beneath the train, and seated on the knee of one of his companions. He was in a stupor, and had a large lump on his brow. His eye was almost closed. The man with the crushed nose now shewed himself an expert surgeon. Whilst Cashel supported the patient on the knee of another man, and the rest of the party kept off the crowd by mingled persuasion and violence, he produced a lancet and summarily reduced the swelling by lancing it. He then dressed the puncture neatly with appliances for that purpose which he carried about him, and shouted in Mellish's ear to rouse him. But the trainer only groaned, and let his head drop inert on his breast. More shouting was resorted to, but in vain. Cashel impatiently expressed an opinion that Mellish was shamming and declared that he would not stand there to be fooled with all the evening.

'If he was my pal 'stead o' yours,' said the man with the broken nose, 'I'd wake him up fast enough.'

'I'll save you the trouble,' said Cashel, coolly stooping and seizing between his teeth the cartilage of the trainer's ear.

'Thats the way to do it,' said the other approvingly, as Mellish screamed and started to his feet. 'Now then. On with you.' He took Mellish's right arm; Cashel took the left; and they brought him away between them without paying the least heed to his tears, his protestations that he was hurt, his plea that he was an old man, or his bitter demand as to where Cashel would have been at that moment without his care.

Lord Worthington had taken advantage of this accident to slip away from his travelling companions, and drive alone to his lodgings in Jermyn Street. He was still greatly excited; and when his valet, an old retainer with whom he was on familiar terms, brought him a letter that had arrived during his absence, he asked him four times whether any one had called, and four times interrupted him by scraps of information about the splendid day he had had and the luck he was in.

'I betted five hundred even that it would be over in quarter of an hour; and then I betted Byron two hundred and fifty to one that it wouldnt. Thats the way to do it: eh, Bedford? Catch Cashel letting two hundred and fifty slip through his fingers! By George though, he's an artful card. At the end of fourteen minutes I thought my five hundred was corpsed. The Dutchman was full of fight; and Cashel suddenly turned weak and tried to back out of the rally. You should have seen the gleam in the Dutchman's eye when he rushed in after him. He made cocksure of finishing him straight off.'

'Indeed, my lord. Dear me!'

'I should think so: I was taken in by it myself. It was only done to draw the poor devil. By George, Bedford, you should have seen the way Cashel put in his right. But you couldnt have seen it: it was too quick. The Dutchman was asleep on the grass before he knew he'd been hit. Byron had collected fifteen pounds for him before he came to. His jaw must feel devilish queer after it. By Jove, Bedford, Cashel is a perfect wonder. I'd back him for every penny I possess against any man alive. He makes you feel proud of being an Englishman.'

Bedford looked on with submissive wonder as his master, transfigured with enthusiasm, went hastily to and fro through the room, occasionally clenching his fist and smiting an imaginary Dutchman. The valet at last ventured to remind him that he had forgotten the letter.

'Oh, hang the letter!' said Lord Worthington. 'It's Mrs Hoskyn's writing – an invitation, or some such rot. Here: lets see it.'

'CAMPDEN HILL ROAD, *Saturday.*

'My dear Lord Worthington – I have not forgotten my promise to obtain for you a near view of the famous Mrs Herbert – Madame Simplicita, as you call her. She will be with us tomorrow evening; and we shall be very happy to see you then, if you care to come. At nine o'clock, Herr Abendgasse, a celebrated German Art critic and a great friend of mine, will read us a paper on the True in Art; but I will not pay you the compliment of pretending to believe that that interests you; so you may come at ten or half-past, by which hour all the serious business of the evening will be over.'

('Well, there is nothing like cheek,' said Lord Worthington, breaking off his perusal. 'These women think that because I enjoy life in a rational way, I dont know the back of a picture from the front, or the inside of a book from the cover. I shall go at nine sharp.')

'I suppose none of your acquaintances take an interest in Art. Could you not bring me a celebrity or two! I am very anxious to have as good an audience as possible for Herr Abendgasse. However, as it is, he will have no reason to complain, as I flatter myself that I have already secured a very distinguished assembly. Still, if you can add a second illustrious name to my list, by all means do so.'

'Very good, Mrs Hoskyn,' said Lord Worthington, looking cunningly at the bewildered Bedford. 'You shall have a celebrity – a real one – none of your mouldy old Germans – if I can only get him to come. If any of her people dont like him, they can tell him so. Eh, Bedford?'

CHAPTER VI

Next evening, Lydia and Alice reached Mrs Hoskyn's house in Campden Hill Road a few minutes before ten o'clock. They found Lord Worthington in the front garden, smoking and chatting with Mr Hoskyn. He threw away his cigar, and returned to the house with the two ladies, who observed that he was somewhat flushed with wine. They went into a parlor to take off their wraps, leaving him at the foot of the stairs. Presently they heard some one come down and address him excitedly.

'Worthington. Worthington. He has begun making a speech before the whole room. He got up the moment old Abendgasse sat down. Why the deuce did you start champagne at dinner?'

'Sh-sh-sh! You dont say so! Come with me; and lets try to get him away quietly.'

'Did you hear that?' said Alice. 'Something must have happened.'

'I hope so,' said Lydia. 'Ordinarily, the fault in these receptions is that nothing happens. Do not announce us, if you please,' she added, to the servant, as they ascended the stairs. 'Since we have come late, let us spare the feelings of Herr Abendgasse by going in as quietly as possible.'

They had no difficulty in entering unnoticed; for Mrs Hoskyn considered obscurity beautiful; and her rooms were but dimly lighted by two curious lanterns of pink glass, within which were vaporous flames. In the middle of the larger apartment was a small table covered with garnet-colored plush, bearing a reading desk and two candles in silver candlesticks, the light from which, brighter than the lanterns, cast strong double shadows from the groups of standing figures. The surrounding space was crowded with chairs, occupied chiefly by ladies. Behind them, along the wall, stood a row of men, among whom was Lucian

Webber. All were staring at Cashel Byron, who was making a speech to some bearded and spectacled gentleman at the table. Lydia, who had never before seen him either in evening dress or quite at his ease, was astonished at his bearing. His eyes were sparkling; his confidence overbore the company; and his rough voice created the silence it broke. He was in high good humor, and marked his periods by the swing of his extended left arm, whilst he held his right hand close to his body and occasionally pointed his remarks by slyly wagging its forefinger.

' – executive power,' he was saying, as Lydia entered. 'Thats a very good expression, gentlemen, and one that I can tell you a lot about. We have been told that if we want to civilize our neighbors, we must do it mainly by the example of our own lives, by each becoming a living illustration of the highest culture we know. But what I ask is, how is anybody to know that youre an illustration of culture? You cant go about like a sandwich man with a label on your back to tell all the fine notions you have in your head; and you may be sure no person will consider your mere appearance preferable to his own. You want an executive power: thats what you want. Suppose you walked along the street and saw a man beating a woman, and setting a bad example to the roughs. Well, you would be bound to set a good example to them; and, if youre men, youd like to save the woman; but you couldnt do it by merely living; for that would be setting the bad example of passing on and leaving the poor creature to be beaten. What is it that you need to know, then, so as to be able to act up to your ideas? Why, you want to know how to hit him, when to hit him, and where to hit him; and then you want the nerve to go in and do it. Thats executive power; and thats whats wanted worse than sitting down and thinking how good you are, which is what this gentleman's teaching comes to after all. Dont you see? You want executive power to set an example. If you leave all that to the roughs, it's their example that will spread, and not yours. And look at the politics of it. I heard a man in the park one Sunday say that in this country we can do nothing; for, says he, if the lords and the landlords, or any other collection of nobs, were to drive us into the sea, what could we do but go? Theres a gentleman laughing at me for saying that; but I ask him what he would do if the police or the soldiers came this evening and told him to turn out of his comfortable house into the Thames? Tell em he wouldnt vote for their employers at the next election, perhaps? Or, if that didnt stop them, tell em that he'd ask his friends to do the same? Thats a pretty executive power! No, gentlemen. Dont let yourself be deceived by people that have staked their money against you. The first thing to learn is how to fight. Theres no use in buying books and pictures unless you know how to keep them and your own head as well. If that gentleman that laughed knew how to fight, and his neighbors all knew how to fight too, he wouldnt need to fear police, nor soldiers, nor Russians, nor Prussians, nor any of the millions of men that may be let loose on him any day of the week, safe though he thinks himself. But, says you, lets have a division of labor. Lets not fight for ourselves, but pay other men to fight for us. That shews how some people, when they get hold of an idea, will work it to that foolish length that it's wearisome to listen to them. Fighting is the power of self-preservation: another man cant do it for you. You might as well divide the labor of eating your dinner, and pay one fellow to take the beef, another the beer, and the third the potatoes. But let us put it for the sake of argument that you do pay others to fight for you. Suppose some one else pays them higher, and they fight a cross, or turn openly against you? Youd have only yourself to blame for giving the executive power to money. Therefore I say that a man's first duty is to learn to fight. If he cant do that, he cant set an example; he cant stand up for his own rights or his neighbors'; he cant keep himself in bodily health; and if he sees the weak ill-used by the strong, the most he can do is to sneak away and tell the nearest policeman, who most likely wont turn up until the worst of the mischief is done.

Coming to this lady's drawing-room, and making an illustration of himself, wont make him feel like a man after that. Let me be understood though, gentlemen: I dont intend that you should take everything I say too exactly – too literally, as it were. If you see a man beating a woman, I think you should interfere on principle. But dont expect to be thanked by her for it; and keep your eye on her: dont let her get behind you. As for him, just give him a good one and go away. Never stay to get yourself into a street fight; for it's low, and generally turns out badly for all parties. However, thats only a bit of practical advice. It doesnt alter the great principle that you should get an executive power. When you get that, youll have courage in you; and, whats more, your courage will be of some use to you. For though you may have courage by nature; still, if you havnt executive power as well, your courage will only lead you to stand up to be beaten by men that have both courage and executive power; and what good does that do you? People say that youre a game fellow; but they wont find the stakes for you unless you can win them. Youd far better put your game in your pocket, and throw up the sponge while you can see to do it.

'Now, on this subject of game, Ive something to say that will ease the professor's mind on a point that he seemed anxious about. I am no musician; but I'll just shew you how a man that understands one art understands every art. I made out from the gentleman's remarks that there is a man in the musical line named Wagner, who is what you might call a game sort of composer; and that the musical fancy, though they cant deny that his tunes are first-rate, and that, so to speak, he wins his fights, yet they try to make out that he wins them in an outlandish way, and that he has no real science. Now I tell the gentleman not to mind such talk. As I have just shewn you, his game wouldnt be any use to him without science. He might have beaten a few second-raters with a rush while he was young; but he wouldnt have lasted out as he has done unless he was clever as well. It's the newness of his style that puzzles people; for, mind you, every man has to grow his own style out of himself; and there is no use in thinking that it will be the same as the last fellow's, or right for the next fellow, or that it's *the* style, and that every other style is wrong. More rot is talked through not knowing that than anything else. You will find that those that run Professor Wagner down are either jealous, or they are old stagers that are not used to his style, and think that anything new must be bad. Just wait a bit, and, take my word for it, theyll turn right round and swear that his style isnt new at all, and that he stole it from some one they saw when they were ten years old. History shews us that this is the way of such fellows in all ages, as the gentleman said; and he gave you Beethoven as an example. But an example like that dont go home to you, because there isnt one man in a million that ever heard of Beethoven. Take a man that everybody has heard of: Jack Randall! The very same things were said of *him*. After that, you neednt go to musicians for an example. The truth is, that there are people in the world with that degree of envy and malice in them that they cant bear to allow a good man his merits; and when they have to admit that he can do one thing, they try to make out that theres something else he cant do. Come: I'll put it to you short and business-like. This German gentleman, who knows all about music, tells you that many pretend that this Wagner has game, but no science. Well, I, though I know nothing about music, will bet you twenty-five pounds that theres others that allow him to be full of science, but say that he has no game, and that all he does comes from his head, and not from his heart. I will. I'll bet twenty-five pounds on it; and let the gentleman of the house be stakeholder, and the German gentleman referee. Eh? Well, I'm glad to see that there are no takers.

'Now we'll go to another little point that the gentleman forgot. He recommended you to *learn* – to make yourselves better and wiser from day to day. But he didnt tell you why it is that you wont learn, in spite of his advice. I suppose that, being a foreigner, he was afraid of hurting your feelings by talking too freely to you. But youre not so thin-skinned as to take offence at a little plain speaking, I'll be bound; so I tell you straight out that the reason you wont learn is not that you dont want to be clever, or that you are lazier than many that have learnt a great deal; but just because youd like people to think that you know everything already – because youre ashamed to be seen going to school; and you calculate that if you only hold your tongue and look wise, youll get through life without your ignorance being found out. But wheres the good of lies and pretence? What does it matter if you get laughed at by a cheeky brat or two for your awkward beginnings? Whats the use of always thinking of how youre looking, when your sense might tell you that other people are thinking about their own looks and not about yours? A big boy doesnt look well on a lower form, certainly; but when he works his way up he'll be glad he began. I speak to you more particularly because youre Londoners; and Londoners beat all creation for thinking about themselves. However, I dont go with the gentleman in everything he said. All this struggling and striving to make the world better is a great mistake; not because it isnt a good thing to improve the world if you know how to do it, but because striving and struggling is the worst way you could set about doing anything. It gives a man a bad style, and weakens him. It shews that he dont believe in himself much. When I heard the professor striving and struggling so earnestly to set you to work reforming this, that, and the other, I said to myself, "He's got himself to persuade as well as us. That isnt the language of conviction." Whose – '

'Really, sir,' said Lucian Webber, who had made his way to the table, 'I think, as you have now addressed us at considerable length, and as there are other persons present whose opinions probably excite as much curiosity as yours – '
He was interrupted by a 'Hear, hear,' followed by 'No, no,' and 'Go on,' uttered in more subdued tones than are customary at public meetings, but with more animation than is usually displayed in drawing-rooms. Cashel, who had

been for a moment somewhat put out, turned to Lucian and said, in a tone intended to repress, but at the same time humor his impatience, 'Dont you be in a hurry, sir. You shall have your turn presently. Perhaps I may tell you something you dont know before I stop.' Then he turned again to the company, and resumed.

'We were talking about effort when this young gentleman took it upon himself to break the ring. Now, nothing can be what you might call artistically done, if it's done with an effort. If a thing cant be done light and easy, steady and certain, let it not be done at all. Sounds strange, doesnt it? But I'll tell you a stranger thing. The more effort you make, the less effect you produce. A *would-be* artist is no artist at all. I learnt that in my own profession (never mind what that profession is just at present, as the ladies might think the worse of me for it). But in all professions any work that shews signs of labor, straining, yearning – as the German gentleman said – or effort of any kind, is work beyond the man's strength that does it, and therefore not well done. Perhaps it's beyond his natural strength; but it is more likely that he was badly taught. Many teachers set their pupils on to strain and stretch so that they get used up, body and mind, in a few months. Depend upon it, the same thing is true in other arts. I once taught a fiddler that used to get a hundred guineas for playing two or three tunes; and he told me that it was just the same thing with the fiddle – that when you laid a tight hold on your fiddle-stick, or even set your teeth hard together, you could do nothing but rasp like the fellows that play in bands for a few shillings a night.'

'How much more of this nonsense must we endure?' said Lucian audibly, as Cashel stopped for breath. Cashel turned, and looked at him.

'By Jove,' whispered Lord Worthington to his companion, 'that fellow had better be careful. I wish he would hold his tongue.'

'You think it's nonsense, do you?' said Cashel, after a pause. Then he raised one of the candles, and illuminated a picture that hung on the wall. 'Look at that picture,' he said. 'You see that fellow in armor – St George and the dragon or whatever he may be? He's jumped down from his horse to fight the other fellow – that one with his head in a big helmet, whose horse has tumbled. The lady in the gallery is half crazy with anxiety for St George; and well she may be. *Theres* a posture for a man to fight in! His weight isnt resting on his legs: one touch of a child's finger would upset him. Look at his neck craned out in front of him, and his face as flat as a full moon towards his man, as if he was inviting him to shut up both his eyes with one blow. You can all see that he's as weak and nervous as a cat, and that he doesnt know how to fight. And why does he give you that idea? Just because he's all strain and stretch; because he isnt at his ease; because he carries the weight of his body as foolishly as one of the ladies here would carry a hod of bricks; because he isnt safe, steady, and light on his pins, as he would be if he could forget himself for a minute and leave his body to find its proper balance of its own accord. If the painter of that picture had known his business, he would never have sent his man up to the scratch in such a figure and condition as that. But you can see with one eye that he didnt understand – I wont say the principles of fighting, but the universal principles that Ive told you of, that ease and strength, effort and weakness, go together. Now!' added Cashel, again addressing Lucian: 'do you still think that notion of mine nonsense?' And he smacked his lips with satisfaction; for his criticism of the picture had produced a marked sensation; and he did not know that this was due to the fact that the painter, Mr Adrian Herbert, was present.

Lucian tried to ignore the question; but he found it impossible to ignore the questioner. 'Since you have set the example of expressing opinions without regard to considerations of common courtesy,' he said shortly, 'I may say that your theory, if it can be called one, is a contradiction in terms.'

Cashel, apparently unruffled, but with more deliberation

of manner than before, looked about him as if in search of a fresh illustration. His glance finally rested on the lecturer's seat, a capacious crimson damask armchair that stood unoccupied at some distance behind Lucian.

'I see youre no judge of a picture,' he said good-humoredly, putting down the candle, and stepping in front of Lucian, who regarded him haughtily, and did not budge. 'But just look at it in this way. Suppose you wanted to hit me the most punishing blow you possibly could. What would you do? Why, according to your own notion, youd make a great effort. "The more effort, the more force," youd say to yourself. "I'll smash him even if I burst myself in doing it." And what would happen then? Youd only cut me and make me angry, besides exhausting all your strength at one gasp. Whereas, if you took it easy – like this – ' Here he made a light step forward, and placed his open palm gently against the breast of Lucian, who, as if the piston-rod of a steam-engine had touched him, instantly reeled back and dropped into the chair.

'There!' exclaimed Cashel, beaming with self-satisfaction as he stepped aside and pointed at Lucian. 'It's like pocketing a billiard ball!'

A chatter of surprise, amusement, and remonstrance spread through the rooms; and the company crowded towards the table. Lucian rose, white with rage, and for a moment entirely lost his self-control. Fortunately, the effect was to paralyse him: he neither moved nor spoke, and only betrayed his condition by his pallor, and the hatred in his expression. Presently he felt a touch on his arm, and heard his name pronounced by Lydia. Her voice calmed him. He tried to look at her; but his vision was disturbed: he saw double; the lights seemed to dance before his eyes; and Lord Worthington's voice, saying to Cashel, 'Rather too practical, old fellow,' seemed to come from a remote corner of the room, and yet to be whispered into his ear. He was moving irresolutely in search of Lydia, when his senses and his resentment were restored by a clap on the shoulder.

'You wouldnt have believed that now, would you?' said
Cashel. 'Dont look startled: youve no bones broken. You
had your little joke with me in your own way; and I had
mine in *my* own way. Thats only— '

He stopped: his brave bearing vanished: he became limp
and shamefaced. Lucian, without a word, withdrew with
Lydia to the adjoining apartment, and left him staring after
her with wistful eyes and slackened jaw.

In the meantime Mrs Hoskyn, an earnest-looking young
woman with striking dark features and gold spectacles, was
looking for Lord Worthington, who betrayed a consciousness of guilt by attempting to avoid her. But she cut off his
retreat, and confronted him with a steadfast gaze that compelled him to stand and answer for himself.

'Who is that gentleman whom you introduced to me? I
have forgotten his name.'

'I am really awfully sorry, Mrs Hoskyn. It was too bad of
Byron. But Webber was excessively nasty.'

Mrs Hoskyn, additionally annoyed by apologies which
she had not invited, and which put her in the ignominious
position of a complainant, replied coldly, 'Mr Byron. Thank
you: I had forgotten,' and was turning away when Lydia
came up to introduce Alice, and to explain why she had
entered unannounced. Lord Worthington seized the chance
of improving Cashel's credit by claiming Lydia's acquaintance for him.

'Did you hear our friend Byron's speech, Miss Carew?
Very characteristic, I thought.'

'Very,' said Lydia. 'I hope Mrs Hoskyn's guests are all
familiar with his style. Otherwise they must find him a little
startling.'

'Yes,' said Mrs Hoskyn, beginning to wonder whether
Cashel could be some well-known eccentric genius. 'He is
very odd. I hope Mr Webber is not offended.'

'If his tact had been equal to the other gentleman's, it
would not have happened to him,' said Lydia. 'It is
really very clever of Mr Byron to knock my cousin down

in the middle of a drawing-room without scandalizing anybody.'

'You see, Mrs Hoskyn, the general verdict is "serve him right,"' said Lord Worthington.

'With a rider to the effect that both gentlemen displayed complete indifference to the comfort of their hostess,' said Lydia. 'However, men so rarely sacrifice their manners to their minds that it would be a pity to blame them. You do not encourage conventionality, Mrs Hoskyn?'

'I encourage good manners, though certainly not conventional manners.'

'And you think there is a difference?'

'I *feel* that there is a difference,' said Mrs Hoskyn, with dignity.

'So do I,' said Lydia; 'but one can hardly call others to account for one's own subjective ideas.'

Lydia went away to another part of the room without waiting for a reply. All this time, Cashel stood friendless, stared at by most of his neighbors, and spoken to by none. Women looked at him coldly lest it should be suspected that they were admiring him; and men regarded him stiffly according to the national custom. Since his recognition of Lydia, his self-confidence had given place to a misgiving that he had been making a fool of himself. He felt lonely and abashed: but for his professional habit of maintaining a cheerful countenance under adverse circumstances, he would have hid himself in the darkest corner of the room. Like many eminent members of his profession, he was rather prone to tears when his feelings were wounded; and his countenance was falling rapidly when Lord Worthington came up to him.

'I had no idea you were such an orator, Byron,' he said. 'You can go into the Church when you cut the other trade. Eh?'

'I wasnt brought up to the other trade,' said Cashel; 'and I know how to talk to ladies and gentlemen as well as to what youd suppose to be my own sort. Dont you be anxious about me, my lord. I know how to make myself at home.'

'Of course, of course,' said Lord Worthington soothingly. 'Every one can see by your manners that you are a gentleman: they recognize that even in the ring. Otherwise, you see – I know you wont mind my saying so – I darent have brought you here.'

Cashel shook his head, but was pleased. He thought he hated flattery: had Lord Worthington told him that he was the best boxer in England – which he probably was – he would have despised him. But he wished to believe the false compliment to his manners, and was therefore perfectly convinced of its sincerity. Lord Worthington perceived this, and retired, pleased with his own tact, in search of Mrs Hoskyn, to claim her promise of an introduction to Madame Szczympliça, which Mrs Hoskyn, by way of punishing him for Cashel's misdemeanor, had privately determined not to keep.

Cashel began to think he had better go. Lydia was surrounded by men who were speaking to her in German. He felt his own inability to talk learnedly even in English; and he felt sure, besides, that she was angry with him for upsetting her cousin, who was gravely conversing with Miss Goff. Suddenly a horrible noise caused a general start and pause. Mr Jack, the eminent composer, had opened the pianoforte, and was illustrating some points in a musical composition under discussion by making discordant sounds with his voice, accompanied by a few chords. Cashel laughed aloud in derision as he made his way towards the door through the crowd, which was now pressing round the pianoforte, at which Madame Szczympliça had just come to the assistance of Jack. Near the door, and in a corner remote from the instrument, he came upon Lydia and a middle-aged gentleman, evidently neither a professor nor an artist.

'Abngas is a very clever man,' the gentleman was saying. 'I am sorry I didnt hear the lecture. But I leave all that to

Mary. She receives the people who enjoy high art upstairs; and I take the sensible men down to the garden or the smoking-room, according to the weather.'

'What do the sensible women do?' said Lydia.

'They come late,' said Mr Hoskyn, and then laughed at his repartee until he became aware of the vicinity of Cashel, whose health he immediately inquired after, shaking his hand warmly and receiving a numbing grip in return. As soon as he saw that Lydia and Cashel were acquainted, he slipped away and left them to entertain one another.

'I wonder how he knows me,' said Cashel, heartened by her gracious reception of a nervous bow. 'I never saw him before in my life.'

'He does not know you,' said Lydia, with some sternness. 'He is your host, and therefore concludes that he ought to know you.'

'Oh! That was it, was it?' He paused, at a loss for conversation. She did not help him. At last he added, 'I havnt seen you this long time, Miss Carew.'

'It is not very long since I saw you, Mr Cashel Byron. I saw you yesterday at some distance from London.'

'O Lord!' exclaimed Cashel, 'dont say that. Youre joking, aint you?'

'No. Joking, in that sense, does not amuse me.'

Cashel looked at her in consternation. 'You dont mean to say that you went to see a – a – Where – when did you see me? You might tell me.'

'Certainly. It was at Clapham Junction, at a quarter past six.'

'Was any one with me?'

'Your friend Mr Mellish, Lord Worthington, and some other persons.'

'Yes. Lord Worthington was there. But where were you?'

'In a waiting-room, close to you.'

'I never saw you,' said Cashel, very red. 'Mellish drove our trap into a ditch and broke it: we had to get home by

train. We must have looked a queer lot. Do you think I was
in bad company?'

'That was not my business, Mr Cashel Byron.'

'No,' said Cashel, with sudden bitterness. 'What did *you*
care what company I kept? Youre mad with me because I
made your cousin look like a fool, I suppose. Thats whats
the matter.'

Lydia, speaking in a low tone to remind him that they
were not alone, said, 'There is nothing the matter, except
that you act and speak like a grown-up boy rather than a
man. I am not mad with you because of your attack upon
my cousin; but he is very much annoyed; and so is Mrs
Hoskyn, whose guest you were bound to respect.'

'I knew youd be down on me. I wouldnt have said a word
if I'd known you were here,' said Cashel dejectedly. 'Lie
down and be walked over: thats what you think I'm fit for.
Another man would have twisted his head off.'

'Is it possible that you do not know that gentlemen never
twist one another's heads off in society, no matter how great
may be the provocation?'

'I know nothing,' said Cashel, with plaintive sullenness.
'Everything I do is wrong. There! Will that satisfy you?'

'I take no pleasure in making you confess yourself in the
wrong; and you cannot have a lower opinion of me than to
think that I do.'

'Thats just where youre mistaken,' said Cashel obstinately. 'I havnt got a low opinion of you at all. Theres such
a thing as being too clever.'

'You may not know that it is a low opinion. Nevertheless,
it is so.'

'Well, have it your own way. I'm wrong again; and youre
right.'

'So far from being gratified by that, I had rather we
were both in the right and agreed. Can you understand
that?'

'I can' say I do. But I give in to it. What more need you
care for?'

'Please, I had rather you understood. Let me try to explain. You think I like to be cleverer than other people. You are mistaken. I should like them all to know whatever I know.'

Cashel laughed cunningly, and shook his head. 'Dont you make any mistake about that,' he said. 'You dont want anybody to be quite as clever as yourself: it isnt in human nature that you should. Youd like people to be just clever enough to shew you off – to be worth beating. But you wouldnt like them to be able to beat you. Just clever enough to know how much cleverer you are: thats about the mark. Eh?'

Lydia made no further effort to enlighten him. She looked at him thoughtfully and said slowly, 'So this perpetual fighting metaphor is the clue to your idiosyncrasy. You have attached yourself to the modern doctrine of a struggle for existence, and look on life as a continual combat.'

'A fight? Just so. What is life but a fight? The curs forfeit or get beaten; the rogues sell the fight and lose the confidence of their backers; the game ones, and the clever ones, win the stakes, and have to hand over the lion's share of them to the moneyed loafers that have stood the expenses; and luck plays the devil with them all in turn. Thats not the way they describe life in books; but thats what it is.'

'Oddly put, and perhaps true. But it is not the creed of the simpleton you pretended to be a moment ago. You are playing with me – revealing your wisdom from beneath a veil of the boyish. My compliments on your excellent acting. I have no more to say.'

'May I be shot if I understand you! I'd rather be a horse than an actor. Come: is it because I raised a laugh against your cousin that youre so spiteful?'

Lydia looked earnestly and doubtfully at him; and he instinctively put his head back, as if it were in danger. 'You do not understand, then?' she said. 'I will test the genuineness of your stupidity by an appeal to your obedience.'

'Stupidity! Go on.'

'But will you obey me, if I lay a command upon you?'

'I will go through fire and water for you.'

Lydia blushed faintly, and paused to wonder at the novel sensation before she resumed. 'You had better not apologize to my cousin: partly because you would only make matters worse: chiefly because he does not deserve it. But you must make this speech to Mrs Hoskyn when you are going: "I am very sorry I forgot myself" –'

'Sounds like Shakespear, doesnt it?' observed Cashel.

'Ah! the test has found you out: you are only acting after all. But that does not alter my opinion that you should apologize.'

'All right. I dont know what you mean by testing and acting; and I only hope you know yourself. But no matter: I'll apologize: a man like me can afford to. I'll apologize to your cousin too, if you like.'

'I do not like. But what has that to do with it? I suggest these things, as you must be aware, for your own sake and not for mine.'

'As for my own, I dont care twopence: I do it all for you. I dont even ask whether there is anything between you and him.'

'Would you like to know?' said Lydia deliberately, after a pause of astonishment.

'Do you mean to say youll tell me?' he exclaimed. 'If you do, I'll say youre as good as gold.'

'Certainly I will tell you. There is an old friendship and cousinship between us; but we are not engaged, nor at all likely to be. I tell you so because you would draw the opposite and false conclusion if I avoided the question.'

'I am glad of it,' said Cashel, unexpectedly becoming very gloomy. 'He isnt man enough for you. But he's your equal, damn him!'

'He is my cousin, and, I believe, my sincere friend. Therefore please do not damn him.'

'I know I shouldnt have said that. But I am only damning my own luck.'

'Which will not improve it in the least.'

'I know that. You neednt have said it. I wouldnt have said a thing like that to you, stupid as I am.'

'Oh, you are impossible: I meant nothing. However, that does not matter. You are still an enigma to me. Had we not better try to hear a little of Madame Szczympliça's performance?'

'I'm a pretty plain enigma, I should think,' said Cashel mournfully. 'I would rather have you than any other woman in the world; but youre too rich and grand for me. If I cant have the satisfaction of marrying you, I may as well have the satisfaction of saying I'd like to.'

'Hardly a fair way of approaching the subject,' said Lydia composedly, but with a play of color again in her cheeks. 'Allow me to forbid it unconditionally. I must be plain with you, Mr Cashel Byron. I do not know what you are or who you are; and I believe you have tried to mystify me on both points –'

'And you never shall find out either the one or the other if I can help it,' put in Cashel; 'so that we're in a preciously bad way of coming to a good understanding.'

'True,' assented Lydia. 'I do not make secrets; I do not keep them; and I do not respect them. Your humor clashes with my principle.'

'You call it a humor!' said Cashel angrily. 'Perhaps you think I'm a duke in disguise. If so, you may think better of it. If you had a secret, and the discovery of it would cause you to be kicked out of decent society, you would keep it pretty tight. And that through no fault of your own, mind you; but through downright cowardice and prejudice in other people.'

'There are at least some fears and prejudices common in society that I do not share,' said Lydia, after a moment's reflection. 'Should I ever find out your secret, do not too hastily conclude that you have forfeited my consideration.'

'You are just the last person on earth I want to be found out by. But youll find out fast enough. Pshaw!' cried Cashel, with a laugh: 'I'm as well known as Trafalgar Square. But I cant bring myself to tell you; and I hate secrets as much as you do; so lets drop it and talk about something else.'

'We have talked long enough. The music is over; and the people will return to this room presently, perhaps to ask me who and what is the stranger that made them such a remarkable speech.'

'Just a word. Promise me that you wont ask any of *them* that.'

'Promise you! No. I cannot promise that.'

'O Lord!' said Cashel, with a groan.

'I have told you that I do not respect secrets. For the present I will not ask; but I may change my mind. Meanwhile we must not hold long conversations. I even hope that we shall not meet. There is only one thing that I am too rich and grand for – mystification. Adieu.'

Before he could reply, she was away from him in the midst of a number of gentlemen, and in conversation with one of them. Cashel seemed overwhelmed. But in an instant he recovered himself, and stepped jauntily before Mrs Hoskyn, who had just come into his neighborhood.

'I'm going, maam,' he said. 'Thank you for a pleasant evening. I'm very sorry I forgot myself. Good-night.'

Mrs Hoskyn, naturally frank, felt some vague response within herself to this address. But, though not usually at a loss for words in social emergencies, she only looked at him, blushing slightly, and offering her hand. He took it as if it were a tiny baby's hand; gave it a little pinch; and turned to go. Mr Adrian Herbert, the painter, was directly in his way, with his back towards him.

'If *you* please, sir,' said Cashel, taking him gently by the ribs, and lifting him aside as if he were a tailor's dummy. The artist turned indignantly; but Cashel was passing the doorway. On the stairs he met Lucian and Alice.

'Good-night, Miss Goff,' he said. 'It's a pleasure to see the country roses in your cheeks.' He lowered his voice as he added, to Lucian, 'Dont you worry yourself over that little trick I shewed you. If any of your friends chaff you about it, tell them that it was Cashel Byron did ıt, and ask them whether they think they could have helped themselves any better than you could. Dont ever let a person come within distance of you while youre standing in that silly way on both your heels. Why, if a man isnt properly planted on his pins, a broom-handle falling against him will upset him. Thats the way of it. Good-night.'

Lucian returned the salutation, mastered by a certain latent dangerousness in Cashel, suggestive that he might resent a snub by throwing the offender over the balustrade. As for Alice, she had entertained a superstitious dread of him ever since Lydia had pronounced him a ruffian. Both felt relieved when the house door, closing, shut him out from them.

CHAPTER VII

SOCIETY was much occupied during Alice's first season in London with one of the accidents of the beginnings of England's destiny in South Africa. When Destiny takes nations into new places, it offers them the choice of marching boldly with it and understanding it, or being led like pigs to market, intensely recalcitrant, scuttling in sudden panics or charging in sudden huffs, and using such rests as its leader gives it, to eat, never to ask Whither? How? or What then? Only when Destiny gives the word to stop eating and march, a useless Why? is raised, whereupon Destiny, out of patience, gives the rope a jerk which fetches the poor pig off his trotters. England, observant of the fact that the pig's line of conduct shifted all moral responsibility to his leader, and got the pig finally to his destination without brain worry, adopted it without hesitation in Africa, with the result that when the king of a considerable people there fell, with his territories, into British hands, the conquest seemed useless, troublesome, and expensive; and after repeated attempts to settle the country on impracticable plans suggested to the Colonial Office by a popular historian who had made a trip to Africa, and by generals who were tired of their primitive remedy of killing the natives, it appeared that the best course was to release the king and get rid of the unprofitable booty by restoring it to him. However, as the pig policy had enabled him to win one battle against English troops, it was thought advisable to take him first to London, and shew him the wonders of English civilization, especially in the matter of cannon and high explosives.

But when the African king arrived, his freedom from English prepossessions made it difficult to amuse, or even to impress him. A stranger to the idea that a handful of private persons could own a country and make others pay them for permission to live and work there, he was unable to understand why such a prodigiously rich nation should be composed chiefly of poor and uncomfortable persons toiling incessantly to create riches, and partly of a class that confiscated and dissipated the riches thus produced without seeming in the least happier than the unfortunate laborers at whose expense they existed. He was seized with strange fears: first for his health, since it seemed to him that the air of London, filthy with smoke, engendered puniness and dishonesty in those who breathed it; and eventually for his life, when he learned that kings of Europe were sometimes shot at in the streets. The queen of England, though accounted the safest of all, had had some half dozen escapes; and the autocrat of an empire huge beyond all other European countries, whose father had been torn asunder in the streets of his capital, lived surrounded by soldiers who shot down every stranger that approached him, even at his own summons; so that he was an object of compassion to the humblest of his servants. Under these circumstances, the African king was with difficulty induced to stir out of doors; and he only visited Woolwich Arsenal – the destructive resources of which were expected to silently warn him against taking the Christian religion too literally – under compulsion. At last the Colonial Office, which had charge of him, was at its wit's end to devise entertainments to keep him in good humor until the time appointed for his departure.

On the Tuesday following Mrs Hoskyn's reception, Lucian Webber, calling at his cousin's house in Regent's Park, said, in the course of conversation:

'The Colonial Office has had an idea. The king, it appears, is something of an athlete, and is curious to witness what Londoners can do in that way. So a grand assault-at-arms is to be held for him.'

'What is an assault-at-arms?' said Lydia. 'I have never been at one; and the name suggests nothing but an affray with bayonets.'

'It is an exhibition of swordsmanship, military drill, gymnastics, and so forth.'

'I will go to that,' said Lydia. 'Will you come, Alice?'

'Is it usual for ladies to go to such exhibitions?' said Alice cautiously.

'On this occasion ladies will go for the sake of seeing the king,' said Lucian. 'The Olympian gymnastic society, which has undertaken the direction of the civilian part of the assault, expects what it calls a flower-show audience.'

'Will you come, Lucian?'

'If I can be spared, yes. If not, I will ask Worthington to go with you. He understands such matters better than I.'

'Then let us have him by all means,' said Lydia.

'I cannot see why you are so fond of Lord Worthington,' said Alice. 'His manners are good; but there is nothing in him. Besides, he is so young. I cannot endure his conversation. He has begun to talk about Goodwood already.'

'He will grow out of his excessive addiction to sport,' said Lucian paternally.

'Indeed!' said Lydia. 'And what will he grow into?'

'Possibly into a more reasonable man,' said Lucian, unabashed.

'I hope so,' said Lydia; 'but I prefer a man who is interested in sport to a gentleman who is interested in nothing.'

'Much might indubitably be said from that point of view. But it is not necessary that Lord Worthington should waste his energy on horse-racing. I presume you do not think political life, for which his position peculiarly fits him, unworthy his attention.'

'Party tactics are both exciting and amusing, no doubt. But are they better than horse-racing? Jockeys and horse-breakers at least know their business: members of parliament do not. Is it pleasant to sit on a bench – even though it be the Treasury bench – and listen to amateur discussions about matters that have been settled for the last hundred years to the satisfaction of everybody who has seriously studied them?'

'You do not understand the duties of a government,

Lydia. You never approach the subject without confirming my opinion that women are constitutionally incapable of comprehending it.'

'It is natural for you to think so, Lucian. The House of Commons is to you the goal of existence. To me it is only an assemblage of ill-informed gentlemen who have botched every business they have ever undertaken, from the first committee of supply down to the last land Act; and who arrogantly assert that I am not good enough to sit with them.'

'Lydia,' said Lucian, annoyed: 'you know that I respect women in their own sphere –'

'Then give them another sphere, and perhaps they will earn your respect in that also. I am sorry to say that men, in *their* sphere, have not won my respect. Enough of that for the present. I have to make some arrangements before I go out. They are of more immediate importance than the conversion of a willing Conservative into a reluctant Women's Suffragist. Excuse me for five minutes.'

She left the room. Lucian sat down and gave his attention to Alice, who had still enough of her old nervousness to straighten her shoulders and look stately. But he did not object to this: a little stiffness of manner gratified his taste.

'I hope,' he said, 'that my cousin has not succeeded in inducing you to adopt her peculiar views.'

'No,' said Alice. 'Of course *her* case is quite exceptional. She is so wonderfully accomplished! In general, I do not think women should have views. There are certain convictions which every lady holds: for instance, we know that Roman Catholicism is wrong. But that can hardly be called a view: indeed it would be wicked to call it so, as it is one of the highest truths. What I mean is that women should not be political agitators.'

'I understand and quite agree with you. Lydia's is, as you say, an exceptional case. She has lived much abroad; and her father was a very singular man. Even the clearest heads, when removed from the direct influence of English life and thought, contract extraordinary prejudices. It is almost a pity that such strength of mind and extent of knowledge should be fortified by the dangerous independence which great wealth confers. Advantages like these bring with them certain duties to the class that has produced them – duties to which Lydia is not merely indifferent, but absolutely hostile.'

'I never meddle with her ideas on – on these subjects. I am too ignorant to understand them. But Miss Carew's generosity to me has been unparalleled. And she does not seem to know that she is generous. I owe more to her than I ever can repay.' 'At least,' Alice added to herself, 'I am not ungrateful.'

Miss Carew now reappeared, dressed in a long grey coat and plain beaver hat, and carrying a roll of writing materials.

'I am going to the British Museum to read,' said she.

'To walk! – alone!' said Lucian, looking at her costume.

'Yes. Prevent me from walking and you deprive me of my health. Prevent me from going alone where I please and when I please, and you deprive me of my liberty – tear up Magna Charta, in effect. But I do not insist upon being alone in this instance. If you can return to your office by way of Regent's Park and Gower Street without losing too much time, I shall be glad of your company.'

Lucian decorously suppressed his eagerness to comply by looking at his watch, and pretending to consider his engagements. In conclusion, he said that he should be happy to accompany her.

It was a fine summer afternoon; and there were many people in the park. Lucian was soon incommoded by the attention his cousin attracted. In spite of the black beaver, her hair shone like fire in the sun. Women stared at her with unsympathetic curiosity, and turned as they passed to examine her attire. Men resorted to various subterfuges to get a satisfactory look without rudely betraying their intention. A few stupid youths gaped; and a few impudent ones smiled. Lucian would gladly have kicked them all without distinction. He suggested that they should leave the path, and make a short cut across the greensward. As they emerged from the shade of the trees, he had a vague impression that the fineness of the weather and the beauty of the park made the occasion romantic, and that the words by which he hoped to make the relation between him and his cousin dearer and closer would be well spoken there. But he immediately began to talk, in spite of himself, about the cost of maintaining the public parks, particulars of which happened to be within his official knowledge. Lydia, readily interested by facts of any sort, thought the subject not a bad one for a casual afternoon conversation, and pursued it until they left the turf and got into the Euston Road, where the bustle of traffic silenced them for a while. When they escaped from the din into the respectable quietude of Gower Street, he suddenly said,

'It is one of the evils of great wealth in the hands of a woman, that she can hardly feel sure – ' Here his ideas fled suddenly. He stopped; but he kept his countenance so well that he had the air of having made a finished speech, and being perfectly satisfied with it.

'Do you mean that she can never feel sure of the justice of her title to her riches? That used to trouble me; but it no longer does so.'

'Nonsense!' said Lucian. 'I alluded to the disinterestedness of your friends.'

'That does not trouble me either. Absolutely disinterested friends I do not seek, as I should only find them among idiots or somnambulists. As to those whose interests are base, they do not know how to conceal their motives from me. For the rest, I am not so unreasonable as to object to a fair account being taken of my wealth in estimating the value of my friendship.'

'Do you not believe in the existence of persons who would like you just as well if you were poor?'

'Such persons would wish me to become poor, merely to

bring me nearer to themselves; for which I should not thank them. I set great store by the esteem my riches command, Lucian. It is the only set-off I have against the envy they inspire.'

'Then you would refuse to believe in the disinterestedness of any man who – who – '

'Who wanted to marry me? On the contrary: I should be the last person to believe that a man could prefer my money to myself. If he were independent, and in a fair way to keep his place in the world without my help, I should despise him if he hesitated to approach me for fear of misconstruction. I do not think a man is ever thoroughly honest until he is superior to that fear. But if he had no profession, no money, and no aim except to live at my expense, then I should regard him as an adventurer, and treat him as one – unless I fell in love with him.'

'Unless you fell in love with him?'.

'That – assuming that such things really happen – might make a difference in my feeling, but none in my conduct. I would not marry an adventurer under any circumstances. I could cure myself of a misdirected passion, but not of a bad husband.'

Lucian said nothing: he walked on with long irregular steps, lowering at the pavement as if it were a difficult problem, and occasionally thrusting at it with his stick. At last he looked up and said,

'Would you mind prolonging our walk a little by going round Bedford Square with me? I have something particular to say.'

She turned and complied without a word; and they had traversed one side of the square before he spoke again.

'On second thoughts, Lydia, this is neither the time nor the place for an important communication. Excuse me for having taken you out of your way for nothing.'

'I do not like this, Lucian. Important communications – in this case – corrupt good manners. If your intended speech is a sensible one, the present is as good a time, and Bedford

Square as good a place, as you are likely to find for it. If it is otherwise, confess that you have decided to leave it unsaid. But do not postpone it. Reticence is always an error – even on the Treasury bench. It is doubly erroneous in dealing with me; for I have a constitutional antipathy to it.'

'Yes,' he said hurriedly; 'but give me one moment – until the policeman has passed.'

The policeman went leisurely by, striking the flags with his heels, and slapping his palm with a white glove.

'The fact is, Lydia, that – I feel great difficulty – '

'What is the matter?' said Lydia, after waiting in vain for further particulars. 'You have broken down twice.' There was a pause. Then she looked at him quickly, and added, incredulously, 'Are you going to get married? Is that the secret that ties your practised tongue?'

'Not unless you take part in the ceremony.'

'Very gallant; and in a vein of humor that is new in my experience of you. But what have you to tell me, Lucian? Frankly, your hesitation is becoming ridiculous.'

'You have certainly not made matters easier for me, Lydia. Perhaps you have a womanly intuition of my purpose, and are intentionally discouraging me.'

'Not the least. I am not good at intuitions, womanly or otherwise. On my word, if you do not confess at once, I will hurry away to the Museum.'

'I cannot find a suitable form of expression,' said Lucian, in painful perplexity. 'I am sure you will not attribute any sordid motive to my – well, to my addresses, though the term seems absurd. I am too well aware that there is little, from the usual point of view, to tempt you to unite yourself to me. Still – '

A rapid change in Lydia's face shewed him that he had said enough. 'I had not thought of this,' she said, after a silence that seemed long to him. 'Our observations are so meaningless until we are given the thread to string them on! You must think better of this, Lucian. The relation that at present exists between us is the very best that our different characters will admit of. Why do you desire to alter it?'

'Because I would make it closer and more permanent. I do not wish to alter it otherwise.'

'You would run some risk of destroying it by the method you propose,' said Lydia, with composure. 'We could not work together. There are differences of opinion between us amounting to differences of principle.'

'Surely you are not serious. Your opinions, or notions, are not represented by any political party in England; and therefore they are practically ineffective, and could not clash with mine. And such differences are not personal matters.'

'Such a party might be formed a week after our marriage – will, I think, be formed a long time before our deaths. In that case I fear that our difference of opinion would become a very personal matter.'

He began to walk more quickly as he replied, 'It is too absurd to set up what you call your opinions as a serious barrier between us. You have no opinions, Lydia. The impracticable crotchets you are fond of airing are not recognized in England as sane political convictions.'

Lydia did not retort. She waited a minute in pensive silence, and then said,

'Why do you not marry Alice Goff?'

'Oh, hang Alice Goff!'

'It is so easy to come at the man beneath the veneer by chipping at his feelings,' said Lydia, laughing. 'But I was serious, Lucian. Alice is energetic, ambitious, and stubbornly upright in questions of principle. I believe she would assist you steadily at every step of your career. Besides, she has physical robustness. Our student stock needs an effusion of that.'

'Many thanks for the suggestion; but I do not happen to want to marry Miss Goff.'

'I invite you to consider it. You have not had time yet to form any new plans.'

'New plans! Then you absolutely refuse me – without a moment's consideration?'

'Absolutely, Lucian. Does not your instinct warn you that it would be a mistake to marry me?'

'No, I cannot say that it does.'

'Then trust to mine, which gives forth no uncertain note on this question, as your favorite newspapers are fond of saying.'

'It is a question of feeling,' he said, in a constrained voice.

'Is it?' she replied, with interest. 'You have surprised me somewhat, Lucian. I have never observed any of the extravagances of a lover in your conduct.'

'And you have surprised me very unpleasantly, Lydia. I do not think now that I had ever had much hope of success; but I thought, at least, that my disillusion would be gently accomplished.'

'Have I been harsh?'

'I do not complain.'

'I was unlucky, Lucian; not malicious. Besides, the artifices by which friends endeavor to spare one another's feelings are petty disloyalties. I am frank with you. Would you have me otherwise?'

'Of course not. I have no right to be offended.'

'Not the least. Now add to that formal admission a sincere assurance that you *are* not offended.'

'I assure you I am not,' said Lucian, with melancholy resignation.

They had by this time reached Charlotte Street; and Lydia tacitly concluded the conference by turning towards the Museum, and beginning to talk upon indifferent subjects. At the corner of Russell Street he got into a cab and drove away, dejectedly acknowledging a smile and wave of the hand with which she tried to console him. Lydia then went to the national library, where she forgot Lucian. The effect of the shock of his proposal was in store for her; but as yet she did not feel it; and she worked steadily until the library was closed and she had to leave. As she had been sitting for some hours, and it was still light, she did not take a cab, and did not even walk straight home. She had heard of a bookseller in Soho who had for sale a certain scarce volume which she wanted; and it occurred to her that the present was a good opportunity to go in search of him. Now there was hardly a capital in Western Europe that she did not know better than London. She soon lost herself in a labyrinth of narrow streets of once fashionable dwelling-houses, long ago turned into small shops or let in tenements, and now succumbing to a slow but steady invasion of large business houses. Nevertheless it was not the bustle of trade that broke the curious Soho quietude. The shops did not seem to do much business; the big counting-houses kept their activity within doors; the few clerks, tradesmen, and warehousemen who were about had the air of slipping across to the public-houses rather than of having urgent affairs in hand. But the place was alive with children, who flocked and chattered and darted about like sparrows, putting their elders out of countenance and making the patiently constructed haunts of commerce their playground.

Lydia noted one small boy looking wistfully through the window of a sweetshop, evidently in the keenest want of money. To him she proposed that he should guide her back to the Bond Street of that region. He embraced the offer greedily, and presently led her thither by way of Lexington Street. She thanked him, and gave him the smallest coin in her purse, which happened to be a shilling. He, in a transport at possessing what was to him a fortune, uttered a piercing yell, and darted off to shew the coin to a covey of small boys who had just raced into view round the corner by the public-house. In his haste, he dashed headlong against one of the usual group outside, a powerfully built young man, who cursed him fiercely. The boy retorted passionately, and then, hurt by the collision, began to cry. When Lydia came up, the child stood whimpering directly in her path; and she, pitying him, patted him on the head and reminded him of all the money he had to spend. He seemed comforted, and scraped his eyes with his knuckles in silence; but the man, who, having received a rude butt in the groin, was stung by Lydia's injustice in according to the aggressor the sympathy due to himself, walked threateningly up to her, and demanded, with a startling oath, whether *he* had offered to do anything to the boy. And, as he refrained from applying any epithet to her, he honestly believed that in deference to Lydia's sex and personal charms he had expressed himself with a dashing combination of gallantry with manly heat of spirit. She, not appreciating his chivalry, recoiled, and stepped into the roadway in order to pass him. Indignant at this attempt to ignore him, he again placed himself in her path, and was repeating his question with increased sternness, when a jerk in the pit of his stomach caused him a severe internal qualm, besides disturbing his equilibrium so rudely that he narrowly escaped a fall against the kerbstone. When he recovered himself he saw before him a showily dressed young man, who thus accosted him:

'Is that the way to talk to a lady, eh? Isnt the street wide enough for two? Wheres your manners?'

'And who are you; and where are you shoving your elbow to?' said the man, with a surpassing imprecation.

'Come, come,' said Cashel Byron admonitorily. 'Youd better keep your mouth clean if you wish to keep your teeth inside it. Never you mind who I am.'

Lydia, foreseeing an altercation, and alarmed by the threatening aspect of the man, sensibly resolved to hurry away and send a policeman to Cashel's assistance. But on turning she discovered that a crowd had already gathered, and that she was in the novel position of a spectator in the inner ring at what promised to be a street fight. Her attention was recalled to the disputants by a violent demonstration on the part of her late assailant. Cashel seemed alarmed for he hastily retreated a step without regard to the toes of those behind him, and exclaimed, waving the other off with his open hand,

'Now you just let me alone. I dont want to have anything to say to you. Go away from me, I tell you.'

'You dont want to have nothink to say to me! Oh! And for why? Because you aint man enough: thats why. What do you mean by coming and shoving your elbow into a man's breadbasket for, and then wanting to sneak off? Did you think I'd 'a bin frightened of your velvet coat?'

'Very well,' said Cashel pacifically: 'we'll say that I'm not man enough for you. So thats settled. Are you satisfied?'

But the other, greatly emboldened, declared with many oaths that he would have Cashel's heart out, and also, if he liked, that of Lydia, to whom he alluded in coarse terms. The crowd cheered, and called upon him to 'go it.' Cashel then said sullenly,

'Very well. But dont you try to make out afterwards that I forced a quarrel on you. And now,' he added, with a grim change of tone that made Lydia shudder, and shifted her fears to the account of his antagonist, 'I'll make you wish youd bit your tongue out before you said what you did a moment ago. So take care of yourself.'

'Oh, I'll take care of myself,' said the man defiantly. 'Put up your hands.'

Cashel surveyed his opponent's attitude with unspeakable disparagement. 'Youll know when my hands are up by the feel of the pavement,' he said. 'Better keep your coat on. Youll fall softer.'

The rough expressed his repudiation of this counsel by beginning to strip energetically. A nameless thrill passed through the crowd. Those who had bad places pressed forward; and those who formed the inner ring pressed back to make room for the combatants. Lydia, who occupied a coveted position close to Cashel, hoped to be hustled out of the throng; for she was beginning to feel faint and ill. But a handsome butcher, who had found a place by her side, held that she was entitled to the post of honor in the front row, and bade her not be frightened. As he spoke, the mass of faces before Lydia seemed to give a sudden lurch. To save herself from falling, she slipped her arm through the butcher's; and he, much gratified, tucked her close to him, and held her up effectually. His support was welcome, because it was needed.

Meanwhile, Cashel stood motionless, watching with unrelenting contempt the movements of his adversary, who rolled up his discolored shirt sleeves amid encouraging cries of 'Go it, Teddy,' 'Give it im, Ted,' and other more precise suggestions. But Teddy's spirit was chilled: he advanced with a presentiment that he was courting destruction. He dared not rush on his foe, whose eye seemed to discern his impotence. When at last he ventured to strike, the blow fell short, as Cashel evidently knew it would; for he did not stir. There was a laugh and a murmur of impatience in the crowd.

'Are you waiting for the copper to come and separate you?' shouted the butcher. 'Come out of your corner and get to work, cant you?'

This reminder that the police might baulk him of his prey seemed to move Cashel. He took a step forward. The excitement of the crowd rose to a climax; and a little man near Lydia cut a frenzied caper and screamed, 'Go it, Cashel Byron.'

At these words, Teddy was frankly terror-stricken. His hands went down hastily; and a pitiable green pallor flitted across his cheek. 'It aint fair,' he exclaimed, retreating as far as he could: 'I give in. Cut it, master: youre too clever for me.' But the cruel crowd, with a jeer, pushed him towards Cashel, who advanced remorselessly. Teddy dropped on both knees. 'What can a man say more than that he's had enough?' he pleaded. 'Be a Englishman, master; and dont hit a man when he's down.'

'Down!' said Cashel. 'How long will you stay down if I choose to have you up?' And, suiting the action to the word, he seized Teddy with his left hand; lifted him to his feet; threw him in a helpless position across his knee; and poised his right fist like a hammer over his upturned face.

'Now,' he said, 'youre not down. What have you to say for yourself before I knock your face down your throat?'

'Dont do it; govnor,' gasped Teddy. 'I didnt mean no harm. How was I to know that the young lady was your fancy?' Here he struggled a little; and his face took a darker hue. 'Let go, master,' he cried, almost inarticulately. 'Youre ch – choking me.'

'Pray let him go,' said Lydia, disengaging herself from the butcher and catching Cashel's arm.

Cashel, with a start, relaxed his grasp; and Teddy rolled on the ground. He went away thrusting his hands into his sleeves, and outfacing his disgrace by a callous grin. Cashel, without speaking, offered Lydia his arm; and, she, seeing that her best course was to get away from that place with as few words as possible, accepted it, and then turned and thanked the butcher, who blushed and became speechless. The little man, he whose exclamation had interrupted the combat, now waved his hat, crying,

'The British Lion for ever! Three cheers for Cashel Byron.'

Cashel turned upon him curtly, and said, 'Dont you make so free with other people's names, or perhaps you may get into trouble yourself.'

The little man retreated hastily; but the crowd responded with three cheers as Cashel, with Lydia on his arm, withdrew through a lane of disreputable-looking girls, roughs of Teddy's class, white-aproned shopmen who had left their counters to see the fight, and a few pale clerks, who looked with awe at the prizefighter and with wonder at the refined appearance of his companion. The two were followed by a double file of little ragamuffins, who, with their eyes fixed earnestly on Cashel, walked on the footways whilst he conducted Lydia down the middle of the narrow street. Not one of them turned a somersault or uttered a shout. Intent on their hero, they pattered along, coming into collision with every object that lay in their path. At last Cashel stopped. They instantly stopped too. He took some bronze coin from his pocket; rattled it in his hand, and addressed them.

'Boys.' Dead silence. 'Do you know what I have to do to keep up my strength?' The hitherto steadfast eyes wandered uneasily. 'I have to eat a little boy for supper every night, the last thing before going to bed. Now, I havnt quite made up my mind which of you would be the most to my taste; but if one of you comes a step further, I'll eat *him*. So away with you.' And he jerked the coins to a considerable distance. There was a yell and a scramble; and Cashel and Lydia pursued their way unattended.

Lydia had taken advantage of the dispersion of the boys to detach herself from Cashel's arm. She now said, speaking to him for the first time since she had interceded for Teddy,

'I am sorry to have given you so much trouble, Mr Cashel Byron. Thank you for interfering to protect me; but I was in no real danger. I would gladly have borne with a few rough words for the sake of avoiding a disturbance.'

'There!' cried Cashel. 'I knew it. Youd a deal rather I had minded my own business and not interfered. Youre sorry for the poor fellow I treated so badly: aint you now? Thats a woman all over.'

'I have not said one of these things.'

'Well, I dont see what else you mean. It's no pleasure to me to fight chance men in the streets for nothing: I dont get my living that way. And now that I have done it for your sake, you as good as tell me I ought to have kept myself quiet.'

'Perhaps I **am** wrong. I hardly understand what passed. You seemed to drop from the clouds.'

'Aha! You were glad when you found me at your elbow, in spite of your talk. Come now: werent you glad to see me?'

'I confess it: very glad indeed. But by what magic did you so suddenly subdue that man? And was it necessary to sully your hands by throttling him?'

'It was a satisfaction to me; and it served him right.'

'Surely a very poor satisfaction! Did you notice that some one in the crowd called out your name; and that it seemed to frighten the man terribly?'

'Indeed. Odd, wasnt it? But you were saying that you thought I dropped from the sky. Why, I had been following you for five minutes before! What do you think of that? If I may take the liberty of asking, how did you come to be walking round Soho at such an hour with a little boy?'

Lydia explained. When she had finished, it was nearly dark. They had reached Oxford Street, where, like Lucian in Regent's Park that afternoon, she became conscious that her companion was an object of curiosity to many of the wayfarers, especially the cabmen and omnibus drivers.

'Alice will think I am lost,' she said, making a signal to a cabman, who made his horse plunge to obey it. 'Goodbye; and many thanks. I am always at home on Fridays, and shall be very happy to see you.'

She handed him a card. He took it; read it; looked at the back to see if there was anything written there; and then said dubiously,

'I suppose there will be a lot of people.'

'Yes, you will meet plenty of people.'

'Hm! I wish youd let me see you home now. I wont ask to go any further than the gate.'

Lydia laughed. 'You should be very welcome,' she said; 'but I am quite safe, thank you. I need not trouble you.'

'But suppose the cabman bullies you for double fare,' persisted Cashel. 'I have business up in Kilburn; and your place is right in my way there. Upon my soul I have,' he added, suspecting that she doubted him. 'I go every Tuesday evening to the St John's Wood Cestus Club.'

'I am hungry and in a hurry to get home,' said Lydia. '"I must begone and live, or stay and die." Come if you will; but in any case let us go at once.'

She got into the cab; and Cashel followed, making some remark which she did not quite catch about its being too dark for any one to recognize him. They spoke little during the drive, which was soon over. Bashville was standing at the open door as they came to the house. When Cashel got out, the footman looked at him with interest and some surprise. But when Lydia alighted, he was so startled that he stood open-mouthed, although he was trained to simulate insensibility to everything except his own business, and to do that as automatically as possible. Cashel bade Lydia goodbye, and shook hands with her. As she went into the house, she asked Bashville whether Miss Goff was within. To her surprise, he paid no attention to her, but stared after the retreating cab. She repeated the question.

'Madam,' he said, recovering himself with a start: 'she has asked for you four times.'

Lydia, relieved of a disagreeable suspicion that her usually faultless footman must be drunk, thanked him and went upstairs.

CHAPTER VIII

ONE morning a handsome young man, elegantly dressed, presented himself at Downing Street, and asked to see Mr Lucian Webber. He declined to send in a card, and desired to be announced simply as 'Bashville'. Lucian had him admitted at once; and, when he entered, condescended to him and invited him to sit down.

'I thank you, sir,' said Bashville, seating himself. It struck Lucian then, from a certain strung-up resolution in his visitor's manner, that he had come on some business of his own, and not with a message from his mistress.

'I have come, sir, on my own responsibility this morning. I hope you will excuse the liberty.'

'Certainly. If I can do anything for you, Bashville, dont be afraid to ask. But be as brief as you can. I am so busy that every second I give you will probably come off my night's rest. Will ten minutes be enough?'

'More than enough, sir, thank you. I only wish to ask one question. I own that I am stepping out of my place to ask it; but I'll risk that. Does Miss Carew know what the Mr Cashel Byron is that she receives every Friday with her other friends?'

'No doubt she does,' said Lucian, at once becoming cold in his manner, and looking severely at Bashville. 'What business is that of yours?'

'Do *you* know what he is, sir?' said Bashville, returning Lucian's gaze steadily.

Lucian changed countenance, and replaced a pen that had slipped from a rack on his desk. 'He is not an acquaintance of mine,' he said. 'I only know him as a friend of Lord Worthington's.'

'Sir,' said Bashville, with sudden vehemence, 'he is no more to Lord Worthington than the racehorse his lordship bets on. *I* might as well set up to be a friend of his lordship because I, after a manner of speaking, know him. Byron is in the ring, sir. A common prizefighter!'

Lucian, recalling what had passed at Mrs Hoskyn's, believed the assertion at once. But he made a faint effort to resist conviction. 'Are you sure of this, Bashville?' he said. 'Do you know that your statement is a very serious one?'

'There is no doubt at all about it, sir. Go to any sporting public-house in London and ask who is the best-known fighting man of the day, and theyll tell you Cashel Byron. I know all about him, sir. Perhaps you have heard tell of Ned Skene, who was champion, belike, when you were at school.'

'I believe I have heard the name.'

'Just so, sir. Ned Skene picked up this Cashel Byron in the streets of Melbourne, where he was a common sailor boy, and trained him for the ring. You may have seen his name in the papers, sir. The sporting ones are full of him; and he was mentioned in The Times a month ago.'

'I never read articles on such subjects. I have hardly time to glance through the ones that concern me.'

'Thats the way it is with everybody, sir. Miss Carew never thinks of reading the sporting intelligence in the papers; and so he passes himself off on her for her equal. He's well known for his wish to be thought a gentleman, sir, I assure you.'

'I have noticed his manner as being odd, certainly.'

'Odd, sir! Why, a child might see through him; for he has not the sense to keep his own secret. Last Friday he was in the library; and he got looking at the new biographical dictionary that Miss Carew contributed the article on Spinoza to. And what do you think he said, sir? "This is a blessed book," he says. "Heres ten pages about Napoleon Bonaparte, and not one about Jack Randall: as if one fighting man wasnt as good as another!" I knew by the way Miss Carew took up that saying, and drew him out, so to speak, on the subject, that she didnt know who she had in her house; and then I determined to tell you, sir. I hope you

147

wont think that I come here behind his back out of malice against him. All I want is fair play. If I passed myself off on Miss Carew as a gentleman, I should deserve to be exposed as a cheat; and when he tries to take advantages that dont belong to him, I think I have a right to expose him.'

'Quite right, quite right,' said Lucian, who cared nothing for Bashville's motives. 'I suppose this Byron is a dangerous man to have any personal unpleasantness with.'

'He knows his business, sir. I am a better judge of wrestling than half of these London professionals; but I never saw the man that could put a hug on him. Simple as he is, sir, he has a genius for fighting, and has beaten men of all sizes, weights, and colors. Theres a new man from the black country, named Paradise, who says he'll beat him; but I wont believe it till I see it.'

'Well,' said Lucian, rising, 'I am much indebted to you, Bashville, for your information; and I shall take care to let Miss Carew know how you have – '

'Begging your pardon, sir,' said Bashville; 'but, if you please, no. I did not come to recommend myself at the cost of another man; and perhaps Miss Carew might not think it any great recommendation neither.' Lucian looked quickly at him as if about to speak, but checked himself. Bashville continued, 'If he denies it, you may call me as a witness; and I will tell him to his face that he lies – and so I would if he were twice as dangerous; but, except in that way, I would ask you, sir, as a favor, not to mention my name to Miss Carew.'

'As you please,' said Lucian, taking out his purse. 'Perhaps you are right. However, you shall not have your trouble for nothing.'

'I couldnt really, sir,' said Bashville, retreating a step. 'You will agree with me, I'm sure, that this is not a thing that a man should take payment for. It is a personal matter between me and Byron, sir.'

Lucian, displeased that a servant should have any personal feelings on any subject, much more one that concerned his mistress, put back his purse without comment, and said,

'Will Miss Carew be at home this afternoon between three and four?'

'I have not heard of any arrangement to the contrary, sir. I will telegraph to you if she goes out – if you wish.'

'It does not matter. Thank you. Good morning.'

'Good morning, sir,' said Bashville respectfully, as he withdrew. Outside the door his manner changed. He put on a pair of cinnamon gloves; took up a silver-mounted walking-stick which he had left in the corridor; and walked from Downing Street into Whitehall. A party of visitors from the country, standing there examining the buildings, guessed that he was a junior lord of the Treasury.

He waited in vain that afternoon for Lucian to appear at the house in Regent's Park. There were no callers; and he wore away the time by endeavoring, with the aid of the library Miss Carew had placed at the disposal of her domestics, to unravel the philosophy of Spinoza. At the end of an hour, feeling satisfied that he had mastered that author's views, he proceeded to vary the monotony of the long summer's day by polishing Lydia's plate.

Meanwhile, Lucian was considering how he could best make Lydia not only repudiate Cashel's acquaintance, but feel thoroughly ashamed of herself for having encouraged him, and wholesomely mistrustful of her own judgment for the future. His secretarial duties had taught him to provide himself with a few well-arranged relevant facts before attempting to influence the opinions of others on any subject. He knew no more of prizefighting than that it was a brutal and illegal practice, akin to cockfighting, and, like it, generally supposed to be obsolete. Knowing how prone Lydia was to suspect any received opinion of being a prejudice, he felt that he must inform himself more particularly. To Lord Worthington's astonishment, he not only asked him to dinner next evening, but listened with interest whilst he expatiated to his heart's content on his favorite theme of the ring.

As the days passed, Bashville became nervous, and sometimes wondered whether Lydia had met her cousin and heard from him of the interview at Downing Street. He fancied that her manner towards him was changed; and he was once or twice on the point of asking the most sympathetic of the housemaids whether she had noticed it. On Wednesday his suspense ended. Lucian came, and had a long conversation with Lydia in the library. Though Bashville was too honorable to listen at the door, he almost hoped that the sympathetic housemaid would prove less scrupulous. But Miss Carew had contrived to leave her servants some self-respect; and Lucian's revelation was made in complete privacy.

When he entered the library, he looked so serious that she asked him whether he had neuralgia, from which he occasionally suffered. He replied with some indignation that he had not, and that he had a communication of importance to make to her.

'What! Another!'

'Yes, another,' he said, with a sour smile; 'but this time it does not concern myself. May I warn you as to the character of one of your guests without overstepping my privilege?'

'Certainly. Do you mean Cheffsky? If so, I am perfectly aware that he is a proscribed Nihilist.'

'I do not mean Monsieur Cheffsky. You understand, I hope, that I do not approve of him, nor of your strange fancy for Nihilists, Anarchists, and other doubtful persons; but I think that even you might draw the line at a prizefighter.'

Lydia lost color, and said, almost inaudibly, 'Cashel Byron!'

'Then you *knew*!' exclaimed Lucian, scandalized.

Lydia waited a moment to recover; settled herself quietly in her chair; and replied calmly, 'I know what you tell me — nothing more. And now will you explain to me exactly what a prizefighter is?'

'He is simply what his name indicates. He is a man who fights for prizes.'

'So does the captain of a man-of-war. And yet society

does not place them in the same class – at least I do not think so.'

'As if there could be any doubt that society does not! There is no analogy whatever between the two cases. Let me endeavor to open your eyes a little, if that be possible, which I am sometimes tempted to doubt. A prizefighter is usually a man of naturally ferocious disposition, who has acquired some reputation among his associates as a bully; and who, by constantly quarrelling, has acquired some practice in fighting. On the strength of this reputation, he can generally find some gambler willing to stake a sum of money that he will vanquish a pugilist of established fame in single combat. Bets are made between the admirers of the two men; a prize is subscribed for, each party contributing a share; the combatants are trained as racehorses, gamecocks, or their like are trained; they meet, and beat each other as savagely as they can until one or the other is too much injured to continue the combat. This takes place in the midst of a mob of such persons as enjoy spectacles of the kind: that is to say, the vilest blackguards a large city can afford to leave at large, and many whom it can not. As the prize-money contributed by each side often amounts to upwards of a thousand pounds; and as a successful pugilist commands far higher terms for giving tuition in boxing than a tutor at one of the universities does for coaching; you will see that such a man, whilst his youth and luck last, may have plenty of money, and may even, by aping the manners of the gentlemen whom he teaches, deceive careless people – especially those who admire eccentricity – as to his true character and position.'

'What is his true position? I mean before he becomes a prizefighter.'

'Well, he may be a skilled workman of some kind; a journeyman butcher, skinner, tailor, or baker. Possibly a discharged soldier, sailor, gentleman's servant, or what not. But he is generally a common laborer. The waterside is prolific of such heroes.'

'Do they never come from a higher rank?'

'Never even from the better classes in their own. Broken-down gentlemen are not likely to succeed at work that needs the strength and endurance of a bull, and the cruelty of a butcher.'

'But what becomes of them in the end? They cannot keep at such work all their lives.'

'They do not. When through age a prizefighter is found to be repeatedly beaten, no one will either bet on him or subscribe to provide him with a stake. Or if he is invariably successful, those, if any, who dare fight him find themselves in a like predicament. In either case his occupation is gone. If he has saved money, he opens a sporting public-house, where he sells spirits of the worst description to his old rivals and their associates, and eventually drinks himself to death or bankruptcy. If, however, he has been improvident or unfortunate, he begs from his former patrons and gives lessons. Finally, when the patrons are tired of him and the pupils fail, he relapses into the dregs of the laboring class with a ruined constitution, a disfigured face, a brutalized nature, and a tarnished reputation.'

Lydia remained silent so long after this that Lucian's magisterial severity first deepened, then wavered, and finally gave way to a sense of injury; for she seemed to have forgotten him. He was about to protest against this treatment, when she looked at him again, and said,

'Why did Lord Worthington introduce a man of this class to me?'

'Because you asked him to do so. Probably he thought that if you chose to make such a request without previous inquiry, you should not blame him if you found yourself saddled with an undesirable acquaintance. Recollect that you asked for the introduction on the platform at Wiltstoken, in the presence of the man himself. Such a ruffian would be capable of making a disturbance for much less offence than an explanation and refusal would have given him.'

'Lucian,' said Lydia: 'I asked to be introduced to my tenant, for whose respectability you had vouched by letting the Warren Lodge to him.' Lucian reddened. 'How does Lord Worthington explain Mr Byron's appearance at Mrs Hoskyn's?'

'It was a stupid joke. Mrs Hoskyn had worried Worthington to bring some celebrity to her house; and in revenge he took his pugilistic *protégé*.'

'H'm!'

'I do not defend Worthington. But discretion is hardly to be expected from him.'

'He has discretion enough to understand a case of this kind thoroughly. But let that pass. I have been thinking upon what you tell me about these singular people, whose existence I hardly knew of before. Now, Lucian, in the course of my reading I have come upon denunciations of every race and pursuit under the sun. Very respectable and well-informed men have held that Jews, Irishmen, Christians, atheists, lawyers, doctors, politicians, actors, artists, flesh-eaters, and spirit-drinkers, are all of necessity degraded beings. Such statements can be easily proved by taking a black sheep from each flock, and holding him up as the type. It seems reasonable to infer a man's character from the nature of his occupation: still, who would act upon an opinion based on that alone? War is a cruel business; but soldiers are not exceptionally bloodthirsty and inhuman men. I am not quite satisfied that a prizefighter is a violent and dangerous man because he follows a violent and dangerous profession – I suppose they call it a profession.'

Lucian was about to speak; but she interrupted him by continuing,

'And yet that is not what concerns me at present. Have you found out anything about Mr Byron personally? Is he an ordinary representative of his class?'

'No: I should rather think – and hope – that he is a very extraordinary representative of it. I have traced his history back to the time when he was a cabin-boy. Having apparently failed to recommend himself to his employers in that capacity, he became errand boy to a sort of *maître d'armes* at Melbourne. Here he discovered where his genius lay; and he presently appeared in the ring with an unfortunate young man named Ducket, whose jaw he fractured. This laid the foundation of his fame. He fought several battles with unvarying success; but at last he allowed his valor to get the better of his discretion so far as to kill an Englishman who fought him with desperate obstinacy for two hours. I am informed that the particular blow by which he felled the poor wretch for the last time is known in pugilistic circles as "Cashel's killer," and that he has attempted to repeat it in all his subsequent encounters, without, however, achieving the same fatal result. The failure has doubtless been a severe disappointment to him. He fled from Australia, and reappeared in America, where he resumed his victorious career, distinguishing himself specially by throwing a gigantic opponent in some dreadful fashion that these men have, and laming him for life. He then – '

'Thank you, Lucian,' said Lydia, rather faintly. 'That is quite enough. Are you quite sure it is all true?'

'My authority is Lord Worthington, and the files of the sporting newspapers. Byron himself will probably be proud to give you the fullest confirmation of the record. I should add, in justice to him, that he is looked upon as a model – to pugilists – of temperance and general good conduct.'

'Do you remember my remarking a few days ago, on another subject, how meaningless our observations are until we are given the right thread to string them on?'

'Yes,' said Lucian, disconcerted by the allusion.

'My acquaintance with this man is a case in point. He has obtruded his horrible profession upon me every time we have met. I have actually seen him publicly cheered as a pugilist-hero; and yet, being off the track, and ignorant of the very existence of such a calling, I have looked on and seen nothing.'

Lydia then narrated her adventure in Soho, and listened

with the perfect patience of indifference to his censure of her imprudence in walking by herself in town.

'May I ask,' he added, 'what you intend to do in this matter?'

'What would you have me do?'

'Drop his acquaintance at once. Forbid him your house in the most explicit terms.'

'A pleasant task!' said Lydia ironically. 'But I will do it – not so much, perhaps, because he is a prizefighter as because he is an impostor. Now go to the writing-table, and draft me a proper letter to send him.'

Lucian's face elongated. 'I think,' he said, 'you can do that better for yourself. It is a delicate sort of thing.'

'Yes. It is not so easy as you implied a moment ago. Otherwise I should not require your assistance. As it is – ' She pointed again to the table.

Lucian was not ready with an excuse. He sat down reluctantly, and, after some consideration, indited the following:—

'Miss Carew presents her compliments to Mr Cashel Byron, and begs to inform him that she will not be at home during the remainder of the season as heretofore. She therefore regrets that she cannot have the pleasure of receiving him on Friday afternoon.'

'I think you will find that sufficient,' said Lucian.

'Probably,' said Lydia, smiling as she read it. 'But what shall I do if he takes offence; calls here; breaks the windows; and beats Bashville? That is what such a letter would provoke *me* to do.'

'He dare not give any trouble. But I will warn the police if you feel anxious.'

'By no means. We must not shew ourselves inferior to him in courage, which is, I suppose, his cardinal virtue.'

'If you write the note now, I will post it for you.'

'No, thank you. I will send it with my other letters.'

Lucian tried to wait; but she would not write whilst he was there. So he left, satisfied on the whole with the success of his mission. When he was gone, she endorsed his draft neatly, and placed it in a drawer. Then she wrote to Cashel thus:—

'Dear Mr Cashel Byron – I have just discovered your secret. I am sorry; but you must not come again. Farewell. Yours faithfully, LYDIA CAREW.'

Lydia kept this note by her until next morning, when she read it through carefully. She then sent Bashville to the post with it.

CHAPTER IX

CASHEL's pupils sometimes requested him to hit them hard – not to play with them – to accustom them to regular right-down severe hitting, and no nonsense. He only pretended to comply; for he knew that a black eye or loosened tooth would be immoderately boasted of if received in combat with a famous pugilist, and that the sufferer's friends would make private notes to avoid so rough a professor. But when Miss Carew's note reached him, he made an exception to his practice in this respect. A young guardsman, whose lesson began shortly after the post arrived, remarked that Cashel was unusually distraught, and exhorted him to wake up and pitch in in earnest. Instantly a blow in the epigastrium stretched him almost insensible on the floor. His complexion was considerably whitened when he was set on his legs again; and he presently alleged an urgent appointment, and withdrew, declaring in a shaky voice that that was the sort of bout he really enjoyed.

When he was gone, Cashel walked distractedly to and fro, cursing, and occasionally stopping to read the letter. His restlessness only increased his agitation. The arrival of a Frenchman whom he employed to give lessons in fencing made the place unendurable to him. He changed his attire; went out; called a cab; and bade the driver, with an oath, drive to Lydia's house as fast as the horse could go. The man made all the haste he could, and was presently told impatiently that there was no hurry. Accustomed to this sort of inconsistency, he was not surprised when, as they approached the house, he was told not to stop, but to drive slowly past. Then, in obedience to further instructions, he turned and repassed the door. As he did so, a lady appeared for an instant at a window. Immediately his fare, with a groan of mingled rage and fear, sprang from the moving vehicle; rushed up the steps of the mansion; and rang the bell violently. Bashville, faultlessly dressed and impassibly mannered, opened the door. In reply to Cashel's half inarticulate inquiry, he said,

'Miss Carew is not at home.'

'You lie,' said Cashel, his eyes suddenly dilating. 'I saw her.'

Bashville reddened, but replied coolly, 'Miss Carew cannot see you today.'

'Go and ask her,' returned Cashel sternly, advancing.

Bashville, with compressed lips, seized the door to shut him out; but Cashel forced it back against him and went in, shutting the door behind him. He turned from Bashville for a moment to do this; and before he could face him again he was tripped and flung down upon the tesselated pavement of the hall. When Bashville was given the lie, and pushed back behind the door, the excitement he had been suppressing since his visit to Lucian exploded. He had thrown Cashel in Cornish fashion, and now desperately awaited the upshot.

Cashel got up so rapidly that he seemed to rebound from the flags. Bashville, involuntarily cowering before his onslaught, just escaped his right fist, and felt as though his heart had been drawn with it as it whizzed past his ear. He turned and fled frantically upstairs.

Lydia was in her boudoir with Alice when Bashville darted in and locked the door. Alice rose and screamed. Lydia, though startled, and that less by the unusual action than by the change in a familiar face which she had never seen influenced by emotion before, sat still, and quietly asked what was the matter. Bashville checked himself for a moment. Then he spoke unintelligibly, and went to the window, which he opened. Lydia divined that he was about to call for help to the street.

'Bashville,' she said authoritatively: 'be silent; and close the window. I will go downstairs myself.'

Bashville then ran to prevent her from unlocking the door; but she paid no attention to him. He did not dare to oppose her forcibly. He was beginning to recover from his panic, and to feel the first stings of shame for having yielded to it.

'Madam,' he said: 'Byron is below; and he insists on seeing you. He's dangerous; and he's too strong for me. I have done my best: on my honor I have. Let me call the police. Stop,' he added, as she opened the door. 'If either of us goes, it must be me.'

'I will see him in the library,' said Lydia composedly. 'Tell him so; and let him wait there for me – if you can speak to him without running any risk.'

'Oh pray let him call the police,' urged Alice. 'Dont attempt to go to that man.'

'Nonsense!' said Lydia good-humoredly. 'I am not in the least afraid. We must not fail in courage when we have a prizefighter to deal with.'

Bashville, white, and with difficulty preventing his knees from knocking together, but not faltering for a second, went devotedly downstairs and found Cashel leaning upon the balustrade, panting, and looking perplexedly about him as he wiped his dabbled brow. Bashville halted on the third stair; and said,

'Miss Carew will see you in the library. Come this way, please.'

Cashel's lips moved; but no sound came from them: he followed Bashville in silence. When they entered the library, Lydia was already there. Bashville withdrew without a word. Then Cashel sat down, and, to her consternation, bent his head on his hand, and yielded to a hysterical convulsion. Before she could resolve how to act, he looked up at her with his face distorted and discolored, and tried to speak.

'Please dont cry,' said Lydia. 'I am told that you wish to speak to me.'

'I dont wish to speak to you ever again,' said Cashel hoarsely. 'You told your servant to throw me down the steps. Thats enough for me.'

Lydia caught from him the tendency to sob which he was

struggling with; but she repressed it, and answered firmly, 'If my servant has been guilty of the least incivility to you, Mr Cashel Byron, he has exceeded his orders.'

'It doesnt matter,' said Cashel. 'He may thank his luck that he has his head on. But *he* doesnt matter. Hold on a bit – I cant talk – I shall get – second wind – and then – ' Cashel raised his head with a curiously businesslike expression; threw himself supinely against the back of his chair; and in that position deliberately rested until he could trust himself to speak. At last he pulled himself together, and said, 'Why are you going to give me up?'

Lydia ranged her wits in battle array, and replied, 'Do you remember our talk at Mrs Hoskyn's?'

'Yes.'

'You admitted then that if the nature of your occupation became known to me, our acquaintance should cease.'

'That was all very fine to excuse my not telling you. But I find, like many another man when put to the proof, that I didnt mean it. Who told you I was a fighting man?'

'I had rather not tell you that.'

'Aha!' said Cashel, with a triumph that was half choked by the remnant of his hysteria. 'Who is trying to make a secret now, I should like to know?'

'I do so in this instance because I am afraid to expose a friend to your resentment.'

'And why? He's a man, of course: else you wouldnt be afraid. You think that I'd go straight off and murder him. Perhaps he told you that it would come quite natural to a man like me – a ruffian like me – to smash him up. That comes of being a coward. People run my profession down, not because there is a bad one or two in it – theres plenty of bad bishops, if you come to that – but because theyre afraid of us. You may make yourself easy about your friend. I am accustomed to get well paid for the beatings I give; and your own common sense ought to tell you that any one who is used to being paid for a job is just the last person in the world to do it for nothing.'

'I find the contrary to be the case with first-rate artists,' said Lydia.

'Thank you,' retorted Cashel sarcastically. 'I ought to make you a bow for that.'

'But,' said Lydia seriously, 'it seems to me that your art is wholly anti-social and retrograde. And I fear that you have forced this interview on me to no purpose.'

'I dont know whether it's anti-social or not. But I think it hard that I should be put out of decent society when fellows that do far worse than I are let in. Who did I see here last Friday, the most honored of your guests? Why, that Frenchman with the gold spectacles. What do you think I was told when I asked what *his* little game was? Baking dogs in ovens to see how long a dog could live red hot! I'd like to catch him doing it to a dog of mine. Aye; and sticking a rat full of nails to see whether pain makes a rat sweat. Why, it's just sickening. Do you think I'd have shaken hands with that chap? If he hadnt been a friend of yours, I'd have taught him how to make a Frenchman sweat without sticking any nails into him. And *he*'s to be received and made much of, while I am kicked out! Look at your relation the general, too! What is he but a fighting man, I should like to know? Isnt it his pride and boast that as long as he is paid so much a day, he'll ask no questions whether a war is fair or unfair, but just walk out and put thousands of men in the best way to kill and be killed – keeping well behind them himself all the time, mind you. Last year he was up to his chin in the blood of a lot of poor blacks that were no more a match for his armed men than a feather-weight would be for me. Bad as I am, I wouldnt attack a feather-weight, or stand by and see another heavy man do it. Plenty of your friends go pigeon-shooting to Hurlingham. *Theres* a humane and manly way of spending a Saturday afternoon! Lord Worthington, that comes to see you when he likes, though he's too much of a man or too little of a shot to kill pigeons, thinks nothing of fox-hunting. Do you think foxes like to be hunted, or that the people that hunt them have such fine feelings that they can afford to call prize-fighters names? Look at the men that get killed or lamed every year at steeplechasing, fox-hunting, cricket, and football! Dozens of them! Look at the thousands killed in battle! Did you ever hear of any one being killed in the ring? Why, from first to last, during the whole century that my sort of fighting has been going on, theres not been six fatal accidents at really respectable fights. It's safer than dancing: many a woman has danced her skirt into the fire and been burnt. I once fought a man who had spoiled his constitution with bad living; and he exhausted himself so by going on and on long after he was beaten that he died of it, and nearly finished me too. If youd heard the fuss that even the old hands made over it, youd have thought a blessed baby had died from falling out of its cradle. A good milling does a man more good than harm. And if all these damned dog-bakers and soldiers and pigeon-shooters and fox-hunters and the rest of them, are made welcome here, why am I shut out like a brute beast?'

'Truly I do not know,' said Lydia, puzzled; 'unless it be that your profession is not usually recruited from our ranks.'

'I grant you that boxers arnt gentlemen, as a rule. No more were painters or poets, once upon a time. But what I want to know is this. Supposing a boxer has as good manners as your friends, and is as well born, why shouldnt he mix with them and be considered their equal?'

'The distinction seems arbitrary, I confess. But perhaps the true remedy would be to exclude the vivisectors and soldiers, instead of admitting the prizefighters, Mr Cashel Byron,' added Lydia, changing her manner: 'I cannot discuss this with you. Society has a prejudice against you. I share it; and I cannot overcome it. Can you find no nobler occupation than these fierce and horrible encounters by which you condescend to gain a living?'

'No,' said Cashel flatly. 'I cant. Thats just where it is.'

Lydia looked grave, and said nothing.

'You dont see it?' said Cashel. 'Well, I'll just tell you all about myself, and then leave you to judge. May I sit down while I talk?' He had risen in the course of his remarks on Lydia's scientific and military acquaintances.

She pointed to a chair near her. Something in the action brought color to his cheeks.

'I believe I was the most unfortunate devil of a boy that ever walked,' he began. 'My mother was – and is – an actress, and a tiptop crack in her profession. One of the first things I remember is sitting on the floor in the corner of a room where there was a big glass, and she flaring away before it, attitudinizing and spouting Shakespear like mad. I was afraid of her, because she was very particular about my manners and appearance, and would never let me go near a theatre. I know nothing about my people or hers; for she boxed my ears one day for asking who my father was, and I took good care not to ask her again. She was quite young when I was a child: at first I thought her a sort of angel. I should have been fond of her, I think, if she had let me. But she didnt, somehow; and I had to keep my affection for the servants. I had plenty of variety in that way; for she gave her whole establishment the sack about once every two months, except a maid that used to bully her and give me nearly all the nursing I ever got. I believe it was my crying about some housemaid or other who went away that first set her abusing me for having low tastes – a sort of thing that used to cut me to the heart, and which she kept up till the very day I left her for good. We were a precious pair: I sulky and obstinate; she changeable and hot-tempered. She used to begin breakfast sometimes by knocking me to the other side of the room with a slap, and finish it by calling me her darling boy and promising me all manner of toys and things. I soon gave up trying to please her or like her, and became as disagreeable a young imp as youd ask to see. My only thought was to get all I could out of her when she was in a good humor, and to be sullen and stubborn when she was in a tantrum. One day a boy in the street threw some mud at me; and I ran in crying, and complained to her. She told me I was a little coward. I havnt forgiven her for that yet – perhaps because it was one of the few true things she ever said to me. I was in a state of perpetual aggravation; and I often wonder I wasnt soured for life at that time. At last I got to be such a little fiend that when she hit me I used to guard off her blows, and look so wicked that I think she got afraid of me. Then she put me to school, telling me I had no heart, and telling the master I was an ungovernable young brute. So I, like a little fool, cried at leaving her; and she, like a big one, cried back again over me, – just after telling the master what a bad one I was, mind you – and off she went, leaving her darling boy and blessed child howling at his good luck in getting rid of her.

'I was a nice boy to let loose in a school. I could speak as well as an actor, as far as pronunciation goes; but I could hardly read words of one syllable; and as to writing, I couldnt make pothooks and hangers respectably. To this day, I can no more spell than old Ned Skene can. What was a worse sort of ignorance was that I had no idea of fair play. I thought that all servants would be afraid of me; and that all grown-up people would tyrannize over me. I was afraid of everybody; afraid that my cowardice would be found out; and as angry and cruel in my ill-tempers as cowards always are. Now youll hardly believe this; but what saved me from going to the bad altogether was my finding out that I was a good one to fight. The bigger boys were like grown-up people in respect of liking to see other people fight; and they used to set us young ones at it, whether we liked it or not, regularly every Saturday afternoon, with seconds, bottleholders, and everything complete, except the ropes. At first, when they made me fight, I shut my eyes and cried; but for all that I managed to catch the other fellow tight round the waist and throw him. After that, it became a regular joke to make me fight; for I always cried. But the end of it was that I learnt to keep my eyes open and hit straight. I had no trouble about fighting then. Somehow, I could tell by instinct when the other fellow was going to hit me; and

I always hit him first. It's the same with me now in the ring: I know what a man is going to do before he rightly knows himself. The power this gave me, civilized me. In the end it made me cock of the school; and, as cock, I couldnt be mean or childish. There would be nothing like fighting for licking boys into shape if every one could be cock; but every one cant; so I suppose it does more harm than good.

'I should have enjoyed school well enough if I had worked at my books. But I wouldnt study; and the masters were all down on me as an idler, though I shouldnt have been like that if they had known how to teach: I have learnt since what teaching is. As to the holidays, they were the worst part of the year to me. When I was left at school I was savage at not being let go home; and when I went home, my mother did nothing but find fault with my schoolboy manners. I was getting too big to be cuddled as her darling boy, you understand. Her treatment of me was just the old game with the affectionate part left out. It wasnt pleasant, after being cock of the school, to be made feel like a good-for-nothing little brat tied to her apron strings. When she saw that I was learning nothing, she sent me to another school at a place in the north called Panley. I stayed there until I was seventeen; and then she came one day; and we had a row, as usual. She said she wouldnt let me leave school until I was nineteen; and so I settled that question by running away the same night. I got to Liverpool, where I hid in a ship bound for Australia. When I was starved out, they treated me better than I expected; and I worked hard enough to earn my passage and my victuals. But when I was left ashore in Melbourne, I was in a pretty pickle. I knew nobody; and I had no money. Everything that a man could live by was owned by some one or other. I walked through the town looking for a place where they might want a boy to run errands or to clean the windows. But I hadnt the cheek to go into the shops and ask. Two or three times, when I was on the point of trying, I caught sight of some cad of a shopman, and made up my mind that I wouldnt be ordered about by *him*, and that since I had the whole town to choose from I might as well go on to the next place. At last, quite late in the afternoon, I saw an advertisement stuck up on a gymnasium; and while I was reading it I got talking to old Ned Skene, the owner, who was smoking at the door. He took a fancy to me, and offered to have me there as a sort of lad-of-all-work. I was only too glad to get the chance; and I closed with him at once. As time went on, I became so clever with the gloves that Ned matched me against a light-weight named Ducket, and bet a lot of money that I would win. Well, I couldnt disappoint him after his being so kind to me – Mrs Skene had made as much of me as if I was her own son. What could I do but take my bread as it came to me? I was fit for nothing else. Even if I had been able to write a good hand and keep accounts, I couldnt have brought myself to think that quill-driving and counting other people's money was a fit employment for a man. It's not what a man would like to do that he must do in this world: it's what he *can* do; and the only mortal thing I could do properly was to fight. There was plenty of money and plenty of honor and glory to be got among my acquaintance by fighting. So I challenged Ducket, and knocked him all to pieces in about ten minutes. I half killed him, because I didnt know my own strength and was afraid of him. I have been at the same work ever since; for I never was offered any other sort of job. I was training for a fight when I was down at Wiltstoken with that old fool Mellish. It came off the day you saw me at Clapham when I had such a bad eye. Wiltstoken did for me. With all my fighting, I'm no better than a baby at heart; and ever since I found out that my mother wasnt an angel, I have always had a notion that a real angel would turn up some day. You see, I never cared much about women. Bad as my mother was as far as being what you might call a parent went, she had something in her looks and manners that gave me a better idea of what a nice woman was like than I had of most things; and the girls I met in Australia and America seemed very small potatoes to me in

comparison with her. Besides, of course they were not ladies.
I was fond of Mrs Skene because she was good to me; and I
made myself agreeable, for her sake, to the girls that came
to see her; but in reality I couldnt stand them. Mrs Skene
said they were all setting their caps at me – women are
death on a crack fighter – but the more they tried it on the
less I liked them. It was no go: I could get on with the men
well enough, no matter how common they were; but the
snobbishness of my breed came out with regard to the
women. When I saw you that day at Wiltstoken walk out
of the trees and stand looking so quietly at me and Mellish,
and then go back out of sight without a word, I'm blest if I
didnt think you were the angel come at last. Then I met you
at the railway station and walked with you. You put the
angel out of my head quick enough; for an angel, after all, is
only a shadowy, childish notion – I believe it's all gammon
about there being any in heaven – but you gave me a better
idea than mamma of what a woman should be, and you
came up to that idea and went beyond it. I have been in love
with you ever since; and if I cant have you, I dont care
what becomes of me. I know I am a bad lot, and have always been one; but when I saw you taking pleasure in the
society of fellows just as bad as myself, I didnt see why I
should keep away when I was dying to come. I am no worse
than the dog-baker, anyhow. And hang it, Miss Lydia, I
dont want to brag; but there are clean ways and dirty ways
in prizefighting the same as in everything else; and I have
tried my best to keep in the clean ways. I never fought a
cross or struck a foul blow in my life; and I have never been
beaten, though I'm only a middle-weight, and have stood up
with the best fourteen stone men in the Colonies, the States,
or in England.'

Cashel ceased. As he sat eyeing her wistfully, Lydia, who
had been perfectly still, said bemusedly,

'I was more prejudiced than I knew. What will you think
of me when I tell you that your profession does not seem half
so shocking now that I know you to be the son of an artist,

and not a journeyman butcher or a laborer, as my cousin told me.'

'What!' exclaimed Cashel. 'That lantern-jawed fellow told you I was a butcher!'

'I did not mean to betray him, but, as I have already said, I am bad at keeping secrets. Mr Lucian Webber is my cousin and friend, and has done me many services. May I rest assured that he has nothing to fear from you?'

'He has no right to tell lies about me. He is sweet on you too: I twigged that at Wiltstoken. I have a good mind to let him know whether I am a butcher or not.'

'He did not say so. What he told me of you, as far as it went, is exactly confirmed by what you have said yourself. I happened to ask him to what class men of your calling usually belonged; and he said that they were laborers, butchers, and so forth. Do you resent that?'

'I see plainly enough that you wont let me resent it. I should like to know what else he said of me. But he was right enough. There are all sorts of blackguards in the ring; theres no use denying it. Since it's been made illegal, decent men wont go into it. All the same, it's not the fighting men, but the betting men, that bring discredit on it. I wish your cousin had held his confounded tongue.'

'I wish you had forestalled him by telling me the truth.'

'I wish I had, now. But whats the use of wishing? I didnt dare run the chance of losing you. See how soon you forbade me the house when you did find out.'

'It made little difference,' said Lydia gravely.

'You were always friendly to me,' said Cashel plaintively.

'More so than you were to me. You should not have deceived me. And now I think we had better part. I am glad to know your history; and I admit that you made perhaps the best choice that society offered you. I do not blame you.'

'But you give me the sack. Is that it?'

'What do you propose, Mr Cashel Byron? Is it to visit my house in the intervals of battering and maiming butchers and laborers?'

'No, it's not,' retorted Cashel. 'Youre very aggravating. I wont stay much longer in the ring now: my luck is too good to last. Anyhow, I shall have to retire soon, luck or no luck, because no one can match me. Even now theres nobody except Bill Paradise that pretends to be able for me; and I'll settle him in September if he really means business. After that, I'll retire. I expect to be worth ten thousand pounds then. Ten thousand pounds, I'm told, is the same as five hundred a year. Well, I suppose, judging from the style you keep here, that youre worth as much more, besides your place in the country; so if you will marry me we shall have a thousand a year between us. I dont know much of money matters; but at any rate we can live like fighting cocks on that much. Thats a straight and businesslike proposal, isnt it?'

'And if I refuse?' said Lydia, with some sternness.

'Then you may have the ten thousand pounds to do what you like with,' said Cashel despairingly. 'It wont matter what becomes of me. I wont go to the devil for you or any woman if I can help it; and I – but wheres the good of saying *if* you refuse? I know I dont express myself properly: I'm a bad hand at sentimentality; but if I had as much gab as any of those long-haired fellows on Friday, I couldnt be any fonder of you, or think more highly of you.'

'But you are mistaken as to the amount of my income.'

'That doesnt matter a bit. If you have more, why, the more the merrier. If you have less, or if you have to give up all your property when youre married, I will soon make another ten thousand to supply the loss. Only give me one good word and, by George, I'll fight the seven champions of Christendom, one down and tother come on, for five thousand a side each. Hang the money!'

'I am richer than you suppose,' said Lydia, unmoved. 'I cannot tell you exactly how much I possess; but my income is about forty thousand a year.'

'Forty thousand a year!' ejaculated Cashel. 'Holy Moses! I didnt think the Queen had as much as that.'

For a moment he felt nothing but mere astonishment. Then, comprehending the situation, he became very red. In a voice broken by mortification, he said, 'I see I have been making a fool of myself,' and took his hat and turned to go.

'It does not follow that you should go at once without a word,' said Lydia, betraying nervousness for the first time during the interview.

'Oh, thats all rot,' said Cashel. 'I may be a fool while my eyes are shut; but I'm sensible enough when theyre open. I have no business here. I wish to the Lord I had stayed in Australia.'

'Perhaps it would have been better,' said Lydia, troubled. 'But since we have met, it is useless to deplore it; and – Let me remind you of one thing. You have pointed out to me that I have made friends of men whose pursuits are no better than yours. I do not wholly admit that; but there is one respect in which they are on the same footing as you. They are all, as far as worldly gear is concerned, much poorer than I. Most of them, I fear, are poorer – much, *much* poorer than you are.'

Cashel looked up quickly with returning hope; but it lasted only a moment. He shook his head dejectedly.

'I am at least grateful to you,' she continued, 'because you have sought me for my own sake, knowing nothing of my wealth.'

'I should think not,' groaned Cashel. 'Your wealth may be a very fine thing for the other fellows; and I'm glad you have it, for your own sake. But it's a settler for me. So goodbye.'

'Goodbye,' said Lydia, almost as pale as he had now become, 'since you will have it so.'

'Since the devil will have it so,' said Cashel ruefully. 'It's no use wishing to have it any other way. The luck is against me. I hope, Miss Carew, that you'll excuse me for making such an ass of myself. It's all my blessed innocence: I never was taught any better.'

'I have no quarrel with you except on the old score of

hiding the truth from me; and I forgive you that — as far as the evil of it affects *me*. As for your declaration of attachment to me personally, I have received many similar ones that have flattered me less. But there are certain scruples between us. You will not court a woman a hundred-fold richer than yourself; and I will not entertain a prizefighter. My wealth frightens every man who is not a knave; and your profession frightens every woman who is not a fury.'

'Then you — Just tell me this,' said Cashel eagerly. 'Suppose I were a rich swell, and were not a —'

'No,' said Lydia, peremptorily interrupting him. 'I will suppose nothing but what is.'

Cashel relapsed into melancholy. 'If you only hadnt been kind to me!' he said. 'I think the reason I love you so much is that youre the only person that is not afraid of me. Other people are civil because they darent be otherwise to the cock of the ring. It's a lonely thing to be a champion. You knew nothing about that; and you knew I was afraid of you; and yet you were as good as gold.'

'It is also a lonely thing to be a very rich woman. People are afraid of my wealth, and of what they call my learning. We two have at least one experience in common. Now do me a great favor by going. We have nothing further to say.'

'I'll go in two seconds. But I dont believe much in you being lonely. Thats only fancy.'

'Perhaps so. Most feelings of this kind are only fancies.'

There was another pause. Then Cashel said,

'I dont feel half so downhearted as I did a minute ago. Are you sure that youre not angry with me?'

'Quite sure. Pray let me say goodbye.'

'And may I never see you again? Never at all? — world without end, Amen?'

'Never as the famous prizefighter. But if a day should come when Mr Cashel Byron will be something better worthy of his birth and nature, I will not forget an old friend. Are you satisfied now?'

Cashel's face began to glow, and the roots of his hair to

tingle. 'One thing more,' he said. 'If you meet me by chance in the street before that, will you give me a look? I dont ask for a regular bow, but just a look to keep me going?'

'I have no intention of cutting you,' said Lydia gravely. 'But do not place yourself purposely in my way.'

'Honor bright, I wont. I'll content myself with walking through that street in Soho occasionally. Now I'm off: I know youre in a hurry to be rid of me. So goodb— Stop a bit, though. Perhaps when that time you spoke of comes, you'll be married.'

'It is possible; but I am not likely to marry. How many more things have you to say, that you have no right to say?'

'Not one,' said Cashel, with a laugh that rang through the house. 'I never was happier in my life, though I'm crying inside all the time. I'll have a try for you yet. Goodbye. No,' he added, turning from her proffered hand: 'I darent touch it: I should eat you afterwards.' He made for the door, but turned on the threshold to say in a loud whisper: 'Mind, I'm engaged to you. I dont say youre engaged to me; but it's an engagement on my side.' And he ran out of the room.

In the hall was Bashville, pale and determined, waiting there to rush to the assistance of his mistress at her first summons. He had a poker concealed at hand. Having just heard a great laugh, and seeing Cashel come downstairs in high spirits, he stood stock still, not knowing what to think.

'Well, old chap,' said Cashel boisterously, slapping him on the shoulder: 'so youre alive yet. Is there any one in the dining-room?'

'No,' said Bashville.

'Theres a thick carpet there to fall soft on,' said Cashel, pulling Bashville into the room. 'Come along. Now shew me that little trick of yours again. Come! dont be afraid: I wont hit you. Down with me. Take care you dont knock my head against the fire-irons.'

'But –'

'But be hanged. You were spry enough at it before. Come!'

Bashville, after a moment's hesitation, seized Cashel, who immediately became grave and attentive, and remained imperturbably so whilst Bashville expertly threw him. He sat thinking for a moment on the hearthrug before he rose. '*I* see,' he said then, getting up. 'Now do it again.'

'But it makes such a row,' remonstrated Bashville.

'Only once more. There'll be no row this time.'

'Well, every man to his taste,' said Bashville, complying. But instead of throwing his man, he found himself wedged into a collar formed by Cashel's arms, the least constriction of which would have strangled him. Cashel again roared with laughter as he released him.

'Thats the way, aint it?' he said. 'You cant catch an old fox twice in the same trap. Do you know any more falls?'

'I do,' said Bashville; 'but I really cant shew them to you here. I shall get into trouble on account of the noise.'

'You come down to me whenever you have an evening out,' said Cashel, handing him a card, 'to that address, and shew me what you know; and I'll see what I can do with you. Theres the making of a man in you.'

'Youre very kind,' said Bashville, pocketing the card with a grin.

'And now let me give you a word of advice that will be of use to you as long as you live,' said Cashel impressively. 'You did a damned silly thing today. You threw a man down – a fighting man – and then stood looking at him like a fool, waiting for him to get up and kill you. If ever you do that again, fall on him as heavily as you can the instant he's off his legs. Double your elbow well under you, and see that it gets into a soft place. If he grabs it and turns you, make play with the back of your head. If he's altogether too big for you, put your knee on his throat as if by accident. But on no account stand and do nothing. It's flying in the face of Providence.'

Cashel emphasized each of these counsels by an impressive tap of his forefinger on one of Bashville's buttons. In conclusion, he nodded; opened the house-door; and walked away in buoyant spirits.

Lydia, standing near the library window, saw him go down the long front garden, and observed how his light alert step, and a certain gamesome assurance of manner, marked him off from a genteelly promenading middle-aged gentleman, a trudging workman, and a vigorously striding youth passing without. The railings that separated him from them reminded her of the admirable and dangerous creatures passing and repassing behind iron bars in the park yonder. But she exulted, in her quiet manner, in the thought that, dangerous as he was, she had no fear of him. When his cabman had found him and taken him off, she went to a private drawer in her desk, and took out her father's last letter. She sat for some time looking at it without unfolding it.

'It would be a strange thing, father,' she said, as if he were actually there to hear her, 'if your paragon should end as the wife of an illiterate prizefighter. I felt a pang of despair when he replied to my forty thousand pounds a year with an unanswerable goodbye. And now he is engaged to me.'

She locked up her father, as it were, in the drawer again, and rang the bell. Bashville appeared, somewhat perturbed.

'If Mr Byron calls again, admit him if I am at home.'

'Yes, madam.'

'Thank you.'

'Begging your pardon, madam, but may I ask has any complaint been made of me?'

'None.' Bashville was reluctantly withdrawing when she added, 'Mr Byron gave me to understand that you tried to prevent his entrance by force. You exposed yourself to needless risk by doing so; and you may make a rule in future that when people are importunate, and will not go away when asked, they had better come in until you get special instructions from me. I am not finding fault: on the contrary, I approve of your determination to carry out your orders; but under exceptional circumstances you may use your own discretion.'

'He shoved the door into my face; and I acted on the impulse of the moment, madam. I hope you will forgive the liberty I took in locking the door of the boudoir. He is older and heavier than I am, madam; and he has the advantage of being a professional. Else I should have stood my ground.'

'I am quite satisfied,' said Lydia a little coldly, as she left the room.

'How long you have been!' cried Alice, almost in hysterics, as Lydia entered. 'Is he gone? What were those dreadful noises? *Is* anything the matter?'

'Dancing and late hours are the matter,' said Lydia. 'The season is proving too much for you, Alice.'

'It is not the season: it is the man,' said Alice, with a sob.

'Indeed? I have been in conversation with the man for more than half an hour; and Bashville has been in actual combat with him; yet we are not in hysterics. You have been sitting here at your ease, have you not?'

'I am not in hysterics,' said Alice indignantly.

'So much the better,' said Lydia gravely, placing her hand on the forehead of Alice, who subsided with a sniff.

CHAPTER X

MRS BYRON, under her stage name of Adelaide Gisborne, was now, for the second time in her career, talked of in London, where she had been for many years almost forgotten. The metropolitan managers of her own generation had found that her success in new parts was very uncertain; that she was more capricious than the most petted favorites of the public; and that her invariable reply to a business proposal was that she detested the stage, and was resolved never to set foot upon it again. So they had managed to do without her for so long that the younger London playgoers knew her by reputation only as an old-fashioned actress who wandered through the provinces palming herself off on the ignorant inhabitants as a great artist, and boring them with performances of the plays of Shakespear. It suited Mrs Byron well to travel with the nucleus of a dramatic company from town to town, staying a week or two in each, and repeating half-a-dozen characters in which she was very effective, and which she knew so well that she never thought about them when she had anything else to think about. Most of the provincial populations received her annual visits with enthusiasm. Among them she found herself more excitingly applauded before the curtain, her authority more despotic behind it, her expenses smaller, and her gains greater than in London, for which she accordingly cared as little as London cared for her. As she grew older she made more money and spent less. When she complained to Cashel of the cost of his education, she was rich. Since he had relieved her of that cost, she had visited America, Egypt, India, and the colonies, and had grown constantly richer. From this great tour she had returned to England on the day when Cashel added the laurels of the Flying Dutchman to his trophies; and the next Sunday's paper had its sporting column full of the prowess of Cashel Byron, and its theatrical column full of the genius of Adelaide Gisborne. But she never read sporting columns, though he kept an eye on theatrical ones.

The managers who had formerly avoided Mrs Byron were by this time dead, bankrupt, or engaged in less hazardous pursuits. One of the actor-managers who succeeded them had lately restored Shakespear to popularity as signally as Cashel had restored the prize ring. Being anxious to produce the play of King John, he made the newly returned actress a tempting offer for the part of Constance, instigating some journalist friends of his at the same time to lament the decay of the grand school of acting, and to invent or republish anecdotes of Mrs Siddons.

This time Mrs Byron said nothing about detesting the stage. She had really detested it once; but by the time she was rich enough to give up the theatre she had worn that feeling out, and had formed a habit of acting which was as irksome to shake off as any other habit. She also found a certain satisfaction in making money with ease and certainty; and she had already made so much that she was beginning to trifle with plans of retirement, of playing in Paris, of taking a theatre in London, and other whims. The chief public glory of her youth had been a sudden triumph in London on the occasion of her first appearance on any stage; and she now felt a mind to repeat this and crown her career where it had begun. So she accepted the manager's offer, and even went the length of privately reading King John from beginning to end.

It happened that one of the most curious documents of the Plantagenet period was a scrap of vellum containing a fragment of a chronicle of Prince Arthur, with an illuminated portrait of his mother. It had been picked up for a trifling sum by the late Mr Carew, and was now in the possession of Lydia, to whom the actor-manager applied for leave to inspect it. Leave being readily given, he visited the house in Regent's Park, which he declared to be an inexhaustible storehouse of treasure. He deeply regretted, he said, that he could not shew the portrait to Miss Gisborne. Lydia replied that if Miss Gisborne would come and look at it, she should be very welcome. Two days later, at noon, Mrs Byron arrived and found Lydia alone. Alice had gone out, feeling that it was better not to meet an actress – one could never tell what they might have been.

The years that had elapsed since Mrs Byron's visit to Dr Moncrief had left no perceptible trace on her: indeed she looked younger now than on that occasion, because she had been at the trouble of putting on an artificial complexion. Her careless refinement of manner was so different from the studied dignity and anxious courtesy of the actor-manager, that Lydia could hardly think of them as belonging to the same profession. Her voice gave a subtle charm to her most commonplace remarks; and it was as different as possible from Cashel's rough tones. Yet Lydia was convinced by the first note of it that she was Cashel's mother. Besides, they had one another's chins.

Mrs Byron, coming to the point without delay, at once asked to see the picture. Lydia brought her to the library, where several portfolios were ready for inspection. The precious fragment of vellum was uppermost.

'Very interesting indeed,' said Mrs Byron, throwing it aside after one glance at it, and turning over some later prints, whilst Lydia, amused, looked on in silence. 'Ah,' she said: 'here is something that will suit me exactly.'

'Do you mean for Constance in King John?'

'Yes.'

'But silk was not made in Western Europe until three hundred years after Constance's death. And that drawing is a sketch of Marie de Medicis by Rubens.'

'Never mind,' said Mrs Byron smoothly. 'What does a dress three hundred years out of date matter when the woman inside it is seven hundred years out? What can be a greater anachronism than the death of Prince Arthur three months hence on the stage of the Panopticon Theatre? I am an artist giving life to a character in romance, I suppose:

certainly not a grown-up child playing at being somebody out of Mrs Markham's History of England. I wear whatever becomes me. I cannot act when I feel dowdy.'

'But what will the manager say?'

'To me? Nothing,' said Mrs Byron; and her calm implied that he had better not. 'Besides, you do not suppose he is a learned person, do you? And as he will wear a suit of armor obviously made the other day in Birmingham, why – !' Mrs Byron shrugged her shoulders, and did not take sufficient interest in the manager's opinion to finish her sentence.

'Is this part of Lady Constance a favorite one of yours?'

'Troublesome, my dear,' said Mrs Byron absently. 'The men look ridiculous in it; and it does not draw.'

'No doubt,' said Lydia, watching her face. 'But I spoke rather of your personal feeling towards the character. Do you, for instance, like portraying maternal tenderness on the stage?'

'Maternal tenderness,' said Mrs Byron with sudden nobleness, 'is far too sacred a thing to be mimicked. Have you any children?'

'No,' said Lydia demurely. 'I am not married.'

'You should get a baby: it will do you good, physically and morally. Maternity is an education in itself.'

'Do you think it suits every woman?'

'Undoubtedly. Without exception. Only think, dear Miss Carew, of the infinite patience with which you must tend a child – of the necessity of seeing with its little eyes and with your own wise ones at the same time – of bearing without a reproach the stabs it innocently inflicts – of forgiving its hundred little selfishnesses – of living in continual fear of wounding its exquisite sensitiveness, or rousing its bitter resentment of injustice and caprice. Think of how you must watch yourself; check yourself; exercise and develop everything in you that can help to attract and retain the most jealous love in the world! Believe me, it is a priceless trial to be a mother. It is a royal compensation for having been born a woman.'

'Nevertheless,' said Lydia, 'I wish I had been born a man. Since you seem to have thought deeply on these matters, I should like to ask you a question. Do you not think that the acquirement of an art demanding years of careful self-study and training – such as yours, for example – is also of great educational value? Almost as good a discipline as motherhood, is it not?'

'Nonsense!' said Mrs Byron decidedly. 'People come into the world ready-made. I went on the stage when I was eighteen, and succeeded at once. Had I known anything of the world, or been four years older, I should have been weak, awkward, timid, and flat: it would have taken me twelve years to crawl to the front. But I was young, passionate, beautiful, and indeed terrible; for I had run away from home two years before, and been cruelly deceived. I learned the business of the stage as easily and thoughtlessly as a child learns a prayer: the rest came to me by nature. I have seen others spend years in struggling with bad voices, uncouth figures, and diffidence; besides a dozen defects that existed only in their imaginations. Their struggles may have educated them; but had they possessed sufficient genius they would have needed neither struggle nor education. Perhaps that is why geniuses are such erratic people, and mediocrities so respectable. I grant you that I was very limited when I first came out: I was absolutely incapable of comedy. But I never took any trouble about it; and by-and-by, when I began to mature a little, and see the absurdity of most of the things I had been making a fuss about, comedy came to me unsought, as romantic tragedy had come before. I suppose it would have come just the same if I had been laboring to acquire it, except that I should have attributed its arrival to my own exertions. Most of the laborious people think they have made themselves what they are – much as if a child should think it had made itself grow.'

'You are the first artist I ever met,' said Lydia, 'who did

not claim art as the most laborious of all avocations. They all deny the existence of genius, and attribute everything to work.'

'Of course one picks up a great deal from experience; and there is plenty of work on the stage. But it is my genius which enables me to pick up things, and to work on the stage instead of in a kitchen or laundry.'

'You must be very fond of your profession.'

'I do not mind it now: I have shrunk to fit it. I began because I couldnt help myself; and I go on because, being an old woman, I have nothing else to do. Bless me, how I hated it after the first month! I must retire soon now. People are growing weary of me.'

'I doubt that. I am bound to assume that you are an old woman, since you say so; but you must be aware, flattery apart, that you hardly seem to have reached your prime yet.'

'I might be your mother, my dear. I might be a grandmother. Perhaps I am.' There was a plaintive tone in the last sentence; and Lydia seized the opportunity.

'You spoke of maternity then from experience, Miss Gisborne?'

'I have one son – a son who was sent to me in my eighteenth year.'

'I hope he inherits his mother's genius and personal grace.'

'I am sure I dont know,' said Mrs Byron pensively. 'He was a perfect devil. I fear I shock you, Miss Carew; but really I did everything for him that the most devoted mother could; and yet he ran away from me without making a sign of farewell. Little wretch!'

'Boys do cruel things sometimes in a spirit of adventure,' said Lydia, watching her visitor's face narrowly.

'It was not that. It was his temper, which was ungovernable. He was sulky and vindictive. It is quite impossible to love a sulky child. I kept him constantly near me when he was a tiny creature; and when he grew too big for that I spent oceans of money on his education. All in vain! He never shewed any feeling towards me except a sense of injury that no kindness could remove. And he had nothing to complain of. Never was there a worse son.'

Lydia remained silent and grave. Mrs Byron looked beside rather than at her. Suddenly she added,

'My poor darling Cashel' (Lydia repressed a start), 'what a shame to talk of you so! You see I love him in spite of his wickedness.' Mrs Byron took out her pocket-handkerchief; and Lydia was for a moment alarmed by the prospect of tears. But Miss Gisborne only blew her nose with perfect composure, and rose to take her leave. Lydia, who, apart from her interest in Cashel's mother, was attracted and amused by the woman herself, induced her to stay for luncheon, and presently discovered from her conversation that she had read much romance of the Werther sort in her youth, and had, since then, employed her leisure in reading every book that came in her way without regard to its quality. Her acquirements were so odd, and her character so unreasonable, that Lydia, whose knowledge was unusually well organized, and who was eminently reasonable, concluded that she was a woman of genius. For Lydia knew the vanity of her own attainments, and believed herself to be merely a patient and well-taught plodder. Mrs Byron happening to be pleased with the house, the luncheon, and the hostess's intelligent listening, her natural charm became so intensified by her good humor that even Lydia was quite fascinated, and began to wonder what its force might have been if some influence – that of a lover, for instance – had ever made Mrs Byron ecstatically happy. She surprised herself at last in the act of speculating whether she could ever make Cashel love her as his father must, for a time at least, have loved Mrs Byron.

When the visitor was gone, Lydia considered whether she was justified in keeping these two apart. It seemed plain that at present Cashel was a disgrace to his mother, and had better remain hidden from her. But if he should for any reason abandon his ruffianly pursuits, as she had urged him to do, then she could bring about a meeting between them; and the truant's mother might take better care of him in the future, besides making him pecuniarily independent of prizefighting. This led Lydia to ask herself what new profession Cashel could adopt, and what probability there was of his getting on with his mother any better than formerly. No satisfactory answer was forthcoming. So she went back to the likelihood of his reforming himself for her sake. On this theme her imagination carried her so far from all reasonable conjecture, that she was shaking her head at her own folly when Bashville appeared and announced Lord Worthington, who came into the room with Alice. Lydia had not seen him since her discovery of the true position of the tenant he had introduced to her; and he was consequently a little afraid to meet her. To cover his embarrassment, he began to talk quickly on a number of commonplace topics. But when some time had passed, he began to shew signs of fresh uneasiness. He looked at his watch, and said,

'I dont wish to hurry you, ladies; but this affair commences at three.'

'What affair?' said Lydia, who was privately wondering why he had come.

'The assault-at-arms. King Whatshisname's affair. Webber told me he had arranged for us to go together.'

'Oh, you have come to take us there. I had forgotten. Did I promise to go?'

'Webber said so. He was to have taken you himself; but he's busy, and has done a good thing for me and put me in his place. He said you particularly wanted to go, hang him!'

Lydia rose promptly and sent for her carriage. 'There is no hurry,' she said. 'We can easily drive to St James's Hall in twenty minutes.'

'But we have to go to Islington, to the Agricultural Hall. There will be cavalry charges, and all sorts of fun.'

'Bless me!' said Lydia. 'Will there be any boxing?'

'Yes,' said Lord Worthington, reddening, but unabashed. 'Lots of it. It will be by gentlemen, though, except perhaps one bout to shew the old king our professional form.'

'Then excuse me whilst I go for my hat,' said Lydia, leaving the room. Alice had gone some time before to make a complete change in her dress, as the occasion was one for display of that kind.

'You look awfully fetching, Miss Goff,' Lord Worthington said as he followed them into the carriage. Alice did not deign to reply, but tossed her head superbly, and secretly considered whether people would, on comparison, think her overdressed or Lydia underdressed. Lord Worthington thought they both looked their best, and reflected for several seconds on the different styles of different women, and how what would suit one would not do at all for another. It seemed to him that Miss Carew's presence made him philosophical.

The Agricultural Hall struck Alice at first sight as an immense tan-strewn barn round which heaps of old packing cases had been built into racecourse stands, scantily decorated with red cloth and a few flags. Lord Worthington had secured front seats in one of these balconies. Just below were the palisades, ornamented at intervals with evergreens in tubs, and pressed against from without by the shilling crowd. Alice remarked that it was little to the credit of the management that these people should be placed so close beneath her that she could hear their conversation; but as Lydia did not seem to share her disgust, she turned her attention to the fashionable part of the audience. On the opposite side of the arena the balconies seemed like beds of flowers in bloom: blacknesses formed here and there by the hats and coats of gentlemen representing the interspaces of clay. In the midst of the flowers was a gaudy dais, on which a powerfully built black gentleman sat in a raised chair, his majestic impassivity contrasting with the overt astonishment with which a row of attendant chiefs grinned and gaped on either side of him.

'What a pity we are not nearer the king!' said Alice. 'I can hardly see the dear old fellow.'

'You will find these the best seats for seeing the assault. It will be all right,' said Lord Worthington.

Lydia's attention was caught by something guilty in his manner. Following a furtive glance of his, she saw in the arena, not far from her, an enclosure about twenty feet square, made with ropes and stakes. It was unoccupied; and near it were a few chairs, a basin, and a sponge.

'What is that?' she asked.

'That! Oh, thats the ring.'

'It is not a ring. It is a square.'

'They call it the ring. They have succeeded in squaring the circle.'

A piercing bugle call rang out; and a troop of cavalry trotted into the arena. Lydia found it pleasant enough to sit lazily admiring the horses and men, and comparing the members of the Olympian Club, who appeared when the soldiers retired, to the marble gods of Athens, and to the Bacchus or David of Michael Angelo. They fell short of the Greek statues in tranquil refinement, and of the Italian in heroic energy as they vaulted over a wooden horse, and swung upon horizontal bars, each cheapening the exploits of his forerunner by outdoing them. Lord Worthington, who soon grew tired of this, whispered that when all that rubbish was over, a fellow would cut a sheep in two with a sword, after which there would be some boxing.

'Do you mean to say,' said Lydia indignantly, 'that they are going to turn a sheep loose and hunt it on horseback with swords?'

Lord Worthington laughed and said yes; but it presently appeared that by a sheep was meant a lean carcass of mutton. A stalwart sergeant cut it in half as a climax to slicing lemons, bars of lead, and silk handkerchiefs; and the audience, accustomed to see much more disgusting sights in butchers' shops, liberally applauded him.

Two gentlemen of the Olympian Club now entered the

inclosure which Lord Worthington called the ring. After shaking hands with one another as well as their huge padded gloves permitted, they hugged themselves with their right arms as if there were some danger of their stomachs falling out if not held tightly in; and danced round one another, throwing out and retracting their left fists like pawing horses. They were both, as Lydia learned from the announcement of their names and achievements by the master of the ceremonies, amateur champions. She thought their pawing and dancing ridiculous; and when they occasionally rushed together and scuffled, she could distinguish nothing of the leading off, stopping, ducking, countering, guarding, and getting away to which Lord Worthington enthusiastically invited her attention, and which elicited alternate jeers and applause from the shilling audience below. When, at the expiration of three minutes, the two dropped supine into chairs at opposite corners of the ring as if they had sustained excessive fatigue, she would have laughed outright if they had not reminded her of Cashel trying to recover himself in her library. At the end of a minute, some one hoarsely cried 'Time!' and they rose and repeated their previous performance for three minutes more. Another minute of rest followed; and then the dancing and pawing proceeded for four minutes, after which the champions again shook hands and left the arena.

'And is that all?' said Lydia.

'Thats all,' said Lord Worthington. 'It's the most innocent thing in the world, and the prettiest.'

'It does not strike me as being pretty,' said Lydia; 'but it seems as innocent as inanity can make it.' Her mind misgave her that she had ignorantly and unjustly reproached Cashel Byron with ferocity merely because he practised this harmless exercise.

The show progressed through several phases of skilled violence. Besides single combats between men armed in various fashions, there were tilts, tent-peggings, drilling and singlestick practice by squads of British tars, who were loudly cheered, and more boxing and vaulting by members of the club. Lydia's attention soon began to wander from the arena. Looking down at the crowd outside the palisades, she saw a small man whom she vaguely remembered, though his face was turned from her. In conversation with him was a powerful man dressed in a yellow tweed suit and green scarf. He had a coarse strong voice, and his companion a shrill mean one, so that their remarks could be heard by an attentive listener above the confused noise of the crowd.

'Do you admire that man?' said Lord Worthington, following Lydia's gaze.

'No. Is he anybody in particular?'

'He was a great man once – in the days of the giants. He was champion of England. He has a special interest for us as the teacher of a mutual friend of ours.'

'Please name him,' said Lydia, intending that the mutual friend should be named.

'Ned Skene,' said Lord Worthington, taking her to mean the man below. 'He has done so well in the colonies that he has indulged himself and his family with a trip to England. His arrival made quite a sensation in this country: last week he had a crowded benefit, at which he sparred with our mutual friend and knocked him about like a baby. Our mutual friend behaved very well on the occasion in letting himself be knocked about. You see he could have killed old Skene if he had tried in earnest.'

'Is that Skene?' said Lydia, looking at him with an earnest interest that astonished and delighted Lord Worthington. 'Ah! Now I recognize the man with him. He is one of my tenants at the Warren Lodge – I believe I am indebted to you for the introduction.'

'Mellish the trainer?' said Lord Worthington, looking a little foolish. 'So it is. What a lovely bay that lancer has! – the second from the far end.'

But Lydia would not look at the lancer's horse. 'Paradise!' she heard Skene exclaim just then with scornful incredulity. 'Aint it likely?' It occurred to her that if he was alluding to his own chance of arriving there, it was not likely.

'Less likely things have happened,' said Mellish. 'I wont say that Cashel Byron is getting stale; but I will say that his luck is too good to last; and I know for a fact that he's gone quite melancholy of late.'

'Melancholy be blowed!' said Skene. 'What should he go melancholy for?'

'Oh, I know,' said Mellish reticently.

'You know a lot,' retorted Skene with contempt. 'I spose you mean the young 'oman he's always talking to my missus about.'

'I mean a young woman he aint likely to get. One of the biggest swells in England – a little un with a face like the inside of a oyster shell, that he met down at Wiltstoken, where I trained him to fight the Flying Dutchman. He went right off his training after he met her – wouldnt do anything I told him. I made so cock sure he'd be licked that I hedged every penny I had laid on him except twenty pound I got a flat to bet agen him down at the fight after I changed my mind. Curse that woman! I lost a hundred pound by her.'

'And serve you right too, you old stoopid. You was wrong then; and youre wrong now, with your blessed Paradise!'

'Paradise has never been beat yet.'

'No more has my boy.'

'Well, we'll see.'

'We'll see! I tell you Ive seed for myself. Ive seed Billy Paradise spar; and it aint boxing: it's ruffianing: thats what it is. Ruffianing! Why, my old missus has more science.'

'Mebbe she has,' said Mellish. 'But look at the men he's licked that were chock full of science. Shepstone, clever as he is, only won a fight from him by claiming a foul, because Billy lost his temper and spiked him. Thats the worst of Billy: he cant keep his feelings in. But no fine-lady sparrer can stand afore that ugly rush of his. Do you think he'll care for Cashel's showy long shots? Not he: he'll just take em on that mahogany nut of his, and give him back one o' them smashers that he knocked out Dick Weeks with.'

'I'll lay you any money he dont. If he does, I'll go back into the ring myself, and bust his head off for it.' And Skene, very angry, heaped epithets on Paradise until he became so excited that Mellish had to soothe him by partially retracting his forebodings, and asking how Cashel had been of late.

'He's not been taking care of himself as he oughter,' said Skene gloomily. 'He's shewing the London fashions to the missus and Fanny: theyre here in the three-and-sixpenny seats, among the swells. Theatres every night; and walks every day to see the Queen drive through the park, or the like. My Fan likes to have him with her on account of his being such a gentleman: she dont hardly think her own father not good enough to walk down Piccadilly with. Wants me to put on a black coat, and make a parson of my-self. The missus just idolizes him. She thinks the boy far too good for the young 'oman you was speaking of, and tells him that she's letting on not to care for him only to raise her price, just as I used to pretend to be getting beat, to set the flats betting agin me. The women always made a pet of him. In Melbourne it wasnt what *I* liked for dinner: it was always what the boy 'ud like, and when it 'ud please him to have it. I'm blest if I usent to have to put him up to ask for a thing when I wanted it myself. And you tell me that thats the lad thats going to let Billy Paradise lick him, I spose. Walker!'

Lydia, with Mrs Byron's charm fresh upon her, wondered what manner of woman this Mrs Skene could be who had supplanted her in the affections of her son, and yet was no more than a prizefighter's old missus. Evidently she was not one to turn a young man from a career in the ring. The theme of Cashel's occupation and the chances of his quitting it ran away with Lydia's attention. She sat with her eyes fixed on the arena, without seeing the soldiers, swordsmen, or athletes who were busy there. Her mind wandered further and further from the place; and the chattering of the people resolved itself into a distant hum and was forgotten.

Suddenly she became conscious of a dreadful looking man coming towards her across the arena. His face had the surface and color of blue granite: his protruding jaws and retreating forehead were like those of an orang-utan. She started from her reverie with a shiver, and, recovering her hearing as well as her vision of external things, heard a burst of applause from a few persons below greeting this apparition. The man grinned ferociously; placèd one hand on a stake of the ring; and vaulted over the ropes. Lydia remarked that, excepting his hideous head and enormous hands and feet, he was a well-made man, with loins and shoulders that shone in the light, and gave him an air of great strength and activity.

'Aint he a picture?' she heard Mellish exclaim ecstatically. ' *Theres* condition for you!'

'Ah!' said Skene disparagingly. 'But aint *he* the gentleman! Just look at him. It's like the Prince of Wales walking down Pall Mall.'

Lydia looked again, and saw Cashel Byron, exactly as she had seen him for the first time in the elm vista at Wiltstoken, approaching the ring, with the indifferent air of a man going through some tedious public ceremony.

'A god coming down to compete with a gladiator,' whispered Lord Worthington eagerly. 'Isnt it, Miss Carew? Apollo and the satyr! You must admit that our mutual friend is a splendid looking fellow. If he could go into society like that, by Jove, the women – '

'Hush,' said Lydia, as if his words were intolerable.

Cashel did not vault over the ropes. He stepped through them languidly, and, rejecting the proffered assistance of a couple of officious friends, drew on a boxing glove fastidiously, like an exquisite preparing for a fashionable promenade. Having thus muffled his left hand so as to make it useless for the same service to his right, he dipped his fingers into the other glove, gripped it between his teeth, and dragged it on with the action of a tiger tearing its prey. Lydia shuddered again.

'Bob Mellish,' said Skene: 'I'll lay you twenty to one he stops that rush that you think so much of. Come: twenty to one!'

Mellish shook his head. Then the master of the ceremonies, pointing to the men in succession, shouted, 'Paradise: a professor. Cashel Byron: a professor. Time!'

Cashel now looked at Paradise, of whose existence he had not before seemed to be aware. The two men advanced towards the centre of the ring; shook hands at arm's length; cast off each other's grasp suddenly; fell back a step; and began to move warily round from left to right like a pair of panthers.

'I think they might learn manners from the gentlemen, and shake hands cordially,' said Alice, trying to appear unconcerned, but oppressed by a vague dread of Cashel.

'Thats the traditional manner,' said Lord Worthington. 'It's done that way to prevent one from pulling the other over, and hitting him with the disengaged hand before he could get loose.'

'What abominable treachery!' exclaimed Lydia.

'It's never done, you know,' said Lord Worthington apologetically. 'It wouldnt be any good, because you cant use your left hand effectively that way.'

Lydia turned away from him, and gave all her attention to the boxers. Of the two, Paradise shocked her least. She saw that he was nervous and conscious of a screwed-up condition as to his courage; but his sly grin implied a wild sort of good humor, and seemed to promise the spectators that he would shew them some fun presently. Cashel watched his movements with a relentless vigilance and a sidelong glance in which, to Lydia's apprehension, there was something infernal.

Suddenly the eyes of Paradise lit up: he lowered his head; made a rush; baulked himself purposely: and darted at

Cashel. There was a sound like the pop of a champagne cork, after which Cashel was seen undisturbed in the middle of the ring, and Paradise, flung against the ropes and trying to grin at his discomfiture, shewed his white teeth through a mask of blood.

'Beautiful!' cried Skene with emotion. 'Beautiful! There aint but me and my boy in the world can give the upper cut like that! I wish I could see my old missus's face now! This is nuts to her.'

'Let us go away,' said Alice.

'That was a very different blow to any the gentlemen gave,' said Lydia, without heeding her, to Lord Worthington. 'The man is bleeding horribly.'

'It's only his nose,' said Lord Worthington. 'He's used to it.'

'Look at that!' chuckled Skene. 'My boy's followed him up to the ropes; and he means to keep him there. Let him rush now if he can. See what it is to have a good judgment!'

Mellish shook his head again despondingly. The remaining minutes of the round were unhappy ones for Paradise. He struck viciously at his opponent's ribs; but Cashel stepped back just out of his reach, and then returned with extraordinary swiftness and dealt him blows from which, with the ropes behind him, he had no room to retreat, and which he was too slow to stop or avoid. His attempts to reach his enemy's face were greatly to the disadvantage of his own; for Cashel's blows were never so tremendous as when he turned his head deftly out of harm's way, and met his advancing foe with a counter hit. There was no chivalry and no mercy in him; but his grace could not have been surpassed by his mother. He revelled in the hardness of his hitting, and gathered fresh vigor as his gloves resounded on Paradise's face or seemed to go almost through his body. The better sort among the spectators were disgusted by the sight; for as Paradise bled profusely, and as his blood smeared the gloves, and the gloves smeared the heads and bodies of both combatants, they were soon stained with it from their waists upward. The managers held a whispered consultation as to whether the sparring exhibition had not better be stopped; but they decided to let it proceed on seeing the African king, who had watched the whole entertainment up to the present without displaying the least interest, now raise his hands and clap them with delight.

'Billy dont look half pleased with hisself,' observed Mellish, as the two boxers sat down for the minute's respite. 'He looks just like he did when he spiked Shepstone.'

'What does spiking mean?' said Lydia.

'Treading on a man's foot with spiked boots,' replied Lord Worthington. 'Dont be alarmed: they have no spikes in their shoes today. And dont look at me like that, Miss Carew. It's not my fault that they do such things.'

Time was called; and the pugilists, who had by dint of sponging been made somewhat cleaner, rose with mechanical promptitude at the sound. They had hardly advanced two steps, when Cashel, though his adversary seemed far out of his reach, struck him on the forehead with such force as to stagger him, and then jumped back laughing. Paradise rushed forward; but Cashel eluded him, and fled round the ring, looking back derisively over his shoulder. Paradise now dropped all pretence of good humor. With reckless ferocity he dashed in; endured a startling blow without flinching; and fought savagely at close quarters. For a moment the falling of their blows reminded Lydia of the rush of raindrops against a pane in a sudden gust of wind. The next moment Cashel was away; and Paradise, whose blood was again flowing, was trying to repeat his manœuvre, to be met this time by a blow that brought him upon one knee. He had scarcely risen when Cashel sprang at him and drove him once more against the ropes with four dazzlingly rapid blows; but this time, with tigerish coquetry, released him by again running away prettily in the manner of a child at play. Paradise, with foam as well as blood at his lips, uttered a howl, and tore off his gloves. There was a shout of protest from the audience; and Cashel, warned by it, tried to get off his gloves in turn. But Paradise was upon him, before he could accomplish this; and the two men laid hold of one another amid a great clamor: Lord Worthington and others rising and excitedly shouting, 'Against rules! No wrestling!' followed by a roar of indignation as Paradise was seen to seize Cashel's shoulder in his teeth as they struggled for the throw. Lydia, for the first time in her life, screamed. Then she saw Cashel, his face fully as fierce as his foe's, get his arm about Paradise's neck; lift him as a coal-heaver lifts a sack; and fling him over his back, heels over head, to the ground, where he instantly dropped on him with his utmost weight and impetus. The two were at once separated by a crowd of managers, umpires, policemen and others who had rushed towards the ring when Paradise had taken off his gloves. A distracting wrangle followed. Skene had climbed over the palisade, and was hurling oaths, threats, and epithets at Paradise, who, unable to stand without assistance, was trying to lift his leaden eyelids and realize what had happened to him. A dozen others, encouraging him to sit up, remonstrating with him on his conduct, or trying to pacify Skene, only added to the confusion. Cashel, on the other side, raged at the managers, who were reminding him that the rules of glove exhibitions did not allow wrestling and throwing.

'Rules be damned!' Lydia heard him shouting. 'He bit me; and I'll throw him to – ' Then everybody spoke at once; and she could only conjecture where he would throw him to. He seemed to have no self-control: Paradise, when he came to himself, behaved better. Lord Worthington descended into the ring, and tried to calm the hubbub; but Cashel shook his hand fiercely from his arm; menaced a manager who attempted to call him sternly to order; frantically pounded his wounded shoulder with his clenched fist; and so outswore and outwrangled them all that even Skene began to urge that there had been enough fuss made. Then Lord Worthington whispered a word more; and

Cashel suddenly subsided, pale and ashamed, and sat down on a chair in his corner as if to hide himself. Five minutes afterwards, he stept out from the crowd with Paradise, and shook hands with him amid much cheering. Cashel was the humbler of the two. He did not raise his eyes to the balcony once; and he seemed in a hurry to retire. But he was intercepted by an officer in uniform, accompanied by a black chief, who came to conduct him to the dais and present him to the African king: an honor he was not permitted to decline.

The king informed him, through an interpreter, that he had been unspeakably gratified by what he had just witnessed, and expressed great surprise that Cashel, notwithstanding his prowess, was neither in the army nor in parliament. He also offered to provide him with three handsome wives if he would come out to Africa in his suite. Cashel was much embarrassed; but he came off with credit, thanks to the interpreter, who was accustomed to invent appropriate speeches for the king on public occasions, and was kind enough to invent an equally appropriate one for Cashel on this.

Meanwhile, Lord Worthington returned to his place. 'It's all settled now,' he said to Lydia. 'Byron shut up when I told him his aristocratic friends were looking at him; and Paradise has been so bullied that he is crying in a corner downstairs. He has apologized; but he still maintains that he can beat our mutual friend without the gloves; and his backers apparently think so too; for it is understood that they are to fight in the autumn for a thousand a side.'

'To fight! Then he has no intention of giving up his profession?'

'No!' said Lord Worthington, astonished. 'Why on earth should he give it up? Paradise's money is as good as in his pocket. You have seen what he can do.'

'I have seen enough. Alice: I am ready to go as soon as you are.'

Miss Carew returned to Wiltstoken next day. Miss Goff

remained in London to finish the season in charge of a friendly lady who, having married off all her own daughters, was willing to set to work again to marry Alice sooner than remain idle.

CHAPTER XI

ALICE was more at her ease during the remnant of the season. Though she had been proud of her connection with Lydia, she had always felt eclipsed in her presence; and now that Lydia was gone, the pride remained and the sense of inferiority was forgotten. Her freedom emboldened and improved her. She even began to consider her own judgment a safer guide in the affairs of everyday than the example of her patroness. Had she not been right in declaring Cashel Byron an ignorant and common man when Lydia, in spite of her warning, had actually invited him to visit them? And now all the newspapers were confirming the opinion she had been trying to impress on Lydia for months past. On the evening of the assault-at-arms, the newsmen had shouted through the streets, 'Disgraceful scene between two pugilists at Islington in the presence of the African king.' Next day the principal journals commented on the recent attempt to revive the brutal pastime of prizefighting; accused the authorities of conniving at it; and called on them to put it down at once with a strong hand. 'Unless,' said a Nonconformist organ, 'this plague spot be rooted out from our midst, it will no longer be possible for our missionaries to pretend that England is the fount of the Gospel of Peace.' Alice collected these papers, and forwarded them to Wiltstoken.

On this subject one person at least shared her bias. Whenever she met Lucian Webber, they talked about Cashel, invariably coming to the conclusion that though the oddity of his behavior had gratified Lydia's unfortunate taste for eccentricity, she had never regarded him with serious interest, and would not now, under any circumstances, renew her intercourse with him. Lucian found little solace in these conversations, and generally suffered from a vague sense of meanness after them. Yet next time they met he would drift into discussing Cashel over again; and he always rewarded Alice for the admirable propriety of her views by dancing at least three times with her when dancing was the business of the evening. The dancing was still less congenial than the conversation. Lucian danced stiffly and unskilfully. Alice, whose muscular power and energy were superior to anything of the kind that Mr Mellish could artificially produce, longed for swift motion and violent exercise. Waltzing with Lucian was like carrying a stick round the room in the awkward fashion in which Punch carries his baton. In spite of her impression that he was a man of unusually correct morals and high political importance, greatly to be considered in private life because he was Miss Carew's cousin, it was hard to spend quarter-hours with him that were asked for by some of the best dancers in her set.

She began to tire of the subject of Cashel and Lydia. She began to tire of Lucian's rigidity. She began to tire exceedingly of the vigilance she had to maintain constantly over her own manners and principles. Somehow, this vigilance defeated itself; for she one evening overheard a lady of rank (who meant her to overhear) speak of her as a stuck-up country girl. For a week afterwards she did not utter a word or make a movement in society without first considering whether it could by any malicious observer be considered rustic or stuck-up. But the more she strove to attain perfect propriety of demeanor, the more odious did she seem to herself, and, she inferred, to others. She longed for Lydia's secret of always doing the right thing at the right moment, even when defying precedent. Sometimes she blamed the dullness of the people she met. It was impossible not to be stiff with them. When she chatted with an entertaining man, who made her laugh and forget herself for a while, she was conscious afterwards of having been at her best with him. But she saw that those whose manners she most coveted were pleasantly at their ease even in stupid society. She began to fear at last that she was naturally disqualified by her comparatively humble birth from acquiring the well-bred air she envied.

One day she conceived a doubt whether Lucian was so safe an authority and example in matters of personal deportment as she had hitherto believed. He could not dance: his conversation was priggish: it was impossible to feel at ease when speaking to him. Was it courageous to stand in awe of his opinion? Was it courageous to stand in awe of anybody? Alice closed her lips proudly and began to feel defiant. Then a reminiscence, which had never before failed to rouse indignation in her, made her laugh. She recalled the scandalous spectacle of the stiff, upright Lucian doubled up in Mrs Hoskyn's gilded armchair to illustrate the prize-fighter's theory of effort defeating itself. After all, what was that caressing touch of Cashel's hand in comparison with the tremendous rataplan he had beaten on the ribs of Paradise? Could it be true that effort defeated itself – in personal behavior, for instance? A ray of the truth that underlay Cashel's grotesque experiment was flickering in her mind as she asked herself that question. She thought a good deal about it; and one afternoon, when she looked in at four at-homes in succession, she studied the behavior of the other guests from a new point of view, comparing the most mannered with the best mannered, and her recent self with both. The result half convinced her that she had been occupied during her first London season in displaying, at great pains, a very unripe self-consciousness – or, as her conscience phrased it, in making an insufferable fool of herself.

Then came an invitation or two from the further west – South Kensington and Bayswater; and here she struck the deeper social stratum of the great commercial middle class, with its doctors, lawyers and clergy. She found it all a huge caricature of herself – a society ashamed of itself, afraid to be itself, suspecting other people of being itself and pretending to despise them for it, and so stifling and starving itself that individuals with courage enough to play the piano on Sunday were automatically extruded by the pressure and shot on to a Bohemian debateable land where they amused themselves by trifling with the fine arts. Alice recognized her own class, but did not on that account spare it the ridicule which, from her point of view as one of Miss Carew's superior set, was due to its insipid funereal dancing, its flagrantly studied manners, its ostentation, its voice and accent warped by the strain of incessant pretending, its habitual insolence to servants, its idolatrous deference to rank, its Sabbatarianism, and a dozen other manifestations of what Alice, not feeling in any way concerned to find the root of the matter, summed up as its vulgarity.

Shortly afterwards, she met Lucian at a dance. He came late, as usual, and gravely asked whether he might have the pleasure of dancing with her. This form of address he never varied. To his surprise, she made some difficulty about granting the favor, and eventually offered him 'the second extra'. He bowed. Just then a young man came up, and, remarking that he thought this was his turn, bore Alice away. Lucian smiled indulgently, thinking that though Alice's manners were wonderfully good, considering her antecedents, yet she occasionally betrayed a lower tone than that which he sought to exemplify in his own person.

When his own turn came, and they had gone round the room twice to the strains of the second extra, they stopped – Alice was always willing to rest during a waltz with Lucian; and he asked her whether she had heard from Lydia.

'You always ask me that,' she replied. 'Lydia never writes except when she has something particular to say, and then only a few lines.'

'Precisely. But she might have had something particular to say since we last met.'

'She hasnt had,' said Alice, provoked by an almost arch smile from him.

'She will be glad to hear that I have at last succeeded in recovering possession of the Warren Lodge from its undesirable tenants.'

'I thought they went long ago,' said Alice indifferently.

'The men have not been there for a month or more. The difficulty was to get them to remove their property. However, we are rid of them now. The only relic of their occupation is a bible, with half the leaves torn out, and the rest scrawled with records of bets, receipts for sudorific and other medicines, and a mass of unintelligible memoranda. One inscription, in faded ink, runs "To Robert Mellish, from his affectionate mother, with her sincere hope that he may ever walk in the ways of this book." I am afraid that hope was not fulfilled.'

'How wicked of him to tear a bible!' said Alice seriously. Then she laughed, and added, 'I know I shouldnt; but I cant help it.'

'The incident strikes me rather as being pathetic,' said Lucian, who liked to shew that he was not deficient in sensibility. 'One can picture the innocent faith of the poor woman in her boy's future. If she could only have foreseen!'

'Inscriptions in books are like inscriptions on tombstones,' said Alice disparagingly. 'They dont mean much.'

'I am glad that these men have no further excuse for going to Wiltstoken. It was certainly most unfortunate that Lydia should have made the acquaintance of one of them.'

'So you have said at least fifty times,' replied Alice deliberately. 'I believe you are jealous of that poor boxer.'

Lucian became quite red. Alice trembled at her own audacity, but kept a bold front.

'Really – it's too absurd,' he said, betraying his confusion by assuming a carelessness quite foreign to his normal manner. 'In what way could I possibly be jealous, Miss Goff?'

'That is best known to yourself.'

Lucian now saw that there was a change in Alice, and that he had lost ground with her. His wounded vanity, like a corrosive acid, suddenly obliterated his impression that she was, in the main, a well conducted and meritorious young woman. But in its place came another impression that she was a spoiled beauty. And, as he was by no means fondest of the women whose behavior accorded best with his notions of propriety, the change was not in all respects a change for the worse. Only he could not forgive her last remark, though he tried not to let her see how it stung him.

'I am afraid I should cut a poor figure in an encounter with my rival,' he said, smiling.

'Call him out and shoot him,' said Alice vivaciously. 'Very likely he does not know how to use a pistol.'

He smiled again; but had Alice known how seriously he entertained her suggestion for some moments before dismissing it as impracticable, she might not have offered it. Putting a bullet into Cashel struck him rather as a luxury which he could not afford than as a crime. And now Alice, quite satisfied that this Mr Webber, on whom she had wasted so much undeserved awe, might be treated as inconsiderately as she used to treat her admirers at Wiltstoken, proceeded to amuse herself by torturing him a little.

'It is odd,' she said, in her best imitation of Lydia's reflective manner, 'that a common man like that should be able to make himself so very attractive to Lydia. It was not because he was such a fine man; for she does not care in the least about that. I dont think she would give a second look at the handsomest man in London, she is so purely intellectual. And yet she used to delight in talking to him.'

'Oh, that is a mistake. Lydia has a certain manner which leads people to believe that she is deeply interested in the person she happens to be speaking to; but it is only manner. It means nothing.'

'I know that manner of hers perfectly well. But this was something quite different.'

Lucian shook his head reproachfully. 'I cannot jest on so serious a matter,' he said, resolving on an attempt to reestablish his dignity with Alice. 'I think, Miss Goff, that you perhaps hardly know how absurd your supposition is. There are not many men of distinction in Europe with whom my cousin is not personally acquainted. A very young girl, who had seen little of the world, might possibly be deceived by the exterior of such a man as Byron. A woman accustomed to society could make no such mistake. No doubt the man's vulgarity and uncouth address amused her for a moment; but –'

'But why did she ask him to come to her Friday afternoons?'

'A mere civility which she extended to him because he assisted her in some difficulty she got into in the street.'

'She might as well have asked a policeman to come to see her. I dont believe that was it.'

Lucian at that moment hated Alice. 'I am sorry you think such a thing possible,' he said. 'Shall we resume our waltz?'

Alice was not yet able to bear an implication that she did not understand society sufficiently to appreciate the distance between Lydia and Cashel.

'Of course I know it is impossible,' she said, in her old manner. 'I did not mean it.'

Lucian, failing to gather from this what she did mean, took refuge in waltzing, in the course of which she advised him to take a dozen lessons from an instructress whom she recommended as specially skilful at getting gentlemen into what she called the smart way of dancing. This sally produced such a chill that at last, fearing lest her new lights had led her too far, she changed her tone and expressed her amazement at the extent and variety of the work he performed in Downing Street. He accepted her compliments with perfect seriousness, leaving her satisfied that they had smoothed him down. But she was mistaken. She knew nothing of politics or official work; and he saw the worthlessness of her pretended admiration of his share in them, although he felt it right that she should revere his powers from the depths of her ignorance. What stuck like a burr in his mind was that she thought him small enough to be jealous of the poor boxer, and found his dancing deficient in smartness.

After that dance Alice thought much about Lucian, and

also about the way in which society regulated marriages. Before Miss Carew sent for her, she had often sighed because all the nice men she knew of moved in circles to which an obscure governess had no chance of admission. She had met them occasionally at subscription balls; but for sustained intimacy and proposals of marriage she had been dependent on the native youth of Wiltstoken, whom she looked upon as louts or prigs, and among whom Wallace Parker had shone pre-eminent as a university man, scholar, and gentleman. Now that she was a privileged beauty in a set which would hardly tolerate Wallace Parker, she found that the nice men were younger sons, poor and extravagant, far superior to Lucian Webber as partners for a waltz, but not to be thought of as partners in home-keeping. Alice had experienced the troubles of poverty, and had met with excellence in men only in poems, which she never seriously connected with the possibilities of actual life. She was quite unconscious of the privation caused by living with meanly-minded people: she was acutely conscious of that caused by want of money. Not that she was indifferent to rectitude as she understood it: nothing could have induced her to marry a man, however rich, whom she thought wicked. She wanted money, good character and social position; but she naturally desired youth and good looks as well; and here it was that she found herself unsuited. For not only were all the handsome, gallant, well-bred men getting deeply into debt by living beyond smaller incomes than that with which Wallace Parker had tempted her, but many of those who had inherited both riches and rank were as inferior to him in appearance and address as they were in scholarship. No man satisfying all her requirements had yet shewn the least disposition to fall in love with her.

One bright forenoon in July, Alice, attended by a groom, went to the Park on horseback. The freshness of morning was upon horses and riders: there were not yet any jaded people lolling supine in carriages, nor discontented spectators sitting in chairs to envy them. Alice, who was a better horsewoman than might have been expected from the little practice she had had, looked well in the saddle. She had just indulged in a brisk canter from the Corner to the Serpentine when she saw a large white horse approaching with Wallace Parker on its back.

'Ah!' he exclaimed, expertly wheeling his steed and taking off his hat at the same time with an intentional display of gallantry and horsemanship. 'How are you, Alice?'

'Goodness!' she cried, forgetting her manners in her astonishment. 'What brings you here; and where on earth did you get that horse?'

'I presume, Alice,' said Parker, satisfied with the impression he had made, 'that I am here for much the same reason as you are – to enjoy the morning in proper style. As for Rozinante, I borrowed him. Is that chestnut yours? Excuse the rudeness of the question.'

'No,' said Alice, coloring a little. 'This seems such an unlikely place to meet you.'

'Oh no. I always take a turn in the season. But certainly it would have been a very unlikely place for us to meet a year ago.'

So far, Alice felt, she was getting the worst of the conversation. She changed the subject. 'Have you been to Wiltstoken since I last saw you?'

'Yes. I go there once every week at least.'

'Every week! Janet never told me.'

Parker implied by a cunning air that he thought he knew the reason of that; but he said nothing. Alice, piqued, would not condescend to make inquiries. So he said,

'How is Miss Thingumbob?'

'I do not know any one of that name.'

'You know very well whom I mean. Your aristocratic patron, Miss Carew.'

Alice flushed. 'You are very impertinent, Wallace,' she said, grasping her riding whip. 'How dare you call Miss Carew my patron?'

Wallace suddenly became solemn. 'I did not know that

you objected to be reminded of all you owe her,' he said. 'Janet never speaks ungratefully of her, though she has done nothing for Janet.'

'I have not spoken ungratefully,' protested Alice, almost in tears. 'I feel sure you are never tired of speaking ill of me to them at home.'

'That shews how little you understand my real character. I always make excuses for you.'

'Excuses for what? What have I done? What do you mean?'

'Oh, I dont mean anything, if you dont. I thought from your beginning to defend yourself that you felt yourself to be in the wrong.'

'I did not defend myself. Dont dare to say such a thing again, Wallace.'

'Always your obedient humble servant,' he replied with complacent irony.

She pretended not to hear him, and whipped up her horse to a smart trot. The white steed being no trotter, Parker followed at a lumbering canter. Alice, in a shame-faced fear that he was making her ridiculous, soon checked her speed; and the white horse subsided to a walk, marking its paces by deliberate bobs of its unfashionably long mane and tail.

'I have something to tell you,' said Parker at last.

Alice did not deign to reply.

'I think it better to let you know at once,' he continued. 'The fact is, I intend to marry Janet.'

'Janet wont,' said Alice promptly.

Parker smiled conceitedly, and said, 'I dont think she will raise any difficulty if you give her to understand that it is all over between *us*.'

'That what is all over?'

'Well, if you prefer it, that there never has been anything between us. Janet believes that we were engaged. So did a good many other people until you went into high life.'

'I cannot help what people thought.'

'And they all know that I, at least, was ready to perform my part of the engagement honorably.'

'Wallace,' she said, with a sudden change of tone: 'I think we had better separate. It is not right for me to be riding about the park with you when I have nobody belonging to me here except a manservant.'

'Just as you please,' he said coolly, halting. 'May I assure Janet that you wish her to marry me?'

'Most certainly not. I do not wish any one to marry you, much less my own sister. I am far inferior to Janet; and she deserves a much better husband than I do.'

'I quite agree with you, though I dont quite see what that has to do with it. As far as I understand you, you will neither marry me yourself – mind, I am quite willing to fulfil my engagement still – nor let any one else have me. Is that so?'

'You may tell Janet,' said Alice vigorously, her face glowing, 'that if we – you and I – were condemned to live for ever on a desert isl— No: I will write to her. That will be the best way. Good morning.'

Parker, hitherto unperturbed, shewed signs of alarm. 'I beg, Alice,' he said, 'that you will say nothing unfair to her of me. You cannot with truth say anything bad of me.'

'Do you really care for Janet?' said Alice, wavering.

'Of course,' he replied indignantly. 'Janet is a very superior girl.'

'I have always said so,' said Alice, rather angry because some one else had forestalled her in that meritorious admission. 'I will tell her the simple truth – that there has never been anything between us except what is between all cousins; and that there never could have been anything more on my part. I must go now. I dont know what that man must think already.'

'I should be sorry to lower you in his esteem,' said Parker maliciously. 'Goodbye, Alice.' Uttering the last words in a careless tone, he again flourished his hat as he pulled up the white horse's head and sped away. It was not true that he was in the habit of riding in the park every season. He had learnt from Janet that Alice was accustomed to ride there in the forenoon; and he had hired the white horse in order to meet her on equal terms, feeling that a gentleman on horseback in the road by the Serpentine could be at no social disadvantage with any lady, however exalted her associates.

As for Alice, his reminder that Miss Carew was her patron rankled in her. The necessity for securing an independent position seemed to press imminently upon her. And as the sole way of achieving this was by marriage, she almost made up her mind to marry any man, whatever his person, age, or disposition, if only he could give her a place equal to that of Miss Carew in the little world of which she had lately acquired the manners and customs.

CHAPTER XII

When the autumn set in, Alice was in Scotland, learning to shoot; and Lydia was at Wiltstoken, preparing her father's letters and memoirs for publication. She did not write at the castle. All the rooms there were either domed, vaulted, gilded, galleried, three sided, six sided, anything except four sided: all in some way suggestive of the Arabian nights' entertainments and out of keeping with the associations of her father's life. In her search for a congruous room to work in, the idea of causing a pavilion to be erected in the elm vista recurred to her. But she had no mind to be disturbed just then by workmen; so she had the Warren Lodge cleansed and limewashed, and the kitchen transformed into a comfortable library, whence, as she sat facing the door at her writing table in the centre of the room, she could see the elm vista through one window, and through another a tract of wood and meadow intersected by the high-road and by a canal, beyond which the prospect ended in a distant green slope used as a sheep run. The other apartments were used by a couple of maidservants, who kept the place swept and dusted, and prepared Miss Carew's lunch, besides answering her bell and going on her errands to the castle. Failing any of these employments, they sat outside in the sun, reading novels.

When Lydia had worked in this retreat daily for two months, her mind became so full of the old life with her father, that the interruptions of the servants became so many shocks recalling her to the present. On the twelfth of August, Phœbe, one of the maids, entered and said,

'If you please, miss, Bashville is wishful to know can he speak to you a moment?'

Permission given, the footman entered. Since his wrestle with Cashel he had never quite recovered his former imperturbability. His manner and speech were as smooth and respectful as before; but his countenance was no longer stead-fast: he was on bad terms with the butler because he had been reproved by him for blushing. On this occasion he came to beg leave to absent himself during the afternoon. He seldom asked favors of this kind, and was never refused.

'There are more people than usual in the road today,' she observed, as he thanked her. 'Do you know why?'

'No, madam,' said Bashville, and blushed.

'People begin to shoot on the twelfth,' she said; 'but I suppose it cannot have anything to do with that. Is there a race, or a fair, or any such thing in the neighborhood?'

'Not that I am aware of, madam.'

Lydia dipped her pen in the ink and thought no more of the matter. Bashville returned to the castle, and attired himself like a country gentleman of sporting tastes before going out to enjoy his holiday.

The forenoon passed away quietly. There was no sound in the Warren Lodge except the scratching of Lydia's pen, the ticking of her favorite skeleton clock, an occasional clatter of crockery from the kitchen, and the voices of the birds and maids without. As the hour for lunch approached, Lydia became a little restless. She interrupted her work to look at the clock, and brushed a speck of dust from her blotter with the feather of her quill. Then she looked absently through the window along the elm vista, where she had once seen, as she had thought, a sylvan god. This time she saw a less romantic object: a policeman. She looked again incredu-lously: there he was still, a black-bearded helmeted man, making a dark blot in the green perspective, and surveying the landscape cautiously. Lydia summoned Phœbe, and bade her ask the man what he wanted.

The girl soon returned out of breath, with the news that there were a dozen more constables hiding among the elms, and that the one she had spoken to had given no account of himself, but had asked her how many gates there were to the park; whether they were always locked; and whether she had seen many people about. She felt sure that a murder had been committed somewhere. Lydia shrugged her shoulders, and ordered luncheon, during which Phœbe gazed eagerly through the window, and left her mistress to wait on herself.

'Phœbe,' said Lydia, when the dishes were removed: 'you may go to the gate lodge, and ask them there what the policemen want. But do not go any further. Stay. Has Ellen gone to the castle with the things?'

Phœbe reluctantly admitted that Ellen had.

'Well, you need not wait for her to return; but come back as quickly as you can, in case I should want anybody.'

'Directly, miss,' said Phœbe, vanishing.

Lydia, left alone, resumed her work leisurely, occasionally pausing to gaze at the distant woodland, and note with transient curiosity a flock of sheep on the slope, or a flight of birds above the tree tops. Something more startling occurred presently. A man, apparently half naked, and carrying a black object under his arm, darted through a remote glade with the swiftness of a stag, and disappeared. Lydia concluded that he had been disturbed whilst bathing in the canal, and had taken to flight with his wardrobe under his arm. She laughed at the idea; turned to her manuscript again; and wrote on. Suddenly there was a rustle and a swift footstep without. Then the latch was violently jerked up; and Cashel Byron rushed in as far as the threshold, where he halted, stupefied at the presence of Lydia and the change in the appearance of the room.

He was himself remarkably changed. He was dressed in a pea-jacket, which evidently did not belong to him; for it hardly reached his middle, and the sleeves were so short that his forearms were half bare, shewing that he wore nothing beneath this borrowed garment. He had on white knee-breeches, soiled with clay and green stains of bruised grass. The breeches were made with a broad flap in front, under which, and passing round his waist, was a scarf of crimson silk. From his knees to his socks, the edges of which had fallen over his laced boots, his legs were visible, naked and muscular. On his face was a mask of sweat, dust, and blood, partly sponged away in black-bordered streaks. Underneath his left eye was a mound of bluish flesh nearly as large as a walnut. The jaw below it, and the opposite cheek, were severely bruised; and his lip was cut through at one corner. He had no hat; his close-cropped hair was disordered; and his ears were as though they had been rubbed with coarse sandpaper.

Lydia looked at him for some seconds, and he at her, speechless. Then she tried to speak; failed; and sank into the chair.

'I didnt know there was any one here,' he said, in a hoarse, panting whisper. 'The police are after me. I have fought for an hour, and run over a mile; and I'm dead beat: I can go no further. Let me hide in the back room; and tell them you havnt seen any one, will you?'

'What have you done?' she said, conquering her weakness with an effort, and standing up.

'Nothing,' he replied, groaning occasionally as he recovered breath. 'Business: thats all.'

'Why are the police pursuing you? Why are you in such a dreadful condition?'

Cashel seemed alarmed at this. There was a mirror in the lid of a paper-case on the table. He took it up, and looked at himself anxiously, but was at once relieved by what he saw. 'I'm all right,' he said. 'I'm not marked. That mouse' – he pointed gaily to the lump under his eye – 'will run away to-morrow. I am pretty tidy, considering. But it's bellows to mend with me at present. Whoosh! My heart's as big as a bullock's, after that run.'

'You ask me to shelter you,' said Lydia sternly. 'What have you done? Have you committed murder?'

'No!' exclaimed Cashel, trying to open his eyes widely in his astonishment, but only succeeding with one, as the other was gradually closing. 'I tell you Ive been fighting; and it's illegal. You dont want to see me in prison, do you? Confound him!' he added, reverting to her question with sudden wrath: 'a steam-hammer wouldnt kill him. You might as well hit a sack of nails. And all my money, my time, my training, and my day's trouble for nothing! It's enough to make a man cry.'

'Go,' said Lydia, with uncontrollable disgust. 'And do not let me see which way you go. How dare you come to me?'

The sponge marks on Cashel's face grew whiter; and he began to pant heavily again. 'Very well,' he said. 'I'll go. There isnt a boy in your stables would give me up like that.'

As he spoke, he opened the door; but he involuntarily shut it again immediately. Lydia looked through the window, and saw a crowd of men, police and others, hurrying along the elm vista. Cashel cast a glance round, half piteous, half desperate, like a hunted animal. Lydia could not resist it. 'Quick!' she cried, opening one of the inner doors. 'Go in there, and keep quiet – if you can.' And, as he sulkily hesitated a moment, she stamped vehemently. He slunk in; and she, having shut the door, resumed her place at the writing table: her heart beating with a kind of excitement she had not felt since, in her early childhood, she had kept guilty secrets from her nurse.

There was a tramping without, and a sound of voices. Then two peremptory raps at the door.

'Come in,' said Lydia, more composedly than she knew. But the asked permission was not waited for. Before she ceased speaking, a policeman opened the door, and looked quickly round the room. He was taken aback by what he saw, and finally touched his helmet to signify respect for Lydia. As he opened his mouth to speak, Phœbe, flushed with running, pushed past him; put her hand on the door; and pertly asked what he wanted.

'Come away from the door, Phœbe,' said Lydia. 'Wait here with me until I give you leave to go,' she added, as the girl moved towards the inner door. 'Now,' she said, turning courteously to the policeman, 'what is the matter?'

'I ask your pardon, mum,' said the constable agreeably. 'Did you happen to see any one pass hereabouts lately?'

'Do you mean a man only partly dressed, and carrying a black coat?' said Lydia.

'Thats him, miss,' said the policeman, greatly interested. 'Which way did he go?'

'I will shew you where I saw him,' said Lydia, rising and going to the door, outside which she found a crowd of rustics around five policemen, who held in custody two men, one of whom was Mellish (without a coat), and the other a hook-nosed man whose like Lydia had seen often on race-courses. She pointed out the glade across which she had seen Cashel run, and felt as if the guilt of the deception was wrenching some fibre in her heart from its natural order. But she spoke with apparent self-possession; and no shade of suspicion fell on the minds of the police.

Several peasants now came forward, each professing to know exactly whither Cashel had been making when he crossed the glade. Whilst they were arguing, many persons, resembling the hook-nosed captive in general appearance, sneaked into the crowd and regarded the police with furtive hostility. Soon after, a second detachment of police came up, with another prisoner and another crowd: Bashville among them.

'Better go in, mum,' said the policeman who had spoken to Lydia first. 'We must keep together, being so few; and he aint fit for you to look at.'

But Lydia had looked already, and had guessed that the last prisoner was Paradise, although his countenance was damaged beyond recognition. His costume was like that of Cashel, except that his girdle was a blue handkerchief with white spots, and his shoulders were wrapped in an old horse-cloth, through the folds of which his naked ribs could be seen, tinged with every hue a bad bruise can assume. As to his face, a crease and a hole amid a cluster of lumps of raw flesh indicated the presence of an eye and a mouth: the rest of his features were indiscernible. He could still see a little; for he moved his puffed and lacerated hand to arrange his blanket, and demanded hoarsely, and with greatly impeded articulation, whether the lady would stand a drain to a poor fighting man what had done his best for his backers. On this some one produced a flask; and Mellish volunteered, provided he were released for a moment, to get the contents down Paradise's throat. As soon as the brandy had passed his swollen lips, he made a few preliminary sounds, and then shouted,

'He sent for the coppers because he couldnt stand another round. I am ready to go on.'

The policemen bade him hold his tongue, and closed round him, hiding him from Lydia, who, without shewing the mingled pity and loathing with which his condition inspired her, told them to bring him to the castle, and have him attended to there. She added that the whole party could obtain refreshment at the same time. The sergeant, who was very tired and thirsty, wavered in his resolution to continue the pursuit. Lydia, as usual, treated the matter as settled.

'Bashville,' she said: 'will you please shew them the way, and see that they are satisfied.'

'Some thief has stole my coat,' said Mellish sullenly to Bashville. 'If youll lend me one, governor, and these blessed policemen will be so kind as not to tear it off my back, I'll send it down to you in a day or two. I'm a respectable man, and have been her ladyship's tenant here.'

'Your pal wants it worse than you,' said the sergeant. 'If there was an old coachman's cape or anything to put over him, I would see it returned safe. I dont want to bring him round the country in a blanket, like a wild Injin.'

'I have a cloak inside,' said Bashville. 'I'll get it for you.' And before Lydia could devize a pretext for stopping him, he disappeared, and she heard him entering the lodge by the back door. It seemed to her that a silence fell on them all, as if her deceit was already discovered. Mellish, who had been waiting for an opportunity to protest against the last remark of the policeman, said angrily,

'Who are you calling my pal? I hope I may be struck

dead for a liar if ever I set eyes on him in my life before.'

Lydia looked at him as a martyr might look at a wretch to whom she was to be chained. He was doing as she had done – lying. Then Bashville, having passed through the other rooms, came into the library by the inner door, with an old livery cloak on his arm.

'Put that on him,' he said; 'and come along to the castle with me. You can see the roads for five miles round from the south tower, and recognize every man on them through the big telescope. By your leave, madam, I think Phœbe had better come with us to help.'

'Certainly,' said Lydia, looking quietly at him.

'I'll get clothes at the castle for the man that wants them,' he added, trying to return her gaze, but failing with a blush. 'Now boys. Come along.'

'I thank your ladyship,' said the sergeant. 'We have had a hard morning of it; and we can do no more at present than drink your health.' He touched his helmet again; and Lydia bowed to him. 'Keep close together, men,' he said, as the crowd moved off with Bashville.

'Ah,' sneered Mellish: 'keep close together, like the geese do. Things has come to a pretty pass when a Englishman is run in for stopping when he sees a crowd.'

'All right,' said the sergeant. 'I have that bundle of colored handkerchiefs you were selling; and I'll find the other man before youre a day older. It's a pity, seeing how youve behaved so well and havnt resisted us, that you dont happen to know where those ropes and stakes are hid. I might have a good word at the sessions for any one that would put me in the way of finding them.'

'Ropes and stakes! Fiddlesticks and grandmothers! There werent no ropes and no stakes. It was only a turn-up: that is, if there was any fighting at all. *I* didnt see none: but I spose you did. But then youre clever; and I'm not.'

By this time the last straggler of the party had disappeared from Lydia, who had watched their retreat from the door of the Warren Lodge. When she turned to go in she saw Cashel cautiously entering from the room in which he had lain concealed. His excitement had passed off: he looked cold and anxious, as if a reaction were setting in.

'Are they all gone?' he said. 'That servant of yours is a good sort. He has promised to bring me some clothes. As for you, youre better than – Whats the matter? Where are you going to?'

Lydia had put on her hat, and was swiftly wrapping herself in a shawl. Wreaths of rosy color were chasing each other through her cheeks; and her eyes and nostrils, usually so tranquil, were dilated.

'Wont you speak to me?' he said irresolutely.

'Just this,' she replied, with passion. 'Let me never see you again. The very foundations of my life are loosened: I have told a lie. I have made my servant – an honorable man – my accomplice in a lie. We are worse than you; for even your wild-beast's handiwork is a less evil than the bringing of a falsehood into the world. This is what has come to me out of our acquaintance. I have given you a hiding-place. Keep it. I will never enter it again.'

Cashel, appalled, shrank back like a child which, trying to steal sweetmeats from a high shelf, pulls the whole cupboard down about its ears. He neither spoke nor stirred as she left the Lodge.

At the castle she went to her boudoir, where she found her maid the French lady, from whose indignant description of the proceedings below she gathered that the policemen were being regaled with bread and cheese, beef and beer; and that the attendance of a surgeon had been dispensed with, Paradise's wounds having been dressed skilfully by Mellish. Lydia bade her send Bashville to the Warren Lodge to see whether any strangers were still loitering about it; and ordered that none of the female servants should return there until he came back. Then she sat down, and tried not to think. But as she could not help thinking, she submitted, and tried to think the late catastrophe out. An idea that she had disjointed the whole framework of things by creating a false belief, filled her imagination. The one conviction she had brought out of her reading was that the concealment of a truth, with its resultant false beliefs, must produce mischief, even though the beginning of that mischief might be as inconceivable as the end. She made no distinction between the subtlest philosophical sophism and the vulgarest lie. The evil of Cashel's capture was measurable, the evil of any lie beyond all measure. She felt none the less assured of that evil because she could not foresee one bad consequence likely to ensue from what she had done. Her misgivings pressed heavily upon her; for her father, a determined sceptic, had left her destitute of the consolations which theology has for the wrongdoer. It was plainly her duty to send for the policeman and clear up the deception she had practised on him. But this she could not do. Her will, in spite of her reason, acted in the opposite direction. And in this paralysis of her moral power she saw the evil of the lie beginning. She had given it birth; and Nature would not permit her to strangle the monster.

At last her maid returned and informed her that the *canaille* had gone away. When she was again alone, she rose, and walked slowly to and fro through the room, forgetting the lapse of time in the restless activity of her mind, until she was again interrupted, this time by Bashville.

'Well?'

He was daunted by her tone; for he had never before heard her speak haughtily to a servant. He did not understand that he had changed subjectively, and was now her accomplice.

'He's given himself up.'

'What do you mean?' she said, with sudden dismay.

'Byron, madam. I brought some clothes to the Lodge for him; but when I got there he was gone. I went round to the gates in search of him, and found him in the hands of the police. They told me he'd just given himself up. He wouldnt give any account of himself; and he looked – well, sullen and beaten-down like.'

'What will they do with him?' she asked, turning quite pale.

'A man got six weeks' hard labor last month for the same offence. Most likely thats what he'll get. And very little for what he's done, as youd say if you saw him doing it, madam.'

'Then,' said Lydia sternly, 'it was to see this' – she shrank from naming it – 'this fight, that you asked my permission to go out!'

'Yes, madam, it was,' said Bashville, with some bitterness. 'I recognized Lord Worthington and plenty more noblemen and gentlemen there.'

Lydia was about to reply sharply; but she checked herself; and her usual tranquil manner came back as she said, 'That is no reason why you should have been there.'

Bashville's color began to waver, and his voice to need increased control. 'It's in human nature to go to such a thing once,' he said; 'but once is enough, at least for me. Youll excuse my mentioning it, madam; but what with Lord Worthington and the rest of Byron's backers screaming oaths and abuse at the other man; and the opposite party doing the same to Byron – well, I may not be a gentleman; but I hope I can conduct myself like a man, even when I'm losing money.'

'Then do not go to such an exhibition again, Bashville. I must not dictate your amusements; but I do not think you are likely to benefit yourself by copying Lord Worthington's tastes.'

'I copy no lord's tastes,' said Bashville, reddening. 'You hid the man that was fighting, Miss Carew. Why do you look down on the man that was only a bystander?'

Lydia's color rose too. Her first impulse was to treat this outburst as rebellion against her authority, and crush it. But her vigilant sense of justice withheld her. 'He was a fugitive who took refuge in our house, Bashville. *You* did not betray him.'

'No,' said Bashville, his expression subdued to one of rueful pride. 'When I am beaten by a better man, I have courage enough to get out of his way and take no mean advantage of him.'

Lydia, not understanding, looked inquiringly at him. He made a gesture as if throwing something from him, and continued recklessly,

'But one way I'm as good as he, and better. A footman is held more respectable than a prizefighter. He's told you that he's in love with you; and if it is to be my last word, I'll tell you that the ribbon round your neck is more to me than your whole body and soul is to him or his like. When he took an unfair advantage of me, and pretended to be a gentleman, I told Mr Lucian of him, and shewed him up for what he was. But when I found him today hiding in the pantry at the Lodge, I took no advantage of him, though I knew well that if he'd been no more to you than any other man of his sort, youd never have hid him. You know best why he gave himself up to the police after your seeing his day's work. But I will leave him to his luck. He is the best man: let the best man win. I am sorry,' added Bashville, recovering his ordinary suave manner with an effort, 'to inconvenience you by a short notice; but I should take it as a particular favor if I might go this evening.'

'You had better,' said Lydia, rising quite calmly, and keeping resolutely away from her the strange emotional effect of being astonished, outraged, and loved at one unlooked-for stroke. 'It is not advisable that you should stay after what you have just – '

'I knew that when I said it,' interposed Bashville hastily and doggedly.

'In going away you will be taking precisely the course that would be adopted by any gentleman who had spoken to the same effect. I am not offended by your declaration: I recognize your right to make it. If you need my testimony to further your future arrangements, I shall always be happy to say that I believe you to be a man of honor.'

Bashville bowed, and said in a low voice, very nervously,

that he had no intention of going into service again, but that he should always be proud of her good opinion.

'You are fitted for better things,' she said. 'If you embark in any enterprise requiring larger means than you possess, I will be your surety. I thank you for your invariable courtesy to me in the discharge of your duties. Goodbye.'

She bowed to him and left the room. Awestruck, he returned her salutation as best he could, and stood motionless after she disappeared: his mind advancing on tiptoe to grasp what had just passed. His chief sensation was one of relief. He no longer dared to fancy himself in love with such a woman. Her sudden consideration for him as a suitor overwhelmed him with a sense of his unfitness for such a part. He saw himself as a very young, very humble, and very ignorant man, whose head had been turned by a pleasant place and a kind mistress. He stole away to pack his trunk, and to consider how best to account to his fellow-servants for his sudden departure.

CHAPTER XIII

ONE afternoon, Lydia, returning from her daily constitutional walk, descried a strange woman on the castle terrace, in conversation with the butler. Though it was warm autumn weather, this person wore a black silk mantle trimmed with fur, and heavily decorated with spurious jet beads. As the female Wiltstokeners always approached Miss Carew in their best raiment, whether it suited the season or not, she concluded that she was about to be asked for a subscription to a school treat, a temperance festival, or perhaps a testimonial to one of the Wiltstoken curates.

When she came nearer, she saw that the stranger was an elderly lady – or possibly not a lady – with crimped hair, and ringlets hanging at each ear in a long-forgotten fashion.

'Here is Miss Carew,' said the butler shortly, as if the old lady had tried his temper. 'You had better talk to her yourself.'

At this she seemed fluttered, and made a solemn curtsy. Lydia, noticing the curtsy and the curls, guessed that her visitor kept a dancing academy. Yet a certain contradictory hardihood in her frame and bearing suggested that perhaps she kept a tavern. However, as her face was, on the whole, an anxious and a good face, and her attitude towards the lady of the castle one of embarrassed humility, Lydia acknowledged her salutation kindly, and waited for her to speak.

'I hope you wont consider it a liberty,' said the stranger tremulously. 'I'm Mrs Skene.'

Lydia became ominously grave; and Mrs Skene reddened a little. Then she continued, as if repeating a carefully prepared and rehearsed speech, 'It would be esteemed a favor if I might have the honor of a few words in private.'

Lydia looked and felt somewhat stern; but it was not in her nature to rebuff any one without strong provocation. She invited her visitor to enter, and led the way to the circular drawing room, the strange decorations of which exactly accorded with Mrs Skene's ideas of aristocratic splendor. As a professor of deportment and etiquette, the ex-champion's wife was nervous under the observation of such an expert as Lydia; but she rose to the occasion and got safely seated without a mistake. For, although entering a room seems a simple matter to many persons, it was to Mrs Skene an operation governed by the strict laws of the art she professed – one so elaborate, indeed, that few of her pupils mastered it satisfactorily in less than half-a-dozen lessons. Mrs Skene soon dismissed it from her mind. She was too old to dwell upon such vanities when real anxieties were pressing upon her.

'Oh, miss,' she began appealingly, 'the boy!'

Lydia knew at once who was meant. But she repeated, as if at a loss, 'The boy?' And immediately accused herself of insincerity.

'Our boy, maam. Cashel.'

'Mrs Skene!' said Lydia reproachfully.

Mrs Skene understood all that Lydia's tone implied. 'I know, maam,' she pleaded. 'I know well. But what could I do but come to you? Whatever you said to him, it has gone to his heart; and he's dying.'

'Pardon me,' said Lydia promptly: 'men do not die of such things; and Mr Cashel Byron is not so deficient either in robustness of body or hardness of heart as to be an exception to *that* rule.'

'Yes, miss,' said Mrs Skene sadly. 'You are thinking of the profession. You cant believe he has any feelings because he fights. Ah, miss, if you only knew them as I do! More tender-hearted men dont breathe. Cashel is like a young child, his feelings are that easily touched; and I have known stronger than he to die of broken hearts only because they were unlucky in their calling. Just think what a high-spirited young man must feel when a lady calls him a wild beast. That was a cruel word, miss: it was indeed.'

Lydia was so disconcerted by this attack that she had to collect herself carefully before replying. Then she said, 'Are you aware, Mrs Skene, that my knowledge of Mr Byron is very slight – that I have not seen him ten times in my life? Perhaps you do not know the circumstances in which we last met. I was greatly shocked by the injuries he had inflicted on another man; and I believe I spoke of them as the work of a wild beast. For your sake, I am sorry I said so; for he has told me that he regards you as his mother; but –'

'Oh no! Far from it, miss. I ask your pardon a thousand times for taking the word out of your mouth; but me and Ned is no more to him than your housekeeper or governess might be to you. Thats what I'm afraid you dont understand, miss. He's no relation of ours. I do assure you that he's a gentleman born and bred; and when we go back to Melbourne next Christmas, it will be just the same as if he had never known us.'

'I hope he will not be so ungrateful as to forget you. He has told me his history.'

'Thats more than he ever told me, miss; so you may judge how much he thinks of you.'

Another pause followed this. Mrs Skene felt that the first round was over, and that she had held her own with a little to spare. But Lydia soon rallied.

'Mrs Skene,' she said penetratingly: 'when you came to pay me this visit, what object did you propose to yourself? What do you expect me to do?'

'Well, maam,' said Mrs Skene, troubled, 'the poor lad has had crosses lately. There was the disappointment about you – the first one, I mean – that had been preying on his mind for a long time. Then there was that exhibition spar at the Agricultural Hall, when Paradise acted so dishonorable. Cashel heard that you were looking on; and then he read the shameful way the newspapers wrote of him; and he thought youd believe it all. I couldnt get that thought out of his head. I said to him, over and over again – '

'Excuse me,' said Lydia, interrupting. 'We had better be frank with one another. It is useless to assume that he mistook my feeling on that subject. I *was* shocked by the severity with which he treated his opponent.'

'But bless you, thats his business,' said Mrs Skene, opening her eyes widely. 'I put it to you, miss,' she continued, as if mildly reprobating some want of principle on Lydia's part, 'whether an honest man shouldnt fulfil his engagements. I assure you that the pay a respectable professional usually gets for a spar like that is half a guinea; and that was all Paradise got. But Cashel stood on his reputation, and wouldnt take less than ten guineas; and he got it too. Now many another in his position would have gone into the ring, and fooled away the time pretending to box, and just swindling those that paid him. But Cashel is as honest and highminded as a king. You saw for yourself the trouble he took. He couldnt have spared himself less if he had been fighting for a thousand a side and the belt, instead of for a paltry ten guineas. Surely you dont think the worse of him for his honesty, miss?'

'I confess,' said Lydia, laughing in spite of herself, 'that your view of the transaction did not occur to me.'

'Of course not, maam: no more it wouldnt to any one, without they were accustomed to know the right and wrong of the profession. Well, as I was saying, miss, that was a fresh disappointment to him. It worrited him more than you can imagine. Then came a deal of bother about the match with Paradise. First Paradise could only get five hundred pounds; and the boy wouldnt agree for less than a thousand. I think it's on your account that he's been so particular about the money of late; for he was never covetous before. Then Mellish was bent on its coming off down hereabouts; and the poor lad was so mortal afraid of its getting to your ears that he wouldnt consent until they persuaded him you would be in foreign parts in August. Glad I was when the articles were signed at last, before he was worried into his grave. All the time he was training he was longing for a sight of you; but he went through with it as steady and faithful as a man could. And he trained beautiful. I saw him on the morning of the fight; and he was like a shining angel: it would have done a lady's heart good to look at him. Ned went about like a madman offering twenty to one on him: if he had lost, we should have been ruined at this moment. And then to think of the police coming just as he was finishing Paradise. I cried like a child when I heard of it; I dont think there was ever anything so cruel. He could have finished him quarter of an hour sooner, only he held back to make the market for Ned.' Mrs Skene, overcome, blew her nose before proceeding. 'Then, on the top of that, came what passed betwixt you and him, and made him give himself up to the police. Lord Worthington bailed him out: but what with the disgrace, and the disappointment, and his time and money thrown away, and the sting of your words all coming together, he was quite brokenhearted. And now he mopes and frets; and neither me nor Ned nor Fan can get any good of him. They tell me that he wont be sent to prison; but if he is' – here Mrs Skene broke down and began to cry – 'it will be the death of him; and God forgive those that have brought it about.'

Sorrow always softened Lydia; but tears hardened her again: she had no patience with them.

'And the other man?' she said. 'Have you heard anything of him? I suppose he is in some hospital.'

'In hospital!' repeated Mrs Skene, checking her tears in alarm. 'Who?'

'Paradise,' replied Lydia, pronouncing the name reluctantly.

'He in hospital! Why, bless your innocence, miss, I saw him yesterday looking as well as such an ugly brute could look: not a mark on him, and he bragging what he would have done to Cashel if the police hadnt come up! He's a nasty low fighting man, so he is; and I'm only sorry that our boy demeaned himself to strip with the like of him. I hear that Cashel made a perfect picture of him, and that you saw him. I suppose you were frightened, maam, and very naturally too, not being used to such sights. I have had my Ned brought home to me in that state that I have poured brandy into his eye, thinking it was his mouth; and even Cashel, careful as he is, has been nearly blind for three days. It's not to be expected that they could have all the money for nothing. Dont let it prey on your mind, miss. If you married – I am only supposing it,' said Mrs Skene in soothing parenthesis as she saw Lydia shrink from the word – 'if you were married to a great surgeon, as you might be without derogation to your high rank, youd be ready to faint if you saw him cut off a leg or an arm, as he would have to do every day for his livelihood; but youd be proud of his cleverness in being able to do it. Thats how I feel with regard to Ned. I tell you the truth, maam, I shouldnt like to see him in the ring no more than the lady of an officer in the Guards would like to see her husband in the field of battle running his sword into the poor blacks or into the French; but as it's his profession, and people think so highly of him for it, I make up my mind to it; and now I take quite an interest in it, particularly as it does nobody any harm. Not that I would have you think that Ned ever took the arm or leg off a man: Lord forbid! or Cashel either. Oh, maam, I thank you kindly; and I'm sorry you should have given yourself the trouble.' This referred to the entry of a servant with tea.

'Still,' said Lydia, when they were at leisure to resume the conversation, 'I do not quite understand why you have come to me. Personally you are most welcome; but in what way did you expect me to relieve Mr Byron's mind by visiting me? Did he ask you to come?'

'He'd have died first. I came down of my own accord, knowing what was the matter with him.'

'And what then?'

Mrs Skene looked around to satisfy herself that they were

alone. Then she leaned towards Lydia, and said in an emphatic whisper,

'Why not marry him, miss?'

'Because I dont choose, Mrs Skene,' said Lydia, with perfect good humor.

'But consider a little, miss. Where will you ever get such another chance? Only think what a man he is: champion of the world and a gentleman as well! The two things have never happened before, and never will again. I have known lots of champions; but they were not fit company for the like of you. Ned was champion when I married him; and my family thought that I lowered myself in doing it, because I was a professional dancer on the stage. The men in the ring are common men mostly; and so ladies are cut off from their society. But it has been your good luck to take the fancy of one thats a gentleman. What more could a lady desire? Where will you find his equal in health, strength, good looks or good manners? As to his character, I can tell you about that. In Melbourne, as you may suppose, all the girls and women were breaking their hearts for his sake. I declare to you that I used to have two or three of them in every evening merely to look at him; and he, poor innocent lad, taking no more notice of them than if they were cabbages. He used to be glad to get away from them by going into the saloon to box with the gentlemen; and then they used to peep at him through the door and get worse than ever. But they never got a wink from him. You were the first, Miss Carew; and, believe me, you will be the last. If there had ever been another, he couldnt have kept it from me; because his disposition is as open as a child's. And his honesty is beyond everything you can imagine. I have known him to be offered eight hundred pounds to lose a fight that he could only get two hundred by winning, not to mention his chance of getting nothing at all if he lost honestly. You know – for I see you know the world, maam – how few men would be proof against such a temptation. There are men high up in their profession – so high that youd as soon suspect the queen on her throne of selling her country's battles as them – that fight cross on the sly when it's made worth their while. My Ned is no low prizefighter, as is well known; but when he let himself be beat by that little Killarney Primrose, and went out and bought a horse and trap next day, what could I think? There, maam: I tell you that of my own husband; and I tell you that Cashel never was beat, although times out of mind it would have paid him better to lose than to win, along of those wicked betting men. Not an angry word have I ever had from him, nor the sign of liquor have I ever seen on him, except once on Ned's birthday; and then nothing but fun came out of him in his cups, when the truth comes out of all men. Oh do just think how happy you ought to be, miss, if you would only bring yourself to look at it in the proper light. A gentleman born and bred, champion of the world, sober, honest, spotless as the unborn babe, able to take his own part and yours in any society, and mad in love with you! He thinks you an angel from heaven – and so I am sure you are, miss, in your heart. I do assure you that my Fan gets quite put out because she thinks he draws comparisons to her disadvantage. I dont think you can be so hard to please as to refuse him, miss.'

Lydia leaned back in her chair, and looked at Mrs Skene with a curious expression which soon brightened into an irrepressible smile. Mrs Skene smiled very slightly in complaisance, but conveyed by her serious brow that what she had said was no laughing matter.

'I must take some time to consider all that you have so eloquently urged,' said Lydia. 'I am in earnest, Mrs Skene: you have produced a great effect upon me. Now let us talk of something else for the present. Your daughter is quite well, I hope.'

'Thank you kindly, maam, she enjoys her health.'

'And you also?'

'I am as well as can be expected,' said Mrs Skene, too fond of commiseration to admit that she was in perfect health.

'You must have a rare sense of security,' said Lydia, watching her, 'being happily married to so celebrated a – a professor of boxing as Mr Skene. Is it not pleasant to have a powerful protector?'

'Ah, miss, you little know,' exclaimed Mrs Skene, falling into the trap baited by her own grievances, and losing sight of Cashel's interests. 'The fear of his getting into trouble is never off my mind. Ned is quietness itself until he has a drop of drink in him; and then he is like the rest – ready to fight the first that provokes him. And if the police get hold of him he has no chance. Theres no justice for a fighting man. Just let it be said that he's a professional, and thats enough for the magistrate: away with him to prison, and goodbye to his pupils and his respectability at once. Thats what I live in terror of. And as to being protected, I'd let myself be robbed fifty times over sooner than say a word to him that might bring on a quarrel. Many a time driving home of a night have I overpaid the cabman on the sly, afraid he would grumble and provoke Ned. It's the drink that does it all. Gentlemen are proud to be seen speaking with him in public; and they come up one after another asking what he'll have, until the next thing he knows is that he's in bed with his boots on, his wrist sprained, and maybe his eye black, trying to remember what he was doing the night before. What I suffered the first three years of our marriage none can tell. Then he took the pledge; and ever since that he's been very good: I havnt seen him what you could fairly call drunk, not more than three times a year. It was the blessing of God, and a beating he got from a milkman in Westminster, that made him ashamed of himself. I kept him to it and emigrated him out of the way of his old friends. Since that, there has been a blessing on him; and weve prospered.'

'Is Cashel quarrelsome?'

The tone of this question awakened Mrs Skene to the untimeliness of her complaints. 'No, no,' she protested. 'He never drinks; and as to fighting, if you can believe such a thing, miss, I dont think he has had a casual turn-up three times in his life: not oftener, at any rate. All he wants is to be married; and then he'll be steady to his grave. But if he's left adrift now, Lord knows what will become of him. He'll mope first – he's moping at present –; then he'll drink; then he'll lose his pupils, get out of condition, be beaten, and – One word from you, miss, would save him. If I might just tell him –'

'Nothing,' said Lydia. 'Absolutely nothing. The only assurance I can give you is that you have softened the opinion I had formed of some of his actions. But that I should marry Mr Cashel Byron is simply the most improbable thing in the world. All questions of personal inclination apart, the mere improbability is enough in itself to appal an ordinary woman.'

Mrs Skene did not quite understand this; but she understood sufficient for her purpose. She rose to go, shaking her head despondently, and saying, 'I see how it is, maam. You think him beneath you. Your relations wouldnt like it.'

'There is no doubt that my relations would be greatly shocked; and I am bound to take that into account – for what it is worth.'

'We should never trouble you,' said Mrs Skene, lingering. 'England will see the last of us in a month or two.'

'That will make no difference to me, except that I shall regret not being able to have a pleasant chat with you occasionally.' This was not true; but Lydia fancied that she was beginning to take a hardened delight in lying.

Mrs Skene was not to be consoled by compliments. She again shook her head. 'It is very kind of you to give me good words, miss,' she said; 'but if I might have one for the boy, you could say what you liked to me.'

Lydia considered far before she replied. At last she said, 'I am sorry I spoke harshly to him, since, driven as he was by circumstances, I cannot see how he could have acted otherwise than he did. And I overlooked the economics of his profession. In short, I am not used to fisticuffs; and what I saw shocked me so much that I was unreasonable. But,' continued Lydia, checking Mrs Skene's rising hope with a warning finger, 'how, if you tell him this, will you make him understand that I say so as an act of justice, and not in the least as a proffer of affection?'

'A crumb of comfort will satisfy him, miss. I'll just tell him that Ive seen you, and that you meant nothing by what you said the other –'

'Mrs Skene,' said Lydia, interrupting her softly: 'tell him nothing at all as yet. I have made up my mind at last. If he does not hear from me within a fortnight, you may tell him what you please. Can you wait so long?'

'Of course. Whatever you wish, maam. But Mellish's benefit is to be tomorrow night; and –'

'What have I to do with Mellish or his benefit?'

Mrs Skene, abashed, murmured apologetically that she was only wishful that the boy should do himself credit.

'If he is to benefit Mellish by beating somebody, he will not be behindhand. Remember: you are not to mention me for a fortnight. Is that a bargain?'

'Whatever you wish, maam,' repeated Mrs Skene, hardly satisfied. But Lydia gave her no further comfort; so she begged to take her leave, expressing a hope that things would turn out to the advantage of all parties. Lydia insisted on her partaking of some solid refreshment, and afterwards drove her to the railway station in the pony-carriage. Just before they parted, Lydia, suddenly recurring to their former subject, said,

'Does Mr Byron ever *think*?'

'Think!' said Mrs Skene emphatically. 'Never. There isnt a more cheerful lad in existence, miss.'

Then Mrs Skene was carried away to London, wondering whether it could be quite right for a young lady to live in a gorgeous castle without any elder of her own sex, and to speak freely and civilly to her inferiors. When she got home she said nothing of her excursion to Skene, who had never been known to keep a secret except as to the whereabouts of a projected fight. But she sat up late with her daughter Fanny, tantalizing her by accounts of the splendor of the castle, and consoling her by describing Miss Carew as a slight creature with red hair and no figure (Fanny having jet black hair, fine arms, and being one of Cashel's most proficient pupils).

'All the same, Fan,' added Mrs Skene, as she took her candlestick at two in the morning, 'if it comes off, Cashel will never be master in his own house.'

'I can see that very plain,' said Fanny; 'but if respectable professional people are not good enough for him, he will have only himself to thank if he gets himself looked down upon by empty-headed swells.'

Meanwhile, Lydia, on her return to the castle after a long drive round the country, had attempted to overcome an attack of restlessness by getting to work on the biography of her father. With a view to preparing a chapter on his taste in literature she had lately been examining his favorite books for marked passages. She now resumed this search, standing perched on the library ladder, taking down volume after volume, and occasionally dipping into the contents for a few pages or so. At this desultory work the time passed as imperceptibly as the shadows lengthened. The last book she examined was a volume of poems. There were no marks in it; but it opened at a page which had evidently lain open often before. The first words Lydia saw were these:

What would I give for a heart of flesh to warm me through
Instead of this heart of stone ice-cold whatever I do!
Hard and cold and small, of all hearts the worst of all.

Lydia hastily stepped down from the ladder, and recoiled until she reached a chair, where she sat and read and re-read these lines. The failing light roused her to action. She replaced the book on the shelf, and said, as she went to the writing-table, 'If such a doubt as that haunted my father, it will haunt me, unless I settle what is to be my heart's business now and for ever. If it be possible for a child of mine to escape this curse, it must inherit its immunity from its father, and not from me – from the man of impulse who never thinks, and not from the rationalizing woman, who cannot help thinking. Be it so.'

CHAPTER XIV

BEFORE many days had elapsed, a letter came for Cashel as he sat taking tea with the Skene family. When he saw the handwriting, a deep red color mounted to his temples.

'Oh Lor!' said Miss Skene, who sat next him. 'Lets read it.'

'Go to the dickens,' cried Cashel, hastily baffling her as she snatched at it.

'Dont worrit him, Fan,' said Mrs Skene tenderly.

'Not for the world, poor dear,' said Miss Skene, putting her hand affectionately on his shoulder. 'Let me just peep at the name – only to see who it's from. Do, Cashel *dear*.'

'It's from nobody,' said Cashel. 'Here: get out. If you dont let me alone, I'll make it warm for you the next time you come to me for a lesson.'

'Very likely,' said Fanny contemptuously. 'Who had the best of it today, I should like to know?'

'Gev him a hot un on the chin with her right as ever I see,' observed Skene, with hoarse mirth.

Cashel moved out of Fanny's reach to read the letter, which ran thus:

'REGENT'S PARK.

'Dear Mr Cashel Byron – I am desirous that you should meet a friend of mine. She will be here at three o'clock tomorrow afternoon. You would oblige me greatly by calling on me at that hour. – Yours faithfully,

LYDIA CAREW.'

There was a long pause, during which there was no sound in the room except the ticking of the clock and the munching of shrimps by the ex-champion.

'Good news, I hope, Cashel,' said Mrs Skene at last, tremulously.

'Blow me if I understand it,' said Cashel. 'Can you make

it out?' And he handed the letter to his adopted mother. Skene stopped eating to see his wife read, a feat which was to him one of the wonders of learning.

'I think the lady she mentions must be herself,' said Mrs Skene, after some consideration.

'No,' said Cashel, shaking his head. 'She always says what she means.'

'Ah,' said Skene cunningly; 'but she cant write it though. Thats the worst of writing: no one cant never tell exactly what it means. I never signed articles yet that there werent some misunderstanding about; and articles is the best writing that can be had anywhere.'

'Youd better go and see what it means,' said Mrs Skene.

'Right,' said Skene. 'Go and have it out with her, my boy.'

'It is short, and not particularly sweet,' said Fanny. 'She might have had the civility to put her crest at the top.'

'What would you give to be her?' said Cashel derisively, catching the letter as she tossed it disdainfully to him.

'If I was, I'd respect myself more than to throw myself at *your* head.'

'Hush, Fanny,' said Mrs Skene: 'youre too sharp. Ned: you oughtnt to encourage her by laughing.'

Next day Cashel paid extra attention to his diet; took some exercise with the gloves; had a bath and a rub down; and presented himself at Regent's Park at three o'clock in excellent condition. Expecting to see Bashville, he was surprised when the door was opened by a female servant.

'Miss Carew at home?'

'Yes, sir,' said the girl, falling in love with him at first sight. 'Mr Byron, sir?'

'Thats me,' said Cashel. 'I say: is there any one with her?'

'Only a lady, sir.'

'Oh damn! Well, it cant be helped. Never say die.'

The girl led him to a door; and when he entered shut it softly without announcing him. The room was a picture gallery, lighted from the roof. At the end, with their backs toward him, were two ladies: Lydia, and a woman whose noble carriage and elegant form would have raised hopes of beauty in a man less preoccupied than Cashel. But he, after advancing some distance with his eyes on Lydia, suddenly changed countenance; stopped; and was actually turning to fly when the ladies, hearing his light step, faced about and rooted him to the spot. As Lydia offered him her hand, her companion, who had surveyed the visitor first with indifference and then with incredulous surprise, exclaimed, in a burst of delighted recognition, like a child finding a long lost plaything, 'My darling boy!' And going to Cashel with the grace of a swan, she clasped him in her arms. In acknowledgment of which, he thrust his red discomfited face over her shoulder; winked at Lydia with his tongue in his cheek; and said,

'This is what you may call the Voice of Nature, and no mistake.'

'What a splendid creature you are!' said Mrs Byron, holding him a little away from her, the better to admire him. 'How handsome you are, you wretch!'

'How d'ye do, Miss Carew,' said Cashel, breaking loose, and turning to Lydia. 'Never mind her: it's only my mother. At least,' he added, as if correcting himself, 'she's my mamma.'

'And where have you come from? Where have you been? Do you know that I have not seen you for seven years, you unnatural boy? Think of his being my son, Miss Carew! Give me another kiss, my own,' she continued, grasping his arm affectionately. 'What a muscular creature you are!'

'Kiss away as much as you like,' said Cashel, struggling with the old schoolboy sullenness as it returned oppressively upon him. 'I suppose youre well. You look right enough.'

'Yes,' she said mockingly, beginning to despise him for his inability to act up to her in this thrilling scene: 'I *am* right enough. Your language is as refined as ever. And why do you get your hair cropped close like that? You must let it grow, and –'

'Now look here,' said Cashel, stopping her hand neatly as she raised it to re-arrange his locks. 'You just drop it, or I'll walk out at that door and you wont see me again for another seven years. You can either take me as you find me, or let me alone. If you want to know the reason for my wearing my hair short, youll find it in the histories of Absalom and Dan Mendoza. Now are you any the wiser?'

Mrs Byron became a shade colder. 'Indeed!' she said. 'Just the same still, Cashel?'

'Just the same, both one and other of us,' he replied. 'Before you spoke six words, I felt as if we'd parted only yesterday.'

'I am rather taken aback by the success of my experiment,' interposed Lydia. 'I invited you purposely to meet one another. The resemblance between you led me to suspect the truth; and my suspicion was confirmed by the account Mr Byron gave me of his adventures.'

Mrs Byron's vanity was touched. 'Is he like me?' she said, scanning his features. He, without heeding her, said to Lydia with undisguised mortification,

'And was *that* why you sent for me?'

'Are you disappointed?' said Lydia.

'He is not in the least glad to see me,' said Mrs Byron plaintively. 'He has no heart.'

'Now she'll go on for the next hour,' said Cashel, looking to Lydia, obviously because he found it much pleasanter than looking at his mother. 'No matter: if you dont care, I dont. So fire away, mamma.'

'And you think we are really like one another?' said Mrs Byron, not heeding him. 'Yes: I think we are. There is a slight –' She broke off, and added with sudden mistrust, 'Are you married, Cashel?'

'Ha! ha! ha!' shouted Cashel. 'No; but I hope to be, some day.' And he ventured to glance again at Lydia, who was, however, attentively observing Mrs Byron.

'Well, tell me everything about yourself. What are you? Now I do hope, Cashel, that you have not gone upon the stage.'

'The stage!' said Cashel contemptuously. 'Do I look like it?'

'You certainly do not,' said Mrs Byron whimsically, 'although you have a certain odious professional air too. What did you do when you ran away so scandalously from that stupid school in the north? How do you earn your living? Or *do* you earn it?'

'I suppose I do, seeing that I am alive. What do you think I was best fit for after my bringing up? Crossing sweeping, perhaps! When I ran away from Panley, I went to sea.'

'A sailor, of all things! You dont look like one. And pray, what rank have you attained in your profession?'

'The front rank. The top of the tree,' said Cashel shortly.

'Mr Byron is not at present following the profession of a sailor, nor has he done so for many years,' said Lydia.

Cashel looked at her, half in appeal, half in remonstrance.

'Something very different indeed,' pursued Lydia, with quiet obstinacy. 'And something very startling.'

'*Cant* you shut up!' exclaimed Cashel. 'I should have expected more sense from you. Whats the use of setting her on to make a fuss and put me in a rage. I'll go away if you dont stop.'

'What is the matter?' said Mrs Byron. 'Have you been doing anything disgraceful, Cashel?'

'There she goes: I told you so. I keep a gymnasium: thats all. Theres nothing disgraceful in that, I hope.'

'A gymnasium!' repeated Mrs Byron, with imperious disgust. 'What nonsense! You must give up everything of that kind, Cashel. It is very silly, and very low. You were too ridiculously proud, of course, to come to me for the means of keeping yourself in a proper position. I suppose I shall have to provide you with –'

'If I ever take a penny from you, may I –' Cashel caught Lydia's anxious look, and checked himself. He lightly retreated a step, a cunning smile flickering on his lips. 'No,' he said: 'it's just playing into your hands to lose temper with you. Make me angry now if you can.'

'There is not the slightest reason for anger,' said Mrs Byron, angry herself. 'Your temper seems to have become ungovernable – or rather to have remained so; for it was never remarkable for sweetness.'

'No?' retorted Cashel, jeering good-humoredly. 'Not the slightest occasion to lose my temper! Not when I am told that I am silly and low! Why, I think you must fancy that youre talking to your little Cashel, that blessed child you were so fond of. But youre not. Youre talking – now for a screech, Miss Carew! – to the champion of Australia, the United States, and England; holder of three silver belts and one gold one; professor of boxing to the nobility and gentry of St James's; and common prizefighter to the whole globe without reference to weight or color for not less than £500 a side. Thats Cashel Byron.'

Mrs Byron recoiled, astounded. After a pause, she said, 'Oh, Cashel, how *could* you?' Then, approaching him again, 'Do you mean to say that you go out and fight those great rough savages?'

'Yes, I do. You can have the gold belt to wear in King John if you think itll become you.'

'And that you *beat* them?'

'Yes. Ask Miss Carew how Billy Paradise looked after standing before me for an hour.'

'You wonderful boy! What an occupation! And have you done all this in your own name?'

'Of course I have. I am not ashamed of it. I often wondered whether you had seen my name in the papers?'

'I never read the papers. But you must have heard of my return to England. Why did you not come to see me?'

'I wasnt quite certain that you would like it,' said Cashel uneasily, avoiding her eye. 'Hallo!' he exclaimed, as he attempted to refresh himself by another look at Lydia: 'she's given us the slip.'

'She is quite right to leave us alone together under the circumstances. And now tell me why my precious boy should doubt that his own mother wished to see him.'

'I dont know why he should,' said Cashel, with melancholy submission to her affection. 'But he did.'

'How insensible you are! Did you not know that you were always my cherished darling – my only son?'

Cashel, who was now sitting beside her on an ottoman, groaned, and moved restlessly, but said nothing.

'Are you glad to see me?'

'Yes,' said Cashel dismally, 'I suppose I am. I – By Jingo!' he cried, with sudden animation, 'perhaps you can give me a lift here. I never thought of that. I say, mamma: I am in great trouble at present; and I think you can help me if you will.'

Mrs Byron looked at him satirically. But she said soothingly, 'Of course I will help you – as far as I am able – my precious one. All I possess is yours.'

Cashel ground his feet on the floor impatiently, and then sprang up. After an interval, during which he seemed to be swallowing some indignant protest, he said,

'You may put your mind at rest, once and for all, on the subject of money. I dont want anything of that sort.'

'I am glad you are so independent, Cashel.'

'So am I.'

'Do, pray, be more amiable.'

'I am amiable enough,' he cried desperately, 'only you wont listen.'

'My treasure,' said Mrs Byron remorsefully. 'What is the matter?'

'Well,' said Cashel, somewhat mollified, 'it's this. I want to marry Miss Carew: thats all.'

'*You* marry Miss Carew!' Mrs Byron's tenderness had vanished; and her tone was shrewd and contemptuous. 'Do you know, you silly boy, that –'

'I know all about it,' said Cashel determinedly: 'what she is; and what I am; and the rest of it. And I want to marry her; and, whats more, I *will* marry her, if I have to break the neck of every swell in London first. So you can either help me or not, as you please; but if you wont, never call me your precious boy any more. Now!'

Mrs Byron abdicated her dominion there and then for ever. She sat with quite a mild expression for some time in silence. Then she said,

'After all, I do not see why you should not. It would be a very good match for you.'

'Yes; but a deuced bad one for her.'

'Really I do not see that, Cashel. When your uncle dies, I suppose you will succeed to the Dorsetshire property.'

'I the heir to a property! Are you in earnest?'

'Of course. Old Bingley Byron, disagreeable as he is, cannot live for ever.'

'Who the dickens is Bingley Byron; and what has he to do with me?'

'Your uncle, of course. Really, Cashel, you ought to think about these things. Did it never occur to you that you must have relatives, like other people?'

'You never told me anything about them. Well, I *am* blowed! But – but – I mean – Supposing he *is* my uncle, am I his lawful heir?'

'Yes. Walford Byron, the only brother besides your father, died years ago, whilst you were at Moncrief's; and he had no sons. Bingley is a bachelor.'

'But,' said Cashel cautiously, 'wont there be some bother about my – at least –'

'My dearest child, what are you thinking or talking about? Nothing can be clearer than your title.'

'Well,' said Cashel blushing, 'a lot of people used to make out that you werent married at all.'

'What!' exclaimed Mrs Byron indignantly. 'Oh, they *dare* not say so! Impossible. Why did you not tell me at once?'

'I didnt think about it,' said Cashel, hastily excusing himself. 'I was too young to care. It doesnt matter now. My father is dead, isnt he?'

'He died when you were a baby. You have often made me angry with you, poor little innocent, by reminding me of him. Do not talk of him to me.'

'Not if you dont wish. Just one thing though, mamma. Was he a gentleman?'

'Of course. What a question!'

'Then I am as good as any of the swells that think themselves her equals? She has a cousin in a government office: a fellow that gives himself out as the Home Secretary, and most likely sits in a big chair in a hall and cheeks the public. Am I as good as he is?'

'You are perfectly well connected by your mother's side, Cashel. The Byrons are only commoners; but even they are one of the oldest families in England.'

Cashel began to show signs of excitement. 'How much a year are they worth?' he demanded.

'I dont know how much they are worth now: your father was always in difficulties; and so was his father. But Bingley is a miser. Five thousand a year, perhaps.'

'Thats an independence. Thats enough. She said she couldnt expect a man to be so thunderingly rich as she is.'

'Indeed? Then you have discussed the question with her?'

Cashel was about to speak, when the maid entered to say that Miss Carew was in the library, and begged that they would come to her as soon as they were quite disengaged. As the girl withdrew, he said eagerly,

'I wish youd go home, mamma, and let me catch her in the library by herself. Tell me where you live; and I'll come in the evening and let you know all about it. That is, if you have no objection.'

'What objection could I possibly have, dearest one? Are you sure you are not spoiling your chance by too much haste? She has no occasion to hurry, Cashel; and she knows it.'

'I am dead certain that now is my time or never. I always

know by instinct when to go in and finish. Heres your mantle.'

'In such a hurry to get rid of your poor old mother, Cashel?'

'Oh, bother! youre not old. You wont mind my wanting you to go for this once, will you?.'

She smiled affectionately; put on her mantle; and turned her cheek towards him to be kissed. The unaccustomed gesture alarmed him: he got away a step, and involuntarily assumed an attitude of self-defence, as if the problem before him were a pugilistic one. Recovering himself immediately, he kissed her, and impatiently accompanied her to the house door, which he closed softly behind her, leaving her to walk in search of her carriage alone. Then he stole upstairs to the library, where he found Lydia reading.

'She's gone,' he said.

Lydia put down her book; looked up at him; saw what was coming; looked down again to hide a spasm of terror; and said, with a steady severity that cost her a great effort, 'I hope you have not quarrelled.'

'Lord bless you, no! We kissed one another like turtle doves. At odd moments she wheedles me into feeling fond of her in spite of myself. She went away because I asked her to.'

'And why do you ask my guests to go away?'

'Because I wanted to be alone with you. Dont look as if you didnt understand. She's told me a whole heap of things about myself that alter our affairs completely. My birth is all right; I'm heir to a county family that came over with the Conqueror; and I shall have a decent income. I can afford to give away weight to old Webber now.'

'Well?' said Lydia sternly.

'Well,' said Cashel unabashed, 'the only use of all that to me is that I may marry if I like. No more fighting or teaching now.'

'And when you are married, will you be as tender to your wife as you are to your mother?'

Cashel's elation vanished. 'I knew youd think that,' he

said. 'I am always the same with her: I cant help it. I cant like a woman through thick and thin merely because she happens to be my mother; and I wont pretend to do it to please anybody. She makes me look like a fool, or like a brute. Have I ever been so with you?'

'Yes,' said Lydia. 'Except,' she added, 'that you have never shewn absolute dislike to me.'

'Ah! *Except!* Thats a very big except. But I dont dislike her. Blood is thicker than water; and I have a softness for her; only I wont put up with her nonsense. But it's different with you – I cant explain how, because I'm not good at sentiment – not that theres any sentiment about it. At least, I dont mean that; but –Youre fond of me in a sort of way, aint you?'

'Yes; I'm fond of you in a sort of way.'

'Well, then,' he said uneasily, 'wont you marry me? I'm not such a fool as you think; and youll like me better after a while.'

Lydia became very pale. 'Have you considered,' she said, 'that henceforth you will be an idle man, and that I shall always be a busy woman, preoccupied with work that may seem very dull to you?'

'I wont be idle. Theres lots of things I can do besides boxing. We'll get on together, never fear. People that are fond of one another never have any difficulty; and people that hate each other never have any comfort. I'll be on the look-out to make you happy. You neednt fear my interrupting your Latin and Greek: I wont expect you to give up your whole life to me. Why should I? Theres reason in everything. So long as you are mine, and nobody else's, I'll be content. And I'll be yours and nobody else's. Whats the use of supposing half-a-dozen accidents that may never happen? Lets take our chance. You have too much good nature ever to be nasty.'

'It would be a hard bargain,' she said doubtfully; 'for you would have to give up your occupation; and I should give up nothing but my unfruitful liberty.'

'I will swear never to fight again; and you neednt swear anything. If that is not an easy bargain, I dont know what is.'

'Easy for me: yes. But for you?'

'Never mind me. You do whatever you like; and I'll do whatever you like. You have a conscience; so I know that whatever you like will be the best thing. I have the most science; but you have the most sense. Come!'

Lydia looked around, as if for a means of escape. Cashel waited anxiously. There was a long pause.

'It cant be,' he said pathetically, 'that youre afraid of me because I was a prizefighter.'

'Afraid of you! No: I am afraid of myself; afraid of the future; afraid *for* you. But my mind is already made up on this subject. When I brought about this meeting between you and your mother, I determined to marry you if you asked me again.'

She stood up quietly, and waited. The rough hardihood of the ring fell from him like a garment: he blushed deeply, and did not know what to do. Nor did she; but without willing it she came a step closer to him, and turned up her face towards his. He, nearly blind with confusion, put his arms about her and kissed her. Suddenly she broke loose from his arms; seized the lappels of his coat tightly in her hands; and leaned back until she hung from him with all her weight.

'Cashel,' she said: 'we are the silliest lovers in the world, I believe: we know nothing about it. Are you really fond of me?'

He could only answer 'Yes' in a constrained way, and stare helplessly and timidly at her. His ineptitude was embarrassing; but she had sense enough to be glad to find him unmistakeably as entire a novice at lovemaking as herself. He remained shy, and was so evidently anxious to go that she presently asked him to leave her for a while, though she was surprised to feel a faint pang of disappointment when he consented.

On leaving the house, he hurried to the address which his mother had given him: a prodigious building in Westminster, divided into residential flats, to the seventh floor of which he ascended in a lift. As he stepped from it he saw Lucian Webber walking away from him along a corridor. Obeying a sudden impulse, he followed, and overtook him just as he was entering a room. Lucian, finding that someone was resisting his attempt to close the door, looked out; recognized Cashel; turned white; and hastily retreated into the apartment, where, getting behind a writing-table, he snatched a revolver from a drawer. Cashel recoiled, amazed and frightened, with his arm up as if to ward off a blow.

'Hallo!' he cried. 'Drop that damned thing, will you! If you dont, I'll shout for help.'

'If you approach me, I will fire,' said Lucian excitedly. 'I will teach you that your obsolete brutality is powerless against the weapons Science has put into the hands of civilized men. Leave my apartments. I am not afraid of you; but I do not choose to be disturbed by your presence.'

'Confound your cheek,' said Cashel indignantly: 'is that the way you receive a man who comes to make a friendly call on you?'

'Friendly *now*, doubtless, when you see that I am well protected.'

Cashel gave a long whistle. 'Oh,' he said: 'you thought I came to pitch into you. Ha! ha! And you call that science – to draw a pistol on a man! But you darent fire it; and well you know it. Youd better put it up, or you may let it off without intending to: I never feel comfortable when I see a fool meddling with firearms. I came to tell you that I'm going to be married to your cousin. Aint you glad?'

Lucian's face changed. He believed; but he said obstinately, 'I dont credit that statement. It is a lie.'

This outraged Cashel. 'I tell you again,' he said, in a menacing tone, 'that your cousin is engaged to me. Now call me a liar, and hit me in the face if you dare. Look here,' he added, taking a leather case from his pocket, and extracting from it a bank note: 'I'll give you that twenty-pound note if you will hit me one blow.' And he put his hands behind him, and placed himself before Lucian, who, sick with fury, and half paralysed by a sensation which he would not acknowledge as fear, forced himself to stand his ground. Cashel thrust out his jaw invitingly, and said, with a sinister grin, 'Put it in straight, governor. Twenty pounds, remember.'

At that moment Lucian would have given all his political and social chances for the strength and skill of his adversary. He could see only one way to escape the torment of Cashel's jeering, and the self-reproach of a coward; for his point of honor, learnt at an English public school, was essentially the same as the prizefighter's. He desperately clenched his fist and struck out. The blow wasted itself on space; and he stumbled forward against Cashel, who laughed uproariously, and exclaimed, clapping him on the back,

'Well done, my boy. I thought you were going to be mean; but youve been game; and youre welcome to the stakes. I'll tell Lydia that you have fought me for twenty pounds and won on your merits. Aint you proud of yourself for having a go at the champion?'

'Sir –' began Lucian. But nothing coherent followed.

'You just sit down for a quarter of an hour, and dont drink any spirits; and youll be all right. When you recover youll be glad you shewed pluck. So goodnight for the present: I know how you feel; and I'll be off. Be sure not to try to settle yourself with wine: itll only make you worse. Ta-ta!'

As Cashel withdrew, Lucian collapsed into a chair, shaken by the revival of passions and jealousies which he had thought as outgrown as the schoolboy jackets in which he had formerly experienced them. He rehearsed the scene a hundred times, not as it had happened, though the recollection of that stung him every moment, but as it might have happened had he, instead of Cashel, been the stronger man. He strove in vain to get on the lower plane, and plume himself on his pluck in having at least dared to strike. There was no escape from his inner knowledge that he had been driven by fear and hatred into a paroxysm of wrath against a man to whom he should have set an example of dignified control. An exhausting whirl in his thoughts, at once quickened and confused by the nervous shock of bodily violence, to which he was quite unused, distracted him. He wanted sympathy, refuge, an opportunity to retrieve himself by doing it all over again the right way. Before an hour had passed he was on his way to the house in Regent's Park.

Lydia was in her boudoir, occupied with a book, when he entered. He was not an acute observer: he could see no change in her. She was as calm as ever: her eyes were not fully open; and the touch of her hand subdued him as it had always done. Though he had never entertained any hope of possessing her since the day when she had refused him in Bedford Square, a sense of intolerable loss came upon him as he saw her for the first time pledged to another – and such another!

'Lydia,' he said, trying to speak vehemently, but failing to shake off the conventional address of which he had made a second nature: 'I have heard something that has filled me with inexpressible dismay. Is it true?'

'The news has travelled fast,' she said. 'Yes, it is true.' She spoke composedly, and so kindly that he choked in trying to reply.

'Then, Lydia, you are the chief actor in a greater tragedy than I have ever witnessed on the stage.'

'It is strange, is it not?' she said, smiling at his effort to be impressive.

'Strange! It is calamitous. I trust I may be allowed to say so. And you sit there reading as calmly as though nothing had happened.'

She handed him the book without a word.

'Ivanhoe!' he said. 'A novel!'

'Yes. Do you remember once, before you knew me very well, telling me that Scott's novels were the only ones you liked to see in the hands of ladies?'

'No doubt I did. But I cannot talk of literature just –'

'I am not leading you away from what you want to talk of. I was about to tell you that I came upon Ivanhoe by chance half an hour ago when I was searching – I confess it – for something very romantic to read. Ivanhoe was a prize-fighter: the first half of the book is a description of a prize-fight. I was wondering whether some romancer of the twenty-fourth century will hunt out the exploits of my husband, and present him to the world as a sort of English nineteenth century Cid, with all the glory of antiquity upon his deeds.'

Lucian made a gesture of impatience. 'I have never been able to understand,' he said, 'how it is that a woman of your ability can habitually dwell on perverse and absurd ideas. Oh, Lydia, is this to be the end of all your great gifts and attainments? Forgive me if I touch a painful chord; but this marriage seems to me so unnatural that I must speak out. Your father left you one of the richest and best-educated women in Europe. Would he approve of what you are about to do?'

'It almost seems to me that he educated me expressly to some such end. Whom would you have me marry?'

'Doubtless few men are worthy of you, Lydia. But this man least of all. Could you not marry a gentleman? If he were even an artist, a poet, or a man of genius of any kind, I could bear to think of it; for indeed I am not influenced by class prejudice in the matter. But a – I will try to say nothing that you must not in justice admit to be too obvious to be ignored – a man of the lower orders, pursuing a calling which even the lower orders despise; illiterate, rough, await-ing at this moment a disgraceful sentence at the hands of the law! Is it possible that you have considered all these things?'

'Not very deeply: they are not of a kind to concern me much. I can console you as to one of them. I have always recognized Cashel as a gentleman, in your sense of the word. He proves to be so: his people are county people and so forth. As to his trial, I have spoken with Lord Worthington about it, and also with the lawyers who have charge of the case; and they say positively that, owing to certain proofs not being in the hands of the police, a defence can be set up that will save him from imprisonment.'

'There is no such defence possible,' said Lucian angrily.

'Perhaps not. As far as I understand it, it is rather an aggravation of the offence than an excuse for it. But if they imprison him, it will make no difference. He can console himself with the certainty that I will marry him at once when he is released.'

Lucian's face lengthened. He abandoned the argument, and said blankly, 'I cannot suppose that you would allow yourself to be deceived. If he is a gentleman, that of course alters the case completely.'

'Lucian,' said Lydia earnestly: 'will you believe that it actually altered the case with me? There is, I know, a plane upon which his past pursuits are wrong; but we are not upon that plane any more than he. The discovery of his rank does not alter the weight of one blow he has ever struck; and yet you have just now admitted that it alters the case completely. It was not prizefighting that you objected to: that was only a pretence: your true repugnance was to the class to which prizefighters belong. And so, worldly cousin Lucian, I silence all your objections by convincing you that I am not going to connect you by marriage with a butcher, bricklayer, or other member of the trades from which Cashel's profession, as you warned me, is usually recruited. Stop a moment: I am going to do justice to you. You want to say that my un-worldly friend Lucian is far more deeply concerned at seeing the phoenix of modern culture throw herself away on a man unworthy of her.'

'That *is* what I mean to say, except that you put it too modestly. It is a case of the phoenix, not only of modern culture, but of natural endowment and of every happy accident of the highest civilization, throwing herself away on a man specially incapacitated by his tastes and pursuits from comprehending her or entering the circle in which she moves.'

'Listen to me patiently, Lucian; and I will try to explain the mystery to you, leaving the rest of the world to misunderstand me as it pleases. First, you will grant me that even a phoenix must marry some one in order that she may hand on her torch to her children. Her best course would be to marry another phoenix; but as she – poor girl! – cannot appreciate even her own phoenixity, much less that of another, she perversely prefers a mere mortal. Who is the mortal to be? Not her cousin Lucian; for rising young politicians must have helpful wives, with feminine politics and powers of visiting and entertaining: a description inapplicable to the phoenix. Not, as you just now suggested, a man of letters. The phoenix has had her share of playing helpmeet to a man of letters, and does not care to repeat that experience. She is sick to death of the morbid introspection and ignorant self-consciousness of poets, novelists, and their like. As to artists, all the good ones are married; and ever since the rest have been able to read in hundreds of books that they are the most gifted and godlike of men, they are become almost as intolerable as their literary flatterers. No, Lucian: the phoenix has paid her debt to literature and art by the toil of her childhood. She will use and enjoy both of them in future as best she can; but she will never again drudge in their laboratories. You say that she might at least have married some one with the habits of a gentleman. But the gentlemen she knows are either amateurs of the arts, having the egotism of professional artists without their ability; or they are men of pleasure, which means that they are dancers, tennis players, butchers, and gamblers. I leave the nonentities out of the question. In the eyes of a phoenix, even the arena – the ring, as they call it – is a better school of character than the drawing room; and a prizefighter is a hero in comparison with the wretch who sets a leash of greyhounds upon a hare. Imagine, now, this poor phoenix meeting with a man who had never been guilty of self-analysis in his life – who complained when he was annoyed, and exulted when he was glad, like a child and unlike a modern man – who was hones and brave, strong and beautiful. You open your eyes, Lucian: you do not do justice to Cashel's good looks. He is twenty-five; and yet there is not a line in his face. It is neither thoughtful, nor poetic, nor wearied, nor doubting, nor old, nor self-conscious, as so many of his contemporaries' faces are – as mine, perhaps, is. The face of a pagan god, assured of eternal youth! I should be mad, since I must marry, to miss such a man.'

'You are mad as it is,' cried Lucian rising, scared and vehement. 'This is infatuation. You no more see the real man as I see him than –'

'Than you can see me as I appear to those who dislike me, Lucian. How do you know that what you see is the real man?'

'I see him as every one sees him except you. That shews that you are infatuated. You know – you *must* know – that you have lost your senses on this subject.'

'I have given you reasons, Lucian. I am open to argument.'

'Argument! Reasons! Do you think that your folly is any the less folly because you have reasons for it? Rational folly is the worst of all folly, because it is armed against reason.'

Lydia opened her eyes fully for the first time during the conversation. 'Lucian,' she said, delightedly: 'you are coming out. I think that is the cleverest thing I ever heard you say. And it is true – frightfully true.'

He sat down despairingly. 'You would not admit it so readily,' he said, 'if you intended it to have the smallest effect on you. Even if all your arguments were good ones, what would they prove? If you really despise the pursuits of gentlemen, is that a reason for respecting the pursuits of prizefighters? Is the ring any the better because you can pretend to think the drawing room worse? – for you do not really hold any such monstrous opinion. How you would scout your own sophistry if I used it in trying to persuade you to conform to social usages!'

'We are drifting back again into mere rationalism, Lucian. However, it is my fault. I began an explanation, and rambled off, womanlike, into praise of my lover. Do not think that I wish to represent my choice as any better than a choice of the least of two evils. I strongly think that Society ought to have made something better of Cashel than a prizefighter; but he, poor fellow, had no choice at all. I once called him a ruffian; and I do not retract the word; though I expect you to forgive him his ruffianism as you forgive a soldier his murders, or a lawyer his lies. When you condemn the others – and with all my heart I say the sooner the better – condemn him, but not before. Besides, my dear Lucian, the prizefighting is all over: he does not intend to go on with it. As to our personal suitability, I believe in the doctrine of heredity; and as my body is frail and my brain morbidly active, I think my impulse towards a man strong in body and untroubled in mind a trustworthy one. You can understand that: it is a plain proposition in eugenics.'

'I know that you will do whatever you have made up your mind to do,' said Lucian desolately.

'And you will make the best of it, will you not?'

'The best or worst of it does not rest with me. I can only accept it as inevitable.'

'Not at all. You can make the worst of it by behaving distantly to Cashel; or the best of it by being friendly with him.'

'I had better tell you,' he said. 'I have seen him since – since – ' Lydia nodded. 'I mistook his object in coming into my room as he did, unannounced. In fact, he almost forced his way in. Some words arose between us. At last he taunted me beyond endurance, and offered me – characteristically – £20 to strike him. And I am sorry to say that I did so.'

'You did so!' said Lydia, turning very pale. 'And what followed?'

'I should say rather that I meant to strike him; for he avoided me, or else I missed my aim. He only gave me the money and went away, evidently with a high opinion of me. He left me with a very low one of myself.'

'What! He did not retaliate!' exclaimed Lydia, recovering her color. 'Oh, he has beaten you on your own ground, Lucian. It is you who are the prizefighter at heart; and you grudge him his superiority in the very art you condemn him for professing.'

'I was wrong, Lydia, but I grudged him you. I know I acted hastily; and I will apologize to him. I wish matters had fallen out otherwise.'

'They could not have done so; and I believe you will yet acknowledge that they have arranged themselves very well. Now that the phœnix is disposed of, I want to read you a letter I have received from Alice Goff, which throws quite a new light on her character. I have not seen her since June; and her mind seems to have grown three years in the interim. Listen to this, for example.'

And so the conversation turned upon Alice.

When Lucian returned to his chambers, he wrote the following note, which he posted to Cashel Byron before going to bed.

'Dear Sir – I beg to enclose you a bank note which you left here this evening. I feel bound to express my regret for what passed on that occasion, and to assure you that it proceeded from a misapprehension of your purpose in calling on me. The nervous disorder into which the severe mental application and late hours of the past session have thrown me must be my excuse. I hope to have the pleasure of meeting you again soon, and offering you personally my congratulations on your approaching marriage. – I am, dear Sir, Yours very truly,

'LUCIAN WEBBER.'

CHAPTER XV

IN the following month Cashel Byron, William Paradise, and Robert Mellish appeared in the dock together, the first two for having been principals in a prizefight, and Mellish for having acted as bottleholder to Paradise. These offences were verbosely described in a long indictment which was to have included the fourth man captured. But against him the grand jury had refused to find a true bill. The prisoners pleaded not guilty.

The defence was that the fight, the occurrence of which was admitted, was not a prizefight, but the outcome of an enmity which had subsisted between the two men since one of them, at a public exhibition at Islington, had attacked and bitten the other. In support of this, it was shewn that Byron had occupied a house at Wiltstoken, and had lived there with Mellish, who had invited Paradise to spend a holiday with him in the country. This accounted for the presence of the three men at Wiltstoken on the day in question. Words had arisen between Byron and Paradise on the subject of the Islington affair; and they had at last agreed to settle the dispute in the old English fashion. They had adjourned to a field, and fought fairly and determinedly until interrupted by the police, who, misled by appearances, mistook the affair for a prizefight.

Prizefighting, Cashel Byron's counsel said, was a brutal pastime, rightly discountenanced by the law; but a fair stand-up fight between two unarmed men, though doubtless technically a breach of the peace, had never been severely dealt with by British juries or British judges, who knew how much it was to our national and manly tolerance of the fist, Nature's weapon, that we owed our freedom from the murderous stiletto of the Italian, the revolver of the cowboy, and the treacherous kick of the French savate player (Mellish, whose favorite spectacle was Devonshire and Lancashire wrestling, murmured in patriotic assent). The case would be amply met by binding over the prisoners, who were now on the best of terms with one another, to keep the peace for a reasonable period. The sole evidence against this view of the case was police evidence; and the police were naturally reluctant to admit that they had found a mare's nest. In proof that the fight had been premeditated, and was a prizefight, they alleged that it had taken place within an enclosure formed with ropes and stakes. But where were those ropes and stakes? They were not forthcoming; and he (counsel) submitted that the reason was not, as had been suggested, that they had been spirited away, which was plainly impossible; but that they had existed only in the excited imagination of the posse of constables who had arrested the prisoners.

Again, it had been urged that the prisoners were in fighting costume. But cross-examination had elicited that fighting costume meant practically no costume at all: the men had simply stripped in order that their movements might be unembarrassed. It had been proved that Paradise had been – well, in the traditional costume of Paradise (Roars of laughter: Paradise grinning in confusion) until the police borrowed a horsecloth to put upon him.

That the constables had been guilty of gross exaggeration was shewn by their evidence as to the desperate injuries the combatants had inflicted upon one another. Of Paradise in particular it had been alleged that his features were obliterated. The jury had before them in the dock the man whose features had been obliterated only a few weeks previously. If that were true, where had the prisoner obtained the unblemished lineaments which he was now, full of health and good humor, presenting to them? (Renewed laughter. Paradise suffused with blushes.) It was said that these terrible injuries, the traces of which had disappeared so miraculously, were inflicted by the prisoner Byron, a young gentleman tenderly nurtured, and visibly inferior in strength and hardihood to his herculean opponent. Doubtless Byron had been emboldened by his skill in mimic combat with softly padded gloves to try conclusions, under the very different conditions of real fighting, with a man whose massive shoulders and determined cast of features ought to have convinced him that such an enterprise was nothing short of desperate. Fortunately the police had interfered before he had suffered severely for his rashness. Yet it had been alleged that he had actually worsted Paradise in the encounter – obliterated his features! That was a fair sample of the police evidence, which was throughout consistently incredible and at variance with the dictates of common sense.

It was unnecessary to waste the time of the jury by comment on the honorable manner in which Byron had come forward and given himself up to the police the moment he learnt that they were in search of him. Such conduct spoke for itself. Paradise would, beyond a doubt, have adopted the same straightforward course had he not been arrested at once, and that too without the least effort at resistance on his part. Surely this was hardly the line that would have suggested itself to two lawless prizefighters.

An attempt had been made to prejudice the prisoner Byron by the statement that he was a notorious professional bruiser. But no proof of that was forthcoming; and if the fact were really notorious there could be no difficulty in proving it. Such notoriety as Mr Byron enjoyed was due, as his friend Lord Worthington had let slip in the course of examination, to his approaching marriage with a lady of distinction. Was it credible that a highly connected gentleman in this enviable position would engage in a prizefight, risking disgrace and personal disfigurement for a sum of money that could be no object to him, or for a glory that would appear to all his friends as little better than infamy?

The whole of the evidence as to the character of the prisoners went to shew that they were men of unimpeachable integrity and respectability. An impression unfavorable to Paradise might have been created by the fact that he was a professional pugilist and a man of hasty temper; but it had also transpired that he had on one occasion rendered assistance to the police, thereby employing his athletic attainments in the interests of law and order. As to his temper, it accounted for the quarrel which the police – knowing his profession – had mistaken for a prizefight.

Mellish was a trainer of athletes: hence the witnesses to his character were chiefly persons connected with sport; but they were not the less worthy of credence on that account.

In fine, the charge would have been hard to believe even if supported by the strongest evidence. But when there was no evidence – when the police had failed to produce any of the accessories of a prizefight – when there were no ropes nor posts, no written articles, no stakes nor stakeholders, no seconds except the unfortunate man Mellish – whose mouth was closed by a law which, in defiance of the obvious interests of justice, forbade a prisoner to speak and clear himself – nothing, in fact, but the fancies of constables who had, under cross-examination, not only contradicted one another, but shewn the most complete ignorance (a highly creditable ignorance) of the nature and conditions of a prizefight, then counsel would venture to say confidently that the theory of the prosecution, ingenious as it was, and ably as it had been put forward, was absolutely and utterly untenable.

This, and much more of equal value, was delivered with relish by an eminent Queen's counsellor, whose spirits rose as he felt the truth change and fade whilst he rearranged its attendant circumstances. Cashel at first listened anxiously. He flushed and looked moody when his marriage was alluded to; but when the whole defence was unrolled, he was awestruck, and stared at his advocate as if he half feared that the earth would gape and swallow such a reckless perverter of known facts. Paradise felt that he was free already: his admiration for the barrister rose to the point of hero-worship. The Judge, and the more respectable persons in court, became extraordinarily grave, as Englishmen will when their sense of moral responsibility is roused on behalf of some glaring imposture. Every one in court knew that the police were right, that there had been a prizefight; that the betting on it had been recorded in all the sporting papers for weeks beforehand; that Cashel was the most terrible fighting man of the day; that Paradise had not dared to propose a renewal of the interrupted contest. And they listened with solemn approbation to the man who knew all this as well as they did, but who was clever enough to make it appear incredible and nonsensical.

It remained for the Judge to sweep away the defence, or to favor the prisoners by countenancing it. Fortunately for them, he had handled the gloves himself in his youth, and was old enough to recall, not without regret, a time when the memory of Cribb and Molyneux was yet green. He began his summing-up by telling the jury that the police had failed to prove that the fight was a prizefight. After that, the sporting spectators, by indulging in roars of laughter whenever they could find a pretext for doing so without being turned out of court, shewed that they had ceased to regard the trial seriously. The lay public retained its gravity to the last.

Finally the jury acquitted Mellish, and found Cashel and Paradise guilty of a common assault. They were sentenced to two days' imprisonment and bound over in sureties of £150 each to keep the peace for twelve months. The sureties were forthcoming; and as the imprisonment was supposed to date from the beginning of the sessions, the prisoners were at once released.

'By Jingo,' said Cashel emphatically as he left the court, 'if we didnt fight fairer than that in the ring, we'd be disqualified in the first round. It's the first cross I ever was mixed up in; and I hope it will be the last.'

CHAPTER XVI

MISS CAREW, averse to the anomalous relations of courtship, made as little delay as possible in getting married. Cashel's luck was not changed by the event. Bingley Byron died three weeks after the ceremony (which was civil and private); and Cashel had to claim possession of the property, in spite of his expressed wish that the lawyers would take themselves and the property to the devil, and allow him to enjoy his honeymoon in peace. The transfer took some time. Owing to his mother's capricious reluctance to give the necessary information without reserve, and to the law's delay, his first child was born some time before his succession was fully established, and the doors of a dilapidated country house in Dorsetshire opened to him. The conclusion of the business was a great relief to his solicitors, who had been unable to shake his conviction that the case was clear enough, but that the referee had been squared. By this he meant that the Lord Chancellor had been bribed to keep him out of his property.

His marriage proved a happy one. To make up for the loss of his occupation, he farmed, and lost six thousand pounds by it; tried gardening with better success; began to meddle in commercial enterprise as director of joint-stock companies in the city; and was soon after invited to represent a Dorsetshire constituency in Parliament in the Conservative interest. He was returned by a large majority; but as he voted just as often with the extreme Radicals as with the party which had returned him, he was speedily called upon to resign. He flatly refused, and held on until the next general election, which he carried as an independent candidate, thanks to a loud voice, an easy manner, the popularity of his own views, and the extent of his wife's information, which he retailed at second-hand. He made his maiden speech in the House unabashed the first night he sat there.

Indeed, he was afraid of nothing except burglars, big dogs, doctors, dentists, and street-crossings. Whenever an accident through any of these was reported, he read it to Lydia very seriously, and preserved the newspaper for quite two days as a document in support of his favorite assertion that the only place a man was safe in was the prize-ring. As he objected to most field sports on the ground of inhumanity, she, fearing that he would suffer in health and appearance from want of systematic exercise, suggested that he should resume the practice of boxing with gloves. But he shook his head. Boxing was too serious a pursuit to him to be either an amusement or a mere exercise. Besides, he had a prejudice that it did not become a married man. He had gone through with it when it was his business; but he had no idea of doing it for pleasure. His career as a pugilist was closed by his marriage.

His admiration for his wife survived the ardor of his first love for her; and her habitual forethought saved her from disappointing his reliance on her judgment. Her children, so carefully planned by her to inherit her intelligence with their father's robustness, proved to her that heredity is not so simple a matter as her father's generation supposed. They were healthy enough, certainly; and in their childhood they were all alike in being precocious and impudent, having no respect for Cashel, and shewing any they had for their mother principally by running to her when they were in difficulties. Of punishments and scoldings they had no experience. Cashel was incapable of deliberate retaliation upon a child; and in sudden emergencies of temper he could always master his hands: perhaps because he had learnt to do so in the ring: perhaps because he remembered his own childhood. Lydia controlled her children, as far as they were controllable, just as she controlled every one else. When she spoke of them to Cashel in private, he seldom said more than that the imps were too sharp for him, or that he was blest if he didnt believe they were born older than their father. Lydia often thought so too; but the care of this troublesome family had one advantage for her. It left her little time to think about herself at the time when the illusion of her love passed away, and she saw Cashel as he really was. She soon came to regard him as one of the children. He was by far the stupidest of them; but he needed her more, loved her more, and belonged to her more than any of them. For as they grew up, and the heredity scheme began to develop results, the boys disappointed her by turning out almost pure Carew, without the slightest athletic aptitude, whilst the girls were impetuously Byronic: indeed one of them, to Cashel's utter dismay, cast back so completely to his mother that when she announced, at thirteen, her intention of going on the stage, he bowed to her decision as to the voice of Destiny.

Alice Goff, when she heard of Lydia's projected marriage, saw that she must return to Wiltstoken and forget her brief social splendor as soon as possible. She therefore thanked Miss Carew for her bounty, and begged to relinquish her post of companion. Lydia assented, but managed to delay this sacrifice to a sense of duty and necessity until a day early in winter, when Lucian, who felt inclined to commit suicide, allowed his cousin to persuade him to offer his hand to Alice. She indignantly refused: not that she had any reason to complain of him, but because the prospect of returning to Wiltstoken made her feel ill-used, and she could not help revenging her soreness upon the first person she could find a pretext for attacking. He, lukewarm before, now became eager; and she, after trampling on him to her heart's content for months, drifted into an engagement, and was promptly married to him by Lydia, who took the matter in hand with her usual decision. She kept Lucian's house, entertained his guests, and domineered over his select social circle with complete success. She was something of a domestic bully; but her empire over her husband and home were never shaken. Lucian found unexpected depth and strength in her nature; and his uxoriousness was only held in check by the fierce impatience with which she sometimes made him feel that the excess of his content was measured by the shortcoming of hers. She invited her brother-in-law and his wife to dinner every Christmas day, and once a year in the season; but she never admitted that Wallace Parker and Cashel Byron were gentlemen, though she invited the latter freely, notwithstanding the frankness with which he spoke of his former exploits to strangers after dinner, without deference to their professions or prejudices. Her respect for Lydia remained so great that she never complained of Cashel save on one occasion, when, at a very special dinner party in her house, he shewed a bishop, whose mansion had been recently broken into and robbed, how to break a burglar's back in the act of grappling with him.

The Skenes returned to Australia and went their way there, as Mrs Byron did in England, in the paths they had pursued for years before. Cashel spoke always of Mrs Skene as 'mother,' and of Mrs Byron as 'mamma.'

William Paradise, though admired by the fair sex for his strength, courage, and fame, was not, like Cashel and Skene, wise or fortunate enough to get a good wife. So exceedingly did he drink that he had but few sober intervals after his escape from the law. He claimed the title of champion of England on Cashel's retirement from the ring, and challenged the world. The world responded in the persons of sundry young laboring men with a thirst for glory and a taste for fighting. Paradise fought and prevailed twice. Then he drank whilst in training, and was beaten. By this time, too, the ring had lapsed into the disrepute from which Cashel's unusual combination of pugilistic genius with honesty had temporarily raised it; and the law, again seizing Paradise as he was borne vanquished from the field, atoned for its former leniency by incarcerating him for six months. The abstinence thus enforced restored him to health and vigor; and he achieved another victory before he succeeded in drinking himself into his former state. This was his last triumph. With his natural ruffianism complicated by drunkenness, he went rapidly down the hill into the Valley of

Humiliation. Becoming noted for his readiness to sell the victories he could no longer win, he only appeared in the ring to test the capabilities of untried youths, who beat him with all the ardor of their age. He became a potman, and was immediately discharged as an inebriate. He had sunk into beggary when, hearing in his misery that his former antagonist was contesting a parliamentary election, he applied to him for alms. Cashel at the time was in Dorset-shire; but Lydia relieved the destitute bruiser, whose condition was now far worse than it had been at their last meeting. At his next application, which followed soon, he was confronted by Cashel, who bullied him fiercely; threatened to break every bone in his skin if he ever dared present himself again before Lydia; flung him five shillings; and bade him begone. For Cashel retained for Paradise that contemptuous and ruthless hatred in which a duly qualified professor holds a quack. The poor wretch, inured to insult and violence from men who had once feared his prowess as he, to give him such credit as he cared for, had never feared Cashel's, thought the abuse natural, and the gift generous. He picked up the money and shambled off to buy a few penceworth of food, which he could hardly eat; and to spend the rest in brandy, which he drank as fast as his stomach would endure it. Shortly afterwards, a few newspapers reported his death, which they attributed to 'consumption, brought on by the terrible injuries sustained by him in his celebrated fight with Cashel Byron.'

NOTE ON MODERN PRIZEFIGHTING

IN 1882, when this book was written, prizefighting seemed to be dying out. Sparring matches with boxing gloves, under the Queensberry rules, kept pugilism faintly alive; but it was not popular, because the public, which cares only for the excitement of a strenuous fight, believed then that the boxing glove made sparring as harmless a contest of pure skill as a fencing match with buttoned foils. This delusion was supported by the limitation of the sparring match to boxing. In the prize ring under the old rules a combatant might trip, hold, or throw his antagonist; so that each round finished either with a knockdown blow, which, except when it is really a liedown blow, is much commoner in fiction than it was in the ring, or with a visible body-to-body struggle ending in a fall. In a sparring match all that happens is that a man with a watch in his hand cries out 'Time!' whereupon the two champions prosaically stop sparring and sit down for a minute's rest and refreshment. The unaccustomed and inexpert spectator in those days did not appreciate the severity of the exertion or the risk of getting hurt: he underrated them as ignorantly as he would have overrated the more dramatically obvious terrors of a prizefight. Consequently the interest in the annual sparrings for the Queensberry Championships was confined to the few amateurs who had some critical knowledge of the game of boxing, and to the survivors of the generation for which the fight between Sayers and Heenan had been described in The Times as solemnly as the University Boat Race. In short, pugilism was out of fashion because the police had suppressed the only form of it which fascinated the public by its undissembled pugnacity.

All that was needed to rehabilitate it was the discovery that the glove fight is a more trying and dangerous form of contest than the old knuckle fight. Nobody knew that then:

everybody knows it, or ought to know it, now. And, accordingly, pugilism is more prosperous today than it has ever been before.

How far this result was foreseen by the author of the Queensberry Rules, which superseded those of the old prize ring, will probably never be known. There is no doubt that they served their immediate turn admirably. That turn was the keeping alive of boxing in the teeth of the law against prizefighting. Magistrates believed, as the public believed, that when men's knuckles were muffled in padded gloves; when they were forbidden to wrestle or hold one another; when the duration of a round was fixed by the clock, and the number of rounds limited to what seems (to those who have never tried) to be easily within the limits of ordinary endurance; and when the traditional interval for rest between the rounds was doubled, that then indeed violence must be checkmated, so that the worst the boxers could do was to 'spar for points' before three gentlemanly members of the Stock Exchange, who would carefully note the said points on an examination paper at the ring side, awarding marks only for skill and elegance, and sternly discountenancing the claims of brute force. It may be that both the author of the rules and the 'judges' who administered them in the earlier days really believed all this; for, as far as I know, the limit of an amateur pugilist's romantic credulity has never yet been reached and probably never will. But if so, their good intentions were upset by the operation of a single new rule. Thus.

In the old prize ring a round had no fixed duration. It was terminated by the fall of one of the combatants (in practice usually both of them), and was followed by an interval of half a minute for recuperation. The practical effect of this was that a combatant could always get a respite of half a minute whenever he wanted it by pretending to be knocked down: 'finding the earth the safest place,' as the old phrase went. For this the Marquess of Queensberry substituted a rule that a round with the gloves should last a specified time, usually three or four minutes, and that a combatant who did not stand up to his opponent continuously during that time (ten seconds being allowed for rising in the event of a knockdown) lost the battle. That unobtrusively slipped-in ten seconds limit has produced the modern glove fight. Its practical effect is that a man dazed by a blow or a fall for, say, twelve seconds, which would not have mattered in an oldfashioned fight with its thirty seconds interval,[1] has under the Queensberry rules either to lose or else stagger to his feet in a helpless condition and be eagerly battered into insensibility by his opponent before he can recover his powers of self-defence. The notion that such battery cannot be inflicted with boxing gloves is only entertained by people who have never used them or seen them used. I may say that I have myself received, in an accident, a blow in the face, involving two macadamized holes in it, more violent than the most formidable pugilist could have given me with his bare knuckles. This blow did not stun or disable me even momentarily. On the other hand, I have seen a man knocked quite silly by a tap from the most luxurious sort of boxing glove made, wielded by a quite unathletic literary man sparring for the first time in his life. The human jaw, like the human elbow, is provided, as every boxer knows, with a 'funny bone'; and the pugilist

1. In a treatise on boxing, by Captain Edgeworth Johnstone, just published, I read, 'In the days of the prize ring, fights lasted for hours; and the knock-out blow was unknown.' This statement is a little too sweeping. The blow was known well enough. A veteran prizefighter once described to me his first experience of its curious effect on the senses. Only, as he had thirty seconds to recover in instead of ten, it did not end the battle. The thirty seconds made the knock-out so unlikely that the old pugilists regarded it as a rare accident, not worth trying for. The glove fighter tries for nothing else. Nevertheless knock-outs, and very dramatic ones too (Mace by King, for example), did occur in the prize ring from time to time. Captain Edgeworth Johnstone's treatise is noteworthy in comparison with the earlier Badminton handbook of sparring by Mr E. B. Michell (one of the Queensberry champions) as throwing over the old teaching of prize-ring boxing with mufflers, and going in frankly for glove fighting, or, to put it classically, cestus boxing.

who is lucky enough to jar that funny bone with a blow practically has his opponent at his mercy for at least ten seconds. Such a blow is called a 'knock-out'. The funny bone and the ten seconds rule explain the development of Queensberry sparring into the modern knocking-out match or glove fight.

This development got its first impulse from the discovery by sparring competitors that the only way in which a boxer, however skilful, could make sure of a verdict in his favor, was by knocking his opponent out. This will be easily understood by any one who remembers the pugilistic Bench of those days. The 'judges' at the competitions were invariably ex-champions: that is, men who had themselves won former competitions. Now the judicial faculty, if it is not altogether a legal fiction, is at all events pretty rare even among men whose ordinary pursuits tend to cultivate it, and to train them in dispassionateness. Among pugilists it is quite certainly very often non-existent. The average pugilist is a violent partisan, who seldom witnesses a hot encounter without getting much more excited than the combatants themselves. Further, he is usually filled with a local patriotism which makes him, if a Londoner, deem it a duty to disparage a provincial, and, if a provincial, to support a provincial at all hazards against a cockney. He has, besides, personal favorites on whose success he bets wildly. On great occasions like the annual competitions, he is less judicial and more convivial after dinner (when the finals are sparred) than before it. Being seldom a fine boxer, he often regards skill and style as a reflection on his own deficiencies, and applauds all verdicts given for 'game' alone. When he is a technically good boxer, he is all the less likely to be a good critic, as Providence seldom lavishes two rare gifts on the same individual. Even if we take the sanguine and patriotic view that when you appoint such a man a judge, and thus stop his betting, you may depend on his sense of honor and responsibility to neutralize all the other disqualifications, they are sure to be exhibited most extremely by the audience before which he has to deliver his verdict. Now it takes a good deal of strength of mind to give an unpopular verdict; and this strength of mind is not necessarily associated with the bodily hardihood of the champion boxer. Consequently, when the strength of mind is not forthcoming, the audience becomes the judge, and the popular competitor gets the verdict. And the shortest way to the heart of a big audience is to stick to your man; stop his blows bravely with your nose and return them with interest; cover yourself and him with your own gore; and outlast him in a hearty punching match.

It was under these circumstances that the competitors for sparring championships concluded that they had better decide the bouts themselves by knocking their opponents out, and waste no time in cultivating a skill and style for which they got little credit, and which actually set some of the judges against them. The public instantly began to take an interest in the sport. And so, by a pretty rapid evolution, the dexterities which the boxing glove and the Queensberry rules were supposed to substitute for the old brutalities of Sayers and Heenan were really abolished by them.

Let me describe the process as I saw it myself. Twenty years ago a poet friend of mine, who, like all poets, delighted in combats, insisted on my sharing his interest in pugilism, and took me about to all the boxing competitions of the day. I was nothing loth; for, my own share of original sin apart, any one with a sense of comedy must find the arts of self-defence delightful (for a time) through their pedantry, their quackery, and their action and reaction between amateur romantic illusion and professional eye to business.

The fencing world, as Molière well knew, is perhaps a more exquisite example of a fool's paradise than the boxing world but it is too restricted and expensive to allow play for popular character in a non-duelling country as the boxing world (formerly called quite appropriately 'the Fancy') does. At all events, it was the boxing world that came under my notice; and as I was amused and sceptically observant, whilst the true amateurs about me were, for the most part, merely excited and duped, my evidence may have a certain value when the question comes up again for legislative consideration, as it assuredly will some day.

The first competitions I attended were at the beginning of the eighties, at Lillie Bridge, for the Queensberry championships. There were but few competitors, including a fair number of gentlemen; and the style of boxing aimed at was the 'science' bequeathed from the old prize ring by Ned Donnelly, a pupil of Nat Langham. Langham had once defeated Sayers, and thereby taught him the tactics by which he defeated Heenan. There was as yet no special technique of glove fighting: the traditions and influence of the old ring were unquestioned and supreme; and they distinctly made for brains, skill, quickness, and mobility, as against brute violence, not at all on moral grounds, but because experience had proved that giants did not succeed in the ring under the old rules, and that crafty middleweights did.

This did not last long. The spectators did not want to see skill defeating violence: they wanted to see violence drawing blood and pounding its way to a savage and exciting victory in the shortest possible time (the old prizefight usually dragged on for hours, and was ended by exhaustion rather than by victory). So did most of the judges. And the public and the judges naturally had their wish; for the competitors, as I have already explained, soon discovered that the only way to make sure of a favorable verdict was to 'knock out' their adversary. All pretence of sparring 'for points': that is, for marks on an examination paper filled up by the judges, and representing nothing but impracticable academic pedantry in its last ditch, was dropped; and the competitions became frank fights, with abundance of blood drawn, and 'knockouts' always imminent. Needless to add, the glove fight soon began to pay. The select and thinly attended spars on the turf at Lillie Bridge gave way to crowded exhibitions on the hard boards of St James's Hall. These were organized by the Boxing Association; and to them the provinces, notably Birmingham, sent up a new race of boxers whose sole aim was to knock their opponent insensible by a right-hand blow on the jaw, knowing well that no Birmingham man could depend on a verdict before a London audience for any less undeniable achievement.

The final step was taken by an American pugilist. He threw off the last shred of the old hypocrisy of the gloved hand by challenging the whole world to produce a man who could stand before him for a specified time without being knocked out. His brief but glorious career completely re-established pugilism by giving a world-wide advertisement to the fact that the boxing glove spares nothing but the public conscience, and that as much ferocity, bloodshed, pain, and risk of serious injury or death can be enjoyed at a glove fight as at an old-fashioned prizefight, whilst the strain on the combatants is much greater. It is true that these horrors are greatly exaggerated by the popular imagination, and that if boxing were really as dangerous as bicycling, a good many of its heroes would give it up from simple fright; but this only means that there is the maximum of damage to the spectator by demoralization, combined with the minimum of deterrent risk to the poor scrapper in the ring.

Poor scrapper, though, is hardly the word for a modern fashionable American pugilist. To him the exploits of Cashel Byron will seem ludicrously obscure and low-lived. The contests in which he engages are like Handel Festivals: they take place in huge halls before enormous audiences, with cinematographs hard at work recording the scene for re-production in London and elsewhere. The combatants divide thousands of dollars of gate-money between them: indeed, if an impecunious English curate were to go to America and challenge the premier pugilist, the spectacle of a match between the Church and the Ring would attract a colossal crowd; and the loser's share of the gate would be a fortune to a curate – assuming that the curate would be the loser, which is by no means a foregone conclusion. At all events, it would be well worth a bruise or two. So my story of the Agricultural Hall, where William Paradise sparred for half a guinea, and Cashel Byron stood out for ten guineas, is no doubt read by the profession in America with amused contempt. In 1882 it was, like most of my conceptions, a daring anticipation of coming social developments, though today it seems as far out of date as Slender pulling Sackerson's chain.

Of these latter-day commercial developments of glove fighting I know nothing beyond what I gather from the newspapers. The banging matches of the eighties, in which not one competitor in twenty either exhibited artistic skill, or, in his efforts to knock out his adversary, succeeded in anything but tiring and disappointing himself, were for the most part tedious beyond human endurance. When, after wading through Boxiana and the files of Bell's Life at the British Museum, I had written Cashel Byron's Profession, I found I had exhausted the comedy of the subject; and as a game of patience or solitaire was decidedly superior to an average spar for a championship in point of excitement, I went no more to the competitions. Since then six or seven generations of boxers have passed into peaceful pursuits; and I have no doubt that my experience is in some respects out of date. The National Sporting Club has arisen; and though I have never attended its reunions, I take its record of three pugilists slain as proving an enormous multiplication of contests, since such accidents are very rare, and in fact do not happen to reasonably healthy men. I am prepared to admit also that the disappearance of the old prizering technique must by this time have been compensated by the importation from America of a new glove-fighting technique; for even in a knocking-out match, brains will try conclusions with brawn, and finally establish a standard of skill; but I notice that in the leading contests in America luck seems to be on the side of brawn, and brain frequently finishes in a state of concussion, a loser after performing miracles of 'science.' I use the word luck advisedly; for one of the fascinations of boxing to the gambler (who is the main pillar of the sporting world) is that it is a game of hardihood, pugnacity, and skill, all at the mercy of chance. The knock-out itself is a pure chance. I have seen two powerful laborers batter one another's jaws with all their might for several rounds apparently without giving one another as much as a toothache. And I have seen a winning pugilist collapse at a trifling knock landed by a fluke at the fatal angle. I once asked an ancient prizefighter what a knock-out was like when it did happen. He was a man of limited descriptive powers; so he simply pointed to the heavens and said 'Up in a balloon.' An amateur pugilist, with greater command of language, told me that 'all the milk in his head suddenly boiled over.' I am aware that some modern glove fighters of the American school profess to have reduced the knock-out to a science. But the results of the leading American combats conclusively discredit the pretension. When a boxer so superior to his opponent in skill as to be able practically to hit him where he pleases not only fails to knock him out, but finally gets knocked out himself, it is clear that the phenomenon is as complete a mystery pugilistically as it is physiologically, though every pugilist and every doctor may pretend to understand it. It is only fair to add that it has not been proved that any permanent injury to the brain results from it. In any case the brain, as English society is at present constituted, can hardly be considered a vital organ.

This, to the best of my knowledge, is the technical history of the modern revival of pugilism. It is only one more example of the fact that legislators, like other people, must learn their business by their own mistakes, and that the first attempts to suppress an evil by law generally intensify it. Prizefighting, though often connived at, was never legal. Even in its palmiest days prizefights were banished from certain counties by hostile magistrates, just as they have been driven from the United States and England to Belgium on certain occasions in our own time. But as the exercise of sparring, conducted by a couple of gentlemen with boxing gloves on, was regarded as part of a manly physical education, a convention grew up by which it became practically legal to make a citizen's nose bleed by a punch from the gloved fist, and illegal to do the same thing with the naked knuckles. A code of glove-fighting rules was drawn up by a prominent patron of pugilism; and this code was practically legalized by the fact that even when a death resulted from a contest under these rules the accessaries were not punished. No question was raised as to whether the principals were paid to fight for the amusement of the spectators, or whether a prize for the winner was provided in stakes, share of the gate, or a belt with the title of champion. These, the true criteria of prizefighting, were ignored; and the sole issue raised was whether the famous dictum of Dr Watts, 'Your little hands were never made, etc.,' had been duly considered by providing the said little hands with a larger hitting surface, a longer range, and four ounces extra weight.

In short, then, what has happened has been the virtual legalization of prizefighting under cover of the boxing glove. And this is exactly what public opinion desires. We do not like fighting; but we like looking on at fights: therefore we require a law which will punish the prizefighter if he hits us, and secure us the protection of the police whilst we sit in a comfortable hall and watch him hitting another prizefighter. And that is just the law we have got at present.

Thus Cashel Byron's plea for a share of the legal toleration accorded to the vivisector has been virtually granted since he made it. The legalization of cruelty to domestic animals under cover of the anesthetic is only the extreme instance of the same social phenomenon as the legalization of prizefighting under cover of the boxing glove. The same passion explains the fascination of both practices; and in both, the professors – pugilists and physiologists alike – have to persuade the Home Office that their pursuits are painless and beneficial. But there is also between them the remarkable difference that the pugilist, who has to suffer as much as he inflicts, wants his work to be as painless and harmless as possible whilst persuading the public that it is thrillingly dangerous and destructive, whilst the vivisector wants to enjoy a total exemption from humane restrictions in his laboratory whilst persuading the public that pain is unknown there. Consequently the vivisector is not only crueller than the prizefighter, but, through the pressure of public opinion, a much more resolute and uncompromising liar. For this no one but a Pharisee will single him out for special blame. All public men lie, as a matter of good taste, on subjects which are considered serious (in England a serious occasion means simply an occasion on which nobody tells the truth); and however illogical or capricious the point of honor may be in man, it is too absurd to assume that the doctors who, from among innumerable methods of research, select that of tormenting animals hideously, will hesitate to come on a platform and tell a soothing fib to prevent the public from punishing them. No criminal is expected to plead guilty, or to refrain from pleading not guilty with all the plausibility at his command. In prizefighting such mendacity is not necessary: on the contrary, if a famous pugilist were to assure the public that a blow delivered with a boxing glove could do no injury and cause no pain, and the public believed him, the sport would instantly lose its following. It is the prizefighter's interest to abolish the real cruelties of the ring and to exaggerate the imaginary cruelties of it. It is the vivisector's interest to refine upon the cruelties of the laboratory, whilst persuading the public that his victims pass into a delicious euthanasia and leave behind them a row of bottles containing infallible cures for all the diseases. Just so, too, does the trainer of performing animals assure us that his dogs and cats and elephants and lions are taught their senseless feats by pure kindness.

The public, as Julius Cæsar remarked nearly 2000 years ago, believes, on the whole, just what it wants to believe. The laboring masses do not believe the false excuses of the vivisector, because they know that the vivisector experiments on hospital patients; and the masses belong to the hospital patient class. The well-to-do people who do not go to hospitals, and who think they benefit by the experiments made there, believe the vivisectors' excuses, and angrily abuse and denounce the anti-vivisectors. The people who 'love animals,' who keep pets, and stick pins through butterflies, support the performing dog people, and are sure that kindness will teach a horse to waltz. And the people who enjoy a fight will persuade themselves that boxing gloves do not hurt, and that sparring is an exercise which teaches self-control and exercises all the muscles in the body more efficiently than any other.

My own view of prizefighting may be gathered from Cashel Byron's Profession, and from the play written by me more than ten years later, entitled Mrs Warren's Profession. As long as society is so organized that the destitute athlete and the destitute beauty are forced to choose between underpaid drudgery as industrial producers, and comparative self-respect, plenty, and popularity as prizefighters and mercenary brides, licit or illicit, it is idle to affect virtuous indignation at their expense. The word prostitute should either not be used at all, or else applied impartially to all persons who do things for money that they would not do if they had any other assured means of livelihood. The evil caused by the prostitution of the Press and the Pulpit is so gigantic that the prostitution of the prize ring, which at least makes no serious moral pretensions, is comparatively negligible by comparison. Let us not forget, however, that the throwing of a hard word such as prostitution does not help the persons thus vituperated out of their difficulty. If the soldier and gladiator fight for money, if men and women marry for money, if the journalist and novelist write for money, and the parson preaches for money, it must be remembered that it is an exceedingly difficult and doubtful thing for an individual to set up his own scruples or fancies (he cannot himself be sure which they are) against the demand of the community when it says, Do thus and thus, or starve. It was easy for Ruskin to lay down the rule of dying rather than doing unjustly; but death is a plain thing: justice a very obscure thing. How is an ordinary man to draw the line between right and wrong otherwise than by accepting public opinion on the subject; and what more conclusive expression of sincere public opinion can there be than market demand? Even when we repudiate that and fall back on our private judgment, the matter gathers doubt instead of clearness. The popular notion of morality and piety is to simply beg all the most important questions in life for other people; but when these questions come home to ourselves, we suddenly discover that the devil's advocate has a stronger case than we thought: we remember that the way of righteousness or death was the way of the Inquisition; that hell is paved, not with bad intentions, but with good ones; that the deeper seers have suggested that the way to save your soul is perhaps to give it away, casting your spiritual bread on the waters, so to speak. No doubt, if you are a man of genius, a Ruskin or an Ibsen, you can divine your way and finally force your passage. If you have the conceit of fanaticism you can die a martyr like Charles I. If you are a criminal, or a gentleman of independent means, you can leave society out of the question and prey on it. But if you are an ordinary person you take your bread as it comes to you, doing whatever you can make most money by doing. And you are really shewing yourself a disciplined citizen and acting with perfect social propriety in so doing. Society may be, and generally is, grossly wrong in its offer to you; and you may be, and generally are, grossly wrong in supporting the existing political structure; but this only means, to the successful modern prizefighter, that he must reform society before he can reform himself. A conclusion which I recommend to the consideration of those foolish misers of personal righteousness who think they can dispose of social problems by bidding reformers of society reform themselves first.

Practically, then, the question raised is whether fighting with gloves shall be brought, like cockfighting, bearbaiting, and gloveless fist fighting, explicitly under the ban of the law. I do not propose to argue that question out here. But of two things I am certain. First, that glove fighting is quite as fierce a sport as fist fighting. Second, that if an application were made to the Borough Council of which I am a member, to hire the Town Hall for a boxing competition, I should vote against the applicants.

This second point being evidently the practical one, I had better give my reason. Exhibition pugilism is essentially a branch of Art: that is to say, it acts and attracts by propagating feeling. The feeling it propagates is pugnacity. Sense of danger, dread of danger, impulse to batter and destroy what threatens and opposes, triumphant delight in succeeding: this is pugnacity, the great adversary of the social impulse to live and let live; to establish our rights by shouldering our share of the social burden; to face and examine danger instead of striking at it; to understand everything to the point of pardoning (and righting) everything; to conclude an amnesty with Nature wide enough to include even those we know the worst of: namely, ourselves. If two men quarrelled, and asked the Borough Council to lend them a room to fight it out in with their fists, on the ground that a few minutes hearty punching of one another's heads would work off their bad blood and leave them better friends, each desiring, not victory, but *satisfaction*, I am not sure that I should not vote for compliance. But if a syndicate of showmen came and said, Here we have two men who have no quarrel, but who will, if you pay them, fight before your constituency and thereby make a great propaganda of pugnacity in it, sharing the profits with us and with you, I should indignantly oppose the proposition. And if the majority were against me, I should try to persuade them to at least impose the condition that the fight should be with naked fists under the old rules, so that the combatants should, like Sayers and Langham, depend on bunging up each other's eyes rather than, like the modern knocker-out, giving one another concussion of the brain.

I may add, finally, that the present halting between the legal toleration and suppression of commercial pugilism is much worse than the extreme of either, because it takes away the healthy publicity and sense of responsibility which legality and respectability give, without suppressing the blackguardism which finds its opportunity in shady pursuits. I use the term commercial advisedly. Put a stop to boxing for money; and pugilism will give society no further trouble.

LONDON, 1901.

MORE ABOUT PENGUINS
AND PELICANS

Penguinews, which appears every month, contains details of all the new books issued by Penguins as they are published. From time to time it is supplemented by the *Penguin Stock List,* which is our list of almost 5,000 titles.

A specimen copy of *Penguinews* will be sent to you free on request. Please write to Dept EP, Penguin Books Ltd, Harmondsworth, Middlesex, for your copy.

In the U.S.A.: For a complete list of books available from Penguins in the United States write to Dept CS, Penguin Books, 625 Madison Avenue, New York, New York 10022.

In Canada: For a complete list of books available from Penguins in Canada write to Penguin Books Canada Ltd, 2801 John Street, Markham, Ontario L3R 1B4.

A selection of recent Penguins

MADAME SOLARIO

Anonymous

Set in Italy at the turn of the century, this strange, evocative novel probes beneath the veneer of a mannered society that is temporarily invaded by a subtle amorality and forbidden sexual passion.

'I have read no novel for years which announces its own distinction with such an air, demanding to be judged by the highest standards ... I read on in willing, fascinated, hypnotized submission' – *Sunday Times* (London)

THE RIDDLE OF THE SANDS

Erskine Childers

Erskine Childers died before a firing squad in Dublin, denounced as a traitor, yet his book was an expression of his loyalty to England and his concern for the nation's defence. Its unique flavour comes from its richly detailed technical background of inshore sailing in the Baltic and North Seas, from its remarkable air of authenticity, and from its evocation of the world of the late 1890s – an atmosphere of intrigue and suspicion that was soon to lead to war.

ONE LAST GLIMPSE

James Aldridge

Set in 1929, *One Last Glimpse* was inspired by a car journey made by Ernest Hemingway and Scott Fitzgerald, described in Hemingway's memoir *A Moveable Feast*. This book is a fictionalized re-creation of the trip, as told by Kit, coopted as chauffeur. But it is also a remarkable and convincing study of the two literary giants and a brilliant evocation of the extraordinary richness of the period: its glamour, vitality and wit.

DEAR ME

Peter Ustinov

'Mr Ustinov's own memory is both abundant and imaginative: hence *Dear Me*, a controversial autobiography, bursting at the seams with uproarious stories, wise saws and modern instances, and ablaze with images' – J. W. Lambert in the *Sunday Times* (London)

'Ustinov has produced an illuminating and joyous book ... He has a penchant for iconoclasm, a gift for the anecdote and the epigram, and a delightful sense of humour. He is, perhaps, as near to that proverbial Renaissance man – humorist, actor, writer – as we have today in the English language' – *Chicago Tribune*

THE NIGHT OF THE TWELFTH

Michael Gilbert

'Michael Gilbert has never been in better form than in this electrifying novel of suspense set in a small English boys' prep school. Three young boys have been kidnapped, cruelly tortured and murdered. The police have very good secret reasons for beginning to focus their attention on the school as harboring the sadistic killer ... – *Publishers Weekly*

A BOY AT THE HOGARTH PRESS

Richard Kennedy

Richard Kennedy started work at the Hogarth Press when he was sixteen. This account of his experiences there is described by John Lehmann as 'absolutely accurate and hilariously funny'. It provides a delightful glimpse into the everyday comings and goings of the Bloomsbury Group and an affectionate recollection of Leonard and Virginia Woolf at work: and, like Lely's portrait of Cromwell, it shows them 'warts and all'.

A BIT OFF THE MAP AND OTHER STORIES

Angus Wilson

It was the decade of rubber plants, Expresso bars and skiffle, of Suez, Teddy Boys and Angry Young Men. These eight short stories are brilliant and incisive reflections on the preoccupations and secrets of the 'respectable' middle classes of the fifties.

THE ABRAMSKY VARIATIONS

Morley Torgov

Leibel Abramsky is haunted by Charles Lindbergh. His son Hershy is obsessed by Thor Heyerdahl, and his grandson, Bert, dreams about making it in the world of Rock.

Three men, three dreams. The result is a pungent, affecting novel about a search for roots and about the interplay of generations, told by a benevolent, clear-eyed humorist.

and a reissue:

A FAIRLY HONOURABLE DEFEAT

Iris Murdoch

Rupert and Hilda are perfectly matched; their only worries a drop-out son and Morgan, Hilda's unstable sister, just back from America.

Enter Julius, Morgan's ex-lover, determined to give Rupert and Hilda's seemingly impregnable marriage a mild jolt. He sets the stage and distributes roles among his unwitting cast with unnerving brilliance and high comedy ... Until the last act with its final inevitable (but not altogether disgraceful) defeat.

THE PENGUIN SHAW

Bernard Shaw's *The Intelligent Woman's Guide to Socialism, Capitalism, Sovietism, and Fascism* was the first Pelican book to be published, in May 1937. Since then many of his plays have been published as Penguins. All of them are complete with Shaw's original prefaces, which put the argument of the play in strong and witty terms and serve as examples of Shaw's individual and assertive prose style. The following are published:

ANDROCLES AND THE LION

THE APPLE CART

BACK TO METHUSELAH

THE DOCTOR'S DILEMMA

HEARTBREAK HOUSE

MAJOR BARBARA

MAN AND SUPERMAN

THE MILLIONAIRESS

PLAYS UNPLEASANT
(*Widowers' Houses, The Philanderer, Mrs Warren's Profession*)

PYGMALION

SAINT JOAN

SELECTED ONE-ACT PLAYS (in 2 vols.)

Also

THE INTELLIGENT WOMAN'S GUIDE TO
SOCIALISM, CAPITALISM, SOVIETISM, AND FASCISM